Water Under the Bridge

by

Catherine Moore

DORRANCE PUBLISHING CO., INC.
PITTSBURGH, PENNSYLVANIA 15222

All Rights Reserved
Copyright © 1999 by Catherine Moore
No part of this book may be reproduced or transmitted
in any form or by any means, electronic or mechanical,
including photocopying, recording, or by any information
storage and retrieval system without permission in
writing from the publisher.

ISBN # 0-8059-4440-0
Printed in the United States of America

First Printing

For information or to order additional books, please write:
Dorrance Publishing Co., Inc.
643 Smithfield Street
Pittsburgh, Pennsylvania 15222
U.S.A.

Dedicated to Tucker and Melissa Moore
for their love and encouragement,
and to Judith Cheney for her artwork.

Contents

Chapter One 1
Chapter Two 15
Chapter Three 32
Chapter Four 42
Chapter Five 48
Chapter Six 58
Chapter Seven 67
Chapter Eight 69
Chapter Nine 74
Chapter Ten 78
Chapter Eleven 86
Chapter Twelve 92
Chapter Thirteen 98
Chapter Fourteen 107
Chapter Fifteen 114
Chapter Sixteen 123
Chapter Seventeen 128
Chapter Eighteen 136
Chapter Nineteen 144
Chapter Twenty 160
Chapter Twenty-one 169
Chapter Twenty-two 182
Chapter Twenty-three 192
Chapter Twenty-four 204
Chapter Twenty-five 233
Chapter Twenty-six 239
Chapter Twenty-seven 244
Chapter Twenty-eight 257
Chapter Twenty-nine 271
Chapter Thirty 281
Chapter Thirty-one 297
Chapter Thirty-two 310
Chapter Thirty-three 318
Chapter Thirty-four 329
Chapter Thirty-five 337
Chapter Thirty-six 347
Chapter Thirty-seven 358

Chapter One

Clarice Creighton pushed open the door to the tiny cabin and stepped out. She climbed the narrow companionway to the quarter deck and walked over to the rail and grasped it with both hands. A soft breeze from the west picked up the ribbons of her hood and curled them around her face. She removed them with her forefinger and tucked them into the lace choker of her blouse.

As she took a long breath of salty air for relief of a butterfly stomach, she noticed that the entire horizon was encircled in pink. She felt glad for the tranquillity of sky and sea. The sunset was the most beautiful she had ever seen. There were a few slowly moving clouds. With the hues of the waning sun upon them, they looked like billowing canopies of lavender and gold hanging over the ship.

There was land in the distance. Church spires were distinctive among the treetops. Only a few moments ago she had heard the captain call through his megaphone, "Land ahoy...Boston ahead."

A thrilling chill of anticipation had run down her spine as she jumped up from her reading and hurriedly put on her cape and hood. She wanted to see for herself.

Robin (the Anthony child, with whom she shared the cabin) was taking a nap and Clarice did not want to wake her, but the opening of the squeaking door awoke her and she soon was on the deck beside her governess.

"Cee Cee, are we there?" Robin asked with excitement in her voice.

"Almost," answered Clarice as she put her arm around the child's shoulder and drew her up to the rail beside her. "See, there is the harbor where we are headed." She hugged her up close and pointed toward the sunset. "Look at that lovely sunset, Robin; if I was an artist I would paint that picture."

The little girl turned from the rail and said, "I'll go and get Mama and Papa; I want them to see it, too." She ran across the deck and went down the steps to the cabins.

Standing there on deck with the wind cooling her face and the salty mist touching her lips, Clarice felt the slow trickle of a tear running down her cheek. She closed her eyes and remembered, remembered all those sorrowful "goodbyes" that had taken place on the wharf in Liverpool. Her mother had looked very ill. It was fear; there was so much fear in Birmingham: her father in his dangerous work, likely to be killed at any moment, and her parents' fears of her making the long ocean voyage to America. She remembered her mother's grief at losing a second daughter, one who had been a help and comfort. She remembered her words: "What will I do without you?"

But the worst fear she remembered, was what might happen to Tom Fellows. He had hated to see her go. He had begged her to marry him. He avowed his love for her with outright weeping and had promised to quit drinking and gambling. She remembered how he stood there holding her hand tightly between his. When she started to go up the gangplank to board the Cordelia he had such a sad expression on his face. He declared that he would follow her to America in a short time and pleaded with her to wait for him. She had returned his embrace and his kiss with a promise to wait. Now she wondered why she hadn't just gone ahead and married him and put off coming to America until they could have come together.

She had wanted to get away from Birmingham very badly, just like her sister, Julia, had wanted to get away seven years ago. Julia had already been living here those past years. First she had lived in Baltimore, and now she was living in New York.

She remembered her father, standing there on the wharf in silence, not saying a word about anything, not even making a comment about the beautiful brig Cordelia. He didn't say "goodbye" but just walked away. Later as the gangplank was drawn up, and she was still standing on the deck looking out at the wharf, she had caught a glimpse of her mother and Tom going through the moving throng, looking for him.

She thought about their long coach trip back to Birmingham. With the weather turning into its regular March meanness, she hoped they wouldn't have any trouble. She knew it would be many months before she would hear from them.

The contract she had with Lord and Lady Anthony came into her mind. Could she be a good governess to a child who had the reputation of being incorrigible? Robin was eight years old and pretty, which made her vain. She was also spoiled and was allowed to be sarcastic.

Noises of hustling feet behind her brought her out of her reminiscence, and when her heart jumped, she opened her eyes and looked around. She realized that the tranquility had transformed into confusion.

The seamen were lowering the mainsail and adjusting the jibs. Some of them were checking the capstan to see if it was working properly for dropping the anchor. There was loud clanking of chains and shouting back and forth between the weary deck crew.

The waves were slapping against the sides of the Cordelia as she was being maneuvered into some kind of favorable position. At one big swing around, Clarice felt like she was headed back to England.

The captain came out onto the deck and lifted his spyglass and took a long look. When he put it down, he announced that a sloop had left the wharf and was on the way out to meet them. This meant that the passengers would transfer to a sloop for debarkation.

Robin and her parents had not yet come to the deck. Clarice returned to her cabin because she had a few last minute things to do. She looked around for small articles belonging to her or Robin, so that nothing would be left. Her memories of the past eight weeks were good. Everything had gone well. She picked up her little diary and jotted down the time of day and the date: May 09, 1773 - Five o'clock P.M.

She gathered up a few books from the floor and tables and put them in the till of her trunk before locking it. It would be left on the Cordelia and unloaded later by the seamen.

She made a mental note to herself that as soon as she was settled she would write a letter to Julia in New York. She would send it with a letter her mother had given her to be sent to Julia. She had so much to tell her.

Crowds of people at the landing wharf were mingling and talking while some were lifting their small spyglasses to their eyes, speculating on the time it would take the passengers to get aboard the sloop and finally arrive at the landing dock.

Governor Thomas Hutchinson had arranged a welcoming party for the Anthonys. He had invited some of Boston's most prominent citizens to meet them at the dock. They had arrived in various carriages, such as chaises, landaus, and landaulets. They had left their vehicles in the hands of their drivers and footmen, who were standing in wait at the hitching places nearby. The governor had a ramp carpeted in red plush, and he and the guests were waiting at this specially reserved place for the king's emissaries and their entourage.

It was just getting dark when the sloop slipped into its mooring and the seamen let down the gangplank. Loud clapping of hands and singing began as the passengers came into view.

The first person to descend the plank was Robin Anthony. Clarice was right behind her trying to keep up while carrying Bo Tay (Beauty), a French poodle; a valise; and a large doll (all possessions of Robin). She was having difficulty holding all the belongings and keeping her balance on the shaky gangplank. She stumbled and almost fell as she set her tiny blue leather-shod feet on American soil. She was glad she had remembered to change from her waterproof boots (which she had worn all during the voyage) into her blue chamois slippers. She had an old-fashioned whimsy that when she wanted a new experience to be perfect, she would wear her blue chamois slippers.

Like a young colt let out of the barn, Robin ran past everyone, not speaking to anyone but crying out loudly while running, "We're here, we're here, hooray, hooray." Some eyebrows were raised, and heads turned to observe such a wild little girl.

When Governor Hutchinson sighted Lord and Lady Anthony coming down the plank, he took off his cockaded tricorn hat and held it across his chest as he bowed low in greeting. He embraced each of them and introduced them to some of the people who were with him.

The emissaries and the governor were escorted to a fashionable new landau drawn by four horses, which had been waiting for them. Clarice and Robin were escorted to a second landau drawn by two horses.

Robin, noticing the difference, immediately screamed that she wanted to ride with her mama and papa. When Clarice explained to her that their carriage would be in sight of her parents' carriage all the way and that it would take only a few minutes to get to the house, she became calm and climbed in. After she was seated, she bounced up again and turned to look at Henry, the footman.

"Why are you black?" she asked him.

"Why are you white?" was his reply.

Then Robin asked her governess why he answered her like that.

"Perhaps in Massachusetts, answers are different," said Clarice.

Henry heard her and said, "You are right, Miss, answers are different here; hardly anyone knows anything—especially answers that make sense."

"See," said Clarice, "we will have to learn more about the people here." In the Anthony household in England there were no black people. The only Negroes Robin had ever seen were in picture books.

The carriages climbed the hill and came to a stop in front of a large house. The first impression of the new home was a very satisfying one to Clarice and Robin.

Flames from flickering candles were like a thousand fireflies playing behind the two hundred and eighty-eight glass panes of eighteen windows.

Henry jumped from his stand on the back of the landau and came to the side of the carriage to assist the passengers to the ground. Clarice handed the poodle to him first, then the doll. He took a long look at his arm load of Robin's possessions and shifted them to his other arm so that he might help Clarice from the carriage. As she stepped down, he said, "Welcome to you; I will be at your service whenever you need me."

"Thank you, I will remember that," Clarice said as she smiled at him.

Then Henry lifted Robin from the carriage and set her down. She followed Clarice toward the house.

Clarice whispered to Robin as they entered the door, "Do you smell what I smell?"

Robin squeezed the hand of her governess and wiggled her nose in response and then asked, "Do you hear what I hear?"

"Yes I do, and I love it," said Clarice.

The music of a harpsichord and the smell of delicious fresh food was the most acceptable welcome in the world as far as Clarice and Robin were concerned.

Small groups of people were standing around in the large hall. Others had congregated in the parlor. Clarice noticed that a receiving line had formed in front of the large bay window shaking hands and making small talk. She and

Robin, however, were whisked quickly toward the stairway by a stiff, buxom woman, who evidently had been assigned the job of seeing that everyone did the right thing at the right time.

"Go up to your rooms; you will find a chambermaid up there to show you about. Bathe and dress properly. You will be notified when it is time for dinner. You are to sit with the guests through the main course but will return to the upstairs parlor for your dessert." She then spoke directly to Robin. "Wash your dirty hands."

Robin gave her a scowling look. Clarice took the child's hand, and they started up the steps.

"Cee Cee, I want to talk to Mama."

"Come on, honey, we will find her; she is probably upstairs getting dressed."

As they were ascending the stairs, Clarice looked back through a large arched doorway into the dining room and caught the eye of a very handsome young man in a long white apron. He was decorating small cakes at a sideboard. She slowed her steps to watch him. He was dipping long-stemmed cherries into brandy one at a time and plunking them into the piled-up whipped cream of each little cake.

She blushed as she caught the twinkle of his deep blue eyes. He also was watching the pretty young lady and the cute little girl going up the stairs. Just as their eyes met, he held up one of the cherries by its stem and as a jest, he twisted it between his thumb and forefinger and bowed. Clarice nodded at him slightly, and Robin giggled.

It was the first time in her life that Clarice had had such a delightful feeling. A thrill had actually skedaddled through her body and weakened her knees. She felt her heart race like it had never raced before. She looked at her feet and knew that her blue chamois slippers were bringing her joy, making her arrival in America a very pleasant one.

At the end of the upstairs hall there was a large bay window like the one in the parlor downstairs. Clarice followed Robin over to it to look out toward town. Robin had been attracted by flashing lights and wanted to see what it was.

"Look, Cee Cee, it's fireworks. Do you think it is to welcome us to Boston?"

A voice behind them answered, "Well I should say not; you are important but not as important as the celebration going on over on the Common. It's the poor folks and the riffraff over there shooting off their firearms and building bonfires. They're having a whomping good time. They got some news today from the colony of Virginia. Tomorrow Sam Adams is going to make a speech, and they want everybody to know about it."

Clarice and Robin just stood there, surprised at what she said.

She continued, "I am Maggie, the chambermaid, I will help you get dressed for dinner."

Robin had a frown on her face as she looked at her. "How do you know all that?" she asked, doubting every word that Maggie had said.

"If you want to believe it is for your arrival in Boston, go ahead, believe what you want to. But the people in Boston are excited over something else. Once they got so excited, there was a big massacre in the street right here in Boston; I lived out at Salem then. I will tell you about that someday." She tickled Robin under the chin and said, "I've already heard that you are a headstrong little miss."

Maggie left the room saying she would be back in a minute with some more of their luggage which she had been bringing to their rooms piece by piece.

Clarice and Robin were glad to be in their own bedchambers which joined each other and each had a separate dressing room.

There was a bowl of warm water waiting on each of their washstands and more in the pitchers. Robin held the sweet smelling towel to her nose and called Clarice to come and smell. It certainly was different from the mildew of the Cordelia.

The room for the governess was almost as elegant as the room for her ladyship, Florence Anthony. Blue silk curtains hung at the large windows. The washbowl and pitcher were Chinese porcelain, hand painted with birds and flowers. The bed had a hand crocheted spread, and the rug was Oriental. Robin's room was the same, except the curtains were pink and there was a little wicker bed for Bo Tay.

Clarice thought her room was the finest room in which she had ever been. She could not help but think of her room at home, and she missed its warmth a little, feeling that she was out of place in the spacious and rich surroundings that were all about her. Her own room at home was small, and she remembered that she often put things away by tucking them under the bed because she had no closets. Her clothes hung on the back of the door. This was very different. The dressing room alone surpassed the size of her room at home.

Robin, being spoiled to all the comforts of life said, when Clarice asked her if she liked her room, "It'll do." She sighed and she said, "I don't think I'm going to like it here."

"Why not?" asked her governess.

"Well, the only people I've said anything to haven't been very friendly. First, that black man gave me a sassy answer. Then that old woman told me to go upstairs when I wanted to speak to Mama, and that chambermaid is a know-it-all."

"Things will get better; you will see. Now you must get dressed for dinner. When we get our 'stomicks' full, we will be happier."

Clarice was always kind to Robin. She was laughing and rubbing her own stomach, trying to make the child smile.

The lovely ball dress that Clarice was putting on had arrived in Boston six weeks before she did. Many trunks and boxes of personal belongings had been shipped ahead to be there in readiness for the parties planned by Governor Hutchinson.

Little did Lady Anthony or Clarice suspect that all the fine velvet and satin dresses as well as the petticoats, hats, coats, and other wearing apparel had been tried on by Maggie and Lola (the cook) and that they had strutted around in front of the long mirrors pretending to be great ladies. Everything had eventually been aired and pressed and the dress being worn by the governess was extremely beautiful and appropriate.

"Look who I found downstairs in the back hall," Maggie said as she came back into the room carrying Bo Tay and the French doll. She handed the poodle to Robin and set the doll in a chair by the window. "The poor little darling was whimpering and looked very forlorn. Had you forgotten him?"

"No," said Robin, "he knows I wouldn't forget him, but I'll bet you scared him."

"Robin…what do you mean?" asked Clarice.

"Look how she looks," responded the child.

Maggie was wearing a white mop cap and a long white pinafore with high-button black shoes that had steel taps on the toes.

Clarice asked, "Maggie, did you see the man who was decorating the cakes at the sideboard?"

"Yes."

"Do you know him?"

"Yes."

"Does he live here…in this house, I mean?"

"No."

After a minute of pause while she struggled with her ribbons and ruffles, Clarice asked more questions. "Why was he doing his work in the dining room instead of the pantry?"

"That's what I would like to know; probably just so he could see who was here and hear what they were saying," Maggie was flippant with her assumption.

She continued, "He is one of Boston's worst rabble-rousers, so I'm told, but he is also the best baker in the province. He makes all the tea cakes and buns served at the government meetings and he makes cakes for most of the grand ladies in Boston. He makes fancies for all the big Rebel parties." Then laughingly she said, "The big Tories, too."

"Maggie, will you help me fasten these damn little buttons?" She clasped her hand over her mouth and apologetically said to Robin, who was sitting on the chair stroking Bo Tay, "Robin, please forgive me; that word just slipped out."

"That's all right Cee Cee; you learned it from me, and I learned it from Papa."

While Maggie buttoned the tiny covered buttons running down the back of Clarice's dress, she was hounded with questions about the baker.

"Maggie, tell me, if he doesn't live here…where does he live?"

"Henry says he lives over his bun shop."

"Where is his bun shop?"

"I think it is on Charles Street."

"Who says he is a rabble-rouser?"

"Jackson said that; he said Henry is, too."

"Who is Jackson?"

"He is the carriage driver and sometimes the house man."

Before Clarice could ask, Maggie said, "And Henry was the footman on the back of the carriage that brought you from the wharf."

Robin was getting very bored with Clarice's and Maggie's questions and answers, and she jumped up from her chair, letting Bo Tay fall to the floor, and loudly interrupted by screaming, "When are we going to have our dinner?"

Clarice walked over to her and lifted her long hair from her shoulders. "If you will bring me your hairbrush, I will brush your hair, then you will be ready when dinner is ready, which I hope will be very soon."

"I don't know where my hairbrush is."

Maggie said, "Come, I think there is one in your bureau drawer; I will find it for you."

Bo Tay scampered ahead of them into Robin's room and jumped up on Robin's bed. Maggie rushed over to the bed and swatted at him to shoo off the crocheted spread.

She yelled at him. "Look here, you rascal, you are not supposed to get on this bed; look there, you have a bed of your own." She pointed at the little wicker dog bed in the corner.

She turned to Robin. "You keep that dog off that bed; he will leave his fleas in that bedspread, and they will lay eggs and make a million more fleas."

Robin looked at Maggie in a quizzical way and stamped her foot. "You are mean to talk to Bo Tay like that. He doesn't have fleas."

"Do you want to wager on that?" asked Maggie.

"What's wager?" asked Robin scornfully.

"Oh, I give up," said Maggie, shaking her head as she went hurriedly back into Clarice's room.

Clarice was sitting in a chair looking out the window. Maggie walked over and stood behind her. She turned and looked at Maggie and asked, "Is that the road to Boston…to Charles Street?"

Maggie answered, "Yes, just follow the walk along the river and you'll get there."

"Will you go with me?"

"If I have a day off from this drudgery."

"How soon will you get a day off?"

Maggie looked uncertain as she said, "From what I hear about our housekeeper, probably never."

Clarice thought a minute, then said, "Oh you mean Marie; well, I'll speak to her."

Then Maggie thought a minute and said, "Who is Marie?"

"Oh, you haven't met her yet? She came with us from England."

"Good Lord—have mercy on us all," said Maggie as she left the room.

Clarice was wondering why Maggie said that, then the maid came hurriedly back into the room and said, "Mrs. Seward is waiting for you and the brat at the foot of the stairs."

"Goody, goody, dinner is ready at last," was the child's joyful expression as she and Clarice went down the stairs.

"Robin, you look very pretty," said the governess to the child.

"You do too, Cee Cee," was the child's reply.

Clarice gave a long, searching look into the dining room, but the head she was looking for was not there.

There were, however, so many powdered wigs and red velvet coats among the blue satin gowns and Spanish lace shawls that it reminded her of a ball she had once attended in England.

As a child she had accompanied her parents to London for a fortnight of celebrating the birth of one of King George III and Queen Charlotte's babies. She couldn't remember which one; they had several children at that time and several since.

Clarice's great aunt (being the cousin of one of the Queen's ladies in waiting) had obtained the position of nursemaid to the new infant. Because of the relationship, the Creightons had been invited to the balls. Not since those parties had Clarice seen such finery and such gaiety.

At the foot of the stairs Mrs. Seward was waiting. A cool smile greeted the two young ladies. "Well...I see you've washed your hands, now you may shake mine." The pompous looking lady extended her hand to Robin.

"I am Mrs. Seward, wife of the captain, who you see standing over there talking to Governor Hutchinson." She continued by looking from Robin to Clarice. "And you are the governess? What, may I ask, is your name?"

"Clarice."

"Clarice who?"

"Clarice Creighton, Mrs. Seward," and she added (just to be facetious) "one of the best names in Birmingham."

"Good evening, Miss Robinette." She was a very pretty lady, but Robin immediately disliked her even more than Mrs. Seward. "I want you to meet my little boy; you and he may get to be playmates very soon."

Clarice followed along after them as Mrs. Hawley led Robin across the parlor to where a young boy was sitting stiffly on a chair, his feet not touching the floor. Clarice estimated his age to be about ten.

"Preston, stand up." It was his mother giving the order. "I want you to meet Robinette; she is going to live here in Boston. You may be seeing a lot of her in the future. Robinette, this is my son Preston, Preston Hawley."

Robin looked bored but not half as bored as Preston.

"Good evening, Robinette," he almost managed to whisper.

Mrs. Hawley nodded to Henry who was serving the needs of the guests. He came over and Mrs. Hawley asked him to put a chair next to Preston's so the young lady could sit there beside him.

Robin said very sternly, "Never mind, I'm not going to sit by him." She immediately pulled at Clarice to move somewhere else. She was looking for her mama and papa. "Where are they?" she asked Clarice.

Mrs. Hawley seemed terribly embarrassed. What she was thinking was not mentionable. Frankly, her opinion of Robinette Anthony was not good. What Preston thought was indiscernible.

Jackson appeared in the archway between the parlor and dining room. He sounded a gong and announced that dinner was served.

Robin brushed through the crowd and found her parents standing near the governor, ready to lead the procession to the table. "Here you are," she cried out in great relief. "May I sit with you?"

Her mother answered her, "I believe the places have been arranged, dear. You are to sit with the Hawley's; they have a son your age who you may talk to."

It was like a ton of bricks had fallen on the child's head, she became so downcast. "I don't like the Hawley's; I've met Preston already."

Clarice stepped up and very softly said to Robin, "I've had Mrs. Seward rearrange the place cards; you will find your card at the opposite end of the table from Preston's." The cards placing the guests in congenial arrangement showed that Clarice would have Robin on her left, but on her right was seated a young portrait painter from Boston named John Singleton Copley. As they sat down he introduced himself to Clarice, and she introduced him to Robin. In the stream of conversation between the three of them, Copley said to Robin, "I suspect you are an aspiring artist. You have hands for drawing."

Robin smiled with pleasure because she loved to draw. "Oh yes," she said, "how did you know?"

"I am an artist myself," he replied, "and it takes one to know one."

"It's funny that you noticed my hands, Mr. Copley. Mrs. Seward noticed them first thing when we arrived."

"Did she ask you if you were an artist?"

"No, she said they were too dirty to shake hands with anybody and to go upstairs and wash them."

"Robin...," said Clarice, "some things we hear are not to be repeated."

Copley laughed heartily.

Toasts were being made to the Anthonys and to the governor. Clarice, Robin, and Copley all lifted their glasses. The dinner was sumptuous, to say the least: large platters of ham, turkey, and fish, garnished with fresh fruit and vegetables. Robin's eyes popped wide open as she filled her plate with too much of everything.

Mrs. Hawley eyed her scornfully as she served Preston's plate with hardly enough for a bird. She didn't consider that it had been almost ten hours since Robin had eaten. Her last meal had been on the Cordelia at eleven o'clock, and there had been much activity since then, enough to make a child's stomach ache with hunger.

When Mr. Copley asked her if he could make a pen and ink portrait of her after dinner, she said, "I will be asleep before that." She knew she had to go to bed, and she asked to be excused as soon as she finished her dinner. Clarice also excused herself to go with Robin to her room.

When they were upstairs, Robin said, "Cee Cee, Mama and Papa aren't paying any attention to me. They hardly knew I was present all evening."

"Don't worry, darling; your mama and papa love you better than anyone in the whole world. They are so busy this evening with their new friends; they will spend more time with you tomorrow."

In spite of the attempt of the governess to comfort her, Robin felt neglected, and she sobbed until she fell asleep.

Clarice was wide awake. There wasn't a sleepy wink in her eyes. She kept refreshing her mind with the sight of the young, tall, handsome, blue-eyed man decorating the cakes. She became restless and wanted to hear more about him, so she pulled the bell cord for Maggie.

"Please tell me some more about the cake man," she asked of her.

"I told you all I know," she sounded put out. "He'll be here again in the morning to pick up his sugar and brandy, maybe you will see him and you can ask him what it is you want to know."

"Oh...Maggie, how will I know when he's here?"

"You will just have to watch for him. Sometimes he rides a horse; sometimes he drives his little chaise, that is if he is delivering."

"Which way does he come?"

"That's hard to tell, unless you know where he's been," Maggie sounded exasperated. "I will ask Henry to let me know when he shows up, and then I will let you know."

"Oh, I do hope Henry will see him."

"Don't worry, Henry will see him. Those two are like peas in a pod." Maggie hesitated for a moment while she hung up Clarice's ball dress, then she said, "I guess Henry knows more about him than anyone, probably more than he knows about himself."

"Maggie that's wonderful. With Henry around here so much I will be able to keep up on the cake man."

"Don't count on Henry to say much; he's close-mouthed. There's something mysterious about that nigger."

"Maggie, don't call Henry that; I don't like it."

"Well, most everyone calls him that, or 'peeper'."

"Peeper? What in the world do they call him 'peeper' for?"

"Don't ask me; I only heard it once. He was coming in the back gate in a run, and one of the soldiers was chasing him and hollering, "Stop that peeper, stop that peeper.

"I asked Lola what it meant; she said she didn't know directly and that she had better not speculate."

Maggie began to grumble a little. Clarice heard her say, "Questions... questions," as she gathered up a few towels from the wash stand and shoved them down the laundry chute then went hurriedly out of the room.

As she galloped down the hall she said to herself, "Heaven help us, this is going to be a strange household. The governess is moonstruck about the baker almost before she got here. Well, she'll find out; so are all the girls in Boston, and he's not about to be tied to any corset strings."

Clarice got out of bed where she had been since Maggie first came into the room. She thought she had better see if Robin was asleep. Tiptoeing into the room next to hers, she encountered Lady Anthony tiptoeing out.

"Oh...my lady, I was just coming in to see if Robin needs a kiver over her."

"She's fine, sleeping like a little lamb. Do you feel like talking for a moment?"

"Yes, your ladyship."

"Then come into my sitting room; Lord Anthony is still at the game table with the governor and a few others who are staying overnight."

Clarice followed Lady Anthony across the hall and into a beautiful room. The two ladies sat down opposite each other on handcarved mahogany chairs.

"Now," said her ladyship, "I must give you some direction. First...regarding yourself...you probably already know that you are a little above every other member of the staff in this household since you are the companion and teacher of my daughter."

"So I presumed," said Clarice.

"But," pointing her finger at Clarice, "you are to obey my orders and requests. I'm sure you remember our agreement between his lordship, myself, and your parents. You are to get my approval before accepting any engagements for social, religious, professional, business, or any other reason whatsoever. Your safety depends on it; so does my daughter's."

Clarice understood, and at the time it didn't dawn on her just how much she was to be curbed.

"And," continued Lady Anthony, "I want to give you some instructions regarding Robin. The long ocean voyage has delayed her studies. We have spoiled her unmercifully. Now she must get down to work. Her Latin is in a deplorable state; she must spend several hours a day at it. That is why it is very important to get started on it first thing tomorrow morning.

"I am told that the third floor has a solarium. We will look at it very soon; it may be ideal for a school room. With so much light, perhaps we can eliminate the use of candles. I worry so much about fire."

She sat silently for a moment as if thinking of something else when Clarice spoke.

"Robin is very curious about her new home and the people who live here. She is also concerned about where Bo Tay is going to run. I believe if we could have one more day to look around and discover places and things she would be more willing to settle down to books."

Clarice had already figured out that she wouldn't have time to find out more about the "Cake Man" if she had to get down to teaching school early the second morning of her arrival.

"Of course you are right, Clarice; you have an excellent mind for which I am grateful. It will be better for Robin to have some time to get to know the place. We will look at the third floor tomorrow, but we will wait a couple of days to begin lessons."

Lady Anthony got up from her chair and walked around the room. She pointed to a portrait on the wall and remarked that it was a good likeness of George II and that she wanted it removed to the downstairs front hall where all who entered could see it. Then she gathered her skirt into her hand and swished out of the room.

Clarice was standing looking at the portrait when her ladyship came hurriedly back exclaiming that she forgot to tell Clarice that she had invited some ladies to tea at four o'clock the next afternoon.

"Let's see if I can remember their names," she said as she laid her finger up to her forehead as if in thought.

"Mrs. James Warren; Mrs. William Brown; Mrs. Seward, who is my coach; and...oh yes, Mrs. Sewell and the governor's daughter-in-law."

She continued, "I would like you and Robin to present yourselves for a few moments around four-thirty. I am very proud of my beautiful daughter and want to show her off to the ladies. I was somewhat surprised at her actions this evening at dinner, not wanting to sit by Preston Hawley."

Clarice jumped to Robin's defense. "You must understand that the child was very tired and abashed by being thrown into elaborate social environment among so many strange faces so suddenly on her arrival. She felt much neglected by you and his lordship. I am sure she will be charming and gracious at your tea party."

"I'm counting on it," said Lady Anthony as she again left the room.

Clarice went back into her own room and began to undress for bed a second time. She was pleased with herself that she had been able to sway Lady Anthony's thinking about beginning school as soon as the morrow. She was delighted to think she might have a chance of seeing the man who had twisted the cherry at her in greeting. She might even get to meet him. She picked up her blue chamois slippers and put them on the chair with a blue dimity dress she had chosen to wear in the morning. It was a very pretty dress with a full skirt and a low neckline that emphasized the fullness of her breasts.

Clarice had developed early. At sixteen she had been proud of herself as she stood in front of her mirror and cupped her hands around her "ripe red apples" as she had called her bosoms.

She remembered that she had glanced over her shoulders, first right then left, to survey the roundness of her buttocks. She thought of the time she was stooping over to pick up some pins her mother had dropped and her father passed by and said to her, "You have enough bait there to trap the wildest cat in the jungle," as he slapped her on the bottom and told her to watch out where she set her trap.

Getting to sleep seemed impossible, although the house was now very quiet. She concluded that all the guests had left or gone to bed.

As she lay there in the dark, she pictured herself in the arms of the tall blond man. She wiggled and softly giggled. This was very strange and she wondered if she was dreaming. She had always shied away from men, but now she wanted to be very close to this one.

Tom Fellows had been her only beau. He had loved her, she was sure of that, but her feelings for him had only been platonic. She had submitted to his kisses, but he had never aroused any sensual desires in her, as just thinking about the cake man was doing. She wondered, Was it the devilment in his eyes?

She realized that she was extremely weary, and she felt nauseated. Sleep was very necessary if tomorrow she was going to be a vivacious and charming person at her lady's afternoon tea. She began her old method of going to sleep, repeating from memory one of Shakespeare's sonnets. Slowly in a whisper her lips were moving:

> ...Fair is my love, but not so fair as fickle;
> Mild as a dove, but neither true nor trusty:
> Brighter than glass, and yet, as glass is brittle:
> Softer than wax, and yet as iron, rusty:
> A lily pale, with damask dye to grace her,
> None fairer, nor none falser to deface her....

But she whispered to herself, "That is certainly not me."

At last she felt relaxed. It had been a long day but a good day. She fell asleep.

Chapter Two

As morning dawned over the high hills of Boston, rain clouds hovered near the earth. Fog was heavy around the new home of the Anthonys.

Clarice looked at the tiny brass clock on her bedside table. (It was a present to her from her father. He had made it for her a few days before sailing.) It was six o'clock and still dark. She was not aware that the sun was blocked out by rain and fog.

She heard soft knocking at her door and someone calling her name. She pulled the linen sheet up to cover her body and called out, "Come in."

Maggie opened the door and came in; she was doing exactly what she had been told to do.

"Good morning, Miss Clarice."

"Good morning, Maggie...Maggie, you can leave off the 'Miss,' just call me Clarice, or Cee Cee, please. It makes me feel like a stranger, and I want us to be close friends. I'm not used to being called Miss Clarice. I need someone else to talk to, besides Robin and Lady Anthony. Will you be my close friend, Maggie?"

Maggie smiled as she said, "Good morning, Cee Cee."

"What about our plans, Maggie? Has he been here?"

"No, have you seen the weather? I don't believe he will come out in this; no one can see the end of their nose."

"What about Henry? If he is here I can give him a message."

Maggie answered, "Better be careful what you say to that one; I told you before, he is a strange character."

She went to the window and drew the blue silk curtains to one side and looked out, then she turned to Cee Cee and remarked, "He's rough; he hangs out with a gang down on the waterfront. He says he's one of the faction; what that means, I don't know."

Clarice got out of bed and poured water from the pitcher into the bowl and doused her face. From behind the towel she said to Maggie, "Will you look in on Robin and see if she is awake?"

Maggie went through the arched doorway into the child's room. Immediately she called back to the governess, "She is not here."

Clarice came to the doorway and, confirming Maggie's discovery, she said, "She probably went and crawled in bed with her parents; she does that when she is disturbed about something."

Maggie picked up the poodle from among the covers and said, "I hope this dog isn't going to be a problem; it's hard enough to keep the linens clean without having dog hairs and fleas to wash away." She put the dog onto the floor and said, "Scat out of here, get down to the kitchen and find yourself some breakfast."

Bo Tay sat down and howled up at her.

Clarice picked him up and petted him as she said, "Come on honey, let's find your mistress."

She went to the bed chamber of her lord and lady and knocked at the door. A grumpy voice belonging to the master answered the knock with a loud, "Yes?"

"It's Clarice, sir. Is Robin in there?"

"No she isn't; she was here about half an hour ago, but she left."

"That's all right, I'll find her."

"Please come back immediately if you don't find her; we don't want her to go anywhere, even in this house, without someone with her."

"Yes sir, I will." She remembered what Lady Anthony had said to her about being cautious and now Lord Anthony, but why?

Maggie came from the bedroom and joined Clarice at the head of the back stairway and they went down together toward the kitchen.

"I suppose she was hungry and went to find some breakfast," said the maid.

Bo Tay was running ahead of them and barking excitedly. "Hush up, Bo Tay, you will awaken Lady Anthony." Clarice was shaking her finger at the dog.

"He must know where Robin is; he is trying to tell us something. Let's see if he leads us to her," said Maggie.

When Bo Tay reached the foot of the stairs, he dashed past the kitchen door in a flash and ran straight to the door that opened into the garden, where he waited with excited bouncing while Maggie and Clarice got to him, and then they all went out into the rain, crossing the garden walk to the gazebo where they found Robin sitting alone but looking very happy.

"Robin, why did you come out here alone? Your mother will be angry with both of us. You are not well enough acquainted with your new home and friends to go any place without me. It may not be safe for you."

The little girl looked at Clarice with mischief in her keen blue eyes. "He left you a note," she said as she held tightly to a piece of paper in her hand.

"Who? Who left me a note?"

"The man who put the cherries on the cakes last night."

"Robin! Robin, you have made my morning. What did he say to you?"

The child couldn't tell if her governess was pleased or offended as she handed her the slightly damp piece of folded parchment.

Clarice hastily unfolded it as Maggie watched with a sheepish grin. The blush on her face was distinctly one of approval. She read:

> Cup cakes or tea cakes
> Whichever you choose
> Your face is so pretty
> You'll never lose.

It was signed with a flowery "J."

The governess turned to Maggie and said, "Then he was here, in spite of the weather."

"So it seems; he's like that, absolutely unpredictable."

As Clarice took Robin's hand and they started to leave the gazebo she said, "Looking like this, it's a good thing I didn't see him. All my plans for the morning were squashed like wet mud. My blue chamois slippers would have been ruined in this weather." She swept her hand downward and outward to indicate mud, rain, and fog.

Maggie looked puzzled, she asked, "What's this about blue chamois slippers?"

"I guess we had better see if we can find some breakfast," Cee Cee said to Robin as they went into the house.

Maggie followed behind them carrying the wet little dog, tenderly shaking him and calling him a "little rascal."

The kitchen had a long trestle table standing in the middle of the floor; it was the servant's table. Being slightly irritated at Robin and the fact her plans were thwarted, Clarice took no notice of the table or the kitchen. "Sit here," she said and the two of them plopped down on the long bench, at the table.

A plumpish woman whom Clarice had not met whisked over to them and said, "You are to eat in the breakfast room; this table is for the hired help."

"Oh, all right. Come on Robin." Clarice took the child by the hand as they moved into an adjoining smaller room with a big bay window overlooking the garden.

The same woman came into the breakfast room carrying a large tray of food and announced that she was Lola, the cook. She placed the tray on a serving stand nearby while she proceeded to fill the sugar bowl.

Robin looked around to see what it held. She saw a plate of sausages, some stewed apples, a half dozen or more fat brown biscuits, a pitcher of milk, almost a pound of butter, and a dish of jam. Her mouth watered while she waited for Lola to put the servings on her plate.

The servant seemed disgruntled and in too much of a hurry. She didn't say anything but kept eyeing first Clarice, then Robin. She attended to her duties quite reluctantly.

Clarice was also silent but eating heartily. Robin was wolfing it down like she had never tasted anything so good. As soon as Lola began scuttling back and forth to the kitchen for more milk and sausages, Clarice said, "Robin, did he say anything when he gave you the note?"

"He said, 'Little lady, will you please give this note to your governess?'"
"That's all?"
"That's all, then he jumped on a horse and galloped down the hill."

Lola began to set things down very hard, to get some attention, because neither Clarice nor Robin had spoken to her, although Robin had looked her over from top to toe.

She kept constantly active around the table where the two were eating. First she rearranged the vase of flowers, then she rearranged the rest of the chairs; she pushed the window curtains aside and vigorously wiped a speck from the glass. Finally she picked up the empty milk pitcher and asked, "Would you like more of anything?"

"No thank you," said Robin.

"No," said Clarice.

She folded her arms across her chest, and, standing slightly askance, she surprised them by boldly asking, "Would you tell me why you are so interested in meeting that smart-alecky, know-it-all, Jason McKenzie?"

"Who?" asked Clarice, looking astonished at such a sudden interrogation.

"Jason McKenzie. Henry's sidekick."

"I'm not sure I know what you're talking about," said Clarice to Lola.

The child spoke up, "You know, Cee Cee, the man who sent you the note."

"Robin,..." scolded the governess, "that is a personal matter. You should keep personal matters to yourself."

Clarice turned to Lola, "Is that his name?" She repeated it, "Jason McKenzie."

Lola felt proud of herself, that she had spoken like that to the "higher ups," so she continued, "I've known him some time now. He comes here every two or three days with buns and sweets; I could have him come oftener if you would like more sweets. He is well known around Boston; he used to come to the place I worked before this almost every day. He furnishes nearly all the taverns and eating establishments with their bread. Now and then he furnishes a bit o' rum too." She laughed and picked up a tray load of the breakfast things and left the room.

Clarice pondered what she had learned while she gazed out the window, then hastily she turned to Robin. "Not another word about the note to anyone, please; too many people know about it already."

"Just you...Maggie...and Lola," said the child.

"And you," said Clarice. "Will you please not tell anyone else?"

Florence Anthony was having tea and biscuits in her sitting room when her husband joined her and gruffly announced that he had the most damnable headache and sour stomach.

"No wonder," replied his lady. "I never saw anyone so gluttonous and so obnoxious as you were last evening." She kept on talking with her mouth full of biscuit. "The governor was not very admirable either. He kept following

Clarice around, giving her the once-over with his sensuous eye. The dear darling never once noticed him."

"No," said Anthony haughtily, "but she was looking for someone. I saw her standing in the reception hall, gazing at the rear entrance as if she expected someone to come through that door." He asked, "Does she know anyone in Boston?"

"Not that I know of. She certainly took good care of Robin; that's all I'm interested in," said her ladyship.

After a moment's hesitation, Florence very frankly asked her husband, "Maurice, did the governor question you about your appointment and your duties here in the colony?"

"He never got around to the actual question; however, he was close a few times. He was full of questions all right."

"What kind of questions?"

"Oh, inquiring about my salary and who was paying it. I think that he may have doubted my being loyal to George III. He seemed a bit preoccupied at times."

"Like when?"

"When he asked if I had met or knew any of the Rebels stirring up unrest here in Boston or any of the other colonies?"

"So what did you tell him?"

"I told him that he and I would meet somewhere soon and have a very confidential talk and he would find out then the people that I know. Florence, we have to keep him in the dark about our real purpose here; I'm depending on you to keep your ears open and your mouth shut and for God's sake and the kingdom, if you see anything touching toward dissension, come to me at once."

Florence said, "I hate all this. I hate the people I met last evening. I wish we had not accepted this mission. I'm going to be sick from the secrecy and snooping and eavesdropping. I hate it." The lady jumped up from her chair and began pacing back and forth while giving Lord Anthony stern and spiteful looks. "I invited some ladies to tea this afternoon, but I wish I could call it off. All I will be doing is watching and listening for some bit of information.

"I asked Clara Seward to come a little earlier to let me in on some of their tricks. I know she is one of our most loyal subjects."

"Be prepared, Florence; they are very wise women and they probably are up to our purposes and they know that you know this town is a hotbed of rebels and some of them are dressed like British Gentry. Just be careful what you talk about.

"I have to go to Boston this morning; I'm going to attend a public meeting, and the speaker will be one of the foremost adversaries. I don't know how long I will be gone. I will send a messenger if anything turns up to keep me in town past six o'clock." He gave his wife, who was now standing in front of a long mirror, a quick peck on her cheek and went into his dressing room.

When he appeared again, he was dressed for town in a scarlet knee-length coat, a ruffled shirt with ruffled cuffs extending over his hands, white silk stockings, shoes with silver buckles, and a cockaded tricorn hat was in his hand.

As he walked past the gold leaf mirror on his way to the door he thought he looked as well dressed as the governor. He called up the stairway to his wife, "Florence, I'm going now," and he said to himself, "If this is a good day I will persuade her to celebrate with me tonight."

Lady Anthony, after watching her husband enter his carriage and depart down the hill, returned to her tea table and had another cup of tea. When she had finished all the biscuits, she delicately wiped her mouth and also her teeth with her napkin. She walked over to the door and pulled the bell cord for Maggie. Maggie was always somewhere on the second floor, and this time she was right outside her lady's door and she came in immediately. She stood in front of her ladyship at attention until given her orders.

"I want you to go out to the cottage and wake up Tomas and Marie. Tell Marie that I want to see her in my sitting room as soon as possible. Oh yes, Tomas, too."

Maggie was well trained, and dutifully she nodded her head as she said, "Yes, my lady." She turned on her heel like a foot soldier at drill and went out the door and down the back stairs, crossed the garden, and knocked on the door of the small brick cottage. No one answered, so she knocked again; still no one answered. Maggie, determined in her mission, gave the door a swift kick causing it to shake on its hinges.

Suddenly, and with anger, a chubby short-legged man with an almost bald head, opened the door and scornfully shouted at Maggie, "Well, what do you want?" He knew she was the upstairs maid by the dress, apron, and mop cap she was wearing.

Maggie, usually quite shy, was ruffled and embarrassed. Her first impression of him was that he was a stuffed shirt and she didn't like him. She said, as she gave him an angry look, "Lady Anthony wants you and your wife to come to her sitting room as soon as possible." She added a little curtly, "You better hurry."

Maggie turned to see him standing in the doorway. She stuck out her tongue at him and went into the back hallway door. She went hurriedly down the long hall and into the kitchen where she found Lola, busy at the long table, folding kitchen towels.

"Where have you been for the last hour, Maggie? You are supposed to help me with all the kitchen chores this morning. There is so much to do after all that big to-do last evening, and Henry was supposed to help me polish all this silver, but he has skipped out, as you might expect."

"I will help you some, Lola, but I still have things to do upstairs."

"Do you suppose I will get any help from that couple in the cottage?" Lola asked as she gave a big sigh of fatigue and hustled about stacking dishes and poking the fire.

"Nope," said Maggie, "they are the official overseers." She continued, "I doubt they will ever come into the kitchen."

Tomas and Marie soon came to the upstairs sitting room where they had been summoned.

Lady Anthony was sitting at a small spindle-legged desk writing her daily instructions to the kitchen. Without turning around to greet her assistants she told them to sit down. After a few more minutes of shuffling papers she got up and changed chairs and sat facing them.

"Now," she said, "we have plans to make, rules to make, and much more. We have lists to compile and invoices to tally." There was silence for a moment while Tomas and Marie nodded their heads in agreement.

"I suppose you have already found out that this is a big house but not as big as our manor house, so you will have approximately the same duties to perform. Neither you nor I nor his lordship, nor Robin, nor Clarice know one iota about any of the others who live here and work for us. So your first duty will be to find out as much as you can about them. Governor Hutchinson has assured us that all of them are faithful, reliable people who are devoted and loyal to England. We will soon find out just by observing and listening."

Her voice became softer when she began to talk about Robin. "She has never been associated with Negroes, and there's no telling what may come out of her mind regarding them. I am depending on Clarice to see that she does not offend them. I trust that no one will offend any of the servants; we do not know them, and I am told that there is much going on in Boston to frighten one, so be careful."

She spoke directly to Tomas. "You are to let them know that you are in charge. You and Marie are potentates of this household except for Lord Anthony, myself, Clarice, and Robin. Clarice comes directly to me if she has any questions or problems."

The two Britons were sitting stiffly on their chairs, their eyes shifting around the room. The lace curtains were blowing at the window and Lady Anthony went over to lower the sash.

She stood there for a few breaths of air before she began to talk again. "Marie," she said, "I will need your help in arranging a small tea party for this afternoon at four o'clock. Tell the cook to prepare something English to serve with the tea. Also see if there are any flowers blooming in the garden. Put some in the vases and urns."

By this time her ladyship was walking back and forth across the room with her forefinger perpendicular across her chin, holding up her lower lip, as if trying to remember something. "Oh yes, Marie, I will be needing a dressmaker and a hairdresser in the very near future, and I will be using them continuously. I want you to find such for me, and be sure they can come here to do their work; I do not intend going to them. Now if you will find the chambermaid and send her to me, you both may go and do what you have to do."

Marie didn't have to go anywhere to find Maggie. She was right outside the sitting room door wiping dust from under the edge of the rug. From the way she was bent over it looked like she had been eavesdropping at the keyhole. Shaking her forefinger at Maggie, she said, "You should be in her ladyship's bedroom straightening her bed."

"Thank you, but I've already attended to my duties in my lady's bedroom," said Maggie curtly.

"Well now she wants to see you immediately, so hop to at once."

Just as Maggie came into the bedroom from the hall, Lady Anthony entered from the sitting room. She spoke, "Maggie, I'm going back to bed for awhile; will you please turn back the sheets?" She untied the ribbons holding her silk robe together and let it fall from her body. Maggie's mouth dropped open in awe. The lady was as nude as a fresh hatched bird. "Don't look so amazed, Maggie; I always sleep naked."

"It's all right with me, your ladyship, if you like it; I'm afraid I would get cold."

"Never, my dear, if his lordship is in bed also."

Maggie fluffed the pillows and gave a big sigh and noticed her ladyship's pretty body and secretly she wished she could sleep naked and have someone to keep her warm. She said, "Your pillow is very soft; would you like a firmer one?"

"No, the pillow is fine." She sat down on the side of the bed and lifted her feet into the soft smooth sheets.

"Maggie, I want to confide in you; I trust you to keep my secret. I pretend to be sick when I'm not. I do it to get out of situations I'm supposed to be in but don't want to be in. I do not want my husband ever to suspect that I'm faking."

"You can trust me, your ladyship; I won't give your secret away." She added, "Do you want me to wake you later?"

"No I'm not going to sleep; I'm going to lie here and think. I'm going to try to like this place, but I hate it so far. Have you noticed any hate expressions on my face, Maggie?"

"No ma'am."

"What did you notice about me, Maggie?"

"Only that you are beautiful, your ladyship."

As the chambermaid left the room she had a sly grin on her face. She knew she had found a way to find favor with the lady: flatter her. She wondered if her mistress was planning a fake sick headache or something else to avoid being at the tea party.

The kitchen was a busy place when Maggie entered it. She noticed that Tomas and Marie had not yet made an appearance. Lola was stirring up a pudding; Henry was polishing silver. He had not skipped out after all as Lola had said. Michael was scrubbing the bottoms of the cooking pots.

She sat down at the table and poured herself a cup of tea. After a few sips she began talking. "I think we are about to have a visit from the residents of the cottage."

Lola began to beat the pudding more vigorously and asked, "When?"

"They will be here momentarily. The ladyship has given them orders to find out all they can about us of the 'lower class' who live here." She continued, "They are going to give us orders and teach us how to serve the king's emissaries. I hope we will learn something new."

"It ain't new to learn to keep your mouth shut," said Henry as he rattled the silver and dropped a spoon on the hard brick floor.

"Or to keep your eyes open," said Lola.

Michael was getting deaf and he couldn't exactly hear what they were talking about, but he supposed they were discussing the new master and mistress. He said, as he nodded his head up and down and pointed his finger at them, "We 'ens do well if we do what we're told and behave ourselfs."

"You are exactly right," came a voice from behind him. It was the voice of authority and Michael began to shake.

Tomas and Marie had heard what he said and they suspected that the others had been making derogatory remarks about them just before they entered the kitchen.

With a loud clearing of his throat and click of his heels Tomas announced their presence. His arms folded across his chest and his shoulders swaying back and forth, he gave a robust hiccup and his short white wig bounced into an askew position on his head, partly covering one eye.

Lola slapped her hand over her mouth to hold back her laughter.

Marie gave him a sharp dig in his side with her elbow, and he straightened his wig and began to talk to the row of foot soldiers standing at attention as Lola, Maggie, Henry, and Michael all jumped to their feet and formed a line in front of them.

"My fellow servants, I wish you to know that I am Tomas Straight and this is my wife, Marie—Mrs. Straight—to you, recently of London, now of Massachusetts. I am the right hand man, or valet, whichever you choose to call it, to his Lordship Maurice Anthony, a very important person in the service of His Majesty George III. I shall be directing, with my wife's help of course, all duties of this staff and household unless her Ladyship Florence Anthony directs me to do differently."

He looked sideways at Marie, as if for approval of what he had just said. She nodded affirmatively and he began again.

"After all, you may as well learn from the start that her ladyship is the director of everything including his lordship and the Lord God Himself."

With a smirking twist of his painted lips, Tomas turned on his heel and left the kitchen. Marie followed right behind him.

The servants sat down at the table with "sour apple" expressions for each other. When Lola put some food on the table they began to eat greedily, more from anger than hunger. Disapproval of Tomas and Marie was evident.

Maggie broke the chilly atmosphere by declaring, "We'll get along all right, you'll see."

Henry looked angrier than the rest when he spoke harshly, "How do you know we'll get along? I don't intend to take any orders from a sneaking British spy."

"Henry, watch what you're saying; you might get yourself put in the stockade."

"Shut up, Lola; I'll say what I please. Anyway I'm not going to be around here much of the time; I got other fish to fry."

Michael looked over the others at Henry who was sitting at the far end of the table and said, "Henry, you and me are free men. We can say some things that other black men can't say, but effen I wus you I would watch my mouth. Don't go around calling somebody a spy. We is all British subjects, and there ain't nobody to spy on."

"Oh hell, Michael, you are too old already. Why don't you go some place and crawl in a hole and die? You talk about us being free men; nobody's free around here. We all do what we're told and pay for doing it."

Maggie had not said anything or hardly moved. She just sat eating slowly, but when she got up from the table she said, "This is a good household, and we had better be thankful we have it so good. As for me, I intend to do the best I know how, to stay satisfied, because when this is over, what will we do? We are only servants. We will lead the line to the chopping block!"

The bell was ringing for Maggie. "See, what did I tell you?" She left the room to answer the bell.

Lola and Henry had something in common that the others did not know about. Lola knew that Henry belonged to one of Boston's street gangs and that he had been in a number of riots and that he always had plenty of money. She and Henry had both come to the Anthony household on orders from the governor.

They had previously worked in a tavern that had closed down because the tavern owner often was too inebriated and unable to attend to his business, causing debts to pile up and employees to fight over the money in the till for their wages.

When Jason McKenzie, who had furnished the tavern with buns and bread, heard of the predicament that his two friends were in, he went to Judge Otis to see if he knew of employment they might obtain, and he in turn contacted the governor who just happened to be in the process of procuring household help for the Anthonys.

Henry and Jason had grown up together. Lola had grown up on the Boston waterfront and had for some years supported herself with the "oldest of the arts." A long spell of smallpox and pneumonia had made her unable to spend long hours outside in the winter time, and she also had become a convert to religious beliefs, mostly of her own fabrication.

She was extremely delighted to get such a situation as the Anthonys. She knew she would be well fed and have a good bed, about the two most important things one could ever hope to attain, as far as she was concerned.

"Where did you go last night, Henry? You were supposed to chop some wood and bring it in. You left before you finished your job," said Lola.

"Didn't you see the glow from the bonfires? We had a hell-raising time over on the Common, and we all got a shilling for being there." Henry looked very pleased with himself as he answered Lola's question.

"I don't believe you, you devil. Who would pay anyone for such disgraceful shenanigans?"

Smiling one of his biggest smiles, Henry said, "Oh, we have a rich sponsor, old gal, a very rich sponsor."

Henry went hastily out the door and across the garden, not taking time to open the gate but doing a handspring over it, and then went striding toward town. He looked like a pirate from the back, his head tied in a red bandanna, his leather breeches squeaking as his knees rubbed together and his heavy boots tapping the stone sidewalk.

"I wonder where he's headed in such a strong-minded manner," said Michael. "I wish I could take him under my wing and teach him to behave."

"Let him alone, Michael; he'll come to the end of his wits someday. I just hope he won't get shot. I've seen the way the British soldiers watch him; they know everything he does." Lola was no dummy. She had been associated with Henry for several years.

Maggie came back to the kitchen and asked, "Where's Henry? I have to talk to him."

"What about?" Lola was curious and concerned for Henry's place. She was afraid he would be dismissed if the Anthonys found out about his actions. She thought perhaps Maggie had said something.

"I want to tell him something that Miss Clarice asked me to tell him."

"He's gone, went hurrying off toward Boston," answered Lola.

"He'll be back about supper time, never misses a good meal," Michael said, then added, "I'll be back then too," as he went outside.

Maggie remembered something as she snapped her fingers and said, "Lola, Lady Anthony has ordered English scones and raspberry jam to be served at her tea this afternoon. I hope you have the scones already and won't have to start baking now, because there is no firewood to heat the oven and Henry has gone and left us without chopping any." She continued, "Jackson might be back in time to chop some, but I doubt it. If his lordship gets to talking to that gang in the tavern, he won't be home before dark."

Lola had a surly expression on her face when she responded to Maggie's orders from Lady Anthony. "I don't know how to make scones, and I'm not going to learn now."

Before Maggie had time to say anything else, the door swung open and Marie came into the kitchen. "So you don't know how to make scones, and you will never learn any younger. Get your cornmeal and milk; put a bowl on the table; put in the meal, about three cups; add the milk until it is soupy; then add some wheat flour to make it like biscuit dough; add some salt. Pound it and pound it and pound it until it is stretchy. Make small round balls of it and bake it in the oven. Be sure each scone is golden brown. Don't ever let me hear you say again that you don't know how to make scones." She was shaking her finger at Lola all the time she was talking.

While Marie was standing there giving directions to Lola, Maggie was standing looking out the window. Lola was almost trembling with fright of the woman, but she quickly began assembling her ingredients for the scones. Marie noticed that there was no firewood to heat the oven. "Where is Henry?" she asked.

"Not here, went to town," said Lola.

"Who gave him permission to go to town?"

"I don't know, Mrs. Straight; Henry don't often wait for permission."

Marie turned to Maggie, but Maggie did not turn around. "Maggie, go and bring in some firewood."

Maggie was braver than she thought when she said, "There isn't any, and besides, that is not my place. I'm the upstairs girl."

"You're what? You're anything I say, and I said that right now you're to bring in some firewood."

Maggie remembered what she had vowed earlier about getting along with Mister Straight. She said, "Oh, all right," and picked up a large basket from near the fireplace and went out to the wood pile.

She picked up an ax that was nearby and began chopping on a huge log that had been hauled to the spot but which had not been sawed or cut. She began to sing as she heaved the ax up and down on the log, knocking off a few chips:

> ...Heave Ho! Away we go
> Off and away today
> Heave Ho! Away we go
> Off and away today
> With bonnie Prince Charlie...

Someone came shyly through the garden gate and walked around the lilac bush, startling Maggie, causing her to drop the ax. "You scared the devil out of me. Truly, what are you doing here?"

A young girl, probably sixteen years old, with curly red hair cut short in front but long in the back and apparently not combed for a week, very slender, with green flashing eyes, wearing a full dark brown skirt to her ankles, a low-necked gathered blouse not quite fresh, as if she had slept in it, looked sheepishly at Maggie. She placed her hands on her hips and, swinging back and forth, took up the ditty Maggie had been singing and sang a different verse:

> ...Over the briny bay today
> Landing on the morrow
> Heave Ho! Away we go
> Bonnie Prince Charlie....

"Truly, if I get the crosscut saw from the shed, will you help me saw this log?" Maggie asked, breaking in on her singing.

"Well maybe, if you pay me."

"Pay you? I can't pay you."

"You can do something for me then."

"And what would that be, for Heaven's sake?"

"Promise me that you will not tell the governess that came with the Anthonys anything about Jason McKenzie, that you won't tell Henry anything about the governess because he talks too much to Jason."

"Why are you so interested in what Jason finds out about the governess or the governess finds out about Jason?"

"Because, damn it, he's mine. I don't want her to ever see him."

"Tell me Truly, how did you find out that there was a governess? What have you heard about her?"

"Well, when we were mixing the dough this morning, Jason remarked that when he was here last night setting up his cakes for the welcoming party, he saw the prettiest girl he had ever seen, and he said she smiled at him. I didn't like her from that minute, and I want you to keep her away from Jason. Henry told me she was the governess."

"Truly, Truly, you are jealous of someone you don't know, have never seen, and may never see. Now I've got to get this wood into the kitchen so let's saw, saw, saw." Maggie went into the shed for the saw while Truly sat on the log and waited.

In a moment or two Maggie was back with the saw. The thing was much too heavy for her and she was out of breath as she and Truly began to use a tool that neither of them had used before.

Together they started to sing their song about "Bonnie Prince Charlie" as they pushed the saw back and forth in rhythm. Soon they had several pieces that Maggie could chop into fireplace logs.

"Help me get some into the kitchen; Lola needs it right away."

They each filled their skirts, and Maggie filled the basket. Their backs were bent under their loads, and when they entered the kitchen they heard a childish giggle. It was Robin laughing at them while Bo Tay was nipping at their ankles and growling furiously.

Truly kicked at Bo Tay and Robin screamed at her. "Don't do that; don't you dare kick Bo Tay...he is my dog."

Truly gave Robin a hateful look; dropped the wood she was carrying into the wood box; and turned toward Robin as she brushed the dirt from her skirt and said, "I guess you are the Anthony kid."

Lola stopped pounding the dough, walked over to Truly, took her by the shoulder, and said, "Get out of here and stay out. I don't want you in this house; you'll only make trouble." Then she shoved her out the door.

Clarice came into the kitchen just in time to see Lola scoffing Truly. She was looking for Robin and called out her name. "Robin, where are you? I've had a hard time keeping up with you today. You are not to come into the kitchen when Lola is busy."

Clarice had heard what Lola said to Truly and had heard Truly say, "But Mama, I want to talk to Maggie, and I'm lonesome for you."

With a questioning glance Clarice exclaimed, "Lola, I didn't know you had a daughter."

"Now you know," said Lola scornfully. "I don't generally let it be known; I'm ashamed of her."

Without saying anything more to Lola, Clarice turned and took Robin's hand, "Come on honey, I believe there is another place we haven't explored today. Shall we go and see it now?"

"What place is it?" asked the child.

"It's the rose garden down by Tomas and Marie's cottage. The roses must be fresh and radiant after the rain."

"How did you know there was a rose garden there, Cee Cee?"

"I was looking out the window for a long time, and I saw it then."

Clarice turned to Maggie and said, "May we have some shears? It would be nice to snip off a few blooms for my lady's tea table."

Maggie opened the small drawer and took out a pair of shears and handed them to Clarice, then she reached to the top shelf and lifted down a basket. "Here take this; you will need something to carry them in."

Clarice thanked her, and she and Robin went skipping out into the garden.

Maggie sat down quickly and wiped her forehead with her apron. "Whew, I'm glad you got rid of Truly just when you did. I feel like we are in for a lot of trouble with that one."

Lola sounded stern enough when she said, "I'll see to it that Truly stays clear of this place."

"How are you going to do that?"

"She's not so big that I can't thrash the devil out of her."

"Yes, you do that, then you've got Henry and Jason to contend with."

When Lord Anthony reached the carriage house which was approximately fifty yards from the main house, he spoke to Jackson who was putting the horse to the chaise that was to take him to town. "Jackson, I want to be taken to Faneuil Hall in Boston. Do you know how to get there? Because I don't."

"Yes suh, I does," answered the faithful servant.

It was only a moment or two before the handsome new chaise went down the hill past the most elegant houses of Massachusetts toward the busy city.

The evening before at the welcoming party Lord Anthony had gotten a run-down on a man he had heard much about before he came to America. He was particularly interested in what this man had to say in the speech he was going to make today at the public hall.

The speaker was well known in Boston. He was a native and member of the press, also a member of the legislature. Governor Hutchinson called Samuel Adams "The Chief Incendiary," said he was a tough, cunning, full-time professional politician, fifty years old, rugged, stern, puritanical, and the first of the new school of eighteenth century revolutionaries.

Lord Anthony was most anxious to hear what such a man had to say. It was public knowledge that Samuel Adams had instigated the organization of the Sons of Liberty and also the Committee of Correspondence.

As the early morning fog lifted, the harbor could be plainly seen. Many masts were swaying in the wind. It was a beautiful sight.

The new ambassador climbed out of his carriage and brushed himself off. He thought he looked every bit as grand and eloquent a person as he should be to represent King George III.

He looked up and down the street for the governor's carriage. He asked Jackson, "Do you see the governor's chaise anywhere?"

"No suh, I doesn't," he replied.

This important man in a strange place would have appreciated a familiar face.

Lord Anthony looked around as he walked toward the large brick building that had been given to Boston in 1742 by Peter Faneuil and where most of the public meetings were held. The building was the hub of trade, the place of markets. This morning, in spite of fog and rain, there was much activity.

Carts of all sizes were being pushed or pulled in every direction. Some were empty, but most were piled high with bags, bundles, or boxes. Some were loaded with crates of chickens or pigs.

The noise was deafening as peddlers, hawkers, farmers, merchants, sailors, or just about every kind of street vendor imaginable was in the process of setting up shop or scrambling around to find a place to set up shop.

A man very elegantly dressed came toward Lord Anthony with his hand outstretched in greeting, "Good Morning, Lord Anthony, I am Andrew Oliver, lieutenant governor and brother-in-law of Governor Hutchinson. I think it is mighty noble of you, sir, to come out in this weather to hear our great little politico lambaste his dear little heart out."

"Wouldn't have missed it for the world," was his lordship's reply.

Oliver then turned around to introduce several men who had come up behind him. "Lord Anthony, this is Mister John Hancock, one of Boston's most prominent citizens. he is a merchant of renown and also owns and operates Hancock's Wharf." The two men nodded and shook hands. "This is Mister John Adams, a lawyer. Here is Mister Bainbridge, Mister Thomas, Mister Prescott, Mister Revere, and Mister Quincy." The greetings were polite but icy.

The men made their way through the bedlam, and on reaching the building they went up to the second floor where the large public hall was already filled. They went about halfway down an aisle and found seats that had been reserved for them.

As Lord Anthony sat down he looked from side to side to surmise the aura and the people who were there. He made a mental inventory of the caliber of the crowd. He could count on his fingers any others besides those in his group who were worth more than a shilling.

The audience was made up mostly of the lower classes; dock workers, blacksmiths, small shop keepers and several onerous characters. Some very young men, probably fourteen to eighteen years old, were leaning against the wall looking too lazy for words. The walls were dirty from previous leaners. A few young children were chasing each other up and down the aisle. Two small boys jumped up on the podium; one grabbed a pitcher of water from the speaker's table and threw it on the other.

Lord Anthony was shaking his head in a reproachful way when he said to Mister Hancock, who was sitting next to him, "Do these children usually attend these gatherings, and are they always this obstreperous?"

Mister Hancock answered, "They are the children of the waterfront. They habitually hang around this building and they live off the refuse of the markets. You can see they are healthy and robust."

"Where do they sleep?" asked Anthony.

"Under overturned boats or carts if it is raining. If it is warm and dry they just lie down on the dock." He continued. "Some don't know who their parents are. Some grow up right here in this area."

"And when they grow up, what then?" Anthony already had a good idea of the outcome, but he had to make conversation.

"When they reach the ages of sixteen or seventeen they join the crew of some merchant ship and become good seamen. We need such men."

"Without an education?" asked Anthony.

"The life they live is an education and a good one, and most important, they are free men with a knowledge of the sea. No one can tie them down." Hancock sounded as if he might like such freedom himself.

Then Anthony asked, "What about the girls?"

Hancock had a slight grin, "What about them? Girls, huh? Oh some find good husbands, some just vanish, others become harlots."

The speaking was about to begin. Two men walked out to the front of the podium. One wore a long wig and the other a queue; each had on a frock coat, knee-length white silk stockings, and black pumps with buckles.

The one with the wig picked up a bell about the size of a teacup and rang it vigorously. About half the people in the hall became exuberant and began to shout, clap hands, and stomp their feet. Whistles and cat calls almost shook the walls.

The bell ringer rang the bell louder and louder. He couldn't get the crowd to calm down. Then the man with the queue stepped up front and waved his arms around. Everyone became quiet like sudden stillness after a storm. Then he began to speak and continued for an hour and a half.

"Mister Otis and Mister Adams make quite a team, wouldn't you say?" Mister Hancock asked Lord Anthony when the applause at the end of the speech ended, and the men were leaving their seats.

Governor Hutchinson never showed up at the meeting and Lord Anthony remarked about it to Andrew Oliver. "It was just as well that the governor didn't hear what Samuel Adams had to say about excessive nepotism in the government."

"Oh well, sir," Oliver replied, "he cannot fill vacancies with people who would be necessarily under scrutiny all the time. He doesn't have time to search out the very desirable from every part of the province."

Lord Anthony paused to shake hands with Otis, who had hurried from the platform to catch up with them. "I was happy to hear Mister Adams," was the comment he made when Mister Otis asked him what he thought of the speaker.

Casually he said, as they approached the exit, "Part of his speech will go down in history, as being the match that ignited the fire."

The men descended the stairs where they paused at a table laden with sweets. There were delicious-looking tea cakes and large glasses of tea and beer.

Anthony looked at the man behind the table who was the caterer and recognized him as the same man who supplied the petits fours for the party at his house the previous evening. As his lordship helped himself to the refreshments his eyes met the caterer's eyes a number of times, but they did not speak. All the men with whom Anthony was now acquainted were enjoying themselves at the table.

Mister Bainbridge was the brunt of much kidding because he was a very fat fellow and was stuffing extra cakes into his pocket. "Well," he said, "as long as John (meaning Hancock) is footing the bill for all this I may as well take my share."

Most of the people who attended the speaking had already gone their separate ways, but the group of seven or eight men in Anthony's crowd lingered around the refreshment table for probably half an hour, talking and smoking.

"I have much to accomplish today and had better be on my way," said his lordship as he held up his hand and wiggled two fingers in a "see you later" motion and walked toward his carriage, which was waiting a short distance away.

Jackson was asleep in the noonday sun, which was now throwing its full force of heat and brightness upon the market place. Some of the stands of fruit and vegetables had been shaded under some kind of makeshift shelter.

Anthony's touch awoke Jackson and he said, "Sure is a busy place today, suh." Jackson felt free to speak even when he wasn't spoken to.

"Oh yes, Jackson, a little like the markets in London."

"Huh, suh? I neber thought London was like this," said the servant.

Lord Anthony climbed into his chaise and told Jackson to drive to Charles Street, "I want to walk around over there and get some ideas of the business climate."

Jackson bobbed his head up and down in obedience and picked up the reins. It was not as far as Anthony had estimated it to be. They were there in about fifteen minutes.

"This is a good place to hitch, suh. There is a little shade for old Stomper." Jackson was a kind man, especially to animals.

"Well and good, Jackson, you wait here; I won't be long." His lordship went striding along toward the row of brick buildings which housed many different establishments for the exchange of goods.

Chapter Three

As Lord Anthony walked along Charles Street and took a few steps down several of the adjoining streets where some of the shops and business establishments were located, he became more and more aware of the dissension that reports to His Majesty had asserted.

He was swearing silently as he read a scrawl on a wall, "To hell with Geo. III."

What are those devils thinking of? he thought.

He stopped in the bakery that he assumed belonged to "McKenzie" and ordered some cinnamon buns. A middle-aged matronly woman came forward to wait on him. "Looks like some more rain, wouldn't you say?" he asked her as she wrapped the buns in brown paper while eyeing his British splendor.

"I ain't one to predict the Lord's doings," was her gruff answer.

"Do you have steady work here?" asked his lordship.

"Mister McKenzie lets me help out sometimes when he's busy somewhere else."

"Would you mind if I asked your name?" (After all, his purpose in Boston was to find out who was antagonistic to the government and who was loyal.) Making friends was a way to start.

"Yes, I would mind, 'cause it ain't none of your business."

Graciously he nodded his head and said, "Thank you for the buns," as he laid one shilling on the counter and started to leave.

"Wait a minute," she yelled, "one more shilling, please."

He threw another shilling down. By this time he was burning under his collar. He walked hurriedly toward the place where Jackson was waiting with the carriage.

"Jackson, I want to go over to Province House. I want to see if the governor is there."

"Yes suh, it's not very far from here."

Lord Anthony walked into the governor's office and found him standing with his arms folded across his chest, looking out the window toward the Old South Meeting House.

His wig and ruffled jabot were laying on the floor in back of him as if he had taken them off angrily and thrown them there.

He turned his head to see who was coming in to his office without knocking at the door. "Come in Anthony, sit down." He was gruff and loud as he walked over to his desk and plopped himself into his chair.

His lordship could see that the governor was upset. "Missed you at the speaking, your Honor." (Anthony didn't have to honor him, but he felt that at the moment a little lift would help.)

"Hell...if I had listened to that jackass this morning, I would probably have exploded right there on the spot; that wouldn't have been becoming to me. I'm trying to keep calm, if possible; I'm getting along in years. I'm sixty-two, but I feel a hundred, especially this morning."

Anthony noticed that his eyes were red, as if he had been crying, but then he remembered last night and said, "You certainly were in good form last evening. Nothing political was bothering you then."

"I guess what I need is a woman. I'm a lonesome man, trying to buck the winds of discontent alone. You understand that, don't you, Anthony?"

He pulled his chair up closer to the desk and placed his clasped hands in front of him while twiddling his thumbs. For a moment or two he held his head down in silence before he said anything more.

Lord Anthony also sat quietly for a moment, reflecting upon this important man. Suddenly, as if with a new spirit, the governor unclasped his hands and began moving small articles around that were in front of him on his desk. "You know, sir, I have much love for Massachusetts: I was born here, I graduated at Harvard, I've held many public offices. My interests have always been for the good of the colony. I was married here; my children were born here. My dear Margaret lies sleeping here in the graveyard. It tears my heart to shreds to see the people rebelling against everything, the way they are. Our people are being torn apart. I only want what's best for them, law and order, obedience and loyalty to the king, better living conditions, good commerce, punishment of crimes; what else can I be expected to do?

"You heard Adams; he and his followers want my removal from the governorship. Also Oliver, the lieutenant governor."

"I met Oliver this morning at the speaking," said Anthony. "I took him to be as fine a gentleman as could be found on the earth."

"Yes he is, but those who seek his removal do not take that into consideration, as hardly any of the rebel faction are gentlemen."

"What are the basic cries of this rebel faction?" asked his lordship.

"There are several requests that just don't make sense. For instance, they are fighting mad because the new judges are to be paid by the crown; also Oliver and I are to be paid by the crown. The Assembly denounces the measure as a violation of the charter and calls my salary a bribe.

"I think perhaps you have read a circulated paper called 'Rights of the Colonists'. Among other things, it denounces the right of the reigning sovereign to establish bishops in America. Now that is downright impious boldness."

The governor continued to talk, but now he was up from his chair, walking back and forth across the room with his hands folded behind his back and was sort of preaching to Lord Anthony.

"They don't want to pay their just taxes; they don't want Parliament to make the rules concerning the colonies. They have these so-called Committees of Correspondence running roughshod from colony to colony carrying tales, telling lies, and stretching small grievances into magnanimous ones. What can be done—tell me—short of bringing troops into Massachusetts?"

Anthony turned around in his chair and coughed while Hutchinson went on ranting and raving. "Some damn son of a bitch in England got hold of some letters I wrote to Tom Whatley—personal letters, mind you—and sent them here to Boston to the Assembly and they were read by Otis and Adams and Hancock, and God knows who else. Now I hear that the contents of the letters are common knowledge and that they are going to be published in the papers. They were among my letters, some that were written by Charles Paxton, Thomas Moffat, Nathe Rogers, and George Rome. My God, Whatley is dead and I can't imagine who the scoundrel is who would do such a thing! Would you have any idea who it might be?"

Anthony shook his head negatively. "No, unless it was Franklin."

"Ben Franklin? Never, never. He wouldn't do a dishonest thing like that."

"The letters were sent to the Reverend Cooper and he handed them to Mister Cushing who is the speaker of the Assembly and he came to me, bringing the letters, and asked me if they were mine, if I had written them? I couldn't deny writing them, but it was five or six days ago, for God's sake."

"What's in them to fire everyone up so?" asked Anthony.

"Oh...I said the colonists did not have the money or the sense to govern themselves, and I said they were money grabbers and rabble-rousers, that criminals should be sent to England for trial, that Parliament ought to pass laws to do away with public, or private, assembly except with written permission from the governor, and that he should have the right to adjourn any meeting whenever he deemed it necessary. I said the king should have absolute rule over the colonies.

"I hoped Whatley would get some ideas from my letters. I wonder what the hell he did get from them. I know I've done myself a great deal of harm." He dropped his head, and in a moment he pulled a handkerchief from his hip pocket and wiped his eyes.

Anthony finally arose from his chair and walked to the governor and put his arm across his shoulder as he spoke to him in soft tones, "Your loyalty to England has grown stronger with the years; everyone knows that. Parliament and the king should be very grateful to you and should compensate you handsomely for your earnest endeavors."

Hutchinson embraced Anthony and said, "Thank you, your lordship, but I fear for this colony—and myself. I'm afraid I don't have much time."

Anthony replied, "I think we ought to cool it for a few days and think what should be done. Maybe we ought to call a meeting and issue an order."

After a slight pause he said, "May 24, two weeks from today, is the king's thirty-fifth birthday. Let's plan a big celebration and invite the whole damn colony to a big shebang, bring them all together and extol all of the king's and parliament's virtues."

"That's a good idea, Anthony; we'll have it at my farm, Milton Hill. It will last all day and all night; we'll eat, drink, and be merry."

Anthony nodded, "For tomorrow we may die."

"Get your man Henry to spread the word; tell him to invite everyone. Make some broadsides and put them up in the Green Dragon and tack them up on trees on the Common. We'll kill the fatted calf and entertain the riffraff, the rabble, the beggars, the scum, and for sure all the big propagandistic fatheads who are going around yelling about freedom."

When the large old grandfather's clock in the corner began to ring out its chimes for four o'clock, Anthony said, "Good Lord, it's late; where did the day go?"

He picked up his hat and cane and started out the door when the governor said, "Wait a minute, I have something to ask you."

"Yes?"

"That young woman, the governess to your child, how old is she?"

"Seventeen, I think."

"She certainly is a beauty; where did you find her?"

"Her father is an iron manufacturer in Birmingham. He makes iron fences, gates, weather vanes, horseshoes, anchors, and any number of things. He was commissioned by the king to make iron statuary for the palace gardens. He also makes firearms."

"Then she's of the gentry?"

"Yes, I would say so; she has a splendid education. Her mother is a Scotswoman, a far distant cousin of my wife, Florence."

"Be sure she gets to the king's birthday party. I want to see more of her," said the governor.

"Now you be careful, Governor; she's vulnerable at her age."

"Oh, most assuredly. I admire her beauty and respect the fact that she is under your jurisdiction."

Lord Anthony left Province House, turning around when he reached the street, even stepping backwards a couple of strides to survey the building. He was wondering if there might be a room there he could use as his office. That close to Hutchinson would be convenient, he thought.

He found Jackson waiting in the carriage, asleep as usual. "Wake up, Jackson; this time we're going home. Maybe supper will be ready."

Jackson said, "Sure hope 'tis, suh, I'se hongry."

When Lord Anthony and Jackson reached Beacon Hill, Anthony asked Jackson to let him off at the front stile. He wanted to look in on his lady's tea party.

As he entered the entrance hall he heard the music from the harpsichord and wondered which one of the Boston ladies was so talented. He went through the arched doorway into the music room and saw Maggie sitting at the mahogany instrument. She was dressed in her gray maid's uniform and wearing her mop cap. This was an astonishment, that she would be entertaining the guests instead of passing refreshments.

He saw Clarice interestingly engaging Mrs. Seward in chitchat, but where was Florence? Nowhere to be seen.

When Clarice saw his lordship taking his seat on a red velvet chair near the door, she hurriedly went over to him.

"Good afternoon, Lord Anthony, we are happy that you have decided to join us."

He smiled at her and stood up and asked her, "Where is her ladyship?"

"Oh, sir, she had a bad headache, but she sent her apologies and said Robin would be her stand-in. Robin is also feeling poorly. Too much going on since we've been here. She will be all right very soon."

"Looks to me like you are doing justice to the occasion," said Lord Anthony. "I will speak to each lady and then go and see about Florence."

After shaking each one's hand and exclaiming that it was indeed a pleasure to be host to so much beauty and grace, he went over toward Maggie, still sitting at the harpsichord, but when he got closer she jumped up and ran out of the music room into the parlor. Crossing that room in a hurry she ran up the back stairs to the third floor where she had a tiny room.

As soon as the Boston ladies left (each in her own liveried carriage), Clarice went looking for Maggie. She found her crying, so afraid she was going to be sternly reprimanded for stepping above her place.

She cried on Clarice's shoulder, "Whoever heard of a servant going to the master's music room, sitting at his harpsichord, and playing it without being asked to do so. I will surely be dismissed."

"Frankly," said Clarice, "I think Lord Anthony was delighted to learn that there is a musician among his household servants. I think that Lady Anthony was the one he was embarrassed about. He knew she didn't have a headache."

"I knew it, too," said Maggie.

They were still in Maggie's room when they heard the dinner bell. Michael was walking around, all over the house, ringing it.

Clarice and Robin, Marie and Tomas, Lord and Lady Anthony were soon on their way to the dining room.

Lord Anthony hesitated and spoke to Tomas. "Round up all the servants and bring them here because I have some good news to tell them."

When they had assembled at the dining room door, he read to them the invitation to the king's birthday party to be held at the governor's house in Milton. He had written it on the governor's gold-edged stationary. He emphasized to them that they would be expected to share in the preparations and be present at the celebrations. He also told them that they were to enjoy themselves to the fullest.

There was so much confusion in the Anthony household after hearing the news of the upcoming celebration of the king's birthday that no one ate much of their dinner.

When Lola came into the dining room to clear away the half full plates of uneaten food she became irritated and proclaimed loudly enough for all to hear that she would not under anyone's persuasion make any cakes or spend any time over the hot coals cooking turkeys, or chickens, for George's birthday.

Lady Anthony called out to her as she was passing through the swinging doors between the dining room and kitchen. "Wait Lola, I have something to say to you and to every one of you," she said as she lifted her hand and pointed her finger at her husband.

"We will have a meeting tomorrow morning and make some plans. This party must be carefully organized. It must be especially festive and friendly. You see, this party has many special purposes. We must impress our friends with the love England has for her colonies."

Lord Anthony scowled down the table, sort of giving an evil eye to all who were seated there. He answered Florence gruffly, "I've already asked Clarice to take charge."

He then got up from his chair and headed for the parlor where demitasse was being served. "Come on, Florence, let's have our coffee."

Clarice and Robin ducked out the French doors and crossed the garden to the gazebo. Tomas and Marie and Florence followed the master into the parlor.

The day was at dusk. It was cool, and ocean breezes were blowing the curls about their faces, but Clarice and Robin could see someone sitting in the gazebo.

It was Jason and Truly.

"What are you two doing here at this time of day?" asked Robin, as she bounced right in front of them, placing her arms akimbo. She gave them a sour look and continued, "Have you heard about the king's birthday party?"

They ignored the question.

Clarice had seated herself and was straightening out her skirt. She was smiling at Jason. She paid no attention to Robin's inquiry as to Jason's and Truly's knowledge of the party. Her mind had already jumped to the conclusion that there was more to the relationship of Jason and Truly than she had heretofore suspected.

Robin stamped her foot and kicked Jason on the shin, "Answer me," she demanded.

Truly leaned out toward her and scornfully replied, "Yes, but who cares?"

Clarice and Jason were looking at each other lovingly, but neither spoke.

After Truly and Robin were calm, Robin sat down beside Clarice but was still frowning because of Truly's answer.

Clarice spoke (making excuses for Robin, as usual), "Robin is very much excited over the prospects of an outing into the country and especially a big celebration."

Jason got to his feet, "Let's go," he said to Truly as he reached out his left hand and pulled her to her feet. He reached out his right hand to Clarice which she accepted and felt his squeeze. He gently said, "I suppose we will see you there. When is the big day anyway? Do you think the likes of Truly and I will be invited?"

Clarice joyfully responded, "I'll see to it."

Jason said, "I hope to see you before that."

Robin left the gazebo and followed them to the garden fence where Jason's horse was tied to the hitching post.

He mounted quickly and helped Truly to mount behind him. The two of them rode off toward Charles Street.

Clarice stood in the gazebo looking after them, and expression of wonderment on her face. She knew she was in love with Jason, but how was she going to get him away from Truly?

Robin was chasing a firefly when she heard Cee Cee calling her, "Come on Robin, it's getting dark. We had better go inside. I will read to you something from Shakespeare."

"I hate Shakespeare," was the child's curt reply. "I want you to make up one of your ghost stories for me."

Candles were flickering as Clarice and Robin climbed the stairs.

The Anthonys were chatting with Tomas and Marie in the front parlor. Lola was busy with her duties in the kitchen.

Robin called to Bo Tay and asked him if he had had his supper. Clarice picked up the little dog from where he was resting on the landing, halfway up the stairs, and carried him to her bedroom.

Henry was sitting at the trestle table in the kitchen, rapidly consuming, by large spoonfuls, the food Lola had scraped from the plates she had just carried from the dining room.

"I think I was about starved," Henry exclaimed with his mouth full. He reached for the large pewter pitcher, tilted it to his mouth, and gulped down the remaining dregs of the cider.

In a choking voice, he said, "Lola, I'm taking some of these leavings (meaning food) to some of the jiggers down on the waterfront; they ain't seen the likes of grub like this in their lifetime."

Lola snatched a gunny sack from the drying line across the corner and jammed it full of bread and meat, apples and jars of honey. She heaved it on to the table and shoved it over to Henry. With a big grunt, she cautioned, "Don't get caught carrying grub to the riffraff. You know they are always causing trouble for the constables."

Henry replied, "I'm not worried about the constables; all I have to do is slip them a shilling and they will lie for me anytime. I play both sides of the crap game."

He took the sack of food, threw it over his shoulder, and shuffled out the door while wiping his mouth on his sleeve. A few minutes later Jackson came into the kitchen and seated himself where Henry had just been.

He said to Lola, "Is there anything to eat? I ain't had a bite since six o'clock this morning; I'se been too busy to eat."

Lola answered him gruffly, "Well, it's your own fault. Why do you go so long, working like a fool, without eating? And what is it that has kept you so busy? Sleeping in the hay?"

She poured out a big stein of tea and put it in front of him, then she slammed a big hunk of roast beef onto his plate (the same one that Henry had used). "I was saving this beef for my friends," she said, "but I guess you are as good a friend as I've got."

"Who are your friends, Lola?" asked Jackson. "Even thems whose right at our elbows mought be carrying a knife for our backs, huh?"

There was something growing on the side of his neck. He said, "I have to chew my grub very slow. I only got two teeth, but this big ole thing on my neck jest kicks the pain all over my head when I'm working my jaws up and down. I wish I knowed somebody to stick it for me."

Lola came closer and looked at it. It was a lump as big as a hen's egg. She picked up a jar of grease from a shelf and standing behind Jackson, she shoved his head to one side as she rubbed a handful of the salty grease into his neck.

Jackson cringed with the pain, but he looked up at Lola and said, "I guess that mought hep some, thank ye."

She stepped back to put the jar back on the shelf and as an afterthought she said, "If you will come with me to my meeting Saturday, I will ask Brother Haskins to lay his hands on you."

Jackson didn't say he would or wouldn't go. He did say, "You asked me what I'se been doing all day. Well, I'll tell ye I ain't been sleeping in the hay.

"After I got through driving his lordship all over Boston from Fanny Hall to Charles Street, to Province House and home, I'se polished the harnesses, I'se washed the chaise. I'se curried old Stomper and Shoo Fly (the horses), I'se swept the stables. I'se gathered the eggs, and fed the chickens, and cleaned the henhouse." (The houses on the hill each kept a few chickens and each had a vegetable garden.) "I'se polished ten pairs of boots. I'se cleaned up Henry's room—"

Here Lola cut in very quickly, "That's enough, you must be crazy to flunky for that shiftless Henry the way you do. One would think that you're his slave. He is very cunning, always sneaking around. Nobody ever knows what he's up to…you can bet it's trouble."

Lola turned toward the hearth and removed her apron and mop cap. She picked up the tail of her skirt and wiped her hands and face and went down into the cellar where she slept. Jackson was still sitting at the table with his head in his hands. As she left the room, she heard him praying.

When Clarice and Robin reached their bedrooms, they discovered that Maggie had turned down their sheets, had hung their silk nightgowns on their bed posts, and had put roses in their vases and scented water in their pitchers.

Clarice was so pleased with all this attention, she wanted to thank Maggie. She pulled the bell cord and within a few minutes Maggie was standing in front of her.

"Oh Maggie, you are so sweet to give so much of your time to Robin and me," were the words she enthusiastically poured out to her.

"It's part of my job," the maid answered. "And here is something else," she said as she took a piece of folded paper and handed it to a surprised Clarice.

"It was from Jason; he had written it an hour or so earlier, just before he met Truly in the gazebo.

Maggie went into Robin's room and found her lying across her bed with her clothes on, hugging Bo Tay up close. She became furious at the child and scolded, "Haven't I told you to keep that dog off this bed? And why haven't you taken off your shoes?"

Robin was sleepy because it was past her usual bedtime; thus she gave the chamber maid a sassy answer, "Because I don't want to take off my shoes, because I want Bo Tay to keep me warm, and because it's none of your business."

Maggie snatched at the poodle. She pushed him into his little wicker bed and began taking off Robin's clothes. By the time she got her into her nightgown the child was asleep. Clarice came into the room while Maggie was hanging up the clothes.

She was looking very pleased as she said, "Guess what, Maggie? Jason wants to meet me in the gazebo tomorrow morning. I do hope Truly won't be there, too."

Maggie didn't respond for a minute or two, then she said rather glumly, "I hope you won't regret it." Then she added, "You can do better."

"But he is so handsome and strong," said Clarice.

Maggie started out of the room, but she turned as if she had thought of something important. "Cee Cee—remember you told me to call you that—I have heard that Jason McKenzie is one of the rabble-rousers of Boston. I have told you this before."

Clarice was getting a little uptight. "What do you mean, rabble-rouser? Is he a thief? A scoundrel? Why do the people patronize his bakery if he is so bad?"

"He is not bad that way, Clarice. It's politics. Liberty for the people, freedom for the colony. The Liberty people do not like the governor, or his sons, or his lieutenant governor. They are against all his office holders and their taxes. That's what I mean by rabble-rousers. They gather in mobs and do destructive things to protest."

Maggie stopped talking for a moment while Clarice was contemplating what she had said, then she went on, "The bonfire gatherings, burning effigies, secret meetings (to talk about breaking away from England), and criticizing Parliament are characteristic of rabble-rousers."

"Well," said Clarice, "I'm not going to let that stop me from loving him. His convictions may have merit. I think maybe I can change his way of thinking if I ever get the chance. I will put his mind on love. He looks to me like he is quite capable of a lot of it."

Maggie left the room, but she was certain that very soon there was going to be big trouble.

Chapter Four

On reaching Jason's place on Charles Street, the two riders dismounted and Jason handed the door key to Truly. He told her to go to his room and sleep there.

He led his horse to the barn and put some hay in his stall and said to the horse, "You better eat and rest because some big excitement may come later tonight and I may need you."

When he started to the back door of his shop, he saw Henry approaching in a hasty gait. He had run all the way from the wharf.

"What's up?" Jason called out to the breathless Henry.

"I heard, just a little while ago when I was at the dock, that the boss of the faction is going to be on the platform on the Common at eight o'clock. I'm rounding up all the Rousers I can locate to be there. Will you come with me?"

"You know damn well I'll come with you." He never got as far as the door. He turned toward the street, and he and Henry went walking hurriedly toward Boston Common.

Jason's room was on the second floor and had one small window. Truly had unlocked the shop door and climbed the dark stairs. She got to the room and walked over to the window. She pulled back the old quilt that Jason kept hanging over it for a curtain.

She saw Jason and Henry going off together. Stamping her foot, she yelled out, "Damn it! I thought you were coming to bed." She knew they were on their way to the Common and quickly decided that she was going with them. She didn't bother to go down the stairs and out the door; instead she opened the window and jumped out. It wasn't very high, and Truly was tough; she didn't hurt herself.

She ran very fast to catch up with the men, but her boot had a flapping sole and it caused her to fall. She became so angry at the moment's delay that she sat down in the street and pulled off her boots and continued running in her bare feet, carrying them. A little later she threw the boots into a pile of trumpery at the edge of the Common.

It was the custom for each person attending the rallies to bring something of no value to burn on the bonfire that they made, to dance around, yell and sing, and throw out insults to Parliament, to the King, and this night to the new emissaries and Governor Hutchinson.

The pile of rubbish into which Truly tossed her boots was for burning, and it was growing larger by the moment. People had brought old chairs, pieces of discarded lumber, logs, old broken furniture, bales of hay, corn cobs soaked in whale grease, etc. Truly's boots stuck out from the top of the pile.

Jason and Henry reached the wild throng several minutes before Truly, who began pushing through the crowd looking for them. Soon she spotted Henry's head. How could she miss it? Henry was conspicuous by his red bandanna, wrapped in pirate fashion around his head.

He and Jason were engaged in back-slapping conversation with a very distinguished looking person who was using a scroll and goose quill pen and was wearing a small bottle of ink tied around his coat button to write down the name of individuals who came up to him to give their identification.

Truly was the only female in that group, however there were several women sitting on the grass some distance away. They were clapping their hands and calling out names, using animation and vulgarity. Truly saw them and ran over to join them, but not before she let Jason and Henry know that she was there.

Jason yelled out after her, "Truly, get the hell away from here; there's going to be some viscious encounters here tonight. I thought I told you to go to bed."

Truly, looking back while running, scornfully hollered back at him, "Well, I thought you were coming to bed with me, but damn it, you ran off with Henry and I was not about to stay there by myself. I want in on the action over here."

The increased yelling caused Jason and Henry to take off toward the fire which someone had started.

Truly saw the flames and remembered her boots, she looked down at her bare feet and said to them, "Them's the only boots we've got. I better go and get them 'cause I don't know where to get some more."

She darted like a flash toward the now briskly burning trash.

Jason saw her as she was dashing toward the big fire. He ran after her, his arms reaching out to her while he kept crying out, "Stop, Truly. What are you doing? Come back." He thought she was going to commit suicide. He ran faster and overtook her.

She screamed out, "My boots, there in the fire, I want them; they are all I have."

Jason then saw what she was screaming about and he jerked her back just as she reached the fire. "You fool," he said, "that skirt was almost in the blaze. You want to burn to death for a pair of boots?"

Just as Jason subdued Truly, someone (a big burly redheaded fellow) gave Henry, who had been running right behind Jason, a big whack on the chin and yelled out, "Let that whore run into the fire; it would be good riddance. She keeps the soldiers in fiery moods every day."

"That's a lie," shouted Jason, who had come to Henry's defense. He whacked the assailant right in the face, knocking him backwards and causing him to fall.

At that moment fistfights broke out all around, and the women over on the grass began to scream and get to their feet and run into the crowd looking for their men.

While the people who had gathered on the Common (to protest the emissaries) were fighting, Truly ran back to Jason's bakery shop.

She did not go to bed but went to the barn instead and climbed up the ladder into the hayloft. She covered herself with hay and lay there trembling.

Truly was very much afraid that Jason and Henry might be killed. She still didn't know why everyone became so angry just because she was trying to retrieve her boots.

The British soldiers who were on patrol that night soon dispersed the crowd. They arrested three or four of the young rebels. This kind of melee was happening often, and no one could ever pin down the ring leaders, so after a good dressing-down those arrested were let go.

The British knew that the Liberty Mongers would meet again soon to set up plans for another "Bonfire Meeting" to arouse the sentiments of the lower classes. They also knew that some of the Boston merchants and professionals were paying the leaders of the troublemakers.

What a contrast! Truly lying there in the hay, in her hot dirty clothes, and Clarice lying in her beautiful bed with her blue silk nightgown pulled up high above her knees. Each had their hands folded across their chests and each was thinking serious thoughts of amorous desire—about the same man. Each wishing, with fast beating hearts, that he would come to her.

Sleep was impossible for either one. Truly was frightened and nervous at every sound. She thought Jason would surely be thrown into the stockade. There was a stockade still in use in Boston, even in this modern time when jails were now being used to lock up the lawbreakers.

Truly had once been put into the stocks, when she was fourteen, but only for a few hours. She had been accused of stealing but was let off because a shop owner (not Jason) paid her fine. He made her scrub his shop floor and wash the windows to reimburse him. Then because she refused to get intimate with him, he kicked her out the door. When she hit the sidewalk on her knees, they were so badly bruised she couldn't walk for weeks.

She went to her mother, who worked as a cleaner in a shop in the same block, for help. Lola did allow her to share her tiny room for a few days and gave her a little food, mostly rotten apples and stale bread, but then she also kicked Truly out.

This all happened before she knew Jason and before the Anthonys came to Boston. Therefore, Truly was well aware of the cruel punishment one could get for doing almost nothing in the area of lawbreaking set up by the British court in Massachusetts.

Clarice, on the other hand, knew nothing of the meeting on the Common, or the fracas, that occurred there because of it.

She had seen the red glow in the sky when she looked out her bedroom window just before getting into bed. She had smelled smoke, but she closed her shutters. She then doused herself, behind her ears and on her neck, with the French perfume that Tom Fellows had given her when they said goodbye on the wharf in Liverpool. Now she never gave one thought to Tom, not even when she used the perfume. Her heart and mind were completely absorbed with Jason McKenzie.

She remembered how he had squeezed her hand earlier that evening when they were in the gazebo. It was an affectionate squeeze and it had sent goosebumps up and down her spine.

She lay there in her bed, the note Maggie had given her tucked into the lace edging of her nightgown. Clarice had memorized it.

She repeated it, "I would like to see you, if you are willing. I will be delivering bread to your house about ten o'clock tomorrow. Will you meet me in the gazebo? If I'm a little late, please wait!" Signed, J. Mc.

Clarice knew he was well educated; every word was correctly spelled, and the punctuation was perfect. She was so pleased.

She absolutely could not lie still, much less sleep, for the anticipation of the next morning.

Truly was tossing and turning in the hayloft, itching from the dry, dusty hay and her dirty clothes. She was so uncomfortable that she mouthed out a few cuss words as she ran her hand under her undergarments to scratch herself.

A moment later she scrambled down the ladder and saw Jason's horse standing in his stall. She walked over to him, threw a bridle on him, and led him out of the barn. She jumped onto his back, patted his neck, and said to him, "Charlie, I have to have a bath. The lice are fighting over the hay seed, and it's driving me mad. Take me to Marsh's Landing. I can swim there, and I can also wash my clothes."

Marsh's Landing was a short and narrow tributary to the Charles River, about five miles from Jason's shop. It was in a sequestered part of the county and once was used as a hiding place for goods stolen from the Canadians during the French and Indian War. The riffraff and derelicts of Boston sometimes hid themselves in the woods surrounding Marsh's Landing.

Truly had often been there to bathe and do her laundry, but only in the daytime. It was two o'clock in the morning when she reached the dark and deserted little creek. She got off Charlie's back and tied him to a bush growing on the bank. She undressed and ran her fingers through her hair. She took a running start and jumped into the cold flowing water.

It felt so good, especially to her itching back. She could feel the hay seed sliding from her shoulder to her derriere. She shook out her red curly locks and ducked her head under the water. She took a few skinny dips, then got out on the bank and picked up her clothes and threw them into the water. She saw them floating away and jumped in and gathered them up and returned to the bank where she was soon pounding them with a small rock against a larger rock. This was an old custom. She had seen her mother do it, and it seemed to get the clothes very clean.

Truly took her time. She would swim a while, then sit on the bank in her cool, wet nakedness, then jump in and swim some more. She was all alone in the woods, and she felt clean and refreshed. She also felt free: free of a hateful mother; free of a mad, threatening mob; even free of Jason and Henry.

She sang a little song. It went like this:

> My dearest is a handsome man,
> Son of a rich man up in town
> His name is John, and his eyes
> Are brown.

Then Truly changed the words and sang it like this:

> My dearest love is a handsome son,
> Of a rich man I never knew,
> His name is Jason
> And his eyes are blue.

It was beginning to be daylight when Truly decided she better put on her wet clothes and start back to Boston. Just as she was about to climb onto Charlie's back, someone laid a hand on her shoulder. She turned quickly, startled to be sure. She saw Henry, very close to her.

"Henry," she cried out, "where did you come from? And why the hell are you here?" She continued, in a voice more angry, "How long have you been here? I was naked in the water; I hate you for spying on me."

Henry sounded apologetic. "I'm sorry," he said, "Jason ordered me to keep an eye on you, sosen you won't get hurt."

Truly was even madder now, "Jason's got no hold on me; I'll get hurt if I have a mind to. I know what he means by 'get hurt.' He won't be my lover, and he won't let anyone else be my lover. I'm beginning to hate him—and you too, Henry. Mind your own business."

Truly was now on Charlie's back; she gave him a dig with her heel and a slap on the hip. The horse bounded off onto the narrow path through the woods, leaving Henry flopped flat on his butt in the damp earth where Truly shoved him when he grabbed at the bridle to stop her. She had seen his intentions and was quick in ridding herself of him.

As she rode toward Boston, she tried to remember her last meal because she felt very hungry. All she could remember was one small bun she had eaten when she first entered Jason's room, before following him and Henry to the Common. It was on a saucer on his dresser and he had taken it and bitten into it. Now she remembered how stale it was. That was eight or nine hours ago.

She patted Charlie's neck and said to him, "Let's go over to the house on the hill, and maybe if Lola is up she will give me some breakfast."

Slapping the reins to hasten Charlie's gait, she said, "I would like some good hog meat, about a dozen biscuits, and some strawberry jam." Then pausing and sighing, she said aloud, as if to the horse, "Who am I supposing that I am, that I'm eating a rich man's grub? Am I Little Miss Robin Anthony? Or maybe I'm her majesty, Lady Anthony, or even maybe I think I'm that high and mighty governess. Giddap, Charlie, I'm starving."

It started to rain and it came down hard, and the wind was blowing the water in sheets. Truly, already in wet clothes, got wetter and wetter. She tightened the reins and asked Charlie to canter. She had water in her face, and it was blinding her eyes. She began to feel very cold.

Truly was having a chill when she tied the horse to the hitching post and bounded through the garden to the kitchen where she hoped to find a big cozy fire. But no one was there and the fire had not been lit; however, it was laid. Jackson had laid the shavings and logs just before day light, but when he saw the rain, he knew everyone would sleep late so he returned to his room over the stables.

Truly found some live coals in the tinderbox and she poured them into the shavings, and the blaze soon burst into a lovely cheerful heat.

She looked into the cupboard and found a few remains of the last evening's meal. After eating from her hands all she could hold of the meat and cold potatoes, she was still standing in front of the cupboard stuffing herself with apple pie when Lola came up the cellar steps and into the kitchen.

She saw Truly immediately and shouted at her, "Truly! Truly! You thief, what are you doing? You've got a nerve sneaking in here stealing food. Get out, get out and stay out."

She grabbed a leather strap from a hook near the cupboard and lashed out at Truly. Just at that moment, Michael came into the kitchen. He felt his heart jump as he jumped between the strap and Truly's back. He caught the lash intended for Truly, right across the face. Blood began to pour from his nose.

Lola screamed at him, "You old fool, get out of the way. This thief is stealing the grub I'm saving for my friends. I'm going to kill her."

Michael, although bleeding badly, held up his hand in front of his face as he approached Lola to take the strap away from her.

He said, "Good Lord, that child is hongray; she is your daughter. How can you do such a thing? Effen you're going to kill her, why didn't you do it when she was borned?"

Lola stopped her stomping and yelling. She looked at Michael and snatched a towel from the line stretched across the corner and wiped his face. She pushed him into a chair and handed him the towel and told him to hold it over his face to catch the blood.

He did as she told him, but not before he saw Truly run across the garden and jump on Jason's horse and ride away toward town.

It was still pouring rain.

Chapter Five

Henry was trudging back toward Boston through the rain. He was wet and cold and felt like he had a broken hip. He had hit the ground so hard when Truly shoved him. He couldn't get up for several minutes, and ever since he had been aching with pain. His boots were leaking and full of water.

"Oh, God!" he said, "I'll be dead with pneumonia when I get home."

Lola saw him trying to get the garden gate open. He was weary and shaking with a chill. It was difficult for him. Just as he got it open and was about to fall, Lola reached him. She carried an old discarded piece of sail cloth that she used for herself when it was raining. She threw it over Henry and took his arm to hold him up until they could get into the kitchen.

She said, "You're such a fool. Why didn't you stay in the tavern, or wherever you were, until it clears up? Oh I know; they threw you out."

Henry said, "Lola, shut up. You don't know a damn thing about me or where I was." Then he asked, "Is Truly here?"

"No she ain't," Lola rudely answered, then added, "I threw her out, the bitch. She's going to get me fired. Why do you ask? Have you seen her?"

Henry, between coughs and sneezes, answered Lola's question. "She took Jason's horse, and where the hell she is now, nobody knows."

"Well, where did she go?" asked Lola.

"I don't give a damn," was Henry's reply. "Jason's always after me to keep an eye on her so she won't get into trouble, but it's a hell of an impossibility."

Henry caught his breath, and, as he gasped, he said, "I feel like burning oil. Lola, get me a swig of rum."

Lola helped him into a chair and stooped to pull off his soaking boots; his feet smelled like rotten potatoes. She flung her head away from the smell and said, "Phew! Henry, you need a foot washing." She sighed and continued. "I can't get you any rum; Tomas locked up the liquor cabinet and told me to call on him to unlock it only when his lordship requested it."

Henry stretched back in his chair and rolled his eyes. He looked frightening. He had a coughing spasm, and Lola covered him with an old coat she took from a nail near the cellar door.

"Henry," she said, "you're sick. I'm going to the stable to get Jackson. Somebody's got to put you to bed."

Lola was gone several minutes, then returned with Jackson who had a bottle sticking out of his hip pocket and an old horse blanket over his arm. He and Lola soon got Henry to the room he called his own and into the flaccid old bed.

He was burning with fever and sweating all over his body.

"I'll go tell Tomas," said Jackson. "Maybe he can get a doctor."

The Anthonys hadn't, at this time, had need of a doctor, and Tomas knew nothing of Boston or Boston doctors.

When Jackson informed Mister Straight, as he called him when talking to him face to face, of Henry's condition, Tomas said, "It will have to wait until Lord Anthony informs me of what to do."

He went straight to his lordship's study, which was an ante-room to the front parlor and was kept locked except when his lordship was in it. He happened to be there when Tomas walked down the hall and knocked on the door.

"Who's there?" came a voice from inside the study.

"Tomas, sir."

"What do you want, Tomas?"

"A doctor, your lordship."

"Who's sick?" questioned his lordship as he opened the door.

"Henry, sir, the black boy."

After a moment's hesitation, Anthony mumbled out, "Well, he'll have to wait until I can find out from the governor's office. I don't recall having heard a doctor's name mentioned. Tell Jackson to bring the chaise around to the front as soon as possible. I'll go and see if I can round up an old sawbones. What's the matter with the boy?"

Tomas shook his head, "I don't know, sir; I haven't seen him."

"Where is he?" asked Anthony.

"I suppose he's in his room over the stables."

"Well, he'll get better when I get back here with the doctor." He added, "Are you sure he's not drunk?"

"Jackson didn't say he was drunk," answered Tomas.

When Henry was in his bed, and having a chill, Jackson pulled the bottle from his hip pocket. He put his arm under Henry's head and raised him up and said, "Here boy, drink this flip; it'll kill your fever."

"Me, too," said Henry as he grasped the bottle and, swallowing greedily and rapidly, finished off the entire contents. In four or five minutes he was sleeping and snoring.

Jackson heeded Tomas's instructions and went to push out the chaise to get ready for the trip to town to find a doctor.

Lola wiped Henry's face with her pinafore; she bent over and kissed him on the cheek and said, "You're like my brother, you ornery cuss, but I ain't got a brother. I just got you."

She left the dingy little room and went back to the kitchen.

Michael was sweeping the hearth. He rested on the broom handle and said to Lola, "Henry's been attenden' them bonfires and spreading rumors that the Anthonys are here to hep the Tories and to see that the British Guards arrest everyone that has a bad word for the tax collectors or any British officer. I wish I could turn him around, at least keep him away from the Commons. Too much is heppenen there. He's going to get shot or put in jail."

Michael began his sweeping again. Lola looked sad when she said, "I am worried about Henry, too—and Jason and Truly and me." Then, as she dumped a bag of potatoes into a large kettle on the hearth, she said, "You, too, Michael, but you're too old to be in any danger; just stay close to the house."

As soon as she opened her eyes, Clarice heard the rain. She pounded her fists into her pillow, "This is unfair...rain, rain again. I might as well be in Noah's ark. Jason would be crazy to get out in this weather."

She got up and went to the window and pulled back the curtain. It was a bad, gloomy day. She folded her hands and began to pray:

"Dear God, may I ask of you a kind favor? I may be a foolish, selfish girl, but I do want to see Jason. Give me that pleasure, please. Please stop the rain, so he won't get wet. If I am asking too much, or you think I am a silly goose, please forgive me. Thank you ever so much. I am sincerely yours, Clarice Creighton."

The prayer boosted her hopes. She went back to bed and laid there in delicious fantasy, pretending that Jason's warm body was close to hers. Actually, Clarice was feeling an exciting surge of passion.

Robin began stirring around in her room and talking to Bo Tay, Clarice aroused herself out of her pleasure and got up.

She went into her dressing room to pick out a dress to put on. She chose a white one with little pink roses embroidered on it with pink ribbons attached to the ruffled cuffs. She held it up to herself and decided it was the one, but she soon changed her mind and took a soft blue from the rack. It had white lace trimming. She held it up in front of her and liked it. There were dozens of dresses from which to choose.

After choosing the blue dress, she sat down at her dressing table and brushed her hair. She noticed that the sounds from Robin's room had ceased, and she went in to see about her. She found the child sleeping, with Bo Tay also sleeping cuddled in Robin's arms.

She tried to quietly remove the little dog from the bed. She knew Maggie would be mad if she caught him there. Her efforts were unsuccessful. When she touched him, he snuggled up closer to Robin. Clarice didn't want to wake the child this early, so she let the poodle be.

Every few minutes she went to the window to see if the rain had let up, but it hadn't. When she heard Lady Anthony tripping down the hall toward her room, she hastily put on her robe and sat down at her dressing table and began to brush her hair again.

She wondered what her ladyship could want, that she was up so early in the morning. She hoped she wouldn't wake Robin. If the child could sleep a few more hours, maybe, thought Clarice, I can write a note to Jason and perhaps a letter to Mama and Papa.

Lady Anthony didn't knock before entering. She opened the door and saw Clarice. "Good morning, my dear; I felt in my bones that you were having a restless night. Is anything the matter? Are you ill or something?"

"Oh no, your ladyship, I couldn't sleep because of the rain. I think Boston is worse than England for rain. I was thinking of Robin's expectations for today and hoping they wouldn't be ruined." (She really was thinking of her own expectations.)

"What expectations?" asked Lady Anthony.

"Oh the plans we were going to make for the birthday celebration, plus looking over her school books and also perhaps getting Jackson and Maggie to drive us around a little bit and show us the town." The last part was a sudden thought on her part, she was very anxious to see Charles Street.

"Well the plans about the party planning and the school books are perfectly all right, but no trips to town, at least for awhile. We must get to know these servants better," was Lady Anthony's response to Clarice's explanations.

"Oh, I do understand," said Clarice. "The rain has ruined everything anyway."

After looking into Robin's room and seeing that she was still asleep, Lady Anthony went back to her own bedroom.

She shook Lord Anthony out of his sleep and told him to get up. "There's been some kind of ruckus in the kitchen. You better go and see if those heathens are fighting."

He stormed back at her, "Florence, you know damn well that Tomas will 'tend to it; that's his job."

Florence answered, "I thought you were the peacemaker. What is your job anyway?"

He got up and angrily answered his wife, while looking for his shoes. "I'm an ambassador of good will, but I doubt the critical disputes going on around here—in this household or out on the streets or anywhere in this damnable colony—will ever be settled."

Florence thought about it for a minute, then she asked, "Don't you like it here?"

Her husband jerked his dressing gown off the bedpost and put it on. While tying his belt around his waist, he went stomping toward the kitchen mumbling something not loud enough for Florence to comprehend.

At nine o'clock Michael was walking through the hall, ringing his bell and calling out like a town crier, "Everyone in the upstairs sitting room at once."

Clarice opened her door and looked out. She was looking for Maggie to ask her if she knew anything about Jason's coming. She had decided that since it was still raining, he wouldn't come anyway.

She hung the blue dress back in the closet and took out a red cotton one. "This will do for such a disapointing day," she said as she laced up the waist with the black ribbons attached to it.

Robin had on the same dress as her mother (only in a miniature size of course), green with beige velvet braid outlining the cuffs and neckline. Her shoes were beige suede. Clarice had combed Robin's hair and put it up on top of her head in a bun.

She and Robin joined Lady Anthony in the sitting room. Lady Anthony complimented her child, as she bent to kiss her cheek.

Robin said, as she released her arms from her mother's neck, "Do you think I look well dressed? Enough for going to town?"

Lady Anthony gave Clarice an inquisitive look as she answered Robin, "My dear, Clarice must have forgotten to tell you. The trip to town has been postponed for a little longer, but you are going to begin your lessons today.

"Maggie has filled the shelves in your schoolroom with wonderful, beautiful books. I know you and Cee Cee are going to enjoy them very much. Those books are lovely stories about places all over the world."

Robin's countenance fell. "I don't want to know about the other places of the world; I just want to know about Boston."

Lady Anthony saw that the others were in the sitting room. She took her seat behind a long table that Michael had set up purposely for her to use.

Boxes had been brought from various closets, where they had been put on arrival, and were now sitting on the floor near the table, waiting to be opened.

Tomas and Marie had shopped all over London, just before sailing for America. They had purchased laces, ribbons, trinkets, perfumes, cloth of different textures, costumes, feathers, and many items for gifts. This merchandise had all been bought and brought along, just in case there might be some celebration, or entertainment, to which it might be useful.

"Now," said Lady Anthony as everyone took a chair facing her, "I will assign each of you a job to do, then a few days before the party, we will meet again and coordinate the whole shebang. Do you understand?" She gave a surveying look over those present and missed Henry from the seated staff.

"Where is the black boy? What's his name? I need him to do some heavy work."

No one answered her. Each had a blank expression on their face. No one dared to say, "Henry's sick."

"Tomas, you must reprimand him. He cannot play hooky with me."

Tomas nodded his head in the affirmative but said nothing.

"Clarice, Lord Anthony has made you the grand potentate of all this pomp and circumstance, but I'm overstepping his authority and taking charge myself. However, you will have a most important part to play in seeing to all of Robin's need."

Clarice answered her, "I am delighted; you can do a much better job than I. After all, you have been to court."

Marie spoke up without being recognized, "So have I."

Clarice was thinking she might have some free time if she didn't have to be supervising all the trivia; she could be seeing Jason—well, maybe.

Jackson was assigned the job of polishing all the carriages and seeing that all the stable hands of other families were asked to do the same. He was also told to wash and brush all the horses the day before the party so they would shine.

"Be sure," she reminded him, "to rub ginger under their tails just before the start of the parade, so that their spirits will be high, as well as their tails. Decorate the harness with red tassels and bows and bells."

Michael was assigned a job which he was not accustomed to doing, but he was most capable of it.

"Michael," Lady Anthony said to him, "you will be in charge of killing and dressing dozens of chickens, but first you have to pen up the selected ones and fatten them until the day of killing.

"Lola, you will roast the chickens and place them on platters to be served. Garnish each platter with mint and wild parsley."

Michael said, "Yes'm, I can do dat."

Lola said, "They won't be fit to eat, because I can't cook chickens."

Lady Anthony remembered Lola's vow not to make any cakes and she didn't want to have any fallen cakes, so she announced that she would hire McKenzie, the baker, to make all the pastries. Everyone smiled at that information.

"Maggie, I've learned just last night that you are a musician. I am sure that Governor Hutchinson has a harpsichord. I want you to practice something to play when we have the musical in the afternoon. You may not be the only one playing, so be prepared with something cheerful.

"Clarice, I want you to teach Robin a recitation, which I want her to do at the musical.

"Maggie, your part, or parts, will be numerous and varied besides performing at the harpsichord. You will be in charge of costuming the people of this house. There are plenty of velvet coats, white knee breeches, buckled shoes, hats, and lace cuffs." She pointed to the boxes. "Everyone must be outfitted in grand style.

"There are also miniature flags. See that every carriage is flying one."

Sighs of relief were noticed as her ladyship got up from her chair to leave. As she went out the door, she turned and said to her staff, "If anyone goofs, they will regret it." Then she said, "Tomas, I want that black boy punished for not being here."

Tomas said, "Yes, my lady," but he mumbled under his breath, "That's not going to be easy."

Marie followed Lady Anthony into her bedroom after observing that Lady Anthony was motioning her to do so.

"Marie," she said, "I have been informed of a dressmaker in Boston who can be hired to fit and sew some clothes for me. Clarice got her name from Mrs. Oliver yesterday at the party. I want you to go there and obtain her services. Jackson will drive you. Take Tomas along for protection."

"When shall I go?" asked Marie.

"This afternoon," said her ladyship.

As Marie walked back to her cottage, she counted on her fingers the ninety-nine dresses she remembered hanging in her ladyship's closet.

The ulterior motive, of course, in obtaining a dressmaker was to acquire a source of gossip. Acquaintance with a Boston businesswoman whose customers were the wives of the richest men, whom she hoped would be liberty-rousers, who was accustomed to political conversations would be of great benefit to Lady Anthony.

Marie told her husband of the afternoon mission and Tomas went to find Jackson, but within a short time Jackson was telling Tomas of Henry's need for a doctor and that trip to town took priority.

Clarice, holding Robin's hand and pulling her along, passed all the others who were leaving the sitting room, heading toward their own stations. She was in a hurry to get to the window at the end of the hall from which she could see the gazebo, although she felt sure Jason wouldn't be there. He wouldn't come in the rain.

Jason wasn't there, but it wasn't because of the rain. It was because he couldn't find his horse. After the bonfire died out and Jason returned home, he went to the barn to pump some water into Charlie's trough and discovered the horse missing. He supposed Truly had taken him, but the rain was now so torrential and cold he changed his mind and believed the horse had been stolen.

Jason knew Truly wasn't dressed for cold rainy weather. She had no warm clothes. In fact, the only clothes she had were the ones she had on. She wasn't likely to be out riding around.

It entered Jason's mind that he had not returned to his shop in time to do the day's baking and he wouldn't have any bread to deliver even if he did find Charlie.

He had Clarice on his mind and felt downhearted that he had not kept his appointment with her. He wasn't sure she had paid any attention to his note. Perhaps she wouldn't have met him anyway.

After pacing the floor back and forth several times and swearing at the weather, he decided to walk over to Beacon Hill and apologize for not bringing their bread. Maybe he would see her and could explain.

He went to his room to change his shirt and fell asleep across the bed. When he awoke several hours later, the morning was already gone. He pounded his head with his hands as he jumped up from his bed. "Who in hell was that girl in my dream? I don't know if it was Truly or Clarice, and why such crazy, erotic lovemaking? That dream was ridiculous. What's the matter with me?"

It was eleven o'clock, and the rain had slackened until it was only a drizzle.

Clarice and Robin were in the schoolroom; they had looked at the books and tried out the goose quill pens with the homemade ink.

Maggie had gathered berries from the pokeberry plants and mashed them into a liquid, which she used for writing. The Anthonys had brought some ink from England and it could be bought in Boston's stationery stores, but Clarice was satisfied with the ink Maggie had made. Robin wasted it away, drawing and scribbling, then discarding her work until the wastebasket was full to overflowing.

Clarice pretended to be interested only in the weather as she kept up her vigil at the window, overlooking the garden. She knew, if Jason should come, she must signal to him in some way that she wanted to see him very much.

She wrote a note while Robin was looking at a book. It said: I was kept by her ladyship until ten-thirty, then I had to commence Robin's lessons. I do want us to meet. If you can come at midnight I will sneak out to see you. Everyone will be asleep. Meet me in the gazebo at twelve midnight. I love you, Clarice.

She knew this would be against everybody's rules, not only Lady Anthony's, but any other way and time was just impossible.

Lessons over. Lunch over. Naps over. Clarice observed that the sun was shining. She was elated. She went to the kitchen looking for Henry. She hadn't learned about his illness. She wanted him to deliver the note to Jason.

Lola had gone back to Henry's room. Michael was the only one in the kitchen. Lord Anthony and Jackson had returned, bringing Doctor Thatcher, whom they had found in his office on Milk Street. Henry was so completely passed out the doctor said he was dog drunk. He asked Jackson to fetch him a bucket of cold water.

Jackson felt obliged to obey the doctor, but he was sure Henry was wet enough since he still had on his rain-soaked clothes. He picked up a cedar bucket and went into the kitchen where a large barrel of water was kept. As he entered the back door, he saw Clarice talking to Michael. She had learned about Henry and was feeling quite upset for two reasons. One was the probability of Henry's dying. Michael had been very sure that Henry had a fever of 210 percent. Clarice didn't have any knowledge of illness, so she believed his exaggeration. And second was wondering who she could depend on to get her note into Jason's hands.

She thought of Truly but discarded that option immediately. She didn't know about Truly taking Jason's horse and riding off to some place instead of returning to Jason's shop, where she usually hung out.

Clarice left the kitchen, thinking she ought to go and see Henry. Then she remembered being told that Lord Anthony, Jackson, Tomas, and Lola were with him. She decided to wait until later.

Clarice returned to the upstairs sitting room where Robin and her mother were having a little afternoon visit and tea party. As soon as Lady Anthony saw Clarice, she knew there was something bothering her. She said, "What is it, my dear? You look like something, or someone, has disappointed you."

"I guess I'm worried about Henry. You know that he is very sick, don't you?"

"Yes, Lord Anthony told me about it. He had to go into town to find a doctor, but why should you be worried? He's nothing to you. You hardly know him."

Robin spoke up in a most knowing fashion. "Because he is a friend of Jason's, and Cee Cee is in love with Jason."

"Robin!" said Clarice with a voice of consternation. "How dare you say such a thing? I hardly know Jason."

"Because he wrote you a note and because he looked at you that way."

"What way, Robin?"

"Like he wanted to kiss you." Robin was wearing a smirk.

Clarice was exasperated at the child. She was embarrassed. She turned quickly and left the room, before Lady Anthony had a chance to say anything. She hadn't been in her own bedroom five minutes until Lady Anthony and Robin followed her and rushed into the room. Robin was looking exceedingly coy and Lady Anthony was looking quite perturbed.

"Clarice," said her ladyship, "have you been carrying on with that low-class shop creature?"

"No, I haven't. In fact, I've only seen him twice. Once at the welcoming reception (only at a distance) and in the gazebo last evening when he was with Truly. I didn't talk to him. Robin told him and Truly about the birthday celebration, and I told him I would see that the two of them were invited."

"Who is Truly?" asked Lady Anthony.

Clarice hesitated to say who Truly was, because Lola had intimated that she didn't want it to be known that Truly was her daughter. Clarice didn't immediately answer; Lady Anthony cleared her throat and stretched her shoulders. Then Clarice said, "She's some relation of Lola's. She doesn't live here, but she stops by now and then to see Lola. She is also a friend of Jason's and Henry's."

"Oh, I see, she's one of them...trash, riffraff. I'm told Boston is a boiling pot of such scum," said Lady Anthony. "I'm telling you, Clarice, have nothing to do with that kind of people."

She reached out to Robin and pulled her up close, hugging her. She said, "My baby here might be in danger."

Robin looked at her mother and stepped back away from her mother's arms and said, "I'm not afraid of Henry or Jason; I like them."

Clarice smiled, but it was a forced smile. "I'll be very careful of what we do and say, but I really believe these people are our friends."

Lady Anthony went out of the room but turned as she closed the door and said, "I won't tell his lordship about Robin's suspicions."

Clarice put her hand in her pocket and fingered the folded note she had written to Jason. Her eyes filled with tears; she was trying to think of a way to get the message to him.

Robin saw the tears and came over to Clarice and put her arms around her. She did love her governess and she knew she had betrayed her.

"Cee Cee," she said, "I'm sorry I told Mama about you and Jason."

"It's all right, Robin, your mother is absolutely right in her advice. She loves us and wants us to be safe. I'm afraid, though, that she is too late with her warnings. My heart is aching for Jason at this very minute."

Clarice pulled the note from her pocket and tore it into a thousand pieces. She then threw the pieces into the water pitcher, knowing they would soon be absorbed with water and the writing would fade away.

She wiped her eyes with the lace cuff of her sleeve and took Robin's hand. "Come, little one, let's go for a walk. The sun is shining brightly and it's so warm. We can walk through the garden and smell the roses."

Chapter Six

After three days had passed and the sun was brilliantly shining again, Jason's horse came home, but riderless. The gate to the barn lot had been left open just in case such a return did occur.

Jason had not been to the Anthonys in all that time. He did not know about Henry's illness or Truly's unknown whereabouts. He assumed all was normal, as usual, at the Beacon Hill address.

Sometimes, when his flour and sugar were dampened by rainy weather, he didn't bake, so he only delivered tea or cider. No orders were on hand for either of these items from Lola.

When he discovered Charlie standing at the barn door with his bridle still on and the reins hanging loosely toward the ground, he walked over to him and petted him. The horse was lank, indicating he hadn't eaten for some time, maybe three days.

After allowing Charlie plenty of time to enjoy his hay and corn, Jason thought it was about time he checked on Truly and Henry. He hadn't seen either of them since the night of the bonfire. He depended on Truly to help him with the baking and on Henry for carrying messages and picking up orders from his customers. He hitched the horse to the chaise and drove to Beacon Hill.

Clarice had spent almost all of her free time watching the road along the garden fence and the hitching post. She didn't want to miss him if he should come. When she saw his chaise slowly making it up the hill, she quickly called to Robin that she was going to the kitchen for some tea. It was almost three o'clock P.M.

Robin immediately caught on, and she dropped the copy book she was working with and followed Clarice down the stairs. Just as Robin landed at the bottom of the stairs she ran into Jason coming in with a basket of honey and tea.

"Hello, Robin," said Jason. "Is everyone all right?"

"Henry's sick," answered the child while looking into the basket. "Where are the cinnamon buns?" she asked.

"Oh, sorry, I could not make any; the sugar was wet and the flour also, but I brought some honey. You can put that on the buns that Lola makes."

"Lola never makes any good ones," Robin replied.

"Did you say that Henry is sick?" asked Jason.

"Yes, he almost died." Then Robin went into the entire story of Jackson and Tomas going for the doctor, of Lola washing his clothes and how he followed Truly to the house. "But," she added, "Truly left and nobody knows where she is, unless she's with you."

"Oh, my goodness," Robin suddenly exclaimed. She had spotted Bo Tay digging like mad under a rose bush. "He mustn't do that," and she rushed out the door to him.

All the time Robin had been talking to Jason, Clarice was waiting, sitting at the trestle table, wishing he would hurry and come into the kitchen before Lola showed up.

When Jason walked through the door from the hall into the kitchen, Clarice's face turned into a precious pink and her lips curled into a loving smile.

"We were worried," she said, "so afraid we couldn't live without your delicious goodies."

"Is that so?" asked Jason. "Well, I was worried that perhaps in my absence, you would forget all about my sweet buns—and me."

"Never," was the reply Clarice gave him. She continued, "I even wrote you a note, but I destroyed it when I knew the rain would keep you away."

"It wasn't the rain. I would go through floods and fires just to look into your eyes. It was my missing horse. I was out looking for him all over Boston. I am glad he knew the way home."

"So that's it?" said Clarice coyly. "I'm second fiddle to a horse."

"Don't be jealous, darling. My horse is a boy."

Clarice's laughter was the most joyful she had had since her arrival in Boston a week ago.

After a few minutes of small talk, Jason started to pick up his empty basket, but he reached for Clarice's hand instead. He pulled her up from her chair and drew her up close, put his arm around her, and kissed her on the lips. He whispered in her ear, "Write me another note; put it under the broken post near the hitching post." He looked around to make sure they were alone, then he drew her up closer, ran his hand up and down her back, and kissed her again. He then released her, stepped back, and kissed her hand.

Clarice was trembling. She was thrilled clear down to her toes. She realized that at least she had felt his warmth. She prayed, Oh, God, make his feelings sincere.

As she went out the door to look for Robin, she saw Jason going into the stables. He was going to see Henry.

Henry was sitting up in his bed when Jason came into the squalid room.

"How are you, you incorrigible devil? What made a tough skunk like you get sick?"

Henry answered, "I guess it was trying to keep up with that damn Truly. I followed her to Marsh's Landing, and I walked all the way back in the rain.

I'm gettin' outta here in a little while, and I'm going to find that bitch and beat the hell out of her."

"Now, now," Jason was firm in his response to Henry's threats. "Don't you lay a hand on Truly. She's only a child. I will take care of her myself."

"In what way?" Henry wanted to know.

"I'll think of a way to make her ashamed of her behavior, but for now I have to go and find her. Maybe she has returned to the bakery, like Charlie did."

Truly had not returned to the bakery; Mrs. Jolly (the buxom clerk) had not seen her. Jason thought perhaps Truly was in someone else's shop along Charles Street. She often combed the area looking for a little job to do.

He first went into the saddle shop next door to his shop and inquired of Mr. Harvey, then he went into the Chandler, on the other side of his shop, and inquired of Mr. Winkler. Neither of them had seen her for a week, or more. Jason thought it strange that she had not been to the bun shop, for she was a cinnamon and cider addict.

He went to his room to look for a sign of her having been there. There was no sign. Truly could not read or write, so there wouldn't have been a note.

He went out again to ask some of the other shopkeepers if they had seen her. The Book House, The Apothecary Shop, The Bootery, the silver smith, and The Raging Bull (a tavern) were all questioned. Truly had not been in any of them.

Now Jason was getting worried. Was she sick and lying in some alley under an old canvas, maybe, or had she been abducted and raped? Was she dead and floating in the river? What was the reason for his rabid concern? Was he trying to avoid thinking of someone else?

When he went into Mr. McGregor's Notions and Potions, he got some advice. "Now McKenzie," said the old Scotsman, "why fret yourself about that lass? She's one of the ablest kind of females. When it comes to taking care of herself, you can bet your last shilling that she ain't sufferin' none for want of food and drink. I'll wager you she's with somebody right now who's settin' her up to a handsome meal."

"Maybe you're right," said Jason. "I shouldn't feel responsible for her and I ought not to be wasting my time, for I know she doesn't want me to. She is an independent little tramp, for sure."

Jason realized that McGregor was right. He put his hands into his pockets and began whistling a tune. He walked with a strutting stride back toward his shop.

His feelings were extremely good, because he was thinking of Clarice. "Oh, what a girl," he said; he could still feel her kiss. He began to walk faster, a passionate sensation came over him. He looked down at his fly; it was bulging way out in front.

He entered his shop and thought he had better get to work. He made up a batch of dough and filled about two dozen loaf pans and put them in his brick ovens.

Talking to himself, he said, "I guess I better go and see about Charlie." He went into the barn; he couldn't concentrate on what he was supposed to do. He forgot about the baking bread and he let it burn until it wasn't fit to sell.

All he could think about was Clarice. "I've got to have that girl," he said. "She is pretty; she is smart. No she isn't smart or she would have nothing to do with me. She let me kiss her; she liked it. What am I thinking about? I must be crazy!"

The oven was smoking; he removed the burnt bread and dumped it out into the trash barrel.

He said, "I better go and see about Charlie; someone may want to borrow him again. Oh for goodness sake, I've already done that. I think I'll make another batch of bread."

"I'm too nervous. Why am I trembling? Is it cold in here?" He threw another log on the fire and punched the coals to make them blaze.

"I think I'm in love. Her kiss was sweet and delicious. She likes me…I don't know her background. Mother told me to be sure I know who I marry. Marry! Why did I say 'marry?' I can't marry; I'm not old enough or rich enough. She wouldn't have me anyway, or they wouldn't allow her to anyway. I might as well forget it."

With trying to forget thinking about Clarice, he went out to the barn again. He said to the horse, "Charlie, where were you for three days? Do you know where Truly is?

"Truly. I better think about Truly. Now there's a girl for the record. Why don't I feel a passion for her? I've known her for years. Perhaps I know her too well.

"Geeze! I must be crazy, I don't care if I ever see her again. She's wild; she'll never settle down. She has no grace.

"Cee Cee is refined, she's settled, she would make a good wife. God! I think I'm in love. Am I old enough to marry? She's old enough, eighteen, I think. I need a wife. Why do I need a wife?

"Charlie," he said to the horse, "help me; I'm in love. I've got to see her. As soon as it's daylight, I'm going to Beacon Hill; if I don't see her I'll die. I don't know what's the matter with me."

Jason was distraught, his thoughts were arousing his passion. He couldn't control himself. Never in his life had he had such feelings. He went back to his room, undressed, and threw himself across his bed. He put a pillow up against his groin. In a moment the pillow was sticky and soggy. He threw it under his bed. He jumped up and pulled his breeches on but no shirt. He ran out into the street and went for a long run, all the way to the river, where he dropped his breeches and jumped into the stream.

He swam for a hundred feet or more, then back, then he stood up in the river (it wasn't deep, about to his waist). He ran his fingers through his hair. He rubbed himself down, first his chest, then his legs. He looked down at his personal belonging and said, "What the hell happened to you?" Then he laughed rapturous laughter (no one would hear; it was very early in the morning) and he said out loud, "Good God, am I going to have to run to the river every time I think of Clarice Anthony?"

He didn't even know her last name.

Jason took his time walking back to Charles Street. He felt so good, fresh from the early morning dip. He was bare-footed, and the earth felt warm to his feet.

He stopped in a clearing to look up and around. The sky was striped with brilliantly colored rays from the rising sun. It was an enormous ball of orange, coming up out of Boston Harbor. He heard a bluebird chirping loudly, singing to his nest of fledglings who were yelling at him for their breakfast. His mate was preening her feathers a short distance away, while swinging on a twig of mulberry bush.

A young rabbit jumped out in front of him and wiggled his ears. Jason laughed and stooped to touch him, but he was too slow. The youngster had hopped on to other explorations.

"Oh, what a beautiful morning!" said Jason.

He was ecstatic, in fact he acted like a completely different person. His outlook on life had greatly changed for the better.

"Love," he said, "I want love. I'm going to be like that bluebird I hear. I'm not going to be scared of love. I love L-O-V-E."

He reached his shop door and opened it to the strong smell of smoke. "Hell fire," he yelled, "I've let the second batch of bread burn up."

After Jason finished cleaning his ovens and fanning the smoke out of his rooms with a sheet that he waved and flung around over his head, he looked in his barrel and saw that he had no more flour.

"That settles it," he said. "No more bread 'til I buy more flour."

He bathed his eyes; they were stinging and twitching from the smoke. He changed his clothes then went to the barn, hitched Charlie to the chaise, and began his drive to Beacon Hill, but he drove to the wharf instead.

"I may find Truly there somewhere among the hucksters," he said to the horse. "She is sometimes keen on helping, especially if she can earn a shilling or two."

Lola was at the wharf doing her marketing. She saw Jason hitching Charlie to a post. She went to him and began tongue-lashing him for not bring bread to the Anthony house. He explained his situation to her, but it didn't soothe her temper one bit. She then began to accuse him of dilly-dallying and not taking care of his business. He admitted having more pressing things on his mind. "What can be more pressing than your business?" Lola scolded. Jason didn't answer that question. He turned and walked away. Lola sighed a big loud, "Huh."

She said, "I think he is looking for Truly." She walked on in the opposite direction, hoping to find a stall where she could buy some fresh cod. There were fewer stalls than usual, and fresh fish of any kind could not be found.

Jason's mind was switching from one thought to another. He sighted a strange schooner, walking near enough to it to read the name Gospel Truth and on the bow Romero.

He saw two black men winding rope. They were naked except for flimsy pants with rolled up cuffs to their knees. "Hello," he called out to them. They didn't answer but went down the hatch.

Jason's curiosity was about to get the best of him. He wondered who they were. He thought, They must be someone's slaves, but whose? He walked on toward the tavern thinking he would get himself something to eat. He realized that he hadn't eaten that morning.

Before reaching the tavern he ran into Lola again. "You still here?" he asked.

"Does I look like I'm here?" she answered, then snarling she said, "Well I sure ain't in heaven."

Jason didn't want to linger; he wanted to get to the tavern. He asked Lola if she would like to go with him to the Merry Mermaid and eat.

"That's no place for a lady," she replied.

Jason snickered, "Who said you are a lady?" She ignored that remark. "I'll go and set in your chaise. Bring me a bun with ham on it; I am hungry."

Lola pulled a pamphlet from her pocket and pretended to be reading. She was embarrassed at her lack of education. She was often seen pretending to be reading.

A ragged stranger passed the chaise and noticed her pamphlet was upside down. He walked closer, and, almost daring to do so, he said, "Good day Miss, would you like me to read your pamphlet to you?" Lola appeared to be grateful for his offering, but she was more grateful because he spoke to her.

"Oh yes," she answered with a blush. She continued, "I left my spectacles at home."

He took the pages from her and read aloud:

> notice:
> To everyone who is loyal to George III and to everyone else who are so ungratefully blessed and outwardly disturbing the peace trying to bring the loyal ones to their stage of dissension and fearfulness. There will be a gathering and speaking at Liberty Tree next Wednesday to install a committee to appoint speakers to make rebuffs to every outcry made to the so-called Patriots of Freedom.

When they reached the house, Lola gathered up her skirt and basket and jumped from the chaise without thanking Jason for the ride home. As she approached the door, she heard a loud commotion coming from inside. Someone was yelling, "Get up." Someone else was yelling, "Come on now, you can get up." Lola knew that voice was Maggie's.

When she opened the door she saw Jackson sprawled out on the floor. She called out excitedly, "What happened?"

Jackson rolled his eyes upward as he said, "I'se fell down the stairs." After helping him get to his feet, Lola went to Robin who had watched and giggled. She gave the child a swift shaking. She said, "Robin, this ain't nothing to laugh about."

Clarice took Robin's hand and led her toward the breakfast room. She called out to Lola, "Hurry and make our lunch."

Jackson was not hurt. He staggered into the kitchen following Lola. Mr. Straight appeared from somewhere following them. He was not concerned about Jackson. He said to Lola, "Why did you stay so long at the market?"

A few minutes later Lola brought a tray of sandwiches made of mint leaves, butter, and honey to the girls in the breakfast room, and Robin threw a fit for biscuits and ham. Clarice did not eat her sandwiches either; she was mad because she did not get to see Jason.

As Lola returned to the kitchen where Tomas was waiting for her, she grumbled under her breath that she was getting tired of flunking for the "Damn Tories."

Later in the afternoon Clarice and Robin went to the gazebo, each carrying a book to read. While there before getting down to reading, they noticed a bundle of what looked like clothing hidden under the bench. Robin said, "Look Cee Cee, someone has left us a present. What do you think it is? Let me examine it closer." She began to squeeze and punch as she tossed about. She poked her finger into the soft paper wrapping and discovered a bright red coat. She tore open the bundle and pulled out the coat. She held it up and determined it to be about size 36 to 40.

Clarice said to Robin, who was fingering the cloth and admiring the buttons, "Let's go and ask Jackson if he knows anything about this." They left the gazebo, forgetting about the books, and hurriedly went toward the house.

They met Lola and Mr. Straight headed for the cottage. Marie was at the big house helping the seamstress fit a dress for Lady Anthony. Robin looked back over her shoulder at Tomas and Lola. She had a big grin on her face as she said to Cee Cee, "Who do they think they're fooling?"

"Keep quiet about what you saw, Robin."

"Why?" questioned the child.

"To prevent trouble."

"Why, I like trouble; it's fun."

"Never mind, Robin; it's wrong to cause trouble."

"Cee Cee, you're too old-fashioned and do not have enough curiosity."

They found Jackson resting by the stable door. Clarice spoke to him. "Jackson, we found this coat in the gazebo. Do you know anything about it?"

"Nome I doesn't; it must be Mr. Straight's. I saw a shadow long about midnight alongside the gazebo and a horse was standing at the gate."

Carrying the bundle under her arm and stepping quickly toward the cottage with Robin following at her heels, Clarice remembered seeing Tomas and

Lola go into the cottage. She quickly changed her mind and decided to put the bundle back under the gazebo bench.

Robin was excited beyond control. She defied her governess's persuasion and ran to the door of the cottage and pushed it open. She saw, to her astonishment, Lola sitting on Tomas's lap and softly caressing his head which she held on her shoulder. This did not hold Robin back, she called out, "Tomas, did you lose a red coat?"

Gruffly he answered, "No, why do you ask?"

"Because Cee Cee and I found one in the gazebo."

Clarice followed Robin to the door of the cottage. She took hold of the child's arm and pulled her back away from the door. "Robin, you must keep it a secret about Tomas and Lola. It's none of your business. Don't tell anyone what you saw. Also, we will put the coat back into the gazebo and forget about it." Then Clarice noticed Robin had taken charge of the coat and was going through the pockets. She had discovered a folded piece of parchment and was unfolding it and reading it. It said, This coat is an exact size and style from which I want twenty-five coats made within the next two weeks. The red material is waiting to be picked up at the lt. governor's office having arrived from England this morning.

"So, that's what it is all about," a sigh of relief came from Clarice.

Robin had an expression of disappointment on her face as she said, "It's for the seamstress who is upstairs with Mama; I think she is a Tory spy. Do you think we ought to tell Papa?" Clarice thought about it for a minute, then said, "No, we will just put it back under the bench in the gazebo and wait to see what happens."

"Cee Cee, I can't see why anyone would need twenty-five coats."

"Robin, you ought to know the coats are for twenty-five different men…soldiers."

Robin shivered as she squeezed Clarice's hand and repeated the word, "Soldiers."

The two walked around the large garden, staying close to the wrought iron fence. They heard a loud noise coming from the intersection at the end of Beacon Hill. Thinking it might involve Jason, Clarice held on tighter to Robin's hand and rushed to the corner of the garden to get a better view of what was going on. They saw a game of horseshoes in progress but also a scuffle between two men with about a dozen men watching and cheering for one or the other of the men doing the fighting.

The girls heard angry words, loud and clear ("Patriot," "Loyalist," "Liar," "Son of a Bitch") and filthy words as well. All of a sudden Clarice and Robin felt quite unsafe, so they ran back toward the house. They saw Lola leaving the cottage and the seamstress entering the gazebo with Marie right behind her.

"Oh my goodness," Robin cried out, "I hope they don't see each other." But they did.

The seamstress picked up the bundle and headed for the street. Lola and Marie rushed toward each other and began a tirade that Clarice did not want Robin to hear.

When Marie knocked Lola down and fell on top of her, pounding her about the head and face, Clarice and Robin began to run faster.

As they closed the door behind them, Clarice said to Robin, "This is certainly a day for fighting."

Robin answered, "But I wanted to watch."

"No, no, Robin, it's evil."

"I like to watch people fight; it makes me laugh."

"Then let's go to your room and have a pillow fight."

Chapter Seven

Governor Hutchinson was following the tradition of his father when he invited four friends to dinner on Saturday evening.

Those in attendance, besides the governor, were Lord Anthony, John Hancock, George Bainbridge, and James Otis. They were standing around greeting each other and pouring their own drinks, waiting for one of the governor's servants to announce that dinner was being served.

Silver mugs of rum were reflecting the flickering candles. The evening was warm and lilac blossoms in a vase were giving off a heady aroma.

The governor, while pointing to a picture of his wife hanging over the mantel, said, "If she wasn't buried here in Boston I would move to England for awhile and rest."

Otis spoke as he hitched up his trousers to sit down, "Don't be a fool, Thomas. She can't be of any help to you. She's as dead as a person can be when they're dead. Why do you consider waiting? Go now and find peace."

Then Hancock spoke. "Your affairs of business could be handled by your sons, couldn't they?"

"Yes, I suppose so," was his reply, "but the wharf is too much now for all of us put together. I would like to sell it."

"Sell it? I thought you were trying to buy some more property along the waterfront. I never knew you to sell anything." George Bainbridge leaned a little forward and continued with a direct question. "How many houses do you now own, Governor?"

"Only eight, in town, and the farm in Milton. I inherited most of my property from my father. I've also acquired a few pieces, which I gave to my sons."

Lord Anthony finally got in a word or two. "I might consider buying a house in the Beacon Hill area if I could get any assurance of being here any length of time. My commission is only for two years. I hope it will be renewed."

"I wouldn't count on it," said Hancock. "These times are unpredictable. There is so much unrest and violence because of it. The farmers, the merchants, the small business people are ready to take drastic action because of the inflation and taxes. They are all hollering for representation in Parliament."

He waited a moment before going on with his statement. "We send petitions to Parliament and also agents to speak in our behalf. We wait and wait for responses, and when they finally come, they are negative. I wouldn't invest in property if I was you, my lord. You may have to abandon it."

Governor Hutchinson was shaking so badly, his cup of brandy spilled over and he had to set it down.

Dinner was ready and a servant came to the door and rang a small bell. The men went single file to their assigned places at the table.

A black man wearing a white jacket stood behind Governor Hutchinson. His head was wrapped in a red turban. First course was a thick soup of turtle and cream, then a large platter of mutton and ham, garnished with fresh sliced apples and grapes. Several different vegetables and breads were passed. A custard with rum sauce was served for dessert. Cuban cigars and more rum were available on the table.

The august men were all pretty well inebriated when they left the dining room to have coffee in the parlor. They sat on velvet chairs, smoking expensive cigars or sniffing snuff. For a while they were silent, as if thinking of something to say, then James Otis spoke up. "The episodes of violence and crime, occurring much too frequently on the Common, are reported to be planned and financed by a committee of nine persons, whose purpose is to cause some action to be taken by the government officials to bring about some relief in regard to poverty, squalor, and ignorance."

Bainbridge again spoke. "I don't think the government is going to do anything; if they were so disposed to help the poor people out of their miseries, who could they get to do their dirty work?"

The governor's face was noticeably red when he cleared his throat and said, "There's always been poor and needy; there has to be, or none of us would have anything. They get paid for any work they do, then they buy beer and rum and lay around drunk for days."

"True, true," said Anthony, "and it's impossible to change them."

Hancock said, in answer to the governor, "Maybe they could be trained as militia."

This remark raised eyebrows, and Bainbridge looked at his silver pocket watch and said, "Fellows, it's time for me to go."

The governor stood up. He said, "I hope to see you all at the celebration on the twenty-fourth. You are invited to Milton Hill for the entire day. Come early."

Hancock replied, "Thomas, that celebration is a bad idea. There are those who would like to repeat the night of August 26, 1765. You are encouraging it. Think about it."

"God! You're right," said the governor, "but it's almost too late to stop it."

Soon Governor Hutchinson was bolting and locking his door. The guests, all except Anthony, were huddled together on the sidewalk, talking in low voices.

Anthony was in his carriage on his way home, his head kept thinking Militia?

Chapter Eight

After leaving Governor Hutchinson's house, Lord Anthony told Jackson to take a longer route back to Beacon Hill.

He said, "I would like to observe the streets and see if I can determine what types of people are out this evening. Drive over to Marlborough Street and go past Province House. Then drive over School Street to Treamont and then to Brattle. Circle around Southback and come in home from Temple Street.

"If any troublemakers are out on the prowl, maybe we can get a good look and discern who they might be."

"Yes sir, we moughtent get a good look at 'em," said Jackson, talking very loudly and looking over his right shoulder, so Lord Anthony could hear him.

At the corner of Marlborough Street and Rawson's Lane, very suddenly and very quietly, four hoodlums came from behind a large privet bush, and almost before Jackson could crack his whip, the four, who wore black hats pulled down over their eyes and false mustaches pasted over their upper lips, attacked the carriage.

They cut the harness loose and slapped the horse on the rump while yelling at him to "Go." He ran off down Marlborough.

Lord Anthony was pulled from his seat inside the carriage and his face shoved down to the ground.

Jackson had jumped from his seat and was lashing at the attackers with his whip.

Lord Anthony was yelling, "What do you want? Why are you attacking us? Stop it—in the name of God and the king."

They ignored his yelling and began rocking the chaise from side to side until it landed on its side in the street, then they lifted it and turned it upside down.

The horse was out of sight; Jackson was still swinging his whip but was not hitting anyone.

The four ruffians gave out loud hee-haws as they ran down Rawson's Lane. Neither Jackson nor Lord Anthony had been able to recognize any of them.

With Jackson's help, Lord Anthony got to his feet. He was swearing and shaking his fist, but it didn't do any good.

Jackson, while holding on to his lordship, said, "I'se hope you isn't hut none. That was a foul think for them meanuns to do. Whose does you recon they is?"

Anthony patted Jackson on the back and said, "Let's just go home; we can't do anything else tonight. The chaise will have to lie here in the street until tomorrow. I think Stomper will be all right; he probably went to his stable. Are you all right, Jackson?" asked Anthony.

"Yes suh, I think I'se up and coming," was the good servant's reply.

Lord Anthony and Jackson walked to the house on Beacon Hill. They went to the front door and knocked. Lord Anthony seldom ever carried keys. He didn't need to because Michael was always near the door to open it, but this Saturday night Lady Anthony had told Michael to go to bed. She had observed that he was coughing and wiping his nose on his handkerchief. She suspected he had a cold.

Lady Anthony was lying in her bed, reading a French novel that she had brought with her to America. A candelabra was giving off plenty of light, showing the beauty of her nude body. (She always slept in the nude.)

She hated the interruption when she heard the knocking. She waited a moment, and there was a second summons, knocking, this time much more vigorous.

She remembered that Michael was not there to open the door because she had sent him to bed. Henry was also still in bed sick. Maggie was way up on the third floor and wouldn't hear the knocking. Clarice and Robin were in their rooms, in bed asleep with the door closed.

She was the only one to answer the door. She laid her book down and got out of bed and put on a very thin lace negligee gown, which she took from her bedpost. She went down the stairs carrying the candelabra.

"Is that you, Maurice?" she called out just before reaching the door.

"Hell yes, Florence. My nose is bleeding, and I'm shaking like the devil. Open the door."

Florence looked at the large brass lock and wondered if she knew how to unlock it. There was a secret lever under the long narrow bar that covered the keyhole. It had to be lifted and pushed aside before the key could be inserted into the keyhole, then the key had to be turned all the way over, and halfway back before the lock would slide back to open the door.

"I'm trying, Maurice, but it won't work. I can't do it. Go around back, come in through the kitchen."

"Good God, Florence! That's two blocks. I can't go that far with my nose bleeding."

"What happened to you Maurice?"

"Florence! Don't ask me that."

Lord Anthony and Jackson (who was holding him up) began their journey around the large brick mansion, which actually was approximately two blocks to the back door.

Florence began her trek back to her bed room. Halfway up the stairs she remembered telling Lola to keep the back door locked, especially at night.

She thought she better arouse someone because she wasn't sure she could unlock the back door either.

In her somnolent state, trying to carry the candelabra, hold her negligee together, and feeling frustrated because she couldn't make the lock work, she headed for the nearest door which was Clarice's bedroom.

She set the candelabra down on a table and knocked lightly. There was no answer. She tried again and still no answer. She turned the door knob, and the door opened.

Walking very quietly over to the bed, hoping not to frighten Clarice, she had a split second of complete surprise. Clarice wasn't in the bed. Florence looked in the dressing room; she wasn't there, either. She wasn't in Robin's room, but Robin was sleeping soundly. Bo Tay was snuggled up against her.

All at once a shiver of fear ran down her spine. Where could she be? Then in a blink she was relieved of her fear.

"Why didn't I think of it? Clarice is up in Maggie's room; they are working on the party decorations."

She fumbled her way down the hall to her own bedroom. She hung her negligee on the bedpost, walked over to the credenza, picked up a bottle of cologne, and sprayed her body all over, then she got into bed, began humming a tune, and wondered why it was taking Maurice so long.

Lord Anthony and Jackson tried the back door and found it locked.

Jackson said, "We'll have to wake up Michael to let us in."

He and his lordship went to the stables to Michael's room. It wasn't easy to wake the old man. He had taken his dram of brandy before he went to bed, as he always did, "Sosen he wouldn't be deviled with nightmares."

After Jackson pulled off his covers and shoved his head around and called his name at least a dozen times, Michael finally sat up on the side of the bed.

He was wearing his red flannel night shirt and a long-tailed red nightcap.

Lord Anthony said, "Good God, Michael, how can you sleep in that getup? You must be sweating all over. Come on, get up; we need you to unlock the back door, so I can get into my house."

Michael was too sleepy to say anything; he just went staggering along to open the door for his lordship.

In the meantime Lord Anthony's nose had stopped bleeding, and he had brushed the dirt off the front of his trousers and jacket. When he got inside his house he felt his way along the wall to the stairs. The candelabra that Florence had left on the table at the top of the stairs was giving off enough light for him to see his way to their bedroom.

Florence was lying in bed, nude. A little beam of light coming through the shutters was dancing up and down her satiny, soft, pink, sweet-smelling body.

She wiggled around a little and reached out her arms to her husband as he came into the room.

"Maurice, dear," she said as she breathed heavily, "come here and let me ease your pain. I can see you've been hurt. Who hurt you, dear? Tell me about it. Don't look so glum."

When his lordship answered her he sounded disgusted, "Oh, no you don't Florence. I'm not falling for you teasing tonight. I've had it. This was a rough evening. A bunch of hoodlums jumped on Jackson and me on our way home. I'm the only one they attacked. I'll tell you about it later. Maybe tomorrow, maybe never. It was too disgusting."

The thought again entered Florence's mind that Clarice was not in her room, but she eased her thinking by second thoughts, that she was being fearful for nothing; of course Clarice was with Maggie.

"Maurice," her ladyship said, "the birthday is just too much work; it's keeping Clarice and Maggie up all night working on all those decorations and frills. Can't we tone it down a little bit?"

"A little bit," answered Anthony, "we're probably going to call the whole thing off. It's too risky. The times are dangerous, and the governor is getting cold feet."

"Cold feet?" exclaimed Lady Anthony. "Why?"

"Well, because, he doesn't want the night of August 26, 1765, repeated."

"I don't remember what happened then," said Florence. "What was it?"

"The low-down rabble of Boston sacked his house, destroyed all his valuables—even his clothes—everything. They damn near ruined him financially and emotionally."

"Let's forget it, Maurice; that was eight years ago. You need some rest. Get into bed."

She threw back the satin sheet and fluffed his pillow and patted it, indicating an invitation for him to put his head on it.

After stretching her arms back over her head and straightening out her body and wiggling her toes, she noticed, as he crawled into bed and slithered over next to her, that his glum had turned to glee.

Florence raised herself from her pillow, reached for the candle, and blew it out. She then put her arms around Maurice and drew him to her. They kissed and held each other tightly and were very quiet and connected for a long time.

The love between this man and woman was sporadic. Florence could be almost unbelievably warm and affectionate at times, but also able to do a complete schizophrenic turn in a moment. Maurice was always on the alert. But this Saturday, she had been alone and lonesome all day. She hated the house. It was rambling and mysterious, overcrafted and under lighted (in spite of the many windows). The higher panes were of stained glass, shading out the light, then large trees too close to the house shut out the sun.

She had walked the halls. There was no one to talk to. Robin, Clarice, and Maggie had spent the whole day in the school room, or Maggie's room, working on costumes or decorations. Lord Anthony had gone early in the morning to Province House and came home only to put on his dinner clothes then head off to the governor's Saturday night dinner. She was now very glad to have Maurice beside her, making love.

After complete relaxation and a feeling of drowsiness, she pulled the sheet over her and turned herself over with her back nestled in Maurice's silky, hairy chest.

Maurice laid his big hand, partly sweating and a little unsteady, on Florence's smooth, plump thigh and said, "Good night, sweetheart."

Chapter Nine

Michael was up and dressed, taking care of his morning chores. He had not been able to get back to sleep after being awakened to open the back door for his lordship.

On his return to his room while crossing the garden, he had observed someone (at least two forms) in the gazebo. He was very cautious not to be seen. He bent over and walked hunched down and stayed behind trees as much as he could.

Michael was not sure it was intruders, but he had heard about hoodlums attacking Lord Anthony and Jackson. He feared they might have followed them home and were planning to break into the house. He didn't know if he should report what he saw or if he should keep it to himself "so he wouldn't arouse more fear in the household." He thought, Just a bunch of mischief makers. May never happen again.

The more he thought about it the more he knew that if his lordship ever found out that he had seen intruders and not reported it, he would surely give him the ax.

He forgot to go to the kitchen for his breakfast; he polished the brass doorknob and knocker twice and examined the door lock more than once. He didn't hear Jackson when he came through the hall, calling him.

Tomas was right behind Jackson. They had a job to do and needed Michael to help. They had to go to Marlborough Street and see about the chaise. Tomas was angered at the idea of his having to go, but Lord Anthony ordered him to get the chaise back into shape immediately. He had to find a carriage repair place and didn't know where there was one.

Jackson knew of a shop that could do the work, but the man who owned the shop, Nathe Frothing, was a hardcore Whig, and he took his sweet time on any work he did for a Tory and charged them unreasonably. He was hateful to them and would not guarantee his work. Actually, he hated working on the elegant carriages the rich Tories, or any government official, owned. Any other carriage repair shop was in Cambridge. It was just too much of a chore to get to Cambridge.

Tomas told Lord Anthony it would be easier, quicker, and cheaper to buy a new chaise.

"But," said Lord Anthony, "this very fine chaise was custom made for me in London, and I want it put back to its original condition. Also I want you to contact the constable and report this brazen act of violence and put in a claim for compensation for my humiliation and damages to my carriage."

Tomas looked perplexed; he didn't know which way to turn.

While Tomas, Jackson, and Michael had gone to Marlborough Street to take care of the removal and repair of the chaise, the others of the Anthony household were in some sort of confusion.

Lady Anthony summoned Maggie to her bedroom as soon as Lord Anthony left it.

"Bring me some very sweet tea, some biscuits with lots of butter, and some apple butter, and I want you to stay with me while I eat; we have to talk."

Maggie went to get the lady's breakfast tray. She met Clarice in the hall carrying a tray to Robin, who, Clarice said, was fretting with a siege of stubbornness, refusing to get up and get dressed.

"What the matter really is," said Clarice, "is that she is bored of being confined; she wants to see the town, and so do I."

"You're not missing much," said Maggie as she went on to do as she had been bidden.

After Lady Anthony had eaten most of her breakfast, still sitting up in bed, she said to Maggie, who was stiffly sitting on a straight back chair (she didn't dare sit in the easy wing chair near the window), "Maggie, there's no need for you and Clarice to work all night on the decorations for the birthday party. We have decided to tone it down, quite a bit. I think you and Clarice have enough to do, doing your regular chores and contending with Robin. You need your sleep."

"Oh! but...." Maggie started to say something.

"Never mind now—I know you are enjoying the preparation, but I must insist, you only work in daytime and only when you have nothing else to do."

Maggie began again, "We haven't done any work at night, your ladyship."

"You haven't?"

"No, not a moment's time after dinner. I have practiced a little bit on the harpsichord. That's all."

"Then what were you two, you and Clarice, doing most of last night about twelve midnight?"

Maggie was beginning to suspect something involving Clarice. "What do you mean, your ladyship? I don't understand."

"Clarice was not in her room for more than an hour. If she wasn't with you, as I suspected, where was she? Do you know?"

Maggie felt the impact of Lady Anthony's question; she had a sudden feeling that somehow Clarice was seeing Jason on the sly. She didn't want to add to her lady's suspicion; she didn't want to do or say anything that would put Clarice in a tight situation.

She sighed and forced a slight cough, placing her hand over her mouth, "No, your ladyship, I don't know. Maybe she went for a walk."

"That...she is forbidden to do and especially at night."

Maggie was showing her nervousness as she was thinking of some other excuse to make up for Clarice. "Maybe she went to do something for Henry; Lola was away last night. You know she, Lola, goes to her meeting every Saturday night and doesn't come home until morning."

"No, I don't know," sneered Lady Anthony. "What meetings?" Then she shook her head as if reviving her thoughts. "Never mind about Lola, for now. Don't change the subject or try to throw me off track. Where was Clarice?"

Maggie was almost in tears. "I'm sure, your ladyship, I have no idea."

"You can be sure, I'll find out. I won't stand for any clandestine meetings on these premises."

She threw back the top sheet and put her feet on the floor. "You may take this tray back to the kitchen now and tell Lola to come to my sitting room at once."

Maggie was so unstrung the dishes rattled on the tray as she carried it back to the kitchen.

"Oh pity Lola," uttered Maggie under her breath and, "Oh, poor Clarice."

There was an Irish crystal vase on a table in front of the south window in Robin's room. The vase had prisms hanging from its rim. Usually the vase was filled with fresh flowers, but yesterday Maggie had removed the wilted ones and had not as yet refilled the vase.

The prisms were in direct sunlight streaming through the window. This was causing iridescent baubles to dance around on the opposite wall. Robin lay there in bed watching the phenomenal antics of the baubles. Her smile was one of delight.

Clarice held the breakfast tray on her lifted knee until she could turn the doorknob to open the door. She saw Robin's smile as soon as she set foot inside the room. She saw the radiant spots on the wall dancing around in kaleidoscopic forms and knew someone from Heaven had lifted Robin's spirit.

When Robin saw Clarice, she jumped out of bed and ran over to the vase. "Look, Cee Cee, I'm going to make them do a different dance," she said as she pointed at the baubles.

"Robin, this is a wonderful Sunday morning. Let's pretend that those little shadows on the wall are angels doing a ballet for us."

"Watch me make them do it and listen to the music," said the child, as she moved the prisms around with her finger, making them tinkle sweetly while the baubles hopped, skipped, and jumped around on the wall.

Clarice had a very happy feeling about so many things that special morning. First and foremost she now knew that Jason loved her, and she had a much friendlier feeling about the people in the Anthony house, that they would be kind and helpful to her if she should ever need them. She had been standing, holding the tray all this time. She set it down on the bed and walked over to the window.

Robin turned for an instant to look out toward the street; she saw a man get off his horse and start toward the house.

"Cee Cee, here comes a man into our house. Who do you suppose he is?"

Clarice knew in an instant that he was a messenger; he had a piece of rolled up parchment in his hand. "It's a messenger," said Clarice, "I wonder if he's bringing good news or bad news."

Robin ran out of the room like a flash and down the hall to her parents' bedroom. Before she got completely into the room she had blurted out, "Mama, there's a messenger at the front door." Then she saw that no one was in the room, so she ran down the hall to the sitting room. Florence was there waiting for Lola.

Any sign of a messenger always brought delightful excitement to Robin. "Mama," she again called out, but before she could say more, her mother had interrupted her. "Good morning, Robin, why are you running around in your night gown? Why aren't you dressed? What do you want?"

Robin immediately knew that her mother was upset. She turned and went sulking back to her own room without saying more.

Clarice knew, when she saw Robin's downcast expression, that the child had not been greeted with open arms, as she should have been, or given a chance to express her reason for such an eager approach to her mother.

"Robin, the angels have finished their ballet and gone away. Come now and eat your breakfast."

"No, I won't, and you can't make me," the sad-looking child sullenly replied.

Chapter Ten

Lola was more than aggravated at having to climb the stairs to the upstairs sitting room. Furthermore, she was angry at having to face Lady Anthony.

"Geeze, God!" she said, "this day is starting off like a monkey's ass—raw! Wonder what she wants."

Lola was about five feet tall and weighed one hundred sixty-five pounds. One would say she was round as a butterball, but paunchy in front and swayback with a butt like a one hundred pound sack of sawdust. She wore her apron tied around her waist, high above her stomach and up under her bosom, with streamer ties hanging down over her butt, which Bo Tay liked to grab hold of and pull backwards.

She always got completely out of breath climbing stairs, and that's the reason she was swearing to herself as she came into Lady Anthony's presence.

"Sit down," said Lady Anthony, "I have some questions to ask you. First, where were you last night? Were you in your room for any part of the evening?"

"No," answered Lola, "I went out."

"Then where were you?"

"I thought I was allowed to go out on Saturday nights."

"That depends on where you go."

"Well, you ought to know I don't go far, and I always come back in time to prepare breakfast."

"I hear you attend some kind of meeting. What is this meeting about?"

"It's about God."

"God? What kind of god?"

"One who does good things."

"Doesn't look like he's done many good things for you."

"Oh yes, but He has, your ladyship. He's cured me of the pox. He's showed me how to get rid of the lice in my hair. He's took me out of the taverns and got me this good home. He's got me some friends, and now I'm learning to read."

"Well, I'm glad you appreciate your situation, but let me give you some warnings. There's a faction of dissenters in this town; they're against the king and the government. Be very careful who your associates are."

"Yes, ma'am, your ladyship, I'm aware of it."

"I'm told you have a relative who visits you; Truly, I believe, is her name. She must be one of the rabble, the trash of Boston. I advise you to have nothing to do with her."

Lola began rolling her thumbs over each other and looking down at her lap. She hoped Lady Anthony wouldn't see her agony. She gave no reply to that advice.

"Now, there's something else," said Lady Anthony, "I do not want that baker coming to this house. We will have to find another baker or you will be required to do the baking. If that man comes near this house I want it reported to me or Lord Anthony."

"May I ask why you no longer want his bread and buns?" asked Lola.

"It's not the bread and buns I object to. It's the man himself. I believe he's dangerous, perhaps conspiring with our enemies. I believe he comes here for other reasons as well."

"I will let him know," said Lola. Actually she was glad he was being dismissed as the Anthony baker. She had always wanted him to prefer Truly to any other girl.

Lady Anthony got up from her chair and reached her hand out to Lola and said, "Lola, you will be well provided for if you fully cooperate with me. Let me know what you know."

She then went over to a mahogany desk and took a shilling from a drawer. She reached for Lola's hand and put the shilling in her palm and closed it.

"That's to help out your meetings," she said.

Lola opened her hand and looked at the coin. "Thank you ever so much, your ladyship. I will keep you informed of all that I know."

When Lady Anthony heard someone at the front door, she stepped out into the hall and looked over the banister to satisfy her curiosity as to who might have come in. It just happened to be Marie, who opened the door for the messenger. She was on her way to her ladyship's sitting room to report, that due to circumstances beyond her control, she had not been able to call on the dressmaker.

She didn't see any other person to open the door, so she opened it and took the parchment (tied with a blue ribbon) from the messenger's hand.

He lifted his hat to her in greeting and said, "It's one fine morning, ma'am." He went back to his horse, not waiting for an answer, because there was no answer needed.

Marie was tempted to open the scroll and learn its contents, but she thought she had better give it to either his lordship or his wife. She knocked on the door of Lord Anthony's study, suspecting he might be in there.

He opened the door on the first knock; said, "Good morning, Marie"; and took the message from her hand. He closed the door, then opened it again and said to Marie, "Bring me something to eat."

His voice was pleasant enough in spite of his frustration over his encounter with the hoodlums the night before.

Lady Anthony's soothing hadn't stayed with him. He was again feeling his anger but was trying to subdue it. He opened the parchment and read:

> To Whom It May Concern,
> Greetings:
>
> Our office has come to the conclusion that a holiday on May 24, 1773, should be done away with.
>
> There will not be public celebrations of any kind in honor of the birthday of King George III, as was heretofore anticipated.
>
> We regret to make such announcement, but due to recent public violence and wrongdoing, we feel it necessary to cancel, in order to keep the peace.
>
> Therefore, the party scheduled for May 24th, at Milton Hill, is no longer possible.
>
> Yours in obedience to the King,
> Thomas Hutchinson,
> Governor of Massachusetts Colony
> 5/15/73

"Well," said Lord Anthony as he threw the paper down on his desk and began pacing the floor, "he has obliterated the very first attempt I made to bring the people together. I hate like the devil to have to tell Florence and Robin about this."

He sat down in his swivel chair, twisting around and thinking about the duty before him. What a disappointment it was going to be.

"Frankly, he said to himself, "it is a good thing to cancel the party. Someone I love may have gotten hurt or even killed. I could have been killed last night if one of them had had a knife or gun."

Maurice Anthony was a peace-loving man. He had often been involved in solving disturbances, street melees of one kind or another, and family squabbles when he served as a prosecuting lawyer in London. He believed in justice and had a reputation of being fair and forgiving to all men.

He laid his head back and closed his eyes and pondered the situation here in Boston. He contemplated the speech he had heard Sam Adams make a few days ago at Faneuil Hall.

Adams had said, "Our people here in Massachusetts and in all of America should have a right to make decisions, a right to choose their judges, their lawmakers, and should have a voice at public meetings. They should have a right to choose their church and a right to approve or disapprove taxes imposed upon them."

Lord Anthony seemed to be agreeing with Adams, when he took hold of his thoughts and said to himself, "This is not right for me. My mind should not be driving in that track; I am here to serve the king."

He jumped up from his chair and went over to the window and looked out. He secretly wished he had not come to America.

He had some kind of sympathy for these Americans. How, he thought, are they ever going to get their freedom without a war? War? What a wicked thought."

Sam Adams had implied that the colonists wanted to be free, absolutely free from England. He had intimated that all the other colonies were in agreement with Massachusetts.

"What if we," meaning his family, "got caught up in a war? But war is impossible; these small colonies cannot finance a war and they have no navy. Sam Adams said they have the guts. Does he realize that blood goes with guts?"

Marie was again knocking on his door and he opened it to the smell of sausage and biscuits and the smile of a happy face, for Marie could put on her very best face for Lord Anthony anytime. She had admired her employer since the day she first saw him.

As he took the tray from her, he covered her hand with his hand and pressed down as a gesture of affection.

He said, "Marie, you always bring something to my soul that cheers me up. I do appreciate your tolerance of me."

Marie felt the thrill of a gracious compliment, but she also felt a sensation like one of desire.

Lady Anthony had made a second stand at the banister; she still was not sure if someone had come in the front door.

She saw Marie starting up the stairs. She began talking to her, "Oh, it's you. Have you been avoiding me? I want to hear what the dressmaker had to say."

Marie waited until she reached the second floor and was within a few feet of her ladyship before she answered her. "I thought you would understand that I have not been able to go and see the dressmaker because the chaise has not been available for my use."

"I know that—Maurice told me, but I didn't put two and two together. I've had so much on my mind."

Lady Anthony led the way into her sitting room. Marie sat down in the chair that Lola had just vacated. The lady sat on a small settee and began talking. "The upcoming party at Milton Hill has got me going in circles." She was lying. Most of the time she spent in bed reading her French novels. Marie was on to her lying, but she said, "Oh I realize how much work is involved, and you trying to put it all together must be exhausting."

"Marie, I think I will be sick before that day ever gets here. I'm so afraid I won't be able to make it. If I do get sick from the strain of it, will you promise me that you will report to me everyone you see talking to Clarice? I have reason to believe that she has a crush on that baker who delivers bread here. I cannot allow her to have associates from the lower element. She must give all her attention to Robin. At least until we find her a suitable gentleman admirer."

"I will do my best," said Marie, but she didn't have any intention to bother with Clarice's flirtations or admirations because she didn't like her. She was jealous of the abilities of the governess. If there was any possibility of Clarice ever finding reason to resign, it would be fine with Marie.

As soon as Marie left the room, Lady Anthony pulled the bell cord for Maggie.

Maggie was a devout churchgoer and had left for the Anglican church which she attended. After jerking on the cord (two jerks for Maggie) and not getting any response, she then pulled for Clarice (three jerks). Clarice came at once.

"Clarice, I have to go back to bed; will you brush my hair? And will you find my husband? (Poor dear, he is a nervous wreck from his ordeal last evening) and tell him to come to my bedroom. I must get his mind on to something else."

Clarice brushed her ladyship's hair, and while doing so reported that Robin's few days at school had been quite rewarding. She had drawn a cartoon head of Governor Hutchinson and delivered it to Henry, who was now out of his bed but not out of his room. Henry, although he couldn't write, could draw and paint pictures. He had added a body to Robin's sketch and put horns and a tail on it. Robin had squealed with laughter.

Lady Anthony wasn't sure she approved of Henry implying that the governor was a devil. Clarice assured her that Robin didn't think bad thoughts about the governor or get the implication that he was a devil just because of the horns and tail.

Lady Anthony thought of asking Clarice about the night before but decided to wait until she had more proof that the girl was seeing the baker. But she thought Clarice was elated beyond her usual degree of happiness. While she was brushing, if she wasn't talking, she was humming.

"Your hair is lovely and soft, your ladyship. It is very becoming when braided and wrapped around your head. Shall I fix it like that for you?"

"Do you think his lordship will like it?"

"Oh, yes, he loves your hair in any style that it is dressed."

"Clarice, you are a treasure. Go ahead and do it that way."

After finishing, Clarice put the brush back on the dressing table and left the bedroom to go and find his lordship.

Lady Anthony slipped out of her negligee and got into bed.

Clarice went downstairs to Lord Anthony's study. She was the first member of the household to whom he read the message from Governor Hutchinson, canceling the party.

Clarice was so surprised she flopped down in a chair and put her head in her hands. For a minute or two, there was complete silence, then she burst out in agonizing sobs. One would have thought she had lost a close relative or friend in death.

Lord Anthony stood beside her and laid his hand on her shoulder. "My dear girl," he said, "it's not the end of the world. There will be another time, probably very soon. We can do something here to celebrate."

Between her sobs, and while wiping her eyes with the hem of her dress, Clarice, gasping for breath, said, "That's just it, 'here.' I was looking forward to getting away from here, getting to see some of Boston and the countryside and some different people."

"Don't you like it here, Clarice?" asked Anthony.

"I'm beginning to hate it," answered the governess.

"You've only been here a week; give yourself some time."

"I guess you're right. I'm acting like a fool."

"Well, you are taking it harder than I expected. Maybe you are not yet adjusted to being away from your parents and your home."

Does he think I am immature? she thought. "Oh, yes, I am; eight weeks at sea adjusted me very well."

She dried her eyes and forced a smile and remembered to tell Lord Anthony (who opened the door and held it for her) that Lady Anthony wanted to see him in her bedroom as soon as possible.

Clarice returned to her room and found Robin asleep. She had not eaten any of her breakfast except the bowl of strawberry jam, of which a good portion was clinging to her chin. Even Bo Tay had strawberry jam in his chin whiskers.

Clarice sat down and held the tray on her lap and finished the food that Robin should have eaten.

"Why did I break down like that? I am really ashamed of myself. I wish Jason would come to me and hold my hand. I do hope I will see him again very soon."

Clarice was feeling her emotions, and her thoughts flashed back to the night before: midnight when she met him in the gazebo. She began to relive that special pleasure.

She felt sure no one had seen her or knew that she had snuck out of the house—not even Robin, who slept through her quiet escape from the bedroom. Nor had anyone heard her as she tiptoed down the back stairs and quickly walked through the garden to the gazebo where Jason was waiting for her.

He was holding the note she had written to him and hidden under the broken post.

"My darling," he said as he held her and kissed her, not once but a dozen times or more, on the lips, the forehead, the neck, her hands. He hugged her and stroked her hair and her back. He pulled her down to his lap and tilted her chin and kissed her again and again.

Sitting there in her chair, Clarice thought she could hear his voice. It was soft and clear in her head and heart. "I could just eat you up, you are so sweet and dear and beautiful," he said.

She remembered that she hardly got in a word, but once between kisses she said, "I love you."

She shivered when she remembered how a noise had startled them, and they hunkered down behind the wainscoting of the gazebo. Jason threw his cape over her. They held each other very close and were as quiet as mice so as not to be discovered. It was Lord Anthony, Jackson, and Michael at the back door.

When they heard Michael locking the back door after he let Lord Anthony into the house, Clarice said to Jason, "I don't know how I'm going to get in, unless Lola has left the cellar door unlocked."

Jason said, "Don't worry, dear, I know how to get into that cellar. I have been there many times."

"But I have never been in the cellar and I don't know how to find the stairway to the kitchen. Is it very dark?" she asked.

Clarice remembered how these admissions of his having been in the cellar grabbed hold of her. She asked, "Jason, were you with Truly when you were in the cellar?"

He laughed as he squeezed her up to his side, "Ha, my darling, you are jealous. What if I was? I hadn't met you then. I will never be with another girl again as long as you will be my girl."

His words sounded so affectionate. However, she still was leery of going through the dark cellar. "Jason," she said, "I'm scared. I can't get through that cellar in the dark."

"I will carry you," Jason assured her. "I know that cellar like the back of my hand."

She thought of her fright and how Jason had taken it all away. She hoped he had not been with Truly; she didn't know if he was teasing her.

She said, "Truly has the whole world to be free in and to look for a sweetheart. I have only this garden, and now that I have found you, I want you to be my sweetheart and no one else's."

She laid her head on his shoulder and he picked her up and carried her across the garden. He kicked the cellar door open with the toe of his boot and carried her into the dark damp room and up the stairs to the kitchen.

As he sat her down, he said, "There now, my dearest, you are safe and sound and I'm so in love I'm going crazy."

Clarice was so gloriously happy and passionately excited that she tapped a little dance through the house until she reached her room. She didn't give another thought to the idea that someone might have heard her.

Clarice looked down at the tray on her lap and came to herself, realizing that she had been in something like a trance, retracing her actions and the ecstasy of that midnight hour.

The happy emotion of midnight and the heartbreaking emotion of this morning clashed like a bolt of lightning splitting a tree. She began to cry again.

Robin awoke and sat up in bed just looking at Clarice and watching her cry. Then without saying anything she got out of bed and walked over to her governess and put her arms around Clarice's neck. "Cee Cee," she said, "why are you crying? Are you homesick? Because I'm homesick, too."

"No, Robin, that's not the reason. I don't know why I'm crying. I don't know if it's because I'm very sad or very happy. I have reason to be either or both. I think it's a little bit of both."

Chapter Eleven

Maggie came back from church. She stopped by Clarice's bedroom. She removed her gloves and laid them and her Bible on a small table. As she laid the book down she patted it and said to Clarice, "You should read this book more often and teach it to Robin."

Clarice gave her a quizzical look and asked, "Do you think I never read the Bible?"

"I have never seen a Bible in your room or among your books," said Maggie as she took a seat on the quilt box under the window.

Robin was leaning against Clarice. She spoke up, "I look at the pictures; the people are funny looking." She went on, "I had a governess when I was five years old who got down on her knees and hollered at God with her eyes shut, and she threw her arms," Robin imitated her character, "up in the air and down and bumped her head on the floor. Mama said she was crazy. She went away and never came back. Papa said if she got caught acting like that she would be sent to prison."

Clarice took Robin's hand to help her off the floor; she hugged her up close. "Don't think about her, Robin. That was her way of talking to God."

Robin said, "It was funny; I laughed at her. She wanted me to get down on my knees, but I didn't want to."

Maggie said solemnly, "Well, it's my opinion that everyone should worship God, and going to church on Sunday is my way." She continued, "There may come a day when one will be thrown into the quad for going to any other church than the Anglican because that is the only true church."

"Maggie, your predictions sometimes are outrageous." This remark of Clarice's evidently irritated Maggie, for she picked up her Bible and gloves and hurried out the door and up the stairs to her room.

Robin went over to the window seat. She sat down and put her feet up and clasped her arms around her knees. "Do you like Maggie?" she asked Clarice.

"Of course I like Maggie. She is the closest friend I have here, except you."

"What about Jason?"

"I am very fond of Jason and you already know that, but he doesn't live here and I'm talking about friends in this house."

"Mama and Papa are your friends, aren't they?"

"Well, they certainly are, but I can't tell them my very own personal thoughts."

"What kind of personal thought?'

"Robin, enough is enough. I'm the teacher; I should be asking the questions."

"Just one more, Cee Cee, please?"

"Oh, all right."

"Did you sneak out to the garden last night to meet Jason?"

Clarice had a very red face; she felt embarrassed. She knew her chagrin was obvious to Robin.

She must have heard me open the door, thought Clarice. "What makes you suspect such a thing?" she asked the child.

"Your blue chamois slippers were covered in sticker tights."

Clarice threw her hand over her mouth, "Stick-tights! Oh, my goodness, I never thought about stick-tights."

She hastily got up from her chair and went around the bed to her night stand, where she had placed the slippers when she took them off. She picked them up and looked at them and began picking off the little seeds, called "beggar lice" by some and "stick-tights" by others.

"Well?" said Robin, looking smug and satisfied.

Clarice knew she was trapped. "Robin, darling, please don't tell anyone. I love Jason and I can't bear it if I don't see him."

"Will you run away with him and leave me?"

"No, I will never do that."

"What are you going to tell Tom," meaning Tom Fellows, "when he comes to America to marry you?"

"Robin, please don't ask that, I haven't decided."

"You talked about loving him when we were on the Cordelia coming to America."

"Yes I did, dear, but I hadn't met Jason then."

Robin's face showed her puzzlement at Clarice's dilemma. "Dear me," said the child as she took the slippers from Clarice's hand and put them on her own feet, "you do have a serious problem."

After a long pause, Clarice selected a book from her book shelf and said to Robin, while flipping the pages, "When you get dressed and brush your hair, we'll go out and sit in the gazebo and I'll tell you some more about my childhood."

"May I wear your slippers?" Robin asked, as she scuffed around the room in them.

"No, Robin, I can't let anyone wear my slippers. I mean, wear them when going someplace. It is all right for you to wear them while you are in my room like you are doing now."

Robin kicked first one foot and then the other as high as she could, sending each slipper flying across the room.

Clarice immediately gathered them up and put them into a brocaded shoe bag and laid it on a shelf in her dressing room. As she did so, she said to the shoes, "Thank you, my sweets, for last night."

Robin went to the window, and, as soon as she drew back the curtain to look out, she called to Clarice, "Cee Cee, there is a fight down on the corner. Come see—do you know who it is?"

Clarice took a quick look and saw three men tearing up a British Union Jack, and two men who had already lost their hats were rolling in the street.

"Let's not look, Robin. Come away from the window." But neither Clarice nor Robin left their stand behind the curtains. The fight got more violent when two fellows passing on horseback jumped off their horses and began belting the men who were tearing up the flag.

The horses were rearing and snorting, evidently scared by the shouting. The men on the ground were being kicked and spat upon. In a moment someone came running from another street flashing a pistol. He shot into the fracas, and one of the men fell into the ditch, face down.

Clarice pushed Robin away from the window, and, holding on to her hand, she ran out into the hall and down the stairs to Lord Anthony's study, pulling Robin along behind her. She knocked on the study door but got no answer.

"Let's go back to the window, Cee Cee; I want to watch the fight."

The two of them ran back to the window in Clarice's room and drew back the curtains. A detail of red-coated soldiers had begun to confer over the dead man. One of them punched at him with his rifle and turned him over.

Blood and mud covered his face. He had on a buckskin jacket with fringed bottom and cuffs.

"Looks like an Indian," said Clarice.

"How do you know what an Indian looks like?" asked Robin.

"There were several Indians standing around the wharf the day we landed. I got a good look at them. Their skin is not red; it is more of a dark tan."

"What do you think an Indian was doing on our street?" Robin asked.

"I believe the two men on horses were chasing him and he ran into the others and they tried to head him off and that started the fight."

"Cee Cee, let's go into the garden and stand up on the seat in the gazebo, and we can watch what the soldiers are going to do with him."

"All right, Robin, let's go." Clarice was as hungry for excitement as Robin was.

They hurriedly went through the house and out the French doors of the dining room, which was the shortest way to get to the gazebo. They hopped up onto the seat and peered through the latticed wall. The view they had of the soldiers and the dead man was perfect. The other men who were involved in the fight were no longer in sight.

Clarice and Robin didn't know that while they were running around looking for Lord Anthony and back to the bedroom, they had missed seeing the paddy wagon that came and unloaded safety guards, who had handcuffed two of them and put them in the wagon to take them to the stocks or jail.

The others had escaped and run away. The two horses were standing off a short distance under a tree. One of the soldiers went to them and picked up their bridles and led them away.

Clarice and Robin continued to watch from the gazebo. Soon they saw someone bring a two-wheeled cart. One of the soldiers picked the dead man up and tossed him into it, and another soldier walked between the shafts and pulled it away.

"Where are they taking him?" asked Robin.

"Perhaps to the morgue or to his home, if he has one," answered Clarice.

"What's a morgue, Cee Cee?"

"That's a place where the bodies of dead people, especially accident victims, are kept until they are identified. If no one ever claims the body it is eventually buried."

"I hope they won't throw him in the river."

"Robin, what made you say that?"

"Because, I heard Lola say that maybe somebody killed Truly and throwed her in the river."

"Robin, your grammar is terrible. The verb is not 'throwed'; it is 'threw.' Now repeat that sentence and say it correctly. Never mind, just forget it. It is such a gruesome thought; you should never think such a thing again."

Clarice put her arm around Robin's shoulder and guided her away from the gazebo. As they started back into the house, Clarice felt a moment of fright. She turned and looked over her shoulder. She thought she saw something, or someone, move slightly under the low growth of the privet bush.

"This has been some kind of morning, very exciting, hasn't it?" she said to Robin.

She then felt a pang of pity for the little girl. She had not, as yet, told her of the cancellation of the party. Perhaps it would be better if her mama and papa should tell her. It might make it easier for her to bear.

"Come on, Robin. Let's see if your Mama would like a little visit with you. You can tell her about the fight we just witnessed."

"No, Cee Cee, I don't want to see mama, not until I am dressed. She was mad at me before, when I went into her sitting room in my nightgown."

Clarice wanted some free time to write a note to Jason, a letter to her sister Julia, and one to her parents.

"Robin, I will help you get dressed. Then I want you to spend some time with your parents. They will be glad to hear you read or sing or recite the poem I've taught you to say at the party."

Under her breath Clarice whispered a prayer, "Oh dear God forgive me; I'm trying to shirk the duty of telling her the sad news."

Clarice and Robin went back into the house through the French doors.

Tomas, Jackson, and Michael were coming in through the back door at the same time, returning from their trip to Marlborough Street. Tomas went directly to Lord Anthony's study and knocked on the door. Michael and Jackson sat down at the trestle table, and Lola gave them each a mug of tea.

"That Mr. Frothing was sort of out of sorts, wouldn't you say?" Jackson asked Michael while they were sitting drinking their tea.

"Yes suh, he was right sassy to Mr. Straight. Does you reckon he'll fix the chaise sos it's in good shape?"

Jackson thought a moment and then replied, "Can't tell; all depends on Frothing's disposition."

Lola came over to the table to refill their tea mugs and asked, "What's wrong with the chaise?"

"Well," said Jackson, "it's smashed in on top, it's bent on the springs, the right wheel is broke in a hundred pieces, and there ain't no shafts on it."

"I can tell you now, Nathe Frothing ain't gonna touch it. I know that old cuss." Lola sternly, with a know-it-all expression, continued to talk. "His Lordship will just have to get a new chaise."

"That's a probability," said Jackson.

Michael's head was bobbing up and down in the affirmative.

Tomas came through the kitchen to tell Jackson and Michael that he didn't find Lord Anthony in his study. He told them to get the landau ready for use because it would have to be the town carriage until the chaise was repaired.

The landau was a very elegant two-seated, four-wheeled vehicle that required either two or four horses. It had red velvet seats, a shiny black divided top, and a step on the back for a footman.

Lola laughed heartily as she interrupted Tomas by saying, "I'll sure look like a grand lady sitting back in that landau when Jackson drives me to market."

Tomas looked her in the eye and said, "I'm pretty sure his lordship will not allow you to go to market in his landau. You're going to have to walk."

"Never, never, never," screamed Lola stamping her foot. "I'm not going to tote that heavy basket back up that hill. Somebody else will have to go to market."

Jackson left the room, following behind Tomas.

Michael went over to the wood box and began to arrange the logs that were left in the box in order to make room for more. "Lola," he said, "you could go oftener and get a lot less, and that way you will be outside more. With summer coming on, it will be nice weather to be outside."

"Won't work," answered Lola gruffly. "I got to have time to do my work here."

"Why don't you let Truly live here? She can stay in the cellar with you and help you here in the kitchen."

"Michael, no one knows where Truly is; she ain't been seen for a week. Besides, her ladyship wouldn't let her stay here." Lola continued to talk. "Henry got up this morning and left. I didn't think he ought to go out yet, but he said he's got to find Truly. I asked him why he wanted to bother. He said he loves the little bitch!"

"Henry loves Truly?" Michael asked with a big sigh of astonishment, and then he said, "That just ain't right; you better talk to him, Lola."

"What ain't right about it?" Then she answered her own question. "You think because he's black and she's white, it ain't all right? Well let me tell you something, old man, her own papa could have been black or Indian or a pirate. I don't know who the hell, which one it was, that knocked me up with her. She ain't as white as I am. She's kind of brown, but she's a woods-colt, and she could have that brownish complexion because of the elements."

Michael was still shifting logs around in the wood box when he said, "Well, that makes it e'n better. Henry could keep an eye on her, and he would be around here more and be a hep."

"I don't care to discuss Henry and Truly anymore. Get your work done and git outta my kitchen."

Michael said, "Lola, don't be such a pile of crabgrass."

He went out the door and headed for the stable, humming as he went along an old tune he had hung onto since he was three years old, in Africa. It sounded like, "the beat, beat, beat, of a lion bone on a thin, thin, skin of a snake drum."

Chapter Twelve

Lord Anthony resentfully left his study. He usually answered Florence's summons as soon as possible. This time he was frustrated because it hadn't been but an hour since he left her. He thought he would be coming back to keeping his records in a few moments, so he didn't lock the door.

He climbed the stairs two steps at a time, reaching Florence's room all out of breath. "What is it you want now, Florence? I have a lot of book work to do. Come on, speak up."

"Maurice, dear, have you decided how we are all going to get out to Milton Hill now that the chaise is no longer usable?"

"Don't worry, Florence, the message that was delivered earlier this morning was from Hutchinson. He canceled the party."

"There's not going to be any celebration?"

Lord Anthony turned and pointed at Florence and stormed at her, "Of any kind. He's afraid of violence. He has every right to be. He's been the victim, more than once." Anthony paused, then continued, "Even Otis, a man of justice, has been beaten and mauled. That's why he acts so crazy at times. Otis outright told Hutchinson to resign and move to England. I think their minds run in the same channel; they're both crazy. Hutchinson said he's thinking of asking Parliament for a leave of absence. I'm going to recommend it.

"Don't think about the party anymore; it's off. The cancellation was a good thing. You and Clarice and the others were going overboard."

Lord Anthony started to leave the room, but Florence took hold of his arm. "Wait a minute, Maurice. Do the others know?"

"Not unless Clarice told them; I told her. I hope she breaks it gently to Robin."

"Maurice, that child was wild with anticipation. She was also looking forward to seeing Peaches." Peaches was Robin's pony, who came to America on the Cordelia with the Anthonys and who was taken to Governor Hutchinson's farm because there was not enough room in the stables and there was no place for Robin to ride.

"Peaches, Peaches? Oh yes, the pony; well she will have to wait. There's no way she's going to see Peaches until we get better acquainted with the people here and find a place for her to ride."

Lord Anthony removed Florence's handhold on his arm and went back to his study.

On reaching the door he slapped his hand up against the side of his face and said, "Geeze, God! I left this door unlocked, even open a crack."

He immediately noticed his wastebasket was upset and wadded papers strewn all around. His desk had also been disturbed. He began picking up the mess and missed the parchment scroll on which the governor's message was written. Someone had taken it. Who?

It was Robin who entered her papa's study. She had on such a pretty new dress and ribbons to match it in her hair. She thought it would be a good time to wish her papa a happy good morning.

Bo Tay was following at her heels. Just as the two of them walked into the study, a mouse jumped from the wastebasket. Bo Tay, with one fierce curl of his lip and a leap, pounced upon the wastebasket, barking furiously. He knocked it over and all that was in it rolled out onto the floor. Robin had seen the mouse, and she climbed up on the chair and turned and sat down on the desk, facing the door. When Bo Tay realized that his prey had gotten away, he sat on his haunches barking at Robin.

As she unseated herself from the desk, she knocked off the parchment scroll. She picked it up and read the message. She turned red with anger at first, then surprise and disappointment overtook her emotions, she ran to her room, and went straight to her bed. She yanked the covers back and climbed in, burying her face in her pillow. Bo Tay jumped in right behind her and took his place under the covers.

Clarice, sitting at her desk in her room, heard the crying child. She knew at once that someone had told her about the party being canceled.

It was going to be hard to console Robin and find something else to take the place of the party planning and the excitement of a day in the country. There just had to be some way the two of them could see the town.

Clarice laid aside her half-written letter and went into Robin's room and crawled into bed with her and Bo Tay. "Robin, dear, I know why you are crying. Someone told you about Governor Hutchinson's decision to cancel the party."

Through sobs Robin cried out, "I hate him. I hate that mean old man. I'm never going to speak to him again. I hate everybody."

"Even me?" asked Clarice.

"I guess I like you a little bit, but only because you are the only one who cares about me. I think I like Jason a little bit too because he loves you."

"Thank you for liking Jason and me, Robin. We both love you very much."

Florence told Maggie, Maggie told Lola, Lola told Jackson, Jackson told Michael, Michael told Tomas, Tomas told Marie. Each person, except Clarice and Robin, seemed very glad to hear it was called off.

Lola still had a very unpleasant thing to do. She had to tell Jason that he was not to come to the Anthony household ever again, that these orders from Lady Anthony had been most emphatic.

Lola had been trying to conjure up a way to get Jason's bakery goods. For several reasons, she wanted the usual procedure to continue, but she had to do as her Ladyship demanded.

As she sat down at the table to make a list of staples she had to buy at market, the thought hit her that she could also buy Jason's baked goodies from his stand at the wharf. That way they could talk to each other and perhaps he would help her look for Truly.

The wharf was one of Truly's favorite hangouts.

When Robin began to feel her hunger later in the afternoon, she suggested to Clarice that they have a tea party in the gazebo.

Clarice said, "I think that is a splendid idea. We will go down to the kitchen and fill a basket with goodies."

Robin still had on her lovely clothes. Clarice told her to get out of bed and put on something more suitable and to remove the ribbons from her hair and put on her hood, for the wind was blowing and it might rain as there were some dark clouds forming over the ocean.

As Clarice and Robin opened the kitchen door they saw a man standing in front of the cupboard. His back was bent over slightly because he was reaching into the lower shelves and bringing out a jug of cider. Robin thought it was Henry. She couldn't see the man's face. He was the only other person in the kitchen.

"Hi, Henry," the child said, and the man turned and faced the two girls. He was extremely shabby, also muddy and pretty badly scratched up around his face. It was hard to tell if he was a white man.

Clarice screamed and jumped in front of the child, pushing her with her hips and telling her to run. "Run upstairs, and get your papa. Stay there with your mama. Lock the door."

Robin ran up the stairs but she stopped at the top and called back to her governess, "Cee Cee, run, come up here."

Clarice was being very brave when she asked the man, "Who are you?" He didn't answer.

She yelled at him. "You have no right to be in our kitchen. Who let you in here?"

Still he did not answer her. His eyes were staring at her. She could see he was emaciated and very unstable on his feet. She thought, Maybe he's drunk, or maybe he's been shot, but she saw no blood other than the scratches on his face, which seemed to be minor. There were no cuts. "Are you that hungry? Is that the reason you broke in here? You did break in didn't you?"

Still only stares and no answers. Clarice was trying to hold on to her wits, when she said, "Sit down at the table, I will fill a plate for you." She thought Keep on talking; be kind. He won't hurt you.

She came closer to him and held out her hand. "Here, let me help you, you are a bit wobbly." She pulled out the bench from the trestle table to make it easier for him to sit down.

She glanced toward the stairs. She hoped Robin would send someone to the kitchen. It seemed such a long time.

Clarice was afraid to turn her back on the stranger. She remembered Lady Anthony's warnings, "We may all be in danger." Clarice said to herself, This poor man is not dangerous; he's scared to death of something or somebody. I wish he would talk.

She was very thankful when she heard Lord Anthony's voice telling Robin, "Stay in there with your mother; keep the door locked." She knew he was on his way.

Lord Anthony saw the poor ragged man sitting at the table and Clarice standing over him pouring milk into a mug. He also saw a plate of meat and bread in front of him.

"Clarice, what in the hell are you doing, feeding this criminal? Why didn't you grab that rifle," he pointed to a rifle stashed in a gun rack over the door, "and shoot him? He's probably planning to kill us."

The man finally spoke. "I wasn't planning to kill anyone. I was almost killed myself and will be killed whenever I show my face in public."

"Who tried to kill you?" Lord Anthony asked.

"Them damn British soldiers," answered the stranger. "One of them shot at me."

"What were you doing?" asked Anthony.

"Me and some others was marking X's across the broadsides advertising the King's birthday."

"And what else?" asked his lordship, "That's not enough lawbreaking to justify killing you."

"We was spittin' on George's picture."

"That's enough," yelled Lord Anthony. "Eat your fill and get out of here, but remember it's the king's food that's filling your belly."

Clarice had sat down on the bench on the opposite side of the table.

Lord Anthony stomped out of the kitchen and went through the garden to Tomas's cottage. He knocked once on the door, but he shoved it open before Tomas could get to it.

He stood staunchly inside the room and said, pointing at Tomas, "How the hell did some vagrant get on to these premises and all the way into our kitchen where he was helping himself to the provisions in our cupboard without being seen?

"Tomas, I want at least two soldiers stationed at this house twenty-four hours a day beginning tomorrow. See to it." He continued, "You may have to call on the Provost Marshall and let him know I demand it. Do you understand?"

Lord Anthony slammed the door so hard the gutter fell from the corner of the cottage. He was swearing to himself, but he said, "Poor devil, he can't be blamed. He was pranking; some of these damn guards like to play war. They're trigger happy." He became so angry he pounded his fist into the palm of his other hand and kicked at the plants growing along the garden walk.

He came back through the kitchen and noticed that Clarice had the stranger engaged in conversation. He heard her ask him, "Are you a member of a gang that causes these acts of violence that so frequently occur in this town? And were you one of the men in the fight at our corner this morning?"

"What fight?" Lord Anthony stopped at the table when he heard Clarice ask the man about a fight he knew nothing about. Again he asked, looking at Clarice, "What fight?"

Clarice told his lordship that she and Robin had witnessed a fight, from the window in her room, and had seen a man killed and later hauled away in a cart.

"Good Lord! Why wasn't I told?"

"We ran to your study immediately, sir, but you weren't there."

"What time was it?"

"About noon, or shortly after twelve o'clock."

"Did you inform anyone at all?"

"No sir, Robin and I have not seen anyone else since then, until now. We were going to get something to eat and take it out to the garden. When we came into the kitchen this man was standing by the cupboard."

"Did he say anything to you?"

"No sir...only to you, when you said he was probably planning to kill us."

"Well, I think all such trash as he is are dangerous. So," he spoke directly to the intruder, "get out, and if you come back here again, a guard will shoot you. I have given orders for him to do just that."

Clarice stood up from her seat at the table and said, "Your lordship, sir, let him finish eating. He needs some strength." She wanted to question him some more.

"That will be all right," answered Lord Anthony, as he lumbered up the stairs to Florence and Robin.

"Did you take part in that fight?" Clarice asked the stranger a second time.

"I was one of the men tearing up the flag. I wouldn't have been tearing up that damn flag, but one of them soldiers was trying to shove it down my throat. I got away and run. I laid low, under a bush in your garden until the fight was all over. I was so scared and hungry and tired that I fell asleep. When I woke up it was so quiet around this house I thought I could get into the kitchen and steal something to eat. I haven't et since day before yesterday. You are very kind to give me this grub.

"I'll admit I hate them damn soldiers, marching around town all the time, eating and drinking and making merry and ordering us Americans to get out of the taverns and ordinaries."

"I can understand your feelings," said Clarice, "but I'm British and the soldiers have orders, too. They are trying to keep the peace."

"Ma'am, thank ye and God bless ye," were the final words of the stranger as he departed.

Clarice put the plate he ate off of over on the trough where there was a stack of dirty dishes. She took a look out the window to see if he went down the hill toward town or up the hill to someplace else.

While she was looking out the window she heard footsteps crossing the kitchen. She turned to see who it was. At that moment, Jason encircled her with his arms and began kissing her.

"My precious beautiful darling. What luck God has bestowed upon me. Just imagine, me, finding an angel in this kitchen."

"Oh Jason, where did you come from? What a wonderful surprise! I've had you pounding in my heart all day. So much as happened to mar the tranquility, but now nothing in the world could make it more perfect than your being here at this moment just when I need you so much."

He led her over to the table and they sat down side by side, very close. She laid her head on his shoulder. He kissed her again and again.

He asked her, "What's wrong, my darling? You are trembling."

"I'm fine now, my dear, but this day has been hectic."

She told him about the fight she and Robin had watched, then about the message from Governor Hutchinson canceling the party and how upset it had made Robin. She told him about the encounter with the intruder. She then began to laugh and cuddle closer to Jason.

He tilted her chin, smoothed her hair back from her face, ran his finger over her lips, and kissing her he whispered, "I can't bear to be away from you; that's why I'm here now. There's no other reason but you, my sweet. After last night, I'm going crazy with love. I've never been like this before."

Clarice, looking into his eyes, responded, "Yes my dear, precious man, I'm crazy with love too, and it's all for you."

She pulled back a little and got hold of herself. She remembered that she would soon be called, if she didn't go to Robin at once. "Jason, darling," she said, "I'm sorry, but I must go before someone comes looking for me. I will put a note under the broken post tomorrow. I love you," she held on to his hand as long as she could while he was backing away from her toward the door and she was backing toward the stairway.

Robin was waiting at the top of the stairs. She said, "I saw him kissing you."

Clarice blushed but responded to Robin, "Oh, Robin, it is too wonderful to believe; I think it must be a dream."

Chapter Thirteen

Jason was crossing the garden to reach his horse when he met Lola; she was returning from a visit with the cook of the Proffitts, the family living about four houses away.

"Good afternoon, Lola; where have you been gallivanting to this warm and beautiful Sunday?"

She didn't answer his question. She greeted him with a haughty, "How do you do, Jason? There's something I have to tell you. Let's set in the gazebo. You need to be settin' down when I tell you."

"Lola, what is so pressing that you are threatening to spoil one of the most beautiful days of my life?"

As they stepped into the gazebo, Jason plucked a rose from a bush nearby. When they sat down, he reached over to Lola, kissed her on the cheek, and tucked the rose under the edge of her mop cap over her ear. He said, "Now tell me what the big news is. Have you heard from Truly?"

"This news is not about Truly," Lola sternly emphasized. "It's from much higher up. It's from 'her majesty', Lady Anthony."

"Oh," said Jason, being flippant, "shall I prostrate myself?"

Lola put her hand on his knee, and she said, "Jason, you are not to come here again. Not even to deliver your bread. Her ladyship suspects you and the governess are into it too deep with each other.

"She was very firm in her orders. She has threatened to put guards here to keep you away." Lola had not yet learned of Lord Anthony's orders to Tomas.

For a minute neither Lola nor Jason said a word. Then Jason jumped to his feet and stepped out of the gazebo to look up at Clarice's window. He saw her standing there. She opened the swinging casement panes and threw him a kiss. He threw one back to her and called out to her, "I'll be back, darling."

He looked at Lola, still sitting in the gazebo. "Lola," he said, "hell or high water, guards or mad dogs, will not keep me away from that girl, and you can give the damn emissaries that message from me. They will have to kill me to keep me away from her. As long as she wants me, I'll come."

Jason left and Lola remained in the gazebo alone for a long time. She had such a feeling of depression she said to herself, "Love is such a splendid thing. It causes so much trouble."

The day darkened, and Lola went inside. She found a mountain of dirty dishes and soiled linen waiting for her to clean up.

In the Anthony household it was the custom for each one to look out for himself for supper on Sunday, although Maggie usually carried a tray to her ladyship. Lord Anthony ended every Sunday drinking rum and eating hunks of cheese and smoking Cuban tobacco.

"I'm glad there's lots of work to do," sighed Lola to herself. "I got to quit thinking of Henry and Truly and Jason and the governess. I've got to think of me."

Tomas came into the kitchen and saw Lola dipping water with a gourd from the barrel by the fireplace and pouring it over the dirty dishes. He picked up a gourd and began also to dip water and pour it over the dishes.

He said, "Lola, you work too hard; you are a very pretty woman, but your smile is warm and encouraging."

"What do you mean, Mr. Straight?" asked the blushing Lola.

"I mean you are a desirable woman. Here let me help you." He reached around her to push some dishes under the water, but he was so close he was pressing himself against her thighs.

She turned to face him, "Why, Mr. Straight, why are you offering to help me? Did your wife throw you out?"

"Oh no, Lola, I just think you're lonesome. You're pretty and desirable and shouldn't be lonesome. I have been admiring you ever since we got here. I also think you are brave and would relish some excitement."

Lola began to rattle the dishes and shove them around. She broke a plate and splashed water out onto the floor.

"Mr. Straight," she said, "I've took my fun from lots of men. There's been wharf rats, vagabonds, scalawags, idiots and numskulls, and all kinds of beggars and thieves, but I ain't never tried it with somebody higher up than I am. I'm not going to run the risk of gettin' caught and losing my good home here with the Anthonys, and I ain't going to discuss this little talk we've had with any other living soul. So consider our love affair ended right here at the start, before it ever gets out of control." What Lola did not know was this: Thoughts of Tomas would keep her awake all night.

Tomas said he was sorry, but he couldn't help the way he felt. He looked disappointed and dejected as he went back to the cottage.

When the kitchen chores were finished Lola went down the cellar steps to her room. She had a piece of a broken mirror propped against the wall and a box to sit on in front of it.

She sat on the box and removed her mop cap. The rose Jason had put over her ear was still in place. She ran her fingers through her hair. She picked up her brush and brushed out her chestnut curls. "Um," she sighed, as she turned her head left to right, "I'm not bad looking. It's nice to know a man thinks I'm pretty. But Tomas Straight? Oh! God please."

That night was long, and Lola couldn't sleep. Tomas had aroused in her a feeling she thought was gone forever. It is true she had almost forgotten what passion felt like, but she said to herself, "I don't want that feeling to return. It makes me want to run away."

Jason didn't go to his room after he left Lola and had heard her message. He rode over to the waterfront and the area around Hancock's Wharf. There, one could always find excitement to stir up energy.

He was hoping perhaps he might run into Henry. He knew Henry was up and about, because he had stopped by his room and Jackson told him that Henry got up from his bed and left with no word as to where he was going.

Charlie was clumping along, Jason was bobbing his head to keep time with Charlie's gait. He was softly whistling a tune to a sad song his mother used to sing to him. He tried to remember the words:

...My love lies dreaming, and I'm so alone.
I know she loves me, but I'm not coming home.
If I come home I'll be shot dead.
Oh how I wish I could be in her bed....

He thought it was the darkest night he had ever seen. The moon that was so bright a little earlier, was nowhere in the sky. A few torches were flaming but not giving off much light. The Merry Mermaid windows showed that candles were lit inside, but there wasn't much of a sound of merry-making going on, probably because it was Sunday.

Jason dismounted and threw Charlie's bridle reins over the hitching pole and went inside. He looked around for a familiar face. The place was not bulging with customers; only sixteen to twenty people were there.

He sat down at a table close to the bar with a couple of fellows he knew; Thomas Moore, who operated a storage business at the wharf, and John Foster, a carpenter-at-large, not long a resident, who had come to Boston from Savannah, Georgia.

Jason spoke first, "Good evening, gentlemen. Do you mind if I sit with you?"

Moore looked through his bushy, drooping eyebrows and said, "Please do sit down and bring us some news. How about a beer?"

Jason motioned with his finger, a sign to the bartender for beer, and in a moment a large mug of the foamy stuff was in front of him.

He began the conversation, "I'm looking for Henry Cook. Does either of you know him? He's black and wears a pirate's bandanna on his head. He has a scar on his lip. He's not a ruffian. Mostly very gentle, that is, if he likes you."

"Why are you looking for him; is he your slave?" asked Foster.

"No, he's a free man, never been a slave. He works for me, and he also works for a family of English gentry recently moved here from England. He does odd jobs," said Jason.

Moore said, "I've seen him here on the dock but not for a week or ten days."

"I've seen him, too," said Foster, and sneeringly he added, "he was with a white girl. It was about two or three weeks ago. She looked like a tramp."

Jason said, "He's been sick with pneumonia, but he got up out of his bed today and left. If you do see him tomorrow—or anytime soon—tell him that J. is looking for him. I will appreciate it."

He never touched his beer, but he threw three shillings down beside it and left the table.

Moore and Foster each grabbed for the mug. Moore had the firmer grip. He drank most of it, then pushed the mug over the table to Foster, who finished it.

Jason mounted Charlie and began his ride across town to Charles Street. He wished he had found Henry. He needed him to pick up the notes from under the broken post and to deliver his notes to Clarice.

He kept thinking, as Charlie slowly carried him home, I must think of a way to be with her. I have to see her and know what is going on with her.

He whispered a prayer as he neared his shop:

"Dear Lord: Maker of Angels and Lovers, of Moon and Stars and all good things. I beg of you to consider this feeble man you have seen cause to place upon this earth and have endowed with desire and passion, oh, so beautiful a gift. Thank you for making me whole and able. Please make me also patient and brave and worthy of such a beautiful young woman. Guide both of us in truth and love and allow us the company and pleasure of each other. We will praise you, dear Lord, and be grateful to you forever. Amen, Your poor humble servant, Jason McKenzie.

Jason felt joy springing out of all the pores of his body, for he was sure God had heard and would answer his prayer.

When he reached his shop, Charlie stopped and snorted as if he was saying, "Here we are, get off and pat my neck, like you always do."

That is not what Jason did. He sat there, his arms crossed at the elbows, for at least ten minutes. He was deeply thinking of what he should do.

At last, as if a bolt of lightning had hit him, he said out loud there in the midnight darkness, "I'll ask her to run away with me and marry me. If she loves me like she says she does, she will do it."

Jason patted Charlie's neck as the horse expected, but he didn't get off. He drew the reins to turn around and said, "Get up, old boy, head for the road to Lynn. I'm going out there right now, to see what kind of condition the house is in for bringing home my bride."

Jason's mother had left him a small farm, twenty acres with a frame house of six rooms. There was a barn and a small lean-to, several cows, and two horses. She also left him the store building on Charles Street and the bakery business. There were living quarters over the store building which he was now using for his home.

Parson Smith, a minister of the town of Lynn, was the caretaker of the farm. He looked after the cows and kept the milk. His wife cleaned the house once a month for the use of the horse, a mare named Panzy, and a small chaise which was badly in need of repair.

Jason tightened the reins on Charlie and said, "If we hurry we'll be there by daylight; that is, if we can catch the first ferry."

The ferry to which Jason was alluding was the public transportation across the Charles River. It operated six times a day from 4:00 A.M. to 10:00 P.M. He wanted to make it in time for the 4:00 A.M. crossing.

The ferry was built like a barge. It was pulled from shore to shore by cables that wound around large wooden wheels. The wheels were turned by horses walking in circles. It took approximately forty-five minutes to cross. It was always loaded to capacity, which was two chaises, two wagons, twenty pedestrians, and five or six horseback passengers, besides a crew of four men, two on each side to keep the cables in line.

While on the ferry, Jason got off his horse and talked with another passenger who was also a horseback traveler and who was on his way to Salem. He introduced himself as Henry Prentiss and said he was a Cooper's apprentice and was going up to Salem to purchase some barrel staves for his boss. He said it was cheaper to buy them already cut and water soaked than it was to do all that work in the Cooper's shop.

Jason wasn't the least bit interested in what Prentiss had to say, but he pretended to be. Jason's mind was whizzing with thoughts and schemes for getting Clarice to marry him and leave the Anthonys.

However, when the ferry reaches its mooring on the north bank of the river and all the passengers were getting off, Jason put out his hand to shake Prentiss's and said, "I would like to talk politics with you some time. I'll drop in at your Cooper's shop if you care to give me the address."

Prentiss said, "It's on the south side, near Griffin's Wharf. We could meet in the Green Dragon Tavern. I work very near the tavern for Joseph Mountford, the Cooper."

Charlie seemed in much vitalized spirit as he took off in a gallop with Jason on his back. He always acted peppier after the ferry ride. It was the only time and place he ever got to be the passenger. Maybe he was happy because he knew that very soon he was going to see Panzy and get a chance to chomp some of the delicious salty sage of the pasture in back of the house where he used to live.

Jason laid the reins down and folded his arms over his chest. He sat back in the saddle and surmised the peaceful landscape.

Charlie knew the way home and he went straight to the yard gate and nickered. Panzy was grazing right at the back door. She came trotting around the house and she and Charlie were immediately rubbing noses and curling their lips at each other over the fence.

Jason sat on Charlie while he took a long look around. It was all very fresh and clean and homey looking. He had been born in that house and spent his boyhood there.

"God," he said, "I've got so much to be grateful for," then he let out a sigh and a deep breath. He dismounted and opened the gate to let Charlie into the yard with Panzy. He didn't see anyone, anywhere.

It was a gorgeous sunrise and not one bit of fog. About a mile away on the horizon, he could see white sails of fishing schooners and one or two tall masts of English Brigs.

Lynn was a busy place; big ships anchored there sometimes for repairs. Everyone predicted that someday in the faraway future, Lynn would be a city of industry. A lot depended on government.

As Jason walked slowly to the door he stopped by his mother's favorite rose bush, which was now in full bloom, and as he bent over to smell it, he said to the bush, "I know Clarice will love plucking a bouquet from you, as Mother did."

He lifted the iron latch and opened the door. The latch was never locked. He went into the house. There was a musty smell from the house being closed most of the time. There were ashes in the fireplace from a fire that had died out several months ago. It didn't look as if Mrs. Smith had been there lately.

Jason sat down in the old wooden rocker and leaned back and closed his eyes. Since he hadn't been to bed all night it was easy for him to fall asleep.

Parson Smith was walking by the house and noticed the door open. He thought his wife had been there and left it open, but when he started to pull the latch toward himself to close the door, he saw the sleeping Jason stretched out in the rocking chair. He quietly entered the house and walked over to him. At first he thought Jason was sick or hurt but soon discovered that was not the case as Jason stirred and straightened himself up, blinking at the sunlight streaming in the door.

The house was built facing east, and when the sun was bright the family room, or meeting room, as Jason's parents called it, was flooded with sunbeams and dancing shadows made by the tall sugar maples on the front pasture.

The house was surrounded by pasture. There was a small garden, now abundant with herbs such as rosemary, basil, tansy, and mint, giving freely of their pungent aromas, which would soon have aroused the sleeping man even if Parson Smith had not come by.

"Dear God! It sure is Jason McKenzie." The Parson was exuberant in his greeting. "Why didn't you let us know you were coming? The missus would'a cooked up a mess of spring lamb. They are just ripe for the slaughtering now. Sure is good to see you."

Jason was trying to get his hand loose from the Parson's. He said, "I didn't know I was coming until I was almost here. I'm so tired and so riled up over the situation in Boston, I had to get out of there for a spell, to think.

"How's the politics here in Lynn? Have there been any shootings, anyone got themselves killed? That is lately, I mean."

The Parson looked down at the ground as he answered Jason. Somehow he felt that he, as a minister of the Gospel, should be able to keep the peace. He said, "There's been lots of nasty talk and lots of threats. The Committee of Correspondence sends one of their men out here every week to make speeches and write down comments. Then there's the town council, nothing but slurs and arguments. The citizens of this town can't get along with one another.

"Tell me, son," continued the Parson, "what about Hutchinson? Is he as bad as he's reported to be? That broadside that one of his soldiers tacked up on a tree in the town square, was an invitation to his farm to celebrate the king's birthday. Is he really going to be that hospitable and generous?"

"No, no," answered Jason, "that's been called off. The governor got cold feet."

"I'll go later and tack up another broadside that it is canceled."

Jason invited the Parson to sit and have some tea.

Hungry for company and some more news, he sat down in the chair that Jason got up from to go to the kitchen.

Looking in the cupboard for tea, Jason found a canister with some tea in it. He had no idea as to its age. Didn't matter, he would try it. He made a fire on the kitchen hearth and found some water in a pitcher which he put on to boil. He found some dark brown sugar; it was full of ants, but he put it in a cup and lit a candle under it and soon it was bubbling syrup which they used to sweeten their tea. There was nothing to go with the beverage.

The two men sat and talked and drank six cups each, and Jason felt ready to walk his fields and see his property again. He was thinking of Clarice every step of the way, hopeful with all his heart that, "she would be happy here."

After a while he came to his senses. "Why, I haven't even asked her; why am I so sure she will marry me?" He said, "Because she loves me, that's why, and I love her."

His thoughts went back to the meeting they had in the gazebo, how she had let him kiss her and caress her, and he could still hear her whispering in his ear that she loved him. He recalled in his memory how he had gently carried her through the dark cellar and how he felt her trembling while in his arms.

Jason felt confident that Clarice would marry him and that they would live in Lynn, in this same house that his father had built and where his mother came as a bride.

His parents had been happy and prosperous, Why can't we do the same? he thought.

It was thrilling to look and see and plan.

"Maybe I will bring the bakery business to Lynn. This town is booming in the shipbuilding business, and I hear there is a shoe manufacturing trade doing well.

"I could, with good planning, raise some corn and barley if I studied the new methods of planting and harvesting."

After walking his boundaries he went to the northwest corner of his northwest field. It was his favorite spot. There was a huge boulder there which had been there for centuries. It probably weighed seventeen or eighteen tons. It changed color according to the weather. When the sun shone warm upon it, it was purple. When the rain was pouring down, it was blue. In the midsummer dry spell it was pink.

His father told stories about it to him, as a child, how pirates had buried gold under it and how Indians used to meet there for council. He remembered how he and two playmates used to chase each other around it and also how it was used for target practice with rifles and bows and arrows. He rubbed his hand over it to feel the nicks. They used to pretend sometimes that it was magic. They would sit cross-legged in front of it and wish for things: boots or coats or, if they were hungry, maybe they would wish for a hot roasted potato or ear of corn.

They had given the rock many different names at many different times. Sometimes they called it Old Blue, sometimes Big Bear, and Jason's favorite was Shiny Squatt. This was because it really looked like it was squatting, and it had been glistening flakes like jewels when the sun was shining on it.

Jason remembered a time when he had waded through deep snow to go to the rock to pray, to ask God to bring home his papa who was out on the sea on a fishing expedition.

He remembered his mother climbing up to the roof with her spy glass, and when she came down saying, "I didn't see any sign of the boats; I'm afraid the flimsy sails could not hold in such a bad storm. I'm thinking they won't return."

But Jason had a lot of faith in God, and since God owned the rock (his father had told him God owned the rock) and it had lasted for hundreds of years, then God would bring his father home from the stormy sea. His father did return in a few days, and there was a celebration to welcome all the fishermen back to their families. They had all returned with hundreds of pounds of fish, and he as a small boy had believed that the rock had something to do with the safe return.

After he had sat there on the ground in front of the rock and meditated for a while, Jason got to his feet and began the walk back to the house. His steps were very slow, and at times he even stopped and closed his eyes, his arms folded across his chest.

Persuading Clarice to marry him was foremost in his thoughts. What a wonderful life they would have here in this busy town. He would probably become very rich and they would have a big family. He would send his sons to Harvard College. Perhaps one might become a lawyer and handle cases for the very poor and not charge them anything. Another might be a doctor and bring new life to young couples and make them happy.

He thought perhaps he would buy a beautiful schooner and he and Clarice would sail to faraway places where the rum and molasses come from, or to Nova Scotia.

His father had sailed there once and brought back an Indian woman to live with them and help his mother. Jason wondered, "What ever became of Shashaw?" She must be about forty years old by now.

Suddenly something whizzed by Jason's face, almost striking him in the eye. He became alert at once and quickened his step. He was aware that he was close to the nest of a sea sparrow; they build nests on the ground. The bird was warning him not to come any closer. They are most protective of their young.

He said to himself, "Gee, I was surely lost somewhere in my future."

On reaching the house and entering, he found Mrs. Smith there waiting for him. She kissed his cheek and remarked how strong and handsome he was. She asked him if he had found a suitable young lady to marry.

When he assured her that he had indeed found his beloved, she asked him if the girl knew her Savior. Stunned by the question, Jason hesitated a moment, then said, "I haven't given her religion a thought." He answered Mrs. Smith, "I'm sure she is a good Christian; she has to be. She never swears or lies or does any promiscuous things."

"How long have you known her?" inquired Mrs. Smith.

"Oh, I'd say about ten days," answered Jason.

"My goodness, my son, you need more time to court her. Your mother would say 'Nay, nay' to you. Do be careful. Do you know if her family is Whig or Tory?"

"She doesn't have any politics. She loves me, and whatever I am, she will be."

Jason was unsure what Clarice felt regarding politics, and when Mrs. Smith asked him about it, he became quite jittery. He changed the subject. "Madam Smith," he said, "I'm going to marry that girl regardless of which way her family thinks. Will you see to getting us a new shuck mattress, a new feather bed, and a new bolster? If there happens to be any linen for sale in this town, will you buy some and make us several new sheets and pillow shams?"

He opened the pouch hanging from his belt and laid out twenty one-pound notes on the table. He said, "If you need more I will return in two weeks or a month, and I will pay you the balance then."

As he started toward the door he turned to face Mrs. Smith and smiled. He said, "The girl's name is Clarice; I don't know her last name."

Mrs. Smith threw her hands up onto her head, "Good Lord, Jason, my friend, you better pray hard."

Jason took a couple of steps to her and kissed her on the cheek. He said, "Thank you for looking after the house and Panzy. I'm heading back to Boston now. I can't stand another day without seeing her."

He had already saddled Charlie, and he was waiting, tied, outside the gate. Panzy was whinnying after them as they went down the pike toward the ferry.

Chapter Fourteen

Lola was trying to think of a way to break the news to Clarice that Jason would not be coming to the Anthony household.

"I'll just come right out with it," she said to herself as she came down extremely hard on the pork shoulder with a meat cleaver, but after a moment of ripping the meat she had second thoughts. "No, that might set her off on a tantrum; I better be more gentle."

Clarice wasn't the kind of person to throw a tantrum, regardless of how she was affected by news or anything adversely touching her feelings or actions.

Lola didn't know this; therefore, she was expecting some negative reaction. Frankly she had cold feet about telling the governess the news she felt would make her very depressed. She finally decided that she would wait until Clarice missed Jason's coming and brought up the subject herself.

Lola did tell Jackson and Michael that evening when the two men were in the kitchen eating their supper. "I got some news for the two of ye," she said, "but ye got to promise not to say anything about it to anyone else. Understand? Everybody will find out about it soon enough.

"Here 'tis. The baker, Jason McKenzie, won't be coming around here anymore. Her ladyship thinks he's making eyes at the governess, and I'll say he is doing that all right. He's going crazy over her and she is him.

"We won't be eating his bread and cakes unless we get them from his store or his stand at the wharf. I'll try to buy something when I go marketing. Keep your eyes out for him around here, because if you see him and don't report it, you'll be in real trouble with Lady Anthony."

Neither Jackson nor Michael liked the news, Lola could tell by the expressions on their faces, but they made no comments.

Michael whispered to Jackson, leaning over against him, "I'm doggone sure that was them two in the gazebo tother night."

After the house was quiet and candles were out, Clarice tiptoed through the back hall and out the door to the garden. She stopped behind a large lilac bush and surveyed the surrounding area. She had a strange feeling that the stranger who had broken into the kitchen on Sunday might still be lurking around. She saw or heard nothing but a mockingbird, who was doing an obbligato, accompanying the crickets and tree frogs who, Clarice imagined, must be performing a "Mid-summer Night's Dream." She darted from behind the bush and ran like a fleeing deer to the broken post and deposited the letter she had spent two hours composing to her own true love.

It had been thirty hours since their last bit of togetherness. What a long, long thirty hours. Why wasn't there a letter from him waiting for her? she wondered. Clarice hurried back very quietly to the house and up to her room. She was satisfied that she had not been seen.

Early next morning two red-coated soldiers appeared at the Anthonys' front door. Tomas was sitting in the entrance hall waiting for them.

When they were admitted, Tomas introduced them to Lord Anthony, who came out of his study. He had observed their arrival by standing at his large oval window, watching.

Tomas said, "Your lordship, this is Corporal Edward Channing, and this is Inspector Sergeant Paul Scott."

Lord Anthony shook their hands, looked them over from head to toe, and asked their ages.

Channing said, "I'm almost eighteen, your lordship."

Scott said, "I've just had my twentieth birthday."

"Young, young, too young," said Lord Anthony, but then he asked, "Are you up to catching scoundrels and thieves, also spies and murderers?" He also said, "This town is bulging with angry people. I think our presence here is resented and we need some protection."

Lord Anthony then directed his talk to Tomas. "Find these soldiers some quarters, select for them a station, and see that they are bountifully fed and made comfortable."

Tomas told the two young officers to follow him, and he led them to the kitchen. He ordered Lola to see that they got the best of everything to eat and to put their meals on the breakfast room table.

Lola became instantly irritated, "With all this extra work," she said, "I'm going to need plenty of help."

Tomas winked at her and said to her, "My dear, you're going to have some help; I'll see that Henry helps you."

Lola wiped her hands on her apron and mumbled to herself, "I might as well be a slave." She looked directly at Corporal Channing and asked, "Are you expecting breakfast now?"

"Yes indeedy we are and plenty of it."

"Geeze," said Lola as she began setting dishes and food on the table in the breakfast room. She was mumbling, "I'm going to find Truly if I have to tramp this town from one end to the other. Henry ain't going to be any help."

About noon, Henry came home.

"Where you been, son?" asked Jackson when he met Henry coming up the garden walk. "We'uns been worried you musta forgot you wus sick. How you feel now?"

"I'm tuckered out, pretty much. I been clean out to Dedham. I went with John Slade as his outrider. He belongs to the Committee of Correspondence, and he had a satchel full of letters and pamphlets to deliver to a man there who was going all the way to Providence, Rhode Island, to give them to a committee member there, who was taking them to New York. I sure wish I could read. I had a chance to read everything. John let me carry the satchel. I felt so good helping him." He said, "Mostly the pamphlets were copies of Sam Adams's speeches and some records of the doings of the Sons of Liberty. He said there was a cutout from the Gazette about the arrival of the Anthonys."

"Are you aiming to take up the out-rider job and quit working here?" asked Jackson.

"Well, I may just do that if Mr. Slade will hire me; however, he is not the only one doing the delivering. They send different members, but I'm going to ask for the duty. Maybe I'll get lucky."

"I hope the best for you, Henry," said Jackson, "but seems to me it's a bit risky. These British soldiers ain't got much use for message carriers. You is apt to get killed."

"Jackson, that can happen right here in this yard or house. What's he doing here anyway?" Henry had sighted the guard. He looked scared when he said that, and a chill ran down his spine.

Inspector Sergeant Paul Scott was pacing along the garden fence.

"Mr. Straight has stationed two guards here, Lord Anthony's orders. They are to keep out intruders and also McKenzie." There, Jackson had let the cat out of the bag; Lola had told him not to tell anyone about McKenzie's banishment.

Henry's eyes changed from mirth to anger in a second, "What about McKenzie?" he asked.

"Well, he has been forbidden to come to this house. He is not to bring any of his bakery goods here or come here for any reason."

"Why, what has Jason don?" Henry was spewing the questions at Jackson fast and furiously.

"I heard Lola say that he was getting too friendly with the governess, or something like that," answered Jackson.

Henry replied, "So they found out; it won't do any good to bar him from coming here. Jason's in love. Man, is he in love. They can't stop it; he's so in love he's crazy. So is she. Miss Clarice is nuts about him. Them soldiers can't stop it. Them two is on fire." Henry went into the kitchen, laughing and clapping his hands.

"Where's Truly?" were the first words he heard Lola say, but she was too busy at the hearth, bent over a large kettle of boiling meat, to stand up and greet him.

"I didn't find her. Nobody's seen her," he answered as he sniffed at the delicious aroma of her cooking.

"You just git back out there and keep on searching and asking until she turns up. I need her here to hep me. I got two more bellies to fill up. I need hep bad." Henry knew who she meant by two more bellies.

"Why don't you poison them and get it over with?" said Henry facetiously.

"I ain't in no mood for your silly talk, Henry. I'm worn out and I'm about to be sick." Lola staggered backwards as she straightened up from the hearth.

Henry stuffed the front of his shirt with biscuits and cold pork chops, which were sitting on the trestle table, and went out toward the stables.

As he crossed the garden a thought came into his mind. "A body can catch a fly quicker with sugar then they can with vinegar. I'll go over to the sergeant and strike up a conversation."

He spoke to Inspector Sergeant Paul Scott, "Good day, Sergeant, I live here. I work for Lord Anthony, so don't shoot me."

"I'm glad you told me that, boy, I was about to billy," the sergeant was swinging his billy around in a circle, "you to Mr. Straight."

Henry didn't like being called "boy"; he felt as big and strong as anybody.

"That won't be necessary; Mr. Straight knows me very well."

At that moment, Tomas came out of his cottage and saw Henry talking to the sergeant. He loudly said to Henry, "Henry, you are in for a good lecture, so come with me to your room."

Tomas strode along with Henry following him to the stables and up the iron stair steps to the loft to Henry's room.

Lola had preceded them by about five minutes and was tidying up Henry's bed. She seemed surprised to see Henry and Tomas entering the room and both looking surly.

Lola spoke. "I didn't know you were coming to your room, Henry. I thought you went to talk to the guard. I will do this another time," and she started to leave.

Tomas put his hand on her arm to halt her movement and said to her, "No, you stay. I need to talk to you." He told Henry to go on about his business, that he would lecture him later.

Henry went down the stairs and sat on a bench near Stomper's stall and began to eat the biscuits and pork chops.

Lola felt goosebumps rising up and down her spine. Tomas, still holding on to her arm but tighter, bent over her and kissed her. Lola blushed and pulled away from him. She said nothing.

When Tomas pushed her back on to the side of the bed then pushed her backwards and fell on top of her, she said, "You oughtn't do that, Mr. Straight."

"Why not?" he asked. "You big brown eyes and dimpled cheeks and juicy lips are irresistible."

"But," said Lola, "someone will see us, and we will both be in trouble."

"No, my dear, we won't be in trouble; no one cares. My wife hates me, and Lord Anthony wouldn't dare do anything to us for fear I might squeal on him. He's been carrying on with my Marie, off and on, ever since we first came to their manor house in London."

"Don't his wife suspect him?" asked the astonished Lola.

"She's too stupid and close-mouthed to notice or care. All she cares about is to be by herself, reading her French novels, stuffing her face, or whining to his lordship about something. She hasn't been out of her upstairs suite, except to the dining room, since the night of our arrival."

"Oh mercy, Mr. Straight, I hadn't noticed." Lola did notice that Tomas had steered her backwards to Henry's bed, and now they were horizontal across it and Tomas was on top of her, smothering her with kisses.

She scrambled hurriedly out of that situation and ran as fast as her fat legs could carry her down the stairs. Henry was still sitting on the bench, finishing his eating. He gulped down a mouthful when he saw Lola making much haste to get away.

"Hey girl, what's the big rush?" Henry called out to her as she ran past him.

"Something's burning," Lola hollered back to him as she flew into the kitchen.

Tomas came down the stairs, to where Henry was sitting, looking very sheepish. He said, "Henry, you are not to go off to town but must stay here and help Lola. The poor thing is overworked."

Henry suspected Tomas of his advances to Lola. He said, "Lola ain't no 'thing'; she's a woman."

Tomas replied, "What a woman, but contrary as the devil." He added, "Come on Henry, there's a big dinner in the works and Lola's about to be promoted, and you'll do the cooking."

The big dinner that Tomas was talking about was a bon voyage celebration for Captain Tucker and Mr. Sewell, who were sailing next day at ten o'clock on the Cordelia. Governor Hutchinson had suggested that Lord and Lady Anthony host the dinner.

Earlier that afternoon Lady Anthony had called Clarice to her sitting room and told her to get her letters ready to be delivered to the Cordelia.

It was good news to Clarice, and she spent the next hour rolling and tying her letters. Then she rolled them all together into a linen cloth and tied it with a ribbon.

Everyone had noticed an expression of loneliness on Clarice's face.

"This," said her ladyship, "will be a good time for them," meaning Clarice and Robin, "to get away from the house for a few hours of diversion."

She went to Lord Anthony's study, the first time she had been there, to ask his permission if they might all go to the wharf to mingle with the passengers and watch the Cordelia hoist her sails and put out to sea.

Lord Anthony really didn't want his family taking up any of his time. He had things to do. At first, his answer was "No." He had to prepare several reports to be sent to Lord North and Dartmouth: reports of dissension, of rabble gatherings, of violence, break-ins, such as happened at his house the previous Sunday, reports of unrest and complaints too numerous to mention. One report was an account of his chaise being attacked and destroyed.

Lady Anthony persisted, and he, out of exasperation at her nagging, finally agreed. He emphasized that Tomas and the two soldier guards were to accompany them and be with them every minute.

The double-seated Landau would take her ladyship, Marie, Clarice, Robin, and Maggie. Tomas would ride alongside. The two soldiers would stand on the back. Jackson would drive.

They would walk from the hitching spot to the mooring and stand together in a row to shake hands with all who were boarding.

The plan that Lord Anthony laid down to his wife was sensible and pleasant. She returned to her room and called for Maggie to tell her the plans and hear her reaction, before telling Clarice and Robin.

When Robin asked Clarice if she had a letter to Tom Fellows in the bundle she was sending to England, Clarice gasped, her eyes got bigger, and she exclaimed, "Oh my God! I forgot Tom."

She untied the bundle so she could include a letter to Tom, which she then had to hurriedly write.

> Dear Tom,
> America is wonderful, that is, what I have seen of it, which isn't much. Lady Anthony thinks it's dangerous and I am mostly confined to the house. She promises that soon Robin and I will be allowed some freedom to go out to stores and parks.
> I miss you, Tom, and I miss my parents. I have not been lonely though, because there has been lots to do. Robin's lessons, getting to know the servants, and friends who come to see the Anthonys.
> I have not yet heard anything from Julia.
> Goodbye, Keep Well, Yours, Clarice

Clarice let Robin read the letter before she rolled it and tied it.

Robin asked, "Why didn't you tell him about Jason?"

Clarice looked at the child and answered her. "Robin, I don't want to upset Tom. There will be plenty of time. I am not sure about Jason, myself. The letter I placed in our secret communication spot is still there. He hasn't picked it up for two days. I'm not sure that he isn't off somewhere with Truly."

"I don't think so, Cee Cee. He loves you."

"I surely hope you are right, Robin, but I feel so downhearted. I feel like he isn't thinking about me."

Maggie came into the room with a big smile on her face and doing a little tap dance as she snapped her fingers to keep time. "Hello," she said. "Aren't you thrilled about our going to the wharf tomorrow morning to see the Cordelia set sail for England?"

"Maggie, do you mean it?" Clarice was beaming all of a sudden. "How do you know we are going?"

"I have just left Lady Anthony. She told me that his lordship has agreed to send us in the landau."

"All of us?" asked Robin.

"Yes, you and Cee Cee, Marie, me, Lady Anthony, and Tomas. I'm so excited," said Maggie.

Clarice went right away into her dressing room and took the bag down from the shelf that held her blue chamois slippers.

"Robin," she said, "don't let me forget to wear these," as she placed the bag on the foot of her bed and returned to the dressing room to select a dress.

"Do you think you might see Jason there?" Maggie heard Robin ask Clarice.

Maggie walked over to Robin and laid her arm across Robin's shoulders, "I know who's going to be there for you to talk to, Preston Hawley. His grandfather is leaving for England. I heard it announced in church. The old man was born in England, and he's going back to live there until he dies."

"Well, I'm not going to speak to him," declared the impudent little girl.

Clarice was thinking, she should write another letter to Jason and carry it to the wharf; she might see him there. She whispered to herself, "If God is good to me, I will see him. I pray he isn't mad at me."

Maggie told Clarice and Robin that it was time to get dressed for the bon voyage dinner, then she left the room.

Before going down the stairs, she called back to Clarice, "Clarice, Henry's back."

Next morning when Clarice opened her eyes and looked at her little brass clock, it was 6:00 A.M. She got out of bed and walked over to the window and drew the curtains back to see what kind of day it was.

The sun was still bouncing like a big golden ball on the harbor. It looked as if it was ten miles wide and the water was reflecting the snowy white clouds. She opened the casement windows and sucked in a long breath of the freshest air she believed she had ever breathed.

"Thank you, my Lord," she said, "for such a promising and beautiful morning. I think I will hurry out to the broken post before anyone gets up. If I'm lucky Channing and Scott will still be sleeping." Their duty began at seven o'clock.

She saw Michael at the hearth as she went silently creeping behind his back. It always seemed much farther when she was trying not to be seen. When she reached the broken post she discovered her own two letters still there. Jason had not been there to get them.

Chapter Fifteen

She brushed more leaves up against the post to better hide them, and with tears streaming down her face she went back to her room. After discovering her letters still there, she didn't care if she was seen or not. Her world suddenly darkened in spite of the glorious morning.

The trip to the wharf was no longer such a great anticipation, except for the hope that she might see Jason there, but if she did see him Lady Anthony would not allow her to speak to him. She even feared that he might ignore her, especially if Truly had demanded it. Clarice had filled her mind with imagery of Jason and Truly together.

She concluded, while getting dressed, that she had to accept her fate whatever it was. Her situation was such that she was helpless.

Robin was up and filled with joy and excitement. It was hard to have to wait two more hours before leaving for the wharf.

Clarice helped her choose a very pretty dress and bonnet and helped her with her shoes and laces. Then she put on her own blue dimity dress, but not with much enthusiasm, and reluctantly she put on her blue chamois slippers, which Robin took from the bag and held out to her, insisting that she would feel better if she wore them.

"Cee Cee," she said, "you told me not to let you forget them."

Clarice hugged the child and assured her that she would be all right and would enjoy the bon voyage gathering at the Cordelia's berth.

There was a large crowd already mingling when the Anthony party arrived. Much laughing and talking was drowning out the clanking and squeaking of the chains holding the many ships in their moorings. The Cordelia looked exceptionally beautiful. She had been sanded and varnished. Her brasses were all polished and gleaming.

The row of well wishers from the Anthony household lined up side by side as his lordship had bidden them to do. Several groups of people were waving flags, and some sailors were scurrying aboard carrying various belongings of those going abroad.

The hustle and bustle was entertaining to Robin. She was exuberant, laughing and squirming around. She tapped her mother's arm, interrupting Lady Anthony's goodbye to old Mr. Sewell.

She said, "Mama, I do wish we were going home on the Cordelia, don't you?"

"It will be our turn someday. Time will fly," her mother assured her.

Maggie whispered to Clarice, who was standing next to her, "Do you see that woman over there?" she nodded toward an elegant-looking couple about a hundred feet away. "Do you see any resemblance to anyone you know?"

People were passing back and forth in front of the couple Maggie was referring to, and the woman had turned and only her profile was visible.

"No," said Clarice.

Maggie threw her hand over her mouth, "Oh my God! It is…it really is."

"Who?" excitedly whispered Clarice to Maggie.

"I think it's Truly! I have to go and see."

Maggie broke out of the line and, twisting and turning, she hurriedly made her way through the crowd to the couple.

She was almost screaming, "My God, Truly! Oh my God! What are you doing? Where did you get those clothes? Who is this man? You better talk fast. Are you crazy?" Maggie was sure Truly was in trouble.

Truly stamped her foot and reached out and shook Maggie, holding her by the shoulder. "Get hold of yourself. Let me say something."

She opened her handbag and pulled out a letter, "Here is a letter my husband wrote to you and Mama. Yes, we are married. Yes, he is my husband."

"You, Truly, are married to this man?"

"Yes I am, and we are sailing to London on the Cordelia."

Maggie had begun to cry.

Truly said harshly, "Now stop that crying. When you get home, read the letter. It will tell you all about it."

By this time Clarice and Robin had broken the rules, left the line, and were approaching the couple.

Maggie yelled at Clarice, "They're married. Truly's married."

Clarice spoke to Truly. "We've been looking everywhere for you. Are you really married? Where? When? Do you know this man?"

"Of course, silly, he's my husband."

"Well then," angrily stormed Robin, "tell us his name, and why did you marry a man with a wooden leg?"

Truly never liked Robin; she answered her scornfully, "It's none of your business."

Maggie looked at the scroll Truly handed to her. It was tied with a red ribbon. She put it into her satchel and said to Clarice, "We'll read it as soon as we get home."

Lady Anthony was craning her neck and shifting her weight from one foot to the other, looking for the three girls who had disobeyed her orders to stay in the line. But she also couldn't help staring at the elegantly dressed couple going up the gangplank.

The lady was wearing a blue silk bonnet with purple ostrich plumes. The pearls around her neck were gleaming as she walked. Her summer coat was blue brocaded moiré with tiny French rosebuds around the hemline. Her shoes were white buckskin with gold filigree ornaments on the toes. She was wearing white crocheted gloves and carrying a beaded handbag.

Lady Anthony had never seen Truly, so she was not overcome with surprise, as was Maggie, Clarice, and Robin.

She surmised that this fine looking couple must do their shopping in Paris or London. She kept sizing them up and down. She noticed the gentleman had a wooden right leg, but it was covered in a white silk stocking, matching his left leg. His shoes were black patent leather with silver buckles. She could tell by the way he walked that his right shoe wasn't flexible. His knee-length coat was velvet, copper colored, and trimmed in gold braid. His hat also had ostrich plumes. He carried a dog head scrimshaw cane with diamond eyes. He looked as if the whole world was his to command, and he kept hugging his wife up closer to him as he steered her along with his arm around her waist.

Lady Anthony asked both Mr. Sewell and Captain Tucker who they were. Mr. Sewell said he never seen them before, and Captain Tucker said he would have to check the passenger list. He wasn't sure what their names were.

After the passengers were all on board and visitors had returned to shore, Clarice and Robin returned to the line, but Maggie was still walking around among the people. Clarice had asked her to look for Jason.

Jason was nowhere to be seen. Robin asked Clarice several times if she had seen him or his little cart of buns and cider, which he usually located somewhere close to a ship that was sailing. He had not come to this sailing.

Clarice began to cry as the Cordelia was towed out of its berth, and she heard the violins begin their charming tunes. Passengers were hugging and kissing each other, huddling in the stern, waving and throwing kisses. Clarice would see those purple plumes waving in the wind. Her crying broke into loud pathetic sobs. Oh, how she wished at that moment that she was going home to England.

Tomas came over to Lady Anthony and said, "It's time to go."

"Please wait," said Robin, "I want to watch the Cordelia fade out of sight." Then she added much more sweetly, "Truly looked so beautiful, I hope she won't be seasick."

Lady Anthony was walking ahead and had not heard Robin's request or Clarice's sobbing.

Maggie joined them and took hold of Clarice's hand and said, "It's not Truly you have to worry about."

When Jackson picked up the reins and said, "Gid ap, go boys," to the horses, he raised the whip and circled it over their rumps.

Paul Scott and Edward Channing must not have been staunchly standing. As the carriage lurched forward they both fell off the backboard into the street. Maybe they were too much inebriated.

Anyway, Robin burst out into loud laughter, Lady Anthony swooned, Clarice began to cry again, Maggie yelled at Jackson to halt, and Marie sat still looking prudish.

Tomas, sitting gallantly astride his gray horse, rode up against the carriage and grossly asked, "What the hell's going on? You look like a bunch of psychopaths on the way to a funeral."

The two guards scrambled to their feet and were running to catch the carriage. Jackson was not aware that anything was amiss.

On arrival at the front stile each one tried to be the first one out before the guards could get off the footboard to assist them.

Clarice exclaimed, while wiping her tears away, "that getting back home was the best part of the day and she wasn't going to be fretting to go any place for a long time."

Michael was waiting inside the front door, and when he saw the carriage drive up, he opened the door to let Bo Tay out.

The little dog went to Robin, and she picked him up and kissed him. "Bo Tay, I'm so glad to see you."

When they were all inside the house, Lola came to the rear of the front hall and called out, "Your lunch is ready."

Robin dropped Bo Tay and bounded toward the dining room.

Clarice ran after her and stopped her. "Don't you dare say one word to Lola about Truly until we have read the letter."

Robin looked abashed; she had already blurted out, "Wait Lola. Guess what?"

They all went into the dining room and seated themselves at the table, except the two guards, who went into the breakfast room, and Jackson, who sat down at the trestle table in the kitchen.

Lola put her hands on her hips and exclaimed, "Three different tables to wait on all at once, who do they think I am, triplet slaves?"

Tomas got up from his seat at the dining room table and said, "I'm going to help Lola; the dear girl can't do it all."

Marie gave him a look that would kill a tiger.

He took a large tray full of food from Lola's hands and carried it into the breakfast room and set it down on the table and told the guards to help themselves.

When they were out of sight in the kitchen, he laid his hand on Lola's shoulder and said, "I love helping you; I love to be near you." Then he patted her on the butt.

Tomas thought Jackson was deaf, but the old man heard what he said to Lola and saw him pat her butt.

Maggie's satchel was laying across her lap and she kept reaching into it to make sure the scroll was still there.

Lady Anthony by now had noticed that all three girls were preoccupied and the scrumptious meal was hardly noticed.

Robin fed most of her cheese soufflé to Bo Tay who was sitting beside her chair. Clarice wrapped her bread and butter into her napkin and put it into her handbag. Maggie only picked at her chicken, scattering it around with her fork. She excused herself before Lola brought in the dessert.

"Where is she going before finishing her meal?" asked the tired Lola.

Tomas stayed in the kitchen with Lola, supposedly helping her, until late afternoon, when Marie came looking for him, so mad she was pulling her hair. Clarice, Maggie, and Robin went directly to the third floor to Maggie's room.

Maggie said, "Since I have the letter I will read it." She untied the red ribbon and unrolled the scroll.

She admired the beautiful handwriting. There was no salutation. She began to read; Clarice and Robin were listening eagerly:

> I married my True Love, you call her Truly, on Wednesday, May 19, 1773, at ten o'clock A.M. in Marblehead, Massachusetts, at the parsonage of Parson Joseph Goode. He heard our vows and read the Holy Scripture.
>
> The parson's wife, their two grown daughters, and my two slaves did the standing up.
>
> I met True Love, Tuesday evening, May 18, at a tavern in Boston called Merry Mermaid. She was very kind to me and kept talking to me when I was extremely tired and needed someone to comfort me.
>
> I fell in love with the girl's warm heart and devilish eyes and her spunky attitude.
>
> I offered her a thousand pounds to marry me, and I was superbly surprised and overjoyed, when she took me up.
>
> I am an orphan child. I was dumped on a trash heap in Madrid, Spain, fifty years ago, when I was about six months old.
>
> A hungry dog scratching for food chewed off my right leg. I was rescued by the city refuse wagon and taken to a hospital where I lived until five years old.
>
> I was adopted then by a couple from Cuba, and they took me there to live in their home.
>
> They had one daughter, seven years old. We grew up together. She married an American shipping merchant and moved to Marblehead, Massachusetts.
>
> Her husband was lost in a shipwreck, and last year she died. They had no children. She left me all her wealth, which included a large house in Marblehead and all of its contents.
>
> True Love and I spent our wedding night there and the next few days.
>
> I told my darling to help herself to my sister's many closets of clothes.
>
> I have also inherited many shipping contracts, and we are going to be very busy.
>
> My parents left me a large sugar plantation and rum manufacturing business in Cuba. I am a very rich man. I have

many slaves. Now I have a beautiful wife to accompany me on my journeys.

I will hire for her the best teachers. I will send her to the best finishing school in the world in Paris.

I will teach her to read and write in French, Spanish, and English.

I have never seen a more sweet, beautiful, willing woman. I love her. Be happy for us and give us your blessing.

I have never been married until now. Let me tell you it is bliss.

I have no relatives. My parents' name was Romero. My name is Don Pedro Romero.

True Love will write to you as soon as she learns how.

Yours forever,
Don Pedro and True Love

P.S. I am leaving my schooner, The Gospel Truth, docked at the Long Wharf here in Boston. I am leaving my two slaves, Tablow and Duncan here with it to look after it and also my house in Marblehead. They are free to sail it if need be. They are honest men, and I trust them explicitly. I have left them plenty of money. Parson Smith will be their monitor, and he also holds their purse.

Please treat them well if you encounter them for any reason. My schooner is moored at Long Wharf, berth number 20.

DPR May 16, 1773

Maggie laid the letter down and smoothed it over with her hand. A tear dropped from her eye and blotted out the line that said, "I have left them plenty of money." She looked at Clarice and Robin; they were both teary-eyed.

Maggie sighed and spoke. "This is nothing to cry about. We should be thanking the Lord. We know Truly craved love, and we also know she was hungry and homeless."

Clarice said, "I'm crying for joy, I think."

Robin said, "I didn't like her; I'm glad she's gone."

Maggie said, "Someone's got to tell Lola."

Clarice said, "Robin wants to do it."

Maggie said, "Good, and I'll read the letter to her."

Clarice said, "I want to see Henry. I have a good many things to say to him." She did not yet know that Jason had been banned from the Anthony household.

Lola was washing the dishes at the water trough. Jackson was polishing the bottoms of the cooper kettles.

Clarice, Maggie, and Robin all came into the kitchen together. Maggie held back the swinging doors as they came in.

"What you all coming down here for?" asked Lola.

Robin haughtily answered her, "We can come down here any time we want to; besides, we've come to see you."

"What about?" Lola turned from her dishwashing, wiped her hands on her apron, and said, "Here, let's sit down; I'm too tired to stand up."

The four sat at the trestle table. Jackson left the room. He knew what they were going to tell Lola. He had heard their talk on the way home from the sailing.

Robin got up and went over to the water trough and got a mug of water. She returned to the bench at the table and was dawdling with her water. Clarice and Maggie were looking around the room but were not saying anything. Robin was putting her finger in the water and sucking it off. She was hesitating, not knowing exactly how to begin.

Lola, becoming exasperated, said, "Well, what do you want to see me about?"

Robin at last said, "Lola, I wish you could have been with us at the wharf this morning to see the Cordelia sail away."

Lola replied, "I've seen sailings before. When I used to work down at the dock, a ship left almost every day."

"But," said Robin, "this one would have been a big surprise."

"Why?" Lola shifted around on the bench.

"Get to the facts of the matter," said Maggie.

"Well," began the child, "we saw Truly."

"Truly?" gasped Lola. "What was she doing? Did you talk to her?"

Robin took a deep breath and blurted out, "She's married, and they left on the Cordelia for England."

At this news Lola jumped to her feet. She yelled out, "I'll be damned, that's just like that little bastard. She'd do anything to get outta working with me." Then she added, "Married? Who'd marry that tramp?"

Clarice then stood up. For a girl of eighteen she could be very authoritative. She leaned across the table toward Lola and said, "Lola, sit down and listen. Truly has made a wise decision. She behaved like a lady, and we believe that her husband really loves her. We are all very happy for her. Now sit still and listen to a letter Maggie has, that her husband wrote to all of us."

Lola was looking very mad when she responded to Clarice, "Why didn't I get the letter? I'm her Mama."

"Yes," said Maggie, "but I'm her best friend, and you were not at the wharf and you can't read."

"Married! Truly married? I can't believe it," sighed Lola as she began to calm down.

Maggie unrolled the scroll and read the letter to Lola. When Maggie finished reading the letter, Lola began to sob. She got up from the table and went down the cellar steps to her room.

Clarice said, "I'll make us some tea. I'm going to wait here until Henry comes."

She poured the water from a large iron kettle into a porcelain teapot, then she spooned in some loose tea leaves. She noticed the canister was almost empty.

She said to Maggie and Robin, "We must remind Lola to buy some tea when she goes to market." Then she added, "Doesn't look like there is much sugar here either."

Tomas came into the kitchen while the three girls were still there drinking their tea. "Where's Lola?" he asked.

"She was quite upset over Truly, and she went down to her room," Maggie told him.

"Why should she be upset over that wharf rat?" asked Tomas.

"Because," said sassy Robin, "Truly's her daughter."

Tomas looked surprised, "Well, I've got to see her about something," he said as he opened the cellar door and went down the steps.

Clarice said, "Maggie, will you go to the schoolroom with Robin and hear her French recitation? That's all there will be time for today."

Maggie and Robin left the kitchen. Clarice reached for a copy of the Gazette and opened it and spread it out on the table and began to read.

People Petition for Governor's Removal. "What's this?" she said to herself as she read. "The People," Clarice wondered who was meant to be "The People." She tried to think who could be finding fault with Governor Hutchinson.

"I think I'll have a talk with Lord Anthony." She read farther, "and his cohorts," it said.

She turned the page and read another column. "Prices to be raised," she read on. "The newly imposed three pence per pound tax on tea would necessarily cause the price to go up."

"Good Lord," she sighed, "I'm glad I'm not in the grocery or ordinary business." She thought of Jason. Could he afford to stay in business? The paper was full of slanderous remarks about the governor being such a coward as to cancel the birthday party.

Then she read the article about, "The Anthony's arrival is just another Leech Game instigated by the governor with the false pretense of being a peacemaker. An Ambassador of good will. But just actually a spy trip to see what the Sons of Liberty was all about."

"Who's writing this slander?" she asked, as she got up from the table and wadded the newspaper into a ball and threw it into the fire.

She forgot all about waiting for Henry. She ran up the stairs, two steps at a time. She went to her water pitcher, poured out some water into the bowl, and dashed it on her face and neck.

"Gee whiz, those news stories got me all hot under the collar, as my Papa used to say when he was fired up about something."

She looked around the room for Robin, then remembered telling Maggie to go with her to the school room for a French lesson. Clarice threw herself across her bed and kicked off her blue chamois slippers.

"There," she said to the slippers. "Today you were working for Truly. You didn't bring me anything but disappointment. I wish I knew why Jason has forsaken me."

Chapter Sixteen

Lady Anthony was not aware that Lord Anthony had been picked up by Governor Hutchinson and taken to Nathe Frothing's carriage shop where Anthony picked out a beautiful new chaise for his very own.

Hutchinson was making a generous gift to Lord Anthony in exchange for a special favor: a visit to his farm for a weekend for Clarice, Robin, and Maggie. The governor had heard that Robin was pining to see her pony, Peaches. He also had a ravenous desire to get a little closer to the beautiful governess. Maggie would be a stand-in as governess while Governor Hutchinson and Clarice dined alone.

When Lord Anthony arrived home in the new chaise, everyone gathered in front of the carriage house to admire it.

Jackson had walked over to Frothing's, leading Stomper to hitch to the new chaise and drive it home.

When they reached the carriage house and stopped, Robin climbed up into the seat beside her papa.

He put his arm around her and said, "You're going to have a nice ride in this lovely new chaise very soon. You are going out to Milton Hill to see Peaches and have a visit with the governor's family for a whole weekend."

Robin at first looked pleased, then her face began to show some anxiety. She asked, "Are you and Mama going, too?"

"No, dear, Clarice and Maggie are going."

"I might be scared way out there in the country. Mama says no place is safe here with 'rabbit rousers' running around everywhere."

Lord Anthony stepped out of the carriage and lifted Robin down. He smiled at his daughter and assured her that there wouldn't be any rabbit rousers at Milton Hill.

He led her by the hand over to where Clarice, Maggie, Marie, Tomas, and Michael were standing.

Lord Anthony said to Clarice and Maggie, "I want you two ladies to meet me and her ladyship in the upstairs sitting room in about half an hour. I have some good news for you."

He and Robin went on ahead into the house. Jackson began unhitching Stomper. The others scattered to wherever they were going. The two guards were standing or walking along Beacon Street in front of the house watching everything and everybody. Clarice and Maggie went straight to Clarice's room.

"Wonder what's brewing now?" said Maggie. She added, "I sure hope it's a trip to town. I've got to get my mind off of you and Jason. Maybe a look into some of the shops would help.

"On second thought," she said, "that would only be temporary. We would be right back here in a few hours. It would be better if we were going some place for a week or more."

"Where would that be?" asked Clarice. She paused a moment.

Maggie didn't answer that question.

Clarice walked over to the window. She saw a chaise; it was stopped about a block away. She recognized the horse; it was Charlie. She saw a black man with his head wrapped in a bandanna. He ran up to the chaise and exchanged something with the driver. What he took from the driver he stuffed into the front of his shirt. Clarice's heart seemed to skip a beat; her breath became short and she began to tremble.

Maggie noticed the way Clarice suddenly became nervous. She went to her and took her hand. "Sit down, Cee Cee, what's wrong?"

"Oh, Maggie, I saw Jason's chaise. He gave something to Henry, and Henry gave something to him. I know it was my letters. I could see it all."

"Through the trees?" asked Maggie. "You could have had an optical illusion, you are so preoccupied with Jason and his letters."

"What I don't understand, Maggie, is why he didn't come to the house. I haven't seen him for a week."

Maggie pulled up a chair close to Clarice; she laid her hand on Clarice's knee as she said, "Clarice, I'm going to tell you something I'm not supposed to tell you, but I can't stand it any longer. Jason has been banned from this house because of you. That's part of the reason for the guards. Lady Anthony thinks you are too good for Jason. She may also be afraid you will neglect Robin, and she also thinks he's some kind of spy."

Clarice became fiery angry all at once. Her face turned red, then she jumped up from her chair and picked up a vase of flowers and threw it across the room, spilling water and flowers all over the bed and wall.

Maggie caught her breath in surprise. She had never seen Clarice even the least bit mad.

Angrily, Clarice said, "I'm going to talk to them," meaning Lady and Lord Anthony. "They have no right to treat me like a prisoner. I've got to have some freedom." She turned again to the window; the chaise had moved on.

Maggie warned her, "Cee Cee, don't go flying off the handle. Sit around awhile and contemplate on what you are going to say and be sure to keep your dignity. You know harsh words will get you nowhere. After all, Lord and Lady Anthony did allow you and Robin to go to the sailing. They will gradually become more lenient, I believe."

Maggie got up from her chair and went to the window and stood by Clarice. She gave her a hug and said, "I'm going to help you as much as I can, for I can't stand to see you heartbroken. Now we better hurry to the sitting room. We're late already."

The news of the trip to Milton Hill was not as well received as his lordship would have liked. Robin said she wanted to see Peaches but she hated the governor because he canceled the party. Clarice absolutely did not want to spend the whole weekend. She said she would enjoy an afternoon's ride and stay for tea, but she thought that was enough.

Maggie's feelings were quite different. She was thinking of Clarice and Robin as well as herself. She said, when asked if she would enjoy the trip, "I most certainly would love it. We are all in need of some diversion. Our minds are too much absorbed with our own inner selves. We seem to think we're in danger. Maybe being in a different atmosphere for a few days will expel some of our anxieties."

Lord Anthony raised his eyebrows and nodded his head, "Good thinking," he said. He also said, "Maggie, I notice you are well educated. I would like to hear your life's story sometime. Would you care to relate it to me?"

Maggie was blushing. She hadn't realized how sensible her opinion had been. She thought, Why would he be interested in my life's story?

Clarice had only said a few words. Her mind was on getting with Henry to get her mail from Jason. Robin was looking skeptical. She secretly felt that these plans to spend a weekend at Milton Hill were actually to cover up something else. The girls were informed to be ready early Friday morning. That was only one day away.

On entering Clarice's room after the conclave in the sitting room, Robin sighed and said, "I'm not sure this trip is worth it, since I hate Governor Hutchinson and I don't want to be away from Bo Tay. May we take him along?"

Clarice answered her, "I don't see why we shouldn't take him."

Maggie remembered she had duties awaiting her in the dining room, as Marie had informed her earlier that she was to set the table every evening for dinner. Tomas had told Marie that Lola didn't have time to do both the dining room and the kitchen work.

As the loyal Maggie was going out the door, Clarice called to her, and she came back to see what she wanted.

"Will you ask Henry to give you the letter he is carrying for me, and will you bring it to me as soon as possible? I feel faint, and I don't want any dinner. Also will you see that Robin has her dinner? She may eat in her room if you will see to it. I thank you, Maggie. You are my friend."

Clarice heard the front door knocker, then she heard voices. Someone had brought a message. She thought perhaps Jason had sent someone with a message for her. Her hopes were high, then she realized that if that were so, she would never see it or hear of it.

Her bed looked inviting, and she decided to take a short nap as Robin had gone into her own room, Bo Tay following.

It was Lord Anthony who answered the door. The message was for him. It was an invitation for his lordship and his lady to attend the graduation exercises at Harvard College to be held on the campus May 31, 1773. Also included was an invitation for the Anthonys to be the guests of Governor Hutchinson and Lieutenant Governor Andrew Oliver to the luncheon and reception following the exercises.

After reading the invitation, Lord Anthony took it to Lady Anthony and sat with her while she read it.

"Maurice," she said, "that day is only four days away. I won't have time to get ready, and it is such a long way over to Cambridge; why don't we send our regrets?"

After waiting a moment for his thoughts to spring forth on her suggestion, she got no answer, just a scornful look and a shake of his head negatively, indicating he was stunned by her remarks and didn't approve of what she said.

Lady Anthony began to talk again, "Besides that, Maurice, the girls will have spent the weekend at Milton Hill and returned. Robin will be full of her experiences, wanting to tell us all about it on Monday. If we are not here it will dampen her enthusiasm, and we may never hear about it."

Lord Anthony got up from his chair and went over to his wife. He took her by the shoulders and shook her. He angrily said, "Florence, you have got to rescue yourself from the doldrums and from what Robin wants. You don't want to do anything but sit in this house. Our job here is to mix and mingle and win respect from the people. You only went to the sailing because you were pining for the Cordelia. Well, we won't be sailing again for two years, so you might as well get over your homesickness and begin to do what you're supposed to do. Stand by me. Now, make up your mind; you're going with me to the graduation."

Florence threw the invitation down on the floor, and, with a scowling expression and mumbling to herself, she went into her dressing room and slammed the door.

Later that evening, Clarice found Jason's letter near the threshold where it had been pushed under the door.

It read:

> My Darling,
> I have to stay away from you for awhile. I'm sure you know why. It's such a mean demand on me. It makes my heart ache for you all the more and my longing for you, such that I might break someone's neck in getting past the guards and all the other barriers.
> I'm so in love with you that I could kill if I have to. No one can subdue my feelings.
> I have so much to tell you about 'Lynn.' I will give all my letters to Henry to deliver to you. That is the safest way.
> I love you more than anybody loves anybody in the entire world.

Here are kisses by the million.

XXXXXXXXXX Jason.
P.S. Oh how I do love you, I want you. Please say you will marry me.

Clarice had never heard Jason mention Lynn. She didn't know what or whom, he meant by Lynn. It gave her much to wonder about.

Maggie was the only one of the four girls enthusiastic about the weekend at Milton Hill.

Marie had managed to ingenuously invite herself. She came bouncing into Clarice's room. "Come on, Cee Cee, get your things together. Be sure to pack some sturdy boots and warm hoods. It's always cold in the country at the turning of the soil." (The end of May was considered planting time for corn and oats.)

Clarice answered grumpily, "The way I feel now, I probably will stay in bed most of the time. It will be up to you to entertain Robin."

Maggie answered, "You will be fine once you get there. I think the strawberries are ripe, and the milk is fresh and rich after the cows have calved. Won't it be fun to watch the calves frolic in the meadow?"

Clarice was bored; she said, "I'm not especially fond of farm life. I came from a bustling manufacturing business community. All our dairy products were brought from somewhere else, but my mother always had a kitchen garden. It was very small; she only raised potatoes and cabbage. We had one little old sour apple tree. I've not been acquainted with any farm animals, except our one carriage mare."

Chapter Seventeen

Next morning after breakfast, Michael and Jackson helped the girls get their valises into the landau. The new chaise had proved to be too small for the four girls and their luggage.

After much kissing by Robin and her parents and waves and goodbyes between the others, Jackson perched on his driver's seat called out to Stomper and Shoo-Fly to, "Git ap and git going."

The city of Boston was busy getting into its day's activities. The girls waved at the British Redcoats patrolling the main thoroughfares. The soldiers bowed, and some even removed their hats. The small Union Jack attached to the dashboard was bright and new. It came with the new chaise but was transferred to the landau for this trip.

Two mounted British guards fell in behind the landau at the intersection of Marlborough and Water Streets.

Robin spread out her cape and reached for Clarice's hand. "Gee whiz, Cee Cee, I feel like Queen Charlotte riding along in her carriage."

About five miles out on the country road Robin called out to Jackson to stop. She and Bo Tay bounded out, and Clarice and Maggie, not knowing why she wanted to get out, jumped out right behind her.

Robin looked at Clarice and said, "Bo Tay wanted to pee, and I want to pick some of these violets."

The ground around their feet was purple with lovely little wood violets that had sprung up through decaying leaves.

"What a splendid thing to do," said Maggie. "We may as well enjoy every moment," as she dashed to another abundant spot.

Marie was sitting stiffly on her seat and scowling at the others, who were picking and smelling their fists full of the tiny spring lovelies. Bo Tay had taken care of his business and was nipping at Robin's heels inviting her to chase him. The two guards had released the reins of their grays and were enjoying their Cuban cigars. Jackson was nodding.

When the carriage was on the way again and violets were in everyone's lap, they began to sing an old ditty that Clarice knew from her childhood. The tune rang out and echoed back from the countryside. She had taught the words and tune to Robin while they were wiling away the time on the Cordelia. It went like this.

> Dear King George, you are so fat.
> Dear King George, where are you at?
> Do not sit around and smile
> Get out of your chair and run a mile
> Be happy and gay all of the way
> Kiss the Queen every day
> Say your prayers and feed the cat
> Dear King George, you're much too fat.

Marie broke into a skimpy smile and raised her hand for silence. She said, "I hope you all are not going to be a rowdy bunch while we're in the governor's house. It will be unbecoming to the Anthonys."

Clarice was forcing herself to be civil. She answered rather curtly, "We know how to behave."

Robin said, "Marie, you're not our boss so keep quiet."

Clarice patted the child's hand and said, "Robin, you too keep quiet."

As the carriage turned into the mile-long driveway between the rows of buttonwood trees, the sun was directly overhead and the shadows from the shimmering leaves seemed like myriad fairies dancing their ballets to greet the distinguished visitors to Milton Hill.

The governor's house was low and rambling but classical with its eight Doric columns. It was surrounded by a low picket fence. Green shutters graced all the windows. The setting was charming and inviting. Two of the governor's daughters-in-law came out to the front steps to greet the visitors.

Robin spoke out abruptly, as soon as her feet his the ground. "Where is my pony? I want to see her right now."

After saying, "Good afternoon," and introducing the others, Marie took Robin by the shoulder and said, "Later, Robin, we must greet everyone first."

Two young boys, probably twelve and fourteen, came out to the porch and picked up some of the luggage and carried it into the house.

"Do they live here?" Robin questioned.

"Yes," answered Sarah, the youngest daughter-in-law, "they are my nephews."

"Good Lord," said Robin, as she kissed Bo Tay on top of his curly little head and set him down on the floor, "I can tell from here that I'm not going to like it here."

As they went into the house, Clarice looked at Sarah and remarked, "Robin is used to taking charge, and she is shy of boys. She will be more pleasant later."

At that moment, Bo Tay spotted two cats sitting at the top of the stairs, and like a shot out of a gun he went bounding up the steps barking furiously.

Of course the cats scampered away so fast they were nowhere in sight when Bo Tay's fat little self reached the upstairs hall, Robin right at his heels.

The two boys stuck their heads out of a door and laughed loudly, sticking their tongues out and putting their thumbs in their ears and wiggling them at Robin, who had stopped short to survey that part of the house. She responded to their gestures by doing exactly what they were doing, only she was also jumping up and down.

Clarice came immediately up the stairs and grabbed Robin by the arm. "Come now, Robin, this is very rude. You are being unladylike. We are here to make friends."

She looked around for the dog. He was standing on his hind legs, on a chair, barking at the two cats who were perched on top of a large bookcase at the end of the hall. They were hissing back at him with their hair standing up on their backs.

Marie came up the steps with a colored maid following her. Maggie was close behind them. "Here, here! What's going on, children? Acting like cats and dogs."

Clarice looked at her and said, "Everything's under control." She turned to the maid and said, "Please show us our rooms. Robin needs a nap."

"I do not, Cee Cee; I need some lunch."

The maid opened a door to a low-ceilinged room. White dimity curtains were blowing out the windows. Two large mahogany four-poster beds with trundle beds underneath stood on one side of the room, and a large chest of drawers was on the opposite side.

A full-length swinging mirror in its handcarved frame graced the other corner. A pitcher of water and washbowl were conveniently ready for the guests. French perfume and scented soap were alongside in a silver container.

Robin went over to the washstand, poured out some water into the bowl, then picked up the perfume and emptied the entire contents into the water. She picked up Bo Tay who had followed them into the room and set him in the water and began stroking him and rubbing him with the soap.

Clarice hadn't noticed what Robin was doing because she had walked over to the window to look out toward the fields and orchard. When she turned around and saw Robin washing Bo Tay, she exclaimed, in a surprised voice, "Robin, what are you doing? That water is for us."

"Well," the child answered, "Bo Tay smelled like a cat."

Very soon they heard the ding-dong of a bell and also heard the two boys scrambling out into the hall and down the stairs, calling out as they hurried, "Come on, you people; that bell is for lunch."

The single file of hungry women going down the steps was more like a circus than a party of refined constituents of King George III.

Right behind Chip and Chuck came Robin; then Clarice, trying to get in arms' reach of the child to slow her down; then Maggie, who was holding up her skirt to keep from tripping over it; then the maid, who should have been in front as a catcher in case someone fell; then Marie, trying to be very dignified;

then Bo Tay, who didn't want to leave his stalking place—to which he had immediately returned after his bath before he had "chewed up a cat"—but who was a coward at heart, especially in such a strange surrounding.

The lunch was set out on a sideboard, and each person was to fill their plate and find a place to sit at the dining room table.

Robin looked over all the food from one end of the sideboard to the other. She asked, as she looked at her hostess, "What's that stuff?"

Sarah answered, "That stuff is very delicious deviled turtle eggs."

"Puke!" Robin exclaimed, "They do look like the devil." She wouldn't try them. She helped her plate to a large slice of chocolate cake and two fried frog legs, which she thought was chicken.

Chip and Chuck were watching Robin eat as they snickered behind their napkins.

When the frog legs were gone and Robin began on her cake, each of the boys began to giggle and call out, "Bee deep, bee deep."

Robin didn't know what the words meant or why they were giggling. She asked to be excused and ran up the stairs, bending at the first step to pick up Bo Tay who seemed delighted to be going back to where the cats were.

Clarice was quite stunned, but silently decided to let her go. Maybe some time in her room alone with only the little dog would give her time to think about her behavior.

Marie and Maggie had been assigned to a guest room which they were to share. This irritated Marie. She felt above Maggie and felt her prestige and authority was diminished by having to share her bedroom with the Anthony's upstairs maid. However, she vowed to endure it, since it would only be for two nights.

Sarah was the only daughter-in-law in evidence for the rest of that day. Mary left for Boston as soon as the Anthony party had settled in at Milton Hill.

Robin was crying in her pillow when Clarice came into the room later in the afternoon.

"Why are you crying, dear?" asked the governess.

"I want to see Peaches and I also want to go home; I hate Chip and Chuck. I know why they were laughing at me, because they stuck their heads into my door and said I had eaten frog and would be covered in warts. I don't believe them. They are silly and mean and tell lies."

Clarice tried to be cool about it all. "Come on, Robin, you're being silly, too. The best way to deal with teasers like Chip and Chuck is to give them a dose of their own medicine or ignore them entirely and pretend they are not here."

"How can we do that, Cee Cee?"

Clarice was beside herself; she didn't know the answer to that. Giving them a dose of their own medicine? She had absolutely no idea what to do.

She said, "For the time being, let's ignore them, and since it's such a lovely afternoon, let's you and I go exploring. Maybe we'll find Peaches."

Clarice invited Marie and Maggie to come with her and Robin. Maggie begged off, insisting that she had brought her sewing kit and had mending to do. Marie said she wanted to catch up on her reading. She was curious to see Governor Hutchinson's extensive library.

Clarice and Robin put on their riding skirts and boots. Sarah told them they would find Peaches in the stone barn.

The walk was a pleasure because for awhile Clarice's mind was not on Jason or his banishment from the house; she appeared to be in great spirits. The country was beautiful and invigorating. They soon came to the stone barn and went in. They found Peaches munching on her feed of apples and shelled corn. Robin ran to the pony and hugged her neck. Then she looked around for a saddle, which Sarah told her was hanging on a tack hook in the tack room.

Clarice saw the gelding she was going to ride, standing in his stall a few feet away. He was a beautiful chestnut brown. She walked over to him, and he bobbed his head in an inquisitive manner. She patted his nose and gave him a lump of sugar, which she took from a small basket near the door, presuming it was meant for the horses as a treat.

Only a short time passed until Clarice and Robin were slow-gaiting down a very unfamiliar country lane. It was almost four o'clock. The sun was no longer overhead but swiftly moving toward a glorious setting.

Robin had studied her Massachusetts map, and she remembered it very well. She remarked that she could almost see the Berkshires. Clarice said she thought the hills they were looking at were called The Blue Hills.

When they had ridden about half a mile, something startled the gelding causing him to rear up on his hind legs. Clarice almost fell off but managed to stay on and keep control.

"Oh my goodness," she exclaimed, "what was that?" She looked around and saw a rock the size of a teacup rolling along the ground. It had barely missed her horse's head.

Robin was a few feet ahead, and she or Peaches had not seen what had happened. In a few seconds the second rock came hurling at the horse; again he became frightened, and Clarice halted him and dismounted. She called out to Robin to wait.

Robin turned Peaches around and rode back to where Clarice was standing in the road. "What's the matter?" she asked.

"Someone is throwing rocks at us, and I'm going to see who it is," Clarice answered and added, "you stay here."

Robin had already dismounted and was tying Peaches to a bush. She said, "I'll bet it's Chip and Chuck."

Clarice started into the woods. As she hurried through the trees, she heard someone running. Robin did not wait as Clarice told her to do; she ran after her governess.

Clarice soon became short of breath and sat down on a log to rest. Robin slowed down to look around. The two boys popped up from behind a clump of huckleberry bushes, laughing and pointing at the girls.

Robin rushed toward them, her riding crop still in her hand, and began lashing out at them, swinging the crop aright and left. The boys turned and began to run farther into the woods. They were headed for their grandfather's house, but they forgot about the goose pond. It was too large to go around and too deep to wade through. They were stopped at the edge.

It was only a moment before Robin caught up with them. She shouted at them, "I hate you." She was so mad her face was red and her chest was heaving with the anger. She ran up to them, standing at the water's edge, and shoved them into the pond.

She stood there yelling at them as they made hasty efforts to get out of the water and mud. "Now you can eat some frogs."

She turned on her heel and fled back to Clarice, who was still sitting on the log but who had seen what Robin had done.

"Robin," she said, "you shouldn't have taken such drastic action; that pond is deep and cold. I hope the boys can get out."

"Cee Cee," answered Robin, "you said we should give them a dose of their own medicine. They have been mean ever since we got here. I don't like them. Let's go home, please."

They waited until they saw the boys crawling up the bank of the pond. When Clarice was sure they were all right, she and Robin went back to their horses. They did not get on their backs but decided to walk along leading them. They soon discovered that the two mischief makers were following slowly along the road behind them.

When Clarice and Robin stopped at the stone barn to put Peaches and the gelding back into their stalls and remove the saddles and bridles, the two boys went on to the house and were about half an hour home before the girls arrived.

Governor Hutchinson had arrived while Clarice and Robin were out. He met them at the front door. "Well, well, my dear young ladies, I'm glad you're finding something to do. How was your ride?"

Sarah had informed him on his arrival that Clarice and Robin were horseback riding.

Robin answered him, "It was disappointing."

Clarice spoke up, "Robin wanted to go farther, but we enjoyed it and will go farther next time." As she talked, she was steering Robin toward the stairs.

Governor Hutchinson cleared his throat and continued his efforts to detain them with conversation. "We are having a scrumptious dinner this evening, so don't tarry too long in your rooms."

Marie came into the hall and spoke coolly to the governor. She went on out onto the verandah.

Maggie came into the hall a moment after Marie and encountered the governor as he was going into his study. He turned toward her and asked, "Are you Maggie?"

"Yes, sir," she said, blushing.

"I hear that you play the harpsichord quite well. Will you play for us this evening?" he asked, gesturing toward the parlor where the instrument was.

"I haven't practiced in a while," she answered, "but I do know a few pieces by heart. If you don't expect perfection, I'll be glad to play something."

"I can't play at all, so I won't know if it's perfect or not, but I thank you and I'll be wonderfully entertained," he said.

Maggie was shaking with pride. She was glad to be worthy of the governor's notice. She and Marie sat on the verandah until the colored maid came to tell them dinner was ready.

Robin told Clarice that she wasn't going to the dining room again and if they expected her to eat they would have to bring it to her room. She exclaimed, as she plunked down on the sofa, that she had seen enough of Chip and Chuck.

Clarice went to Sarah and explained Robin's inconsiderate request. Sarah understood and sent the maid up to the guest room with a tray full of delicious food.

Robin was hungry, probably from the fresh air of the country and the excitement of the afternoon. She ate heartily, and when Clarice returned to the room later to invite her to the parlor to hear Maggie play, she found her asleep in her bed.

The parlor was a lively place after the evening meal. Fresh flowers, mostly geraniums and sweet williams, were placed on the tables and mantel. The maid stood near the door holding a silver tray of sweet meats and posies.

When Maggie entered the room she looked lovely in a pink blouse and yellow skirt. Her big brown eyes revealed her self-esteem. The governor's invitation to play had fluffed her exuberance more than any of her family had ever seen.

Clarice smiled at her and walked across the room and hugged her and whispered, "Play something for Jason and me."

She took a yellow blossom from the tray and tucked it into Maggie's chignon.

Maggie sat down on the bench and spread her skirt out flamboyantly. She gave a quick bow toward the governor and began with a brisk rendition of "God Save the King."

Everyone stood up. When that piece was finished, Maggie announced that her next piece would be "Drink to Me Only With Thine Eyes and I Will Pledge with Mine." She invited them to sing along with her.

When that piece was finished, the governor said, "Ben Jonson wrote that dear song in 1616."

"The next number will be a musical recitation," announced Maggie. She began softly playing an old lullaby, and, while looking Clarice in the eye, she recited in a low melodious voice:

> Where has your beloved gone, O fairest of women?
> Which way did your beloved go? That we may help you seek him?

Why is your beloved more than any other, O fairest of women?
Why is your beloved more than any other, That you give us this charge...?
Then the dear maiden answered,
My beloved's cheeks are like beds of spices
His lips are lilies and drop liquid myrrh.
His hands are golden rods set in topaz
His body is ivory overlaid with lapis lazuli
His legs are pillars of marble in sockets of finest gold
His whispers are sweetness itself wholly desirable
Such is my beloved, Such is my darling.

Hark, Hark, fair maiden, Here comes your beloved
Bounding over the mountains, Leaping over the hills
Your beloved is like a gazelle, or a young wild goat
There he stands outside our wall, Peeping in at the windows
Glancing through the lattice
Your beloved calls out to you
He said, Rise up my darling, My fairest, Stop weeping
Come away with me
For lo, the winter is past
The rains are over and gone
The flowers appear on the earth
And the time of singing of birds has come
The turtle-dove's cooing will be heard in our land;
The green figs will ripen on the fig tree
And the vines will give forth their fragrance
Rise up, my darling;
Come away with me.

[*Excerpts from the Bible's Songs of Solomon.]

Chapter Eighteen

There was complete silence as the tune faded away. The governor who sat next to Clarice on the sofa noticed her tears. He reached for her hand and pressed it gently. Tears were also running down his cheeks.

He said, "That was from the 'Songs of Solomon.' It gets more beautiful each time I hear it, and putting it to music makes it more lovely."

Maggie, getting up from the harpsichord, felt someone's eyes watching her from the stairway through the banister. Of course it was Robin, who had awakened from her napping.

"Come on down here," said the governor when he also noticed her. "You have missed a wonderful musical."

"No, I haven't; I saw it," said the child, then added, "I want to do my recitation that I learned for the birthday party which you canceled."

"I'm sorry that I had to do that, Robin, but please come down here and entertain us now. We would love to hear your recitation."

"Come, stand by me," said Clarice.

Robin came slowly down the steps and went to Clarice's side. She was tousled from sleeping in her clothes. Clarice straightened the child's hair and smoothed her dress and kissed her as she held on to her hand.

Robin spied Chip and Chuck sitting cross-legged on the floor in front of their Aunt Sarah.

Clarice and Maggie each gasped for breath when Robin blurted out in anger, "They've got to leave," as she pointed her finger at the boys, "or else I won't say a word." Chip and Chuck immediately got to their feet and ran out of the room.

Robin's recitation was something about "Apple Blossoms" and "Honey Bees." It was not a very memorable poem, but she said it without pause. Everyone clapped and praised her.

Clarice pulled her down on to the sofa between herself and the governor. "Robin," she said, "I'm proud of you and I'm ashamed of you. It was rude and uncalled for to cause Chip and Chuck to leave the room. They might have liked your recitation."

Robin ducked her head but didn't respond to Clarice.

The governor said, "My grandsons nearly always deserve some scolding or rebuff of some sort; they are pranksters at heart. They were most anxious to visit with us this weekend. I believe, Robin, they really wanted to get to know you."

"Well, I don't want to know them any better than I do already," said Robin as she squirmed into a more comfortable position, snuggling closer to Clarice.

One by one the guests were quitting the parlor. When Clarice and Robin stood up to leave, Governor Hutchinson held on to Clarice's hand.

"You stay and chat awhile with me," he said. "Marie and Maggie can look after Robin."

Clarice blushed as she sat back down beside the governor. After all, thought she, what excuse can I give the governor, my host?

He looked at her smiling and said, "I get very lonesome for some feminine conversation. My daughters-in-law only want to talk of their children or their husbands. I want to know more about you and your family and your home in England. I want to hear how you like it here and if you have been homesick."

Clarice cleared her throat and fingered her ribbons. "Really, Governor, there is very little of anything of interest to tell. I am not from a rich family. My family is very well educated but poor. My father owns a small iron foundry. He is very creative with his grills and gates and statuary. I am adventurous and I begged my mamma and papa to sign me on with Lord and Lady Anthony as governess.

"I wanted to get away from the dank smell of Birmingham. The smoke was very bad there. I hope my parents will also come to America within a year or two."

The governor asked, "Didn't you have a sweetheart you hated to leave?"

"Yes, but I believed he wanted to settle down and work there in an iron foundry and if we married my life would always be the same, and I thought if I left he might follow me."

"Do you think now he will follow you?"

"Yes, but I'm all out of the notion to marry him. I like what I am doing."

The governor released his hold on Clarice's hand and stood up, then he said, "Would you like to go for a walk? The moon is full and it's almost as light as midday. I would like to show you our goose pond. It shimmers and bubbles and reflects the trees. It is a pretty sight in the moonlight."

Clarice was stunned by the invitation. She would rather have run upstairs. She felt queasy. Then she got hold of herself and said, "Sure, but not a long walk, I will start to sneeze in the night air." She was determined to handle with dignity what she was suspecting.

She took a knitted shawl from a peg near the front door (must have belonged to Sarah or Mary), and threw it around her shoulders. She clasped the governor's arm, as she said, "This really is a moonlit night," when they stepped off the porch.

The wind was blowing softly, and the trees were making summer music. Clarice began telling the governor about what happened that afternoon. She said, "I have already seen the goose pond in the sunlight, and my memories of it are not too joyful. I was ashamed of Robin's behavior, her hasty actions, but in a way I didn't blame her. Your grandsons need some discipline."

"Yes, I will agree, but they are left alone too much. Let's not discuss children; let's discuss something more adult."

He stopped and faced Clarice, "Do you mind if I kiss you? I haven't kissed a woman in many years, and I want the joy of a pretty girl's lips."

Clarice was not at all surprised. She knew already, from the way he had squeezed her hand, that he was seeking a more intimate relationship.

"Why, Governor Hutchinson, I'm amazed at you. You ought to be able to woo any woman you want."

"That's why I'm asking you; you have captured my heart."

She smiled and said, "I suppose one little kiss won't hurt anything, but understand, that's as far as it goes."

"I hope, my dear, you didn't think I had other advances in mind."

They gradually slowed their walk to a standstill under a large oak tree. The governor put his arm around Clarice's shoulder. He put his hand behind her head and pulled her lips up to his and kissed her on the mouth. She did not flinch or pull away.

He stepped back and said to her, "That was sweeter than honey, and I loved it and hope you did too."

Clarice smiled and was glad she had not refused. She knew no one else would ever know and she had made a sad old man feel young again.

She took the governor's arm and said, "Shall we continue our walk? I think the frogs are sitting on the bank of the pond waiting to serenade us."

"After that kiss, my dear, I think I can sleep very well. I feel a wonderful dream coming on. I'm ready to get into bed."

They did not go any farther but returned to the house.

Sarah was waiting for them in the parlor. She got up from her chair to meet them, "Papa, you are not yourself. You never go out walking in the night air."

The governor ignored her; he winked at Clarice and went through the hall toward his bedroom.

Then Sarah spoke directly to Clarice, "Robin is acting strange, like she may be ill. Maggie has been putting cold cloths on her head."

Clarice hurried to Robin's room and found Maggie there comforting the feverish child.

"What's hurting you, Robin? You were all right when I left the house to go for a walk with the governor, not thirty minutes ago. How could you get sick so quick?"

The child answered in a whimperish voice, "I don't know, but I think it is this place. I want to go home."

The maid knocked on the door and announced to Maggie, who opened it, that Chip and Chuck were also sick and red as beets and vomiting.

"Find Sarah and let her know," Clarice called across the room when she heard what the maid said to Maggie.

"Heavens above, it's too late in the day to go for a doctor; what shall we do?"

Maggie said, "I'll go to the kitchen and make some tea. Maybe she will fall asleep after she drinks some hot tea."

Clarice was hovering over Robin. She picked up Bo Tay and put him in the bed at Robin's side. She turned the lamp to a lower flame and moved a chair closer to the bed.

"I will stay right here beside your bed, darling. Now don't fret; everything will be all right very soon."

Maggie returned with the tea, and Clarice held Robin's head up while she drank a few swallows. Sarah was in the boys' room giving them some of the tea.

Clarice asked Maggie to check with Sarah to see what she thought might be the cause of the sudden illness of the children. Maggie returned after a short time had passed and said that the boys were having chills and she believed it was measles.

The governess and the maid were too much concerned for Robin to go to bed; they stayed in her room all night. When morning sunlight began to peep through the shutters, Clarice opened the window and drew the curtains back. When she went to the bed she noticed that Robin was covered in red spots.

"My Lord, Maggie, it is measles. Just look at Robin."

Maggie ran over to the window and closed it and drew the curtains. "We must keep the room dark for at least twenty-four hours or else Robin may go blind."

"Who told you that?" questioned Clarice. "I think that must be an old wives' tale."

"We need a doctor. I will go and awake Sarah and see if she knows how we can get a doctor to come out here from Boston."

When Clarice went out into the hall, she saw the maid sitting on a chair just outside the boys' room. She asked the maid how the boys were and she answered that Miss Sarah had spent the night in their room cooling them off (meaning that she had been wiping their faces with cool wet cloths).

The maid knocked on the door and Sarah came out. When Clarice asked her about the doctor, she said that Governor Hutchinson had already sent a messenger to town but that it would probably be several hours before Dr. Thatcher could possibly arrive at Milton Hill.

Clarice returned to Robin's room and told the child that a doctor would soon be there. The door opened and Marie came into the room. Before anyone could speak, Robin burst out into hilarious laughter, while pointing her finger at Marie.

The auspicious Marie had her head wrapped around with a long white stocking. Her face was swollen to twice its normal size. Large red welts were standing out on her cheeks and a big one on the end of her nose. Her eyes were almost shut. Clarice ran to her and caught her to keep her from falling. She helped her to a chair.

Maggie poured her a cup of hot tea. As she offered the tea, Marie said, "My God, Clarice, I think I'm going to die." Marie had not heard about the boys and Robin being down with the same ailment. Marie continued while Clarice held a wet cloth to her face, "What is the matter with me? I'm as hot as fire."

"We think the boys and Robin have measles, and I think you must have the same thing," said Clarice.

"Measles is a child's disease!" exclaimed the pitiful Marie. "I never had any of the children's diseases," she said as she began to shake with chills.

Clarice and Maggie helped her into Clarice's bed, covered her, and assured her that she was not going to die.

Robin's laughter at Marie's funny looks had subsided, and she was whimpering while hugging the dog.

Clarice asked Maggie if she thought there was any possibility of breakfast, "I'm hungry," she said.

Maggie said she would go to the kitchen and see about it. When she reached the kitchen she saw no one. "I suppose it will be all right if I do it."

She began looking into the cupboards. Very soon a tasty and nourishing breakfast was served up on trays and delivered to each of the sick people.

The colored maid and Maggie had pitched right in. All the servants of the Hutchinson house had escaped to their own quarters, afraid of the measles. Word had spread rapidly when Governor Hutchinson and one of his black men left early for Boston. They had overheard the talk about someone going for a doctor.

About noon, Dr. Thatcher arrived and promptly pronounced the illness as red measles. He at once slapped a quarantine on the entire household.

He motioned Clarice and Marie to follow him into the hall where they joined Sarah. "I will have to ask you ladies to see to it that no one leaves this house for ten days. We doctors have our hands full in town. There are many cases of this pesky sickness, and we have no idea where it came from but we must curb it at once.

"I don't believe your cases are too severe, but the patients must be kept separated and the rooms must be kept dark. Continue giving them hot sassafras tea, and keep them quiet. I will return in a few days to check on them. By all means don't let them scratch. Bathe them with warm water to which you have added quite a bit of alcohol."

Dr. Thatcher picked up his hat and returned to his chaise. He waved back to Sarah who was watching from the porch.

Clarice said to Marie, "I hope Robin won't throw a fit when she hears about the quarantine."

"I doubt that she will take it calmly," replied Marie. "I am not brave about it myself; I hate it. I want to be back in our cottage with Tomas."

Clarice hung her head but said nothing. She went slowly back to Robin's bedside. Maggie was still there. She had propped the child up with pillows.

Robin asked anxiously, "Cee Cee, are we leaving today?"

"No, dear, you have to get over the measles before we can go home." She added, "We're quarantined."

"What's quarantined?" asked Robin.

Maggie quickly replied, "Don't think about it. Don't think about anything but resting, eating, and getting well. Quarantine means everything will be just fine in a few days."

When Dr. Thatcher reached his office he immediately dispatched a messenger with a note to the Anthony house with the news of the outbreak of measles and the quarantine for ten days at the Hutchinson country estate.

"Good Lord!" exclaimed Lord Anthony. "The girls won't be home for ten days. I wonder if the governor is also quarantined."

He soon found out the governor had escaped the confinement by leaving before the doctor arrived and was safely established in his town house in the center of Boston.

Chip and Chuck were out of their rooms in only two days. Sarah said it was impossible to keep them corralled in their bedroom. They were sneaking out every time someone left their side.

Robin did just the opposite; she wouldn't come out of her room, even when she felt much better. She was enjoying the attention Clarice and Maggie were pouring on.

However, Maggie was also waiting on Marie, who was not doing so well. Clarice was trying to keep her mind off Jason by reading books and playing backgammon with Robin.

The governor had sent out a few new books, Goody Two Shoes and Gulliver's Travels.

Robin didn't want Clarice to put them down. She said, "Cee Cee, just keep on reading until the end."

"Robin Anthony, you must understand I have other things to do. Right now, it is time to sponge you off."

Clarice turned to get the bowl of water, she picked up the bottle and poured denatured alcohol into the bowl. Later, she noticed Robin licking her arms and Bo Tay licking her feet and legs. Robin was giggling at full speed between her licks.

"What are you doing, child?" asked the bewildered governess.

"I like the soap," answered Robin.

Clarice knew it was the alcohol and not the soap. She was torn between her continuing the alcohol or not continuing it. She asked Maggie what she would do.

Maggie said, "Let her lick it; maybe she would heal quicker."

Clarice frowned at her answer, but she had so much confidence in Maggie's judgment that she shrugged her shoulders and said, "All right."

In about an hour Robin was calling Cee Cee who was dozing in her chair.

"What do you want, Robin?"

"I want to be sponged off again; I feel too hot."

"No you don't, Robin. It is not time for another bath."

"Well, I want one anyway," scornfully answered the child.

When Clarice did not get up and get the washbowl, Robin jumped out of bed and ran over to the washstand where the bath water was and began dousing her arms with the water.

Clarice softly said, "Robin, you are going to be sicker than you are, and you won't get to go home for a long time." She was thinking this statement might make the child more aware of what she was doing.

Robin said, "I will get back in bed, but I won't eat anything until I die. I hate you, Cee Cee, and I hate Maggie and Marie and everyone."

"It's all right, Robin. We don't mind your hating us; we know you are being bad because you are tired of being sick. Bo Tay is sleeping so peacefully. Why don't you try to sleep?"

"I will if you give me a bath."

Clarice decided to leave her alone for awhile. As she left the room she took the alcohol and the water pitcher with her. She closed the door behind her and went downstairs.

As she walked through the hall she met the colored maid, who held out a small package to her. "Here," said the maid, "is something a messenger left for you."

"For me?" exclaimed Clarice, seeming quite surprised.

She handed the pitcher to the maid and took the package. She saw a scroll attached to the package. Her heart jumped as she read, "For Miss Clarice." She knew it was from Jason. She recognized his handwriting. She returned to her room and opened it. It contained a dozen of the prettiest petits fours she had ever seen.

Robin reached for one at once, one with little red candy cherries on it. She smiled sincerely when she said, "This looks just like the one I had at the welcome reception."

Clarice hardly heard her. She was quite absorbed with the letter.

Jason had spread out his heart and soul with words of love and affection, also explaining his loneliness and heartbreak at her absence. Clarice clasped the letter up to her heart and began to sob.

Robin, with her mouth full of cake, went to her governess and put her arms around her. "Please stop crying, Cee Cee, and eat one of the cakes. He loves you so much. Someday soon you two will be together. I'm going to talk to Papa when we get home and make him allow Jason to come to see you."

"Oh, Robin, dear. In the Bible it says, 'A little child shall lead them.' Please don't forget."

"Cee Cee, may I give Chip and Chuck, each, one of the cakes?"

"Why yes, dear, but I thought you weren't speaking to them."

"I haven't yet, but I'm going to apologize to them and forgive them. If they have had measles, like me, that is punishment enough. Besides, I am going home soon and won't ever see them again."

"Don't count on that," said Clarice.

Robin got a chance to ride Peaches once more along with Chip and Chuck on their ponies and Clarice on the chestnut brown gelding that she rode before. They also enjoyed a picnic by the Goose Pond and had another musical.

On the tenth day Thatcher arrived at Milton Hill and sounded the "All Clear Quarantine Lift."

Chapter Nineteen

The house party was over and the Anthony family was on the way home in Governor Hutchinson's "coach and four" with his driver and footman in charge. It was one-fourth of the way into the month of June.

There was quite a celebration to welcome them home. Lola decorated the dining room with daisies and roses and tied yellow ribbons on the chair backs. She baked a jam cake and made mulberry punch. Henry drew cartoon pictures and put them at each one's plate for place cards.

They sat around the table and each told of some adventure they had experienced during the past ten days. Lady Anthony began by telling of her trip to Harvard with Lord Anthony and Governor Hutchinson to attend the Commencement Exercises.

Lola kept up her chattering while carrying food back and forth to the table: how much she had enjoyed her respite from so much work, that their being away had given her time to patch her aprons and get a little rest. She finally admitted, though, that she was happy that they were all back safe and sound, only she hoped they didn't bring her the measles.

What she didn't tell them was that while they were at Milton Hill she spent a great deal of her time in the cottage with Tomas and when she had work to do in the kitchen Tomas was there helping her. He also accompanied her to market.

After the meal was over and everyone, except Maggie, had left the dining room, Lola sat down beside her and leaned close to her as she talked.

"Henry went to see the men on the schooner that belongs to Don Pedro, the one that's called The Gospel Truth, and he found them there living in luxury. He found out their names are Tablow and Duncan. He told me," she was talking in a low voice right into Maggie's face, "that them two is different than any slaves he has ever seen before. They is more like big rich men than slaves.

"They do as they pleases. Seems like money is plentiful. They has plenty of cigars and rum. They don't wait on nobody, and they take the schooner out whenever they want to.

"Henry says they speak Spanish to each other but speak English to him. He said he invited them over here to meet me, but I ain't expectin' they'll come. He says he thinks they are afraid Truly will have a mind to change Don Pedro's way of thinking about them and it will make a difference in the way they are treated by the master.

"I told him to tell them that Truly don't know nothing about changing anybody's mind. She ain't never been nothin' but a slave herself."

Maggie was bored; she moved her chair back to get up, "Come on, Lola, I will help you do these dishes. I am so glad for Truly, that she has someone to love her and care for her. I've been wishing I had someone to love and care for me."

Lola became very quiet as if wishing for the same thing.

Maggie went out toward the gazebo, where she sat for awhile. She whispered under her breath, "Good Lord, Lola's grammar is terrible; it is very tiring to listen to her."

When the day was over and everyone was in their own room, Clarice sat by her window with her elbows on her knees and her hands cupping her chin, with tears seeping from her eyes. She was watching for Jason's chaise to come along the street. She could see the guard, Channing, standing near the garden gate, and she knew it would be impossible for Jason to put a letter in the broken post while he was there.

She whispered to herself, "I wish I had a gun; I feel like I could shoot him," meaning the guard. "It is mean of him to be so dutiful that he can't look the other way sometimes."

June was not unlike May. It lolled along day after day with the same old anxieties and frustrations. Lola was grouchy, Jackson was poorly, Michael was lazy, and Lady Anthony pretended a lot of headaches. Tomas and Marie were suspecting each other and being snide about it. Henry was away most of the time. Jason kept busy but not near the Anthony house, although thoughts of Clarice filled his heart and mind.

Lord Anthony was hardly ever at home except from late night hours until early morning. He was working hard, attempting to understand the agonies of the Sons of Liberty, The Committee of Correspondence, The Safety Committee, and The Provincial Council and trying to find out who belonged to the Loyal Nine. His head was full of wonderment and his hands were full of problems.

Robin was invited to the Adams's for an afternoon of puzzles and games. At the insistence of her mother she went but hated every minute of it.

Nabby had said to her, "You are a Tory; we don't care much for Tories."

Robin asked, "What is a Tory?"

"A Tory is a king lover," said Nabby.

"Then I'm a Tory and I like being a Tory. Even my dog is a Tory."

Clarice did not accompany Robin to the Adams's. Tomas rode in the chaise with her and left her there. He returned in a couple of hours to pick her up. Clarice begged off, claiming to have vertigo. She was in a bad, withdrawn, almost depressive mood. The poor girl was lovesick and lonesome.

One afternoon, three of Boston's most prominent ladies called on Lady Anthony. They came together in a fine carriage accompanied by their maids.

Michael opened the door and Lady Anthony met them and greeted them, cool as an iceberg. She told Maggie to show the maids to the breakfast room and serve them some tea.

Mrs. Adams called after her "girl" to come back shortly, that they wouldn't be staying long; "This is only a courtesy call." The maids stiffened their backs and sized up Maggie. They were not wearing maid uniforms and looked rather shabby compared to Maggie's starched and prim look.

Mrs. Bainbridge gazed all around at all the elegant furnishings: the paintings, harpsichord, mirrors, velvet chairs, and Oriental rugs. She said to Lady Anthony, "It must be quite rewarding to be in the king's service. I suppose Governor Hutchinson is responsible for the furniture in this house. You surely didn't ship all this from England?"

"Oh my, no! We won't be here long enough for that."

"Did he also acquire the servants for you?"

"Yes, everything was ready for us when we arrived. It was well organized."

"You are quite fortunate to have such a capable governess for your child."

"Yes, I am; she came with us and will return with us."

Mrs. Bainbridge was still talking. Mrs. Adams was stiffly sitting on the settee.

"I hear your daughter is very beautiful; I would like to meet her." Mrs. Adams already knew Robin from the afternoon she visited Nabby.

"Thank you," said Lady Anthony, "Robin is in her French class at the moment, and it would not be right to distract her. She has a hard enough time with her languages."

Lady Anthony dared not risk the possibility of Robin saying something negative or asking an embarrassing question.

When the ladies were leaving, Mrs. Clark, who had not said a word after she said "Good Afternoon" when arriving, sided up to Lady Anthony and felt of her ladyship's silk peau-de-soie sleeve. Stroking it she said, "Oh dear, what perfectly handsome silk. I presume you brought it with you. No American lady that I know of could afford it."

Her ladyship's reply was, "Then you must acquire some silkworms and put them to work for you."

July began with storms and squalls. Businesses closed when the wind and rain got too blustery. Jason did not go out with his cart of bakery goods when the weather was bad. He rarely came along Beacon Street. He was becoming more and more the stranger.

Henry was away for two or three weeks at a time. He had taken the job of Outrider to Committeeman John Slade and was going as far as New York with him. Judge Otis warned Henry not to go into Virginia, where he might be shanghaied into slavery.

John Slade always lied to anyone who asked about Henry's ownership. He would say, "Henry is my slave." Slade and Henry got along splendidly. For fear of being captured, Henry agreed to have his feet shackled and even allowed Slade to tie a rope around his leg and lead him along as if on a leash, especially in New York.

The two were good friends, and once when Slade became too much inebriated and was thrown into jail, Henry asked to be put in with him.

When being questioned, Henry slipped and gave his address as Beacon Hill, Boston, while Slade gave his address as Goose Lane, Chelsey. The jailer suspected that Henry was a runaway slave or stolen property.

The two of them stayed in the lockup for two weeks while investigations were in progress. Slade finally admitted that he had stolen Henry and was taking him to Virginia to sell him. They were turned out of jail and ordered to get out of New York before dark.

The judge decided that the New York courts were too snowed under with runaway slave cases already to bother with this confusing one; besides, it was too hot. Matter of fact he was in sympathy with his Southern planter friends, and actually hoped Slade would get a high price for such a strong black buck. He was not at all concerned that Slade might have stolen him or that Slade was lying, since Slade had slipped him five pounds.

Ever since the return from Milton Hill, Robin had been urgently begging to go somewhere again. Clarice did not discourage her from this plea because she wanted to go someplace also. She hated the control of her freedom.

Maggie was not denied her liberty to go where and when she pleased. She went to church every Sunday, and when Lola went out and about, to do shopping, sometimes Maggie accompanied her. Maggie even went shopping in Boston by herself. She drew a small salary of five pounds each month. She always gave one tenth to her church and spent the rest.

Having been born of French parents, she inherited a love of sweet-smelling colognes and soaps. These luxuries took a good part of her salary, but as she said, "People never back away from me when I come up close to them."

It was a sunny morning, and right after breakfast Robin asked her governess if she could take Bo Tay for a walk all by herself. She bluntly said, "I'm tired of everyone, even you."

"Why, Robin dear, I'm sorry to hear that, but I think it will be all right if you promise not to go any farther than the garden gate."

Robin called for Bo Tay and the child and dog left the house.

Clarice stood near the window overlooking the garden. She didn't see Channing or Scott but presumed they were close by. She could see Jackson wiping down the benches and lattice of the gazebo. She was watching Robin tripping along the garden path, Bo Tay at her heels.

Seeing that traffic was heavy along the street, she thought, If Robin goes near the gate I will go out there. Lady Anthony will be upset with me if she finds out that I allowed Robin to do this.

Jackson was also watching the child from the gazebo. To get her attention and perhaps entice her back to the gazebo, he took out a French harp from his pocket and began to play a snappy tune.

Robin came running back to the gazebo, "Jackson," she said, "I didn't know you knew how to play the harmonica."

"Ya, and I can dance, too." He began a lively tap. He reached for Robin's hand and led her into the rhythm. She got the beat in a second and began to laugh and snap her fingers.

Clarice smiled and felt much better; Jackson had rescued Robin from her melancholy. She went out to join them. As she approached the gazebo she began clapping her hands and humming.

Jackson was now really warmed up, and Robin was dancing with him in perfect time. Bo Tay was sitting on his hind legs howling.

When Jackson's breath became so short he had to rest, he sat down on the bench and wiped his sweaty face with his sleeve. He said, "Lordy, Lordy, I ain't as young and agile as I used to be."

"Where did you learn to dance like that?" asked Clarice.

"Oh, I reckon I'ze picked it up from the jiggers down at the wharf. Miss Robin here is pretty good at it. We'ze enjoyed it mightily."

"Yes," said Robin, "but I hope Mama doesn't find out about it. She won't let me dance anything but the minuet. I hate it; it is too slow."

Clarice looked around and asked Jackson, "Where are the guards?"

He answered, "Isn't you heard? Lord Anthony told Mr. Straight to let 'em go. His lordship said we don't need 'em anymore since that spy is not coming here...Mr. Straight sent 'em back to headquarters. That was four or five days ago. I ain't seed 'em since."

Clarice responded with, "Jackson, that's wonderful news. I felt their eyes following me every time I came outside. They were so unfriendly."

"Them guards is all lak that; they is also being watched. They has to do what they is told to do."

Jackson saw Michael coming, tottering along the path, carrying a bucket of water. He went to him to assist him. He said, "Michael, what are you doing out in this hot sun? You ought to be inside."

"I'se watering the beans," said the old man.

Jackson took the bucket from him and said, "Here, I'll do it for you; you go and wait in the gazebo."

Clarice, Robin, and Bo Tay were already entering the house through the French doors.

That same evening, Governor Hutchinson's chaise appeared at the front stile of the Anthony home and picked up Lord Anthony. Clarice was just entering the hall when she saw his lordship kissing Lady Anthony and Robin goodbye.

As the chaise drove away, Robin ran to her governess and announced in exuberant tones that her papa was going with Governor Hutchinson to Rhode Island and wouldn't be back for two weeks. Clarice felt her heart sink, because she knew Robin hadn't asked her papa to release the ban on Jason.

When Clarice and Robin were in their room again, Clarice asked Robin, "Did you speak to your papa about you know what? You said you would talk to him."

The child interrupted, "You mean Jason?"

"Yes."

"No, I was scared to."

"Why on earth would you be scared?"

"Because I heard Mama telling Papa that she was afraid you might run away with Jason. I don't want him to take you away."

"Robin, I told you before, I won't leave you, ever…but I must be allowed to see Jason. I love him; we enjoy each other's company. He tells me about things going on in Boston. He knows I am eager to learn. He knows I don't get much information from reading the papers. Usually they are taken away before I get to read them."

"Well, Cee Cee, I will talk to Papa when he gets back."

"Why don't you talk to your mother? Being a woman, she might understand how I feel."

"But Cee Cee she is the one who wanted Jason banned in the first place."

"I suppose you are right, Robin; talking to her ladyship wouldn't do any good."

Later on in July, Clarice received two letters, one from her parents and one from Tom Fellows. Good news of her parents' good health and well-being lifted her spirits to some degree. Tom's letter, however, brought disturbing news. He had joined the British regulars and asked to be sent to Massachusetts as soon as his training was over.

It would take about six weeks of training before he would sail. He implied, with much anticipation, he hoped to be near her in a few months.

Clarice realized that she had to write him immediately and let him know that she had someone else and was very happy with her new-found love. As she was preparing her parchment and looking for her pen, the thought came to her that Tom was probably on his way already and by the time her letter reached England, he most likely would be in Boston.

Clarice told Maggie about it, and Maggie replied that it was very good news that, "Perhaps you won't moon so much over Jason." This didn't sit well with Clarice; she felt everyone, even Maggie, was trying to break up her relationship with Jason.

Robin went into her own room, picked up her French doll, and began undressing her. She became angry at a button that wouldn't unbutton and she threw the doll down on the floor and walked to the window, talking to herself. "Why do I have to be the one to bring them together again? Why is it that Papa and Mama are so against Jason? I like his cinnamon buns. I want him to come again. I think I will run away and I will leave a note telling them I will come back when Jason can come again. I can't get out of the garden with Scott and

Channing watching my every move. I hate this place. I wish Jason would kill Scott and Channing."

"Robin, who are you talking to? I heard you; you sounded mad." It was Clarice coming up behind Robin, who was still standing at the window.

"Cee Cee, I've decided to do something."

"What is it that you are going to do?"

"I won't tell you or anyone."

"Robin, you don't have to do anything. I heard you say, 'Why do I have to be the one to bring them together again?' Please be a good girl, Robin; I have enough on my mind as it is."

"You poor thing," said Robin, "too many sweethearts."

Lady Anthony was indulging herself by sponging off her naked body with cool, scented water and taking sips of apple cider that had been spiked with cinnamon.

On hearing a soft knock at the door she pulled her silk chemise over her body and threw her crepe-de-chine shawl around her shoulders as she went over to open it.

When she saw Robin standing there she held out her hand to the coy, smiling child, "Come in, dear, are you all right?"

"Mama, I want to talk to you about something important."

"Why...Robin, yes dear." She sat down and pulled the child up close to her knees. "Now tell your mama what it is that is so important."

"Well," she hesitated and moved around a bit, "Cee Cee is very unhappy and she cries sometimes, and she doesn't listen when I'm talking. She even writes notes or letters while I'm reciting my lessons."

"Do you think she is homesick?" asked her ladyship.

"No, she's in love with Jason McKenzie."

"The baker?"

"Yes, and you and Papa won't let him come here anymore, and she doesn't get to see him."

"But we were told when we were negotiating with her parents that she was going to marry a young man there in Birmingham when we return in two years."

"I know that, but then she met Jason and she wants to see him. Won't you please change your mind? Cee Cee thinks he is a fine person."

Lady Anthony felt sympathy for her little girl. She hugged her as she said, "You dear baby, how compassionate you are to be so concerned about your governess."

Robin was very quiet, her head hanging down.

Lady Anthony spoke again, "Please don't worry about Cee Cee; she will get over Jason McKenzie. She is young and foolish right now."

While still holding her child up close, her ladyship thought about what she had said and she began talking more in the complimentary style. "Clarice is beautiful and smart, and trained to be gracious; she can get many suitors and admirers. She should attend to her duties and forget that common street vendor."

This last remark really upset Robin's apple cart, and she tore herself away from her mother's arms and ran angrily out of the room.

As she ran down the hall, her eyes spotted the hall closet. She opened the door and saw a large empty sea chest standing there. She grabbed Bo Tay, who had joined her as she came out of her mother's room. She crammed him into the chest, she reached for the door and closed it, then she climbed into the chest and pulled the lid down. She said, as she felt the tightness of the lid, "Gee whiz, it's dark in here."

Lady Anthony sat down in front of her mirror and continued her sponging. She hummed a little tune as her thoughts went meandering through her brain. Clarice is intelligent; she will come to her senses soon and forget about the baker.

Thinking that Robin had had enough time to convince her mother, Clarice went to Lady Anthony's door and knocked as she called out, "Robin are you here? Can you come with me now? It is time for stories."

There was a sudden reply from Lady Anthony. "Don't you know where Robin is, Clarice? You must keep closer watch on her. She is only and child and an eager one at that. She was here talking to me but ran out of the room like she was mad at me."

"Why would Robin be mad at you, your ladyship?"

"I am not sure...I did not grant her request. You probably know what the request was."

Clarice whirled around and ran down the hall, calling out for the child in an excited manner. Robin heard her name being called, but she ignored it as she grinned and squeezed Bo Tay, while hunkering farther down in the sea chest. After checking in her room and Robin's room, Clarice ran down to the kitchen and spread the alarm, "Robin is missing," she cried out.

Lola and Michael began to search the kitchen and stables. Jackson walked around the garden, calling her name and looking behind shrubbery and trees. Tomas or Marie couldn't see how she could possibly have gotten into their cottage without being seen, but they searched all the cupboards and closets anyway.

Maggie came in from a shopping spree in Boston, carrying numerous packages. As she passed through the hall she heard Bo Tay scratching and whimpering from inside the closet. She opened the door and he came out. He went only a few feet before he returned to the closet door and scratched to get back in. Maggie said to him, "Look here, I haven't time to play games."

She was starting up the third flight of stairs when she saw Clarice running breathlessly up the back stairs.

"Maggie, have you seen Robin? We can't find her. Everyone is frantic. Where can she be?"

"No, I haven't seen her. I have just come in. It is my day to shop and I have been to town." Then she remembered Bo Tay. "Bo Tay was here in the hall closet," she said, pointing to the closet door. "He was scratching to get out. Do you suppose Robin is in the closet?"

The girls almost ran over each other getting to the closet. They found no one.

Robin was now aware of the excitement she was causing and she was enjoying it. She quietly left the closet and went into her mother's room when she knew her mother was not there.

Florence had joined the others in the search and was now in Lord Anthony's study. She noticed a pile of letters on his lordship's desk. She said to herself, "I will come back and read these letters. I want to know who is writing them and what they say."

Seeing Clarice and Maggie and realizing that they looked scared, she said, "Have you any idea where Robin is and why she is not on these premises?"

"No, your ladyship, and I am very scared," said the governess.

Tomas came into the hall and Lady Anthony rushed up to him, "Tomas, send Jackson to Boston right away to the constable's station to report Robin is missing and tell them to get some men out at once to look for her." Lady Anthony had begun to show her nervousness in an angry way. "Where are the guards? What's their name...Channing or Scott? Find them at once and bring them to me. I must question them."

Robin got into her mother's bed and covered herself with the counterpane, completely hiding herself. Florence was downstairs excitedly running from room to room. The others were still searching and calling.

When Jackson arrived with the constable, the questioning began. He directed his questions at each one in a manner of suspicion.

Lady Anthony took him by the shoulder, shaking him, she said, "Officer, don't stand there asking questions; get your men out and about town to find my child."

Robin fell asleep; Bo Tay was on the bed beside her, but not under the covers, and he began to bark to wake her. Maggie heard the little dog and followed the sound into Lady Anthony's room. Clarice then heard the dog and Lady Anthony saw Clarice running toward the house. She ran after her, then the Constable ran after Lady Anthony, followed by Tomas and Marie, all running into her ladyship's room.

It was quite an audience that met Robin's eyes when she quit rubbing them and sat up in her mother's bed. Bo Tay was high-stepping around over the bed, looking very pleased.

Lady Anthony screamed out at the child, "Robin, you have given us a terrible scare. Even the constable has come out from town to look for you."

"Yes, I did and I'll do it again or something worse if you don't let Jason come to see Cee Cee; and besides that, I want some of his cinnamon buns."

The child slid out of the high-post bed and picked up Bo Tay and twisted backwards out of the room, slamming the door and latching it on the outside. Lady Anthony, the constable, Maggie, Clarice, Tomas, and Marie were all trapped in the bedroom.

Clarice ran to the door but couldn't open it. She backed up against it and burst into hysterical laughter. In a moment all the rest—except Lady Anthony and the constable—were laughing.

Then the constable spoke, "I think we've been had."

When Robin reached the kitchen, to where she ran as fast as she could, she stormed at Lola, who was sitting at the trestle table, "I want something sweet to eat, like a cinnamon bun, right now."

"We don't have any buns, Robin. Where were you?"

"Don't change the subject, Lola. Send Henry to Jason's shop right this minute to get some buns."

Lola pointed her finger at Robin. Scornfully she said, "You have got no right to tell me what to do, you brat."

Robin picked up a small wooden bowl from the table and hurled it at Lola, barely missing her head. "You are a mean old Whig and King George hates Whigs and you'll probably be put in jail."

Jackson entered the kitchen, coming in from the garden, "Whereabouts is Mister Straight or Miss Clarice?" he asked, directing his question at Lola.

Robin answered haughtily, "Locked up with Mama and Maggie, and they're going to stay locked up until Mama lets Jason come back."

"What do you mean, 'locked up?'" asked Lola.

"That's it," answered Robin, "locked up."

Lola spoke positively to Jackson, "Go get Tomas quick."

Robin blurted out, "I told you, he's locked up, so is Marie."

Lola and Jackson were dumbfounded, "I'se better git Michael, he's got extra keys."

"Don't need a key," said Robin, "I bolted the H. and L."

"Then you go, Jackson," said Lola.

"I doesn't usually go on the second floor," said Jackson. "I'll go git Michael to go let 'um out."

Jackson went out into the garden, where only a few moments before he had encountered Michael tottering along the garden walk in the hot sun and had warned him to get out of the heat. He didn't see the old man anywhere. He didn't see him sitting in the gazebo where he sometimes rested. Where can he be when I needs him? thought Jackson. He called out, "Michael, where is you? We need you to do something in a hurry." He got no answer.

Jackson glanced toward the garden and saw a dark pile of something behind a rose bush. It was Michael, all in a heap, his feet pulled up against his chest. Jackson shook him. Michael was dead. Jackson said, "Oh God...oh God," as he stepped high and fast back to the house.

Lola and Robin were still at the table sitting beside each other having apple pie doused with heavy cream. Jackson passed by them and went up the back stairs, headed for the bolted door. "Guess he couldn't find Michael," said Lola. She added, after a few more bites, "He tries to shift a lot of his duties onto Michael or Henry. I think he thinks he is 'Cock-of-the-walk' around here because Lord Anthony talks to him the most."

"My papa doesn't talk much to anybody but Governor Hutchinson, and I'll tell you a secret, Lola—my papa is fooling around with Marie."

Lola cringed. She wondered if Robin knew about her and Tomas. She said, "I love secrets, Robin; they keeps me in my prime."

"What's prime?" asked Robin, wide-eyed with her mouth full of pie.

"Girlish," answered Lola.

"Oh, you mean young and foolish?" Robin was repeating what her mama said about Clarice.

"Yes," answered Lola.

Within the next moment a procession of people came down the stairs single file, each looking as if they were in shock. They passed by Lola and Robin and hurried out the door and down the garden walk. Lola and Robin jumped up from the table and followed along in the rear, craning their necks to see what the mad rush was all about.

Tomas remarked later to Lady Anthony, "It's a good thing the constable was here; I wouldn't have known what to do."

"Yes," responded Lady Anthony, "with his lordship away, it is a good thing."

A wagon painted black with one horse and one driver came and took Michael's body away. Jackson followed the wagon, driving the chaise. Henry and Lola were the only other people accompanying the wagon. They rode in the chaise feeling very grand, both dressed in their very best clothes.

There was, on the outskirts of Boston, a burying ground called Potter's Field. There was always an open grave waiting. It was free. The people of Boston contributed to its upkeep by dropping a pence or two into the "poor boxes" placed around town in public meeting places and churches.

Money from these boxes bought Michael a plain wooden box which was standing beside the open grave. Henry and Jackson lifted his body from the wagon and wrapped it in a clean linen sheet, which Maggie had contributed. Henry and Jackson placed the body in the box and Jackson nailed the lid down. When it was lowered into the grave Lola burst out in sobs. Henry comforted her a few moments while Jackson knelt down on his knees and prayed. His voice was soft and mellow, tears were running down his face:

> Oh, Lord, listen to me.
> Our good 'ole brother has now come before ye
> Beggin' for to be let in to a restful home.
> Ye promised to prepare a place for him,
> I hope ye didn't forget.
> Have mercy on us here who 'members him
> 'Cause he helped us and we loved him.
> Thank ye for our good blessin's.
> Please take care of yeself.
> We kindly beg ye to 'member us.
> This is Jackson and Henry and Lola.

Jackson got to his feet.

Lola went over to the chaise and picked up a bouquet of flowers that Clarice and Robin had gathered and sent along. She walked over to the grave and pitched the bouquet onto the lowered box.

As she walked away she said, "Goodbye, Michael, I'll miss your stumblin' around in the kitchen."

The summer lagged on for Clarice. She and Robin and Maggie worked among the flower beds and spent many hours in the gazebo. Clarice remarked that it was such a relief not to be watched every minute. None at the Anthony house had heard from Scott or Channing. Someone at the wharf told Henry that they had been sent to New York.

Robin was invited to spend a week at Braintree visiting Nabby Adams, but she declined, saying she hated the country.

Clarice received a letter from Jason almost every time Lola went to the market. Also every time Henry was in town, Jason would meet up with either of them and give them a letter for Clarice. She, in turn, had a letter ready to go whenever they were going out.

One bright September day Clarice and Robin were in the garden gathering leaves to press in a book. Robin saw Jason's chaise. It was turning the corner at the foot of Beacon Hill and was headed toward the Anthonys. "Cee Cee, look quick, here comes Jason."

Clarice hadn't seen Jason since the end of May. She ran toward the street waving both arms and calling out, "Jason, oh Jason." Robin was at Clarice's side, also waving and shouting.

When Jason stopped at the garden gate, he didn't step out of the chaise, he jumped out and jumped over the fence. Their arms were around each other in an instant, and their lips were pressed in kissing. His feet were dancing all around, and he was lifting Clarice off the ground and swinging her around, kissing her lips and her cheeks.

Then Jason let loose of Clarice and grabbed Robin, lifting her off the ground and kissing the top of her head and her cheeks.

"This is the happiest moment I've ever had in my life," said the jubilant Jason.

Clarice was so happy and breathing so hard she could hardly get the words out, "Oh, my darling, I can't believe it's you. You are so much more mature and so handsome. You have aged. You are an older man. I love you."

"Yes, dear, grieving for you has made an old man out of me." He held her hands and moved back from her and looked lovingly into her eyes.

"Jason, are you here because Lord Anthony has lifted the ban?"

"Yes, my darling. He and I met in the Green Dragon and had a long talk. When he found out that I am not 'poor' but a man with a home, a business, and a farm, he changed his opinion of me...at least temporarily. There are some other things he has not found out, but he did find out that I'm going to marry you as soon as possible."

"Oh, my darling, did you hear from my mama and papa?"

"Yes, I had a letter in August. They both said, 'If I love you like I said I did and you love me, they are willing for the marriage and send us their blessings.' Lord Anthony admitted it would be hard to prevent such a marriage. He even said, 'It must be God's will.'"

Jason stayed with Clarice in the gazebo for an hour, then he said, "I have to go to an important meeting; I will see you soon."

Clarice and Robin followed him to the gate, and as he drove away they were all throwing kisses at each other. They heard Jason singing as he went down the hill. Clarice and Robin held hands and swung each other around in circles, singing "Ring around the Roses" while laughing and hugging and prancing along.

As the two girls entered the door, Clarice sang out, "Jason's back."

"What's all the glory shoutin' about?" asked Lola, who had not seen Jason come or go but was now seeing the joyful antics of Robin and Clarice.

"Lola, Lola, glorious news…Jason is back. Papa gave him permission to come back; aren't you glad? Now we can eat cake every day." Robin was showing her happiness at the probability of Jason's goodies. She said, "Lola, don't you ever make buns again; Jason's are much better."

Lola clapped her hands, "Hooray, I won't. When will he be here with the first batch?"

"Maybe very soon, maybe tomorrow. I don't think he said when he would return," said the child.

Jason did return, early next morning. He brought a large basket filled with an assortment of sweet buns, cinnamon buns, hard rolls, light bread, corn muffins, chocolate cake, and cream puffs.

"Here are sweets for the sweet," he said as he set the basket down on the table. He returned to the chaise and brought in a second basket filled with presents, wrapped in different shades of silk and tied with streamers of bright colored yarn. Each present had a name on it.

Lola pulled the cord, summoning Clarice and Robin back to the kitchen. They had left when Jason went out the door to return to his chaise for the basket of presents.

The amazing thing about all this was the elegance of Jason's attire. He was dressed in his very best clothes: brown velvet knee-length coat; buff breeches, very tight; white silk stockings; black shoes with silver buckles; and on his head a white queue tied back with a black ribbon.

He reached out for Clarice as he put the basket of presents on the table. He drew her up to his side. "Robin, hand me that tiny little box tied with the blue string," he said.

Robin's eyes were sparkling as she did as Jason asked. He handed the little present to Clarice and said, as he kissed her, "With all my love, my darling."

Clarice's hand was shaking, her body was trembling, but she was beaming with happiness as she pulled the blue silk wrapping off the little box. Inside was a plain gold ring with two tiny pearls inset in it, so close together they were touching.

"Jason, Jason, my dearest, you are so thoughtful." She put her arms around his neck and kissed him. "I am so proud to be your girl."

He released her arms from his neck and put the ring on her finger and kissed it. He said, "I will always love you; this ring is my promise."

He then said to Robin, "The pink package is for you."

Robin eagerly took off the wrapping and found a small silver box. The top of the box was a hand-painted porcelain portrait of a young girl holding a small French poodle in her arms.

Robin's face showed her delight. She put her arms around Jason's neck and kissed him on the cheek as she said, "Jason, I think this is my picture."

"It is, Robin. I had Paul Revere make it from the sketch he made of you. The poodle is Bo Tay."

"I love it. I love it. I'm going to show it to Mama right now."

There were some more presents in the basket. Eventually they would reach the recipients they were intended for: pure silk handkerchiefs edged with tatting lace for Maggie, Marie, and Lola; and an ostrich feather fan for Lady Anthony; Cuban cigars for Tomas, Jackson, Henry, and Lord Anthony.

"My darling, you have been a busy man getting all these presents and wrapping. Besides, I haven't told you yet how handsome you are this day or how much I love you. You are truly my prince charming."

"Thank you, dear. I have to go now; there is pressing business I am elected to tend to." He held her and kissed her again as he said, "My life depends on it."

"Will you be coming back here soon?" she asked.

"Yes, probably. Everything will be the same, only I will be working harder. I will be busy long hours into the night."

"I think he's going to a council meeting because he is so dressed up. But didn't you think he looks like a lord?" Robin asked.

"Well...yes...sort of, but he's American and they don't have lords."

"Only one," said Maggie, who had just come into the kitchen and heard them talking about Jason.

Robin saw to it that everyone got the present intended for them.

She and Clarice began reading The Life and Poems of John Milton.

Maggie told Lady Anthony that John Milton was too much for Robin. She said it might make her addle-brained.

Lady Anthony paid Maggie no mind. She had pointed out to Clarice that she wanted Robin taught the "Theological Virtues: Faith, Hope, and Charity."

The month of October was warm and bright. Clarice carried an armful of books to the gazebo every morning from which she and Robin read. Sometimes Lola prepared for them a basket of lunch: ripe red apples, hunks of clabber cheese, biscuits with ham, and hard-boiled eggs.

Now and then Maggie would join them for lunch, and once Jason stopped by with cinnamon buns fresh from his ovens. He also brought a bundle of peppermint sticks, which were a rare treat, for Robin's mother forbade her to have candy except at Christmas.

One day when lessons were finished, Clarice walked away across the garden to stand by the broken post and reminisce of the days, not too long gone, when her anxiety would almost get the better of her.

Maggie and Robin sat in the gazebo and talked. Maggie was clasping Robin's hand and bounding it up and down on her leg. She said, "Robin, do you realize that Cee Cee has a birthday coming up very soon? She will be eighteen, and I think we ought to celebrate with a party. Her birthday is November second. I think it will still be warm. We can decorate the gazebo and have it here." She was looking all around as if imagining how it would look decorated.

Robin said, "Oh yes, let's do it. But how do you know that her birthday is November second? She never told me about her birthday."

"Here's how I know," said Maggie. "One day not long ago Cee Cee and I were straightening out the bureau drawers to put away the clean linens. We noticed an old copy of the Boston Gazette lining the drawer. We pulled it out carefully as it was yellow with age. It was dated December 12, 1770. The heading of an article at the bottom of the page caught our eyes. It read, 'Marie Antoinette Gives Up Her Jewels.' We read on. The story printed there was about an elegant celebration in France, at the Palace of Versailles to honor Marie Antoinette on her birthday, November second, and her marriage which had taken place in the preceding May.

"Clarice said, as we read on, 'Why, that is my birthday also.' I asked if it was also the same year."

"'Exactly,' she said." Maggie was repeating Clarice's words.

Robin seemed puzzled. She sighed, then said, "I don't understand why they didn't celebrate the wedding in May."

"The news item didn't say why, but," Maggie said to Robin, "I have heard that the Daupin, Louis XVI, would have nothing to do with Marie Antoinette, his young bride, for a long, long time. He was shy and angered at any attempt his family made to bring them together. So in November when her birthday was near, her family and attendants decided to make a big celebration, in hopes they would dance and sing together and become good friends and lovers. They were married but not even friendly.

"While the celebration was in progress, a raging fire broke out in the palace and spread rapidly to the houses nearby and the stables and grounds. Many hundreds of people were burned to death or seriously wounded.

"Marie Antoinette went out among the dead and knelt beside them and prayed. When the fire died out and collectors for the poor and burned were out taking alms, Marie gave her jewels and pledged her income—which was exceedingly much.

"At this time Louis XVI noticed her beauty. Her grief was overwhelming. He felt much tenderness toward her, and from then on he began to pay her a little bit of attention, such as smiles when passing."

"I thought she was the queen," said Robin.

"Not yet," said Maggie. "She won't be the queen until Louis XV is dead and her husband XVI ascends the throne of France."

"Then she is going to be eighteen on November second," said Robin. She thought about it for awhile and suggested to Maggie that they make it royal by making a crown for Clarice and pretending she is going to be the queen of Massachusetts.

"That will be a lot of fun," Maggie replied.

"Let's ask Jason to make a cake." Robin was beaming with pride as she stood out in front of Maggie and spread her skirts in a curtsy.

Clarice came back to the gazebo and with an expression of sadness said, "I hope Jason is busy with his bakery business and not meddling with the tea arguments."

Everyone had heard that trouble was brewing over the new tea tax imposed on the people of the colonies, supposedly to pay for the British soldiers patrolling the streets. There was inflammatory conversation in every tavern, shop, wharf, meeting place of worship, and street corner.

The people in general had picked up a slogan: "Taxation without representation is tyranny."

In a couple of days Robin and Maggie got together and planned the royal birthday party for Clarice. It was supposed to be a surprise, but that didn't work out because Clarice was always so close to Robin; she overheard the whispering. She was beside herself with enthusiasm and elated at the prospect of seeing Jason.

Maggie made lovely invitations written in both French and English. She drew a small crest and crown on the inside of the eight-by-six inch parchment card which she rolled and tied with ribbon.

Lady Anthony, Marie, Lola, Tomas, Lord Anthony, Jason, and Jackson each received one handed to them by Robin. Clarice insisted she send one by messenger to Nabby Adams.

Robin said, "But Nabby won't come because she doesn't like me."

"Do you like her, Robin?" asked Clarice.

"Sometimes I do, when she stops talking about Tories being mean."

Robin cornered Jason on his next delivery to the house and gave him his invitation and asked him to make a big cake and decorate it with a little crown of swirled sugar.

"Why a crown?" asked Jason as he looked into Robin's smiling eyes.

"Because it is Marie Antoinette's birthday, too."

"All right, I'll try to make a crown but just because you asked me to."

"Please come early, Jason. Cee Cee will be watching for you every second."

"You can bet I'll be early," he assured the happy child.

Chapter Twenty

November second turned out to be a little hazy at first, but the gazebo was brilliant with autumn leaves, ribbons, and candles glowing from the hurricane candle holders placed on the tables. There was a pile of presents enticing Robin to touch, shake, and smell every one.

Waiting for Jason turned into moments of anxiety. Clarice, wearing her blue velvet dress and her blue chamois slippers, kept eagerly watching for Jason's chaise to come around the corner.

He never came.

Jason was busy nailing broadsides up on trees announcing a meeting to be held on November third at Liberty Tree. The broadside said in bold letters:

> Gentlemen:
> You are desired to meet at Liberty Tree next Wednesday, November Third, at twelve o'clock noon, then and there to hear the persons to whom the tea shipped by The East India Company is consigned, make a public resignation of their office as consignees, and also swear that they will reship any tea consigned to them by the said company by the first vessel sailing for London.
> Signed O.C. Secretary

At the bottom of the broadside there was a drawing of a hand with an index finger pointing to these words, Show me the man that dares take this down.

Jason hadn't forgotten the birthday party; he had made the cake and decorated it, and it was in his shop waiting to be taken to Clarice. He had intended having Henry deliver it, he knew he wouldn't make it in time, but Henry never showed up at the shop.

When he ran into Henry on Brattle Street, he asked him to go and get the cake and deliver it to Beacon Hill with the note he quickly wrote: My darling, Happy Birthday, I am sorry to miss the party, but this business I am in at the moment is urgent. I will make it up to you later. Love, J.

John Slade was waiting for Henry to join him in front of Faneuil Hall. They were going out through the province to put the broadsides up in every tavern, ordinary, and town hall.

Henry took the note and put it in his jacket, but he did not go to Charles Street to pick up the cake.

When he reached the Anthony house he ran to the kitchen door and called, "Lola, come here and get this note for Clarice. It's from Jason. He ain't comin'."

Lola took the note from his hand and started to ask him something, but he was gone like a flash and never turned to look back.

Lola went straight to the gazebo with the note. "Here is a note," she handed it to Clarice, "from Jason. Henry brought it and he was in such a hurry he didn't tell me anything."

Clarice read the note and began to tremble, she sat down and said to Maggie, Robin, and Lola (who had remained to hear what the note said), "Jason won't be here; he is busy doing something else." She sighed and continued, "I wonder what can be so pressing as to keep him from my birthday party...."

Maggie spoke up, "Well, we will celebrate anyway. Come on everyone, join hands, form a circle, and sing." Clarice would not join in, but the others danced around and sang a little ditty.

> Pretty brown eyes, don't weep and sigh,
> Your true love will come by and by.
> He'll bring a cake and apple pie
> He'll bring a kiss and a kite to fly.

Robin was laughing and Maggie was humming. Clarice wiped her eyes and began hugging each one and thanking them for the merry tune and the work they had done to make the birthday jolly, but her heart was heavy, not because of the absence of Jason but for a fear she had that he might be killed. She knew he had enemies.

Explaining the Broadsides

The East India Tea Company was to deliver more than three hundred chests of tea, shipped in three different vessels, to especially appointed consignees who had agreed to accept the cargoes and pay the customs charge including the three pence per pound tax. This plan excluded many merchants who had previously been buyers of East India Tea.

The angered citizens, led by the Sons of Liberty, called a meeting and voted to ask the consignees to resign their commitments of accepting the cargoes of tea. A committee was appointed to notify each consignee that the citizens of Boston requested them to resign and send the tea back to London. They were to meet at noon on November third under the Liberty Tree to publicly resign their commissions.

Jason McKenzie was delegated by the Club Nine (Loyal Nine) to head a crew of volunteers to see to the publishing and displaying over one hundred broadsides notifying every citizen of the province to meet at noon on November third, 1773, to witness the signing.

At the appointed day and time the consignees never showed up. After waiting for more than an hour the people who had gathered there began to get rowdy and when someone yelled, "Let's go get 'em; they're at Clarke's Warehouse," the mad rush began.

At Clarke's warehouse the consignees were in meeting to discuss the situation they were in. When the angry mob reached the warehouse, they broke open the doors and rushed up the stairs, yelling and calling names. They were met by about twenty men who used chairs, canes, or anything they could lift as weapons to bang and bash at the rioters. The fighting was angry and noisy. The old wooden staircase wobbled and creaked, threatening to collapse.

In a short while the crowd outside blockaded the building and taunted those inside to come out. The besiegers finally, after an hour or so, began to pall and straggle away. Nothing had been accomplished, only some insulting and despicable behavior.

There were meetings every day and evening throughout November: the Sons of Liberty, the Club Nine (John Hancock's flock of followers), and the Committee of Correspondence (meeting throughout the thirteen colonies).

Messages were arriving pledging fidelity to the Common Cause, that no tea from the East India Company would be landed.

Explaining the Club Nine

The Club Nine was a secret club (it was supposedly supported by Samuel Adams and John Hancock). It met in a second floor room over a distillery at Hanover Square. The room was called Liberty Hall. The Liberty Tree stood nearby.

Since the club was a secret organization, the names of the members were in doubt, but those suspected of being the most active, causing much controversy in and around Boston, were John Avery, Jr.; Henry Bass; Thomas Chase; Steven ——- (somebody); Tom Crafts, a painter, ironic that his name was Crafts; George Trott; Benjamine Eads, who was a reporter for the activities, etc.; John Will Smith; and Jason McKenzie, a baker who had a sidekick named Henry Cook, a free black man of about twenty-five.

These men were the actual perpetrators of slanderous publications against some of Boston's most prominent citizens, namely the governor and his sons and their relatives who held government office.

Many of the rich Tories, especially the Clarkes, the Faneuils, and the Lieutenant Governor Andrew Oliver's family were the victims of violence and abuse during these troubled times.

There was a town meeting being held almost every day. The squabble over the East India Tea was the main issue. The townspeople in general wanted it shipped back to London. The consignees wanted it to be unloaded at their warehouses and held there. Very little was accomplished at any of the meetings, other than name calling, swearing, drinking, and threats.

The Club Nine (history later called it the Loyal Nine) called a meeting, and Henry Cook called on each member with a message. The message asked for volunteers to assemble in a back room at Merry Mermaid Tavern on a specified night and hour to hear a very important plea. The aim of the plea was not explained. Even Henry did not know what the meeting had in mind.

Not every day in November was going to be a bad day. Lady Anthony wrote a charming note to Jason, inviting him to have dinner with them on the fourteenth to announce the date and plans for his and Clarice's wedding. She asked Maggie to deliver it to him several days ahead of time so he would not be tied up with something else.

When Clarice and Jason had approached his lordship and ladyship some time ago, with their desire to marry and asked their permission, they had received a rather cool response and were told to postpone their plans for a year until Clarice served out her indenture agreement.

Since then the sweethearts had been in unhappy states. Jason had been so preoccupied with the tea controversy that he had not been coming to the house as often. He had employed a young boy to do his delivering for him, and Mrs. Jolly was doing the baking and shop work.

Maggie took the note from Lady Anthony and went to the kitchen. She told Lola to detain Jason when and if he came until she could give him the note from her ladyship.

Lola asked, "What's the note about? Is her majesty going to forbid him to come here again?"

Maggie was uptight at Lola's assumptive question.

"I doubt it; I think they understand each other better now. I suppose we will find out what the note has to say eventually."

"Do you want me to take care of it 'til Jason shows up?" asked Lola.

"No, it is entrusted to me. You just be sure that he doesn't get away before I see him." Maggie didn't trust Lola, although she knew she couldn't read.

Next day Jason came hustling into the kitchen. He sternly said to Lola, "Pull your bell cord for my girl; I want to give her a kiss, then I've got to run. I have to meet a fellow at Griffin's wharf about some paint and some plans."

First Lola pulled for Maggie, then Clarice. Clarice came bouncing down the steps; she was full of pep and smiles. She knew when Lola was telling her Jason was there "by a peculiar sound of the bell."

Maggie was a moment or two behind her, just in time to witness the passionate embrace between the two lovers.

"Here's something for you from Lady Anthony," said Maggie, holding out the note.

"For me?" Jason seemed surprised as he released Clarice and took the paper from Maggie's hand. He began to glow with an expression of approval as he said to the girls facing him, "Hear ye! Listen to this." He began to read:

> Dear Jason,
> Lord Anthony and I have decided that the love you and Clarice have for each other was made in Heaven, and ought not to be interfered with in any manner by anyone.
> We are pleased to give each of you our blessings, and we want you to come to dinner on Sunday, November fourteenth. We will spend the afternoon helping the two of you make your plans.
> Looking forward to that day, I am
> Sincerely, Florence Anthony

Jason hugged and kissed Clarice again, and on second thought he planted a kiss on the cheek's of each of the others standing there.

He ran to Charlie, who was waiting at the garden gate. He said to the horse as he picked up the bridle rein, "Think of that, old boy, will you? Everything is going to be just fine."

Charlie shook his head back and forth and snorted.

Lola told Clarice that Jason was meeting someone at Griffin's wharf to buy paint and make plans. This news left Clarice in a wonderment. She hadn't heard anything about Jason painting something. She was satisfied though, because he had informed her once that women were not supposed to know anything about men's business. He also told her that women were for loving and cooking. She laughed to herself when she thought about how little she knew about cooking.

The dinner on the fourteenth was a happy occasion. Jason and Clarice were fully in bloom. Lady Anthony took the place of an ecstatic mother of the bride, suggesting food for the reception and names of friends to invite.

The date of the wedding decided upon was to be December seventeenth, the same date as Lord and Lady Anthony's wedding. The place would be in the parlor of the Anthony home.

Maggie was to be the bridesmaid, Robin the flower girl, Lord Anthony would give the bride away, Henry would be best man, Governor Hutchinson would perform the ceremony.

December seventeenth was still five weeks away. Everyone would have plenty of time to prepare for the wedding and reception and also for making changes in the household.

Maggie agreed to make Clarice's wedding dress. She began searching the shops of Boston for satin and lace. She selected a picture of a French coquette from one of Lady Anthony's novels and was copying it for design. Marie was ordering Tomas around, demanding that he obtain one hundred clean and substantial chairs to be placed in the parlor for the guests.

Robin was busy at making paper roses to carry and strew along the stairway and hall in front of the bride. Jackson was putting extra wax on the chaise as Jason was borrowing it to take Clarice out to the Dedham Inn for a weekend honeymoon.

Henry asked John Slade to loan him his formal clothing to wear. He wanted to look elegant and aristocratic as Jason's best man.

Lady Anthony stayed at her desk hours into the night writing a hundred invitations.

Robin asked her mother not to invite the Hawleys, she didn't want to see Preston. Lady Anthony answered her in a stern voice, "I don't want to see any of these people either, but your papa says I have to. So you will have to see them also, including Preston, but you don't have to talk to him."

Monday morning when Clarice went to her window to check the weather as she did every morning as soon as she awoke, she was startled to see a company of militia marching along Temple Street. A thought came to her that John Hancock's company of cadets was out for practice and on the way to breakfast at the Cawing Crow, an eating and drinking place on Hawkins Street.

She had heard Lola speak of the place, of raucous behavior by the soldiers and riffraff of Boston. Once when she asked Jason if he ever gone there, he answered her, "Who do you think I am? What kind of person do you take me for? That place is run by the devil," but she saw him turn toward Lola and wink. That made her doubt his truthfulness.

She watched the cadets march on until they were out of sight. She couldn't get that scene out of her mind all day. She resolved to question Jason about it, but he never came to Beacon Hill that day. He never came again to the Anthony house until Wednesday, then he was in such a hurry he didn't wait until Clarice could get down stairs to meet him. He put the order of bread on the trestle table and said to Lola, "Tell my sweetheart that I will be back this evening. Tell her to meet me in the gazebo at seven o'clock. I will have only a minute to kiss her."

Clarice did herself over in a beautiful dress and hairdo and went to the gazebo at seven. There she waited over an hour; she got very cold. A chilly November wind was whipping the dried vines, still clinging to the lattice, causing their debris to break loose and huddle in little piles under the benches, where in the summer the crickets and grasshoppers did their love dances.

She gave up the waiting and went back into the house, entering through the French doors and crossing the dining room to avoid Lola, whom she knew was waiting with a hundred questions and remarks as to why Jason stood up his best girl.

Clarice was well aware that there was trouble brewing, and she was partly angry and partly sick with anxiety as to why Jason wouldn't confide in her.

The week went on; Jason never came to the house, nor did he send any messages. Clarice had her fears that perhaps he was getting cold feet about marrying her.

On the evening of the seventeenth, Lord and Lady Anthony, dressed in their finest, were driven away in a carriage belonging to someone else, another couple in formal dress. The couples were in gay spirits when they left the Anthony house.

Robin and Clarice were watching the departure from the parlor window. The child said to her governess, "Mama told me they were going to Mr. Richard Clarke's house to a party to welcome home Mr. Jonathan Clarke who has just come home from England. Papa told me I mustn't tell anyone where they have gone, but you know I don't keep secrets from you."

"I wonder why it is such a secret," said Clarice.

"Because of the rabble-rousers," answered the child. "Papa told Mama that the rabble-rousers are very dangerous. Do you know, Cee Cee…that Papa thinks Jason is a rabble-rouser? That at every meeting and party he not only provides goodies, he also provides information (that he learns from the king's men), to Samuel Adams and Mr. Bainbridge and Mr. John Hancock."

Clarice was amazed at Robin's abstruse suspicions of Jason. It was obvious that she completely believed her father.

"Robin, you can't believe that Jason is a spy or that he would do anything to hurt any of our closest friends." There was a bit of suspicion running through her own mind.

Jason arrived an hour early to help set up the buffet in the huge Clarke dining room. He was furnishing the petit fours, cream candy, and minted crumpets.

The guests were arriving in couples and bunches, laughing and bowing, kissing and hugging. It was a happy joyful bunch of friends and neighbors, eager to hear the news from England that Jonathan Clarke had brought home. Especially were they eager to hear about the tea ships and the bargains made with the East India Tea Company.

Right in the middle of the chitchat and greetings, a mob began to gather outside, and the prediction of Lord Anthony, that there might be violence, came true. First they shouted profane language and spat on the steps of Richard Clarke's house. Then they began to throw rocks and break windows.

The ladies rushed to the second floor and huddled in a bedroom. One of Mr. Clarke's guests opened a window and shouted at the mob to disperse or be fired upon. None of the rioters subsided their shouting and rock throwing.

Someone ran to the open window and fired a pistol over the heads of the mob, hitting no one but scaring some of them to turn and run. The rock throwing had ceased, and they were standing in groups talking as if plotting more mischief.

Jason came out to the front stoop and while waving his arms over his head to signal quietness, he gave out several shrill whistles and when the crowd had become still he began to talk to them; he knew them well.

"Friends and fellow countrymen, there is no use to disgrace yourselves in order to obtain whatever it is you want. Your desires will be much easier and faster accomplished by quiet and peaceful negotiating. Go home now and on

Friday come to the public meeting at Faneuil Hall, and there, perhaps, with proper procedure you may be heard."

When Lady Anthony rang her bell for Maggie the next morning, the briskly alert maid answered quickly for she could tell by the sound of the bell that her ladyship was much annoyed at something.

Before Maggie had time to say, "Good morning," Lady Anthony said, "Maggie, my dear, I simply hate every cobble stone, every roof top, every blade of grass; in fact, I hate everything about this horrible place, even its people. Do you know that a gang of ruffians tried to kill us last evening at the Clarke's? Some one of the gang was shooting off a pistol." Lady Anthony having escaped to the second floor didn't know that it was one of Clarke's guests doing the shooting. "Maggie I want to go home to London. I am afraid for my husband and child. To live in constant fear is not to my liking."

After a pause, she asked Maggie to bring her breakfast, reminding herself that no one at the party ever sat down to supper, and she hadn't eaten since noon the day before.

She ate her food with a ravenous appetite, saying nothing more to Maggie. When she finished eating she went to her sitting room. She sat for awhile gleaning what she could from the Boston Gazette which she snatched from Jackson's hand as he was bringing it into the house. She didn't even say "Good morning" to the abashed servant.

Clarice went early to see if there was a letter in the broken post. She and Jason were still using this method of communication, although it was no longer a secret. Sometimes when Jason was very busy and could not spend any time with Clarice, he would leave some token of his love in the old familiar posting place.

There was nothing there this time but a little green frog. "You can't possibly take the place of a letter from Jason," Clarice said to him, as she lifted him out of the soft rotten wood nest he had made for himself and put him in the dried leaves under the rosebush.

Robin opened her window and called down to Clarice, "Cee Cee, why are you out so early? Are you worried about Jason?"

"Yes, Robin, I am," answered the governess. "I don't understand his avoiding me so close to our wedding day."

She came back into the house and went to her room. Robin was sitting in the middle of Clarice's bed, holding Bo Tay.

Clarice plopped down into her armchair, picked up the tail of her dress, and wiped her eyes. Robin just stared at her but said nothing. She let loose of Bo Tay and told him to go and comfort Cee Cee. The little dog jumped from the bed, ran across the room, and jumped into Clarice's lap.

The governess couldn't help but love the little dog; he was very affectionate, licking her face and nuzzling her neck.

Maggie entered the room, and laying across her outstretched arms was the beautiful wedding dress she was making for Clarice.

"Clarice," she said, "you have to try on this dress before I can add the finishing touches. Come now, stand up and let me drop it over your head."

The skirt was full and flowing. Clarice looked beautiful in it. The bodice was molded around Clarice's "prefect red apples." The lace at the neckline was teasing and causing Clarice to blush as she ran her fingers around the tiny rose buds peaking out of the lace.

"Oh Maggie, this is too lovely for words. I am so happy I can't stand it. I think I will just die if anything happens to prevent our marriage."

Robin asked Maggie if she has been working on her dress and her own dress.

"I still have two weeks, Robin. I will get all the dresses finished by December seventeenth."

Robin summoned her mother into Clarice's room to give her approval, and that's when Lady Anthony announced that, "Madame Alexander, the couturier of Boston, is almost finished with my dress. It is powder blue grosgrain under lavender georgette, and it is ten yards around the bottom. It has a powder blue ruff standing up around my neck which tickles my earlobes and keeps me smiling."

Now all the females were in happy spirits. Clarice, it seemed, had forgotten that there was no message in the broken post.

The meeting on Friday, November nineteenth, was called to order by the governor. He began with a didactic speech, as if he were scolding children. The people began to hiss and boo. There was more than two thousand to shout at the governor.

He yelled out through his megaphone. "This state of the province is in possession of the process of government, in other words 'Mob Rule.'" A bit more calmly he said, "I have tried with all my power and strength to preserve peace and suppress all riotous assemblies but without success." He spoke of the violence that occurred at Richard Clarke's house, also his warehouse.

One of his council members, sitting away back in the audience yelled out, "The only way to prevent rioting and violence is for the tea consignees to resign right now."

After that the wrangling began and the people were very noisy. Nothing could possibly be resolved. The governor pounded his gavel very hard on the table and adjourned the meeting. He went straight to Milton Hill.

Later that day Richard Clarke wrote a letter to his sons empowering them to make whatever agreements they thought suitable. He vowed to fully support them in their decision. He then vanished from Boston. It was reported that he took his necessary belongings and went to his estate in the country.

The governor, after two more unsuccessful riotous meetings, which were just as agonizing to him as anything could be, decided to stay in Milton. Actually he was too tired and sick to govern.

It was evident now, in all corners of the province of Massachusetts, that England and the colonies were in a most unhappy situation—that Governor Hutchinson had become the most unpopular governor in colonial history.

Chapter Twenty-One

On a designated night Samuel Adams and John Hancock met at the Merry Mermaid. They knew if they were followed there nothing would be suspected because they were frequent customers of the establishment. They were early for the meeting so called. They had two or three beers before going into the back room.

The Club Nine members began showing up one or two at a time. When all were assembled, Samuel Adams began to talk.

"Friends, something drastic has to be done. We cannot dilly and dally over the imposition of the tea tax, and it is most evident that our government is not going to do anything but stall until they think we will give up and allow the tea to be unloaded. The ships are just sitting out there waiting for us to say, 'To hell with it,' and tuck our tails and go on crawling to British slavery."

Everyone in the room clapped hands.

Samuel Adams said, "Now Mr. Hancock has some words on the subject."

John Hancock, without any opening speech, said, rather excitedly, "Let's dump the damn stuff into the sea."

There was such a "hurrah," that Adams stood up, waving his arms and shushing the men. "Keep quiet," he uttered, "we don't want to let anyone out there," meaning in the tavern, "to know that we are in here." He sat down again.

John Hancock asked if anyone had any objection to dumping the tea. No one showed his hand. All were in favor of the procedure.

"Now," said Mr. Hancock, "it will take more than a hundred men. We must recruit some very patriotic men thoroughly dedicated to our cause, who believe in our freedom. If some, or all, of you will go out into the province if necessary to find them and talk with some of the men, if they are willing to take part in the 'tea party' and will swear to keep it a deep, dark secret until the actual time, then take their names and give them a time to meet for discussion."

Sometime during the next week the Gazette printed an announcement that had arrived from the Philadelphia Committee of Correspondence which said, "Our Tea Consignees have all resigned and Boston need not fear, the tea will not be landed here or New York. We fear you will shrink at Boston. You have failed us in the importation of tea from London and we fear this tea will be landed.

"May God give you virtue enough to save the Liberties of your Country."

Activities around the family fireside began to be quite subdued. Lady Anthony, it seemed, had lost much of her enthusiasm for the wedding and was staying locked in her bedroom. The reason, everyone suspected, was because her husband hardly ever came home. He was even sleeping at Province House or at the town home of the governor. Also he had been assigned a body guard, as Lady Anthony found out.

She sent a note to Maggie asking her to question Jackson to get some information about Lord Anthony's whereabouts and his political activities. She hated not being able to keep up with his progress.

Clarice was so worried about Jason she stayed in her room waiting for her bell to ring to announce his arrival. She believed that Henry would come home any minute with a message. She hadn't seen Jason for a week.

Robin was pouting and being very rude to everyone, refusing to eat or do her lessons. It was the frustrations of Clarice and her mother rubbing off on her.

Lola came home from market, grumbling to Maggie that the situation at the market was pitiful; there was no one there selling their produce. She said to Maggie, "I asked my old potato man where everybody was and he said, 'They's all at Fanny Hall or at Old South Church trying to cut each other's throats over the damn tea.'

"When I asked him why he wasn't there, too, he said, 'Hell, I don't want nuthin' to do with that gang of idiots, they ain't got sense enough to just dump the damn tea into the harbor and be done with it. That'd sure show 'em.'"

Maggie looked into Lola's market basket; all she saw was a shoulder of pork and some very small potatoes. "Is this all you bought, Lola?"

"Yes, it is, and it took every bit of the money her ladyship gave me. I didn't have enough left to buy myself a stein of beer."

The Dartmouth sailed into Boston Harbor on November 28 and sent a small boat ashore with the mail and messages. It anchored astern off the admiral's flagship at Castle William. Word of the ship's arrival was hastily dispatched to the Committee of Correspondence and Samuel Adams.

A courier, briefed in advance, was soon galloping off to Milton to notify Governor Hutchinson. Both Samuel Adams and Governor Hutchinson moved at once to handle their opposing tactics.

Orders went out to the Dartmouth from the Committee of Correspondence to bring the ship to town. Also orders went out, by Governor Hutchinson, to keep the ship in safe waters off the Castle William.

At the same time, the Club Nine was having printed a public notice which the members were displaying in every tavern and ordinary and tacking up on buildings that read as follows:

Friends Brethren CountrymenThat worst of plagues, the detested tea, shipped for this port by the East India Company, is now arrived in this harbor; the hour of destruction or manly oppositions to the machinations of tyranny stares you in the face; every friend to his country, to himself and posterity, is now called upon to meet at Faneuil Hall at nine o'clock this day (Monday), at which time the bells will ring to make a united and successful resistance to this last, worst, and most destructive measure of administration.

The Dartmouth was assigned twenty-five guards because of its other carges, expected and needed by Boston merchants. It moved into Rowe's Wharf where the guards stood by until all the goods ordered by merchants were unloaded. It was reported that British marines would board the ship and overpower the guards. In order to move the goods to safer storage, the ship moved to Griffin's Wharf and dropped anchor. None of its tea cargo was disturbed.

If the marines should attempt to unload any of the tea, or disturb it in any way, the Club Nine would certainly recruit armed rabble to the resistance.

A Boston merchant eager for action informed the club that not one pistol could be bought in Boston. A mad rush to buy arms had depleted the supply.

Every time loud noises permeated the atmosphere, Lady Anthony pulled her window shades and put chairs and tables against her door. She had frightful memories of the night at Mr. Clarke's house and felt sure it was going to happen at her house.

She knew well that Lord Anthony's appeasement mission was a failure. The fog was so heavy on the morning of December sixteenth that vehicles on Boston streets were moving at a snail's pace and burning their lanterns. The foghorns were making mournful sounds, and pedestrians were bumping into each other.

Clarice tossed and turned all night, getting up every hour to open her shutters a crack and peer out into the night. She was obsessed with her own personal feelings and had no thoughts concerning the unusual activities of the town.

It was December sixteenth, and the rehearsal for her wedding was to be at five o'clock and a dinner following at seven. She had not seen or heard from her fiancé for a week; she didn't know if he was dead or alive. He had told her several times that he was in danger.

Lola came up the back stairs and, after knocking, entered Clarice's room. She had brought a pot of tea and a plate of scones, which she could now make to perfection.

"Here missy, I know you have been pacing the floor, so have some tea," the forbidden fruit, "and quit your worryin' about Jason. He'll be here on time; you'll see."

Robin came into the room, looking sleepy and inquisitive. She plopped down in a chair and picked up the little dog and held him on her lap. She didn't say anything but began to sob and sniffle. Clarice fell on her knees beside the child and began to cry also.

Lola had a moment of anguish on her face as she said, "Why are you two acting like the world is comin' to an end?"

Clarice answered, "It my be, Lola, that is, for me anyway. I can't stand it if anything has happened to Jason. If he doesn't show up for the rehearsal, I'm breaking out of here to go and find him."

Lord Anthony came home a little before noon and gruffly told his wife not to disturb him, he had to have a little rest. As he laid himself down on the bed, he groaned and mumbled that he had been trying to answer the governor's messages, and every hour on the hour he had been rushing across the street to Old South Church to see what was going on at the meeting assembled there.

Florence told him to hush up and sleep. She removed his boots and loosened his shirt and pulled his trousers off. She massaged his feet and then she noticed that he was sleeping, but fitfully. She kissed his lips and his cheek and covered him, then tiptoed out of the room.

Robin encountered her mother in the hall. Her ladyship reached for the child's hand and led her over to the settee where they sat down.

"I know, dear, why you are so quiet. You are sorry that Clarice is getting married."

"No, Mama, that's not the reason. I have a headache from hearing those bells. They haven't stopped ringing for a minute since I woke up. Bo Tay has howled for hours. I'm sick of it."

"Yes, I am tired of the bells and the whistles, and I hate the awful look on your papa's face. He acts like doomsday is coming."

"Is it because he doesn't like Jason and doesn't want Cee Cee to marry him?"

"That's part of it, but he's worried about his friends, the Clarkes and the governor's sons and some others who are now isolated at the fort for their own protection."

"Is somebody trying to kill them?" asked the weary child.

"No, I don't think that is the reason they are there."

"Well, I still don't understand why the bells don't stop ringing."

Maggie was dusting and brushing the parlor furniture when Lola came to her, and, looking down-mouthed, she said, "Henry ain't showed up yet with the desserts for the rehearsal dinner; I wonder where he's at."

"He will be here in time, Lola. Stop your fretting. You know Henry; he's always late."

In a short time Lord Anthony was up from his nap and leaving the house again before the afternoon had gotten underway.

Lady Anthony called after him as he went out, "Be sure to be back here by five o'clock. I don't want to be embarrassed by your absence."

His lordship turned as he climbed into his carriage, "Just cancel the rehearsal; no one can be here today. I know the governor won't be here, and Copley won't be here to sketch the bride and groom."

Lady Anthony mumbled to herself, "Disgusting, disgusting," as she went into the hall and rang the bell for Lola.

Lola came to the hall and met her ladyship who was hurriedly writing a note at the hall desk.

"If Henry comes here within the next couple of hours, give him this note."

Lola said, "Yes, your ladyship, I will."

"Now," said Lady Anthony, "I'm going to bed and rest. I hope I will be alert during the rehearsal."

Lola was so curious to know what the note said, and she could not read. So she rang Maggie's bell immediately on reaching the kitchen.

"Here Maggie, read this for me," she said to the maid, when she answered the bell.

Maggie took the note, opened it, and looking aghast at Lola said, "This is for Henry; I must not read it to you."

Lola was quiet for a moment, thinking, trying to conjure up a plea that would cause Maggie to give in and read the note to her.

Lola said, "Oh, Maggie, you know how these people are. Is someone going to hurt somebody?"

"No Lola. Lady Anthony wants to hire Henry to follow her husband."

"What for?" asked Lola.

"She does not explain why, Lola."

Lola busied herself unnecessarily with punching the coals, with rearranging the kettles, with shuffling the logs in the wood box. After a few minutes she began to talk again.

"His lordship ain't been payin' much attention to Marie lately."

She paused for a moment then said rather jokingly, "Maybe he's found him another wench in town. Do you think?"

"No. No Lola. He's involved in the meetings between the political factions who are squabbling over the tea tax."

"Now Maggie, I don't believe his lordship has that much importance. The governor tooks care of all the politics."

Maggie said, "So be it, Lola, you're right," and she left the kitchen.

At that moment Tomas walked in. He had an ax in his hand that he was returning to the kitchen. "Hi there, my precious, I haven't been able to come to see you for a day or two because Lady Anthony ordered me to chop some greens for decorations, and I decided that while I was about it I might as well get us a Christmas tree. I've been out to Hyram Scott's farm two days in a row. Did you miss me?"

"Yes, I did."

"Well, I sure learned a lot talking to that old man. He says the colony is headed for war and Samuel Adams is trying to hurry it up."

"Don't think on it, Tomas; I don't believe it will happen."

"He says that's what all the fuss over the tea is about. To rile the rabble into shooting the soldiers."

"Don't talk about it, Tomas. Do you want some scones and tea? Sit down at the table. I want to warm your blood."

Tomas drank his tea and remained quiet for a short while.

Lola sat beside him wearing an expression of admiration.

He noticed her smile and covered her hand with his and sweetly said, "Let's go down in the cellar. Do you want to?"

"I sure do," said the smiling Lola, "I have two whole hours before I have to start cooking dinner."

Lola and Tomas were still in the cellar when loud knocking on the door brought Lola quickly up the stairs to the kitchen.

Henry was standing there, holding a rolled up piece of parchment. "Ring your bell for Clarice," he said, "I have to give her this and I have to wait for an answer."

"Is it from Jason?" Lola wanted to know.

"Yes, it's urgent, and I'm in a hurry."

"I guess he ain't comin' to the rehearsal; that's going to hurt Clarice pretty bad," said Lola as she jerked furiously on the bell cord.

Clarice, expecting Jason, was hurrying down the stairs when she saw Henry. She was overcome with fright as her shaking hands slowly unrolled the parchment.

Henry said to Lola, "Go back downstairs; this is very private and personal business." He felt like Clarice would burst out crying, and Lola must not know the reason.

Clarice read the note. It said, Pack a bag, simple warm clothes, disguise yourself, meet me in the gazebo right after midnight tonight. Our wedding must take place somewhere else. There will be no formal ceremony. I will explain later, I love you. Please send your answer by Henry. Jason.

For a moment or two Clarice just stood there as if in a trance, then she said to Henry, "Tell Jason I will do as he says; I will meet him right after midnight."

Henry left her standing in the middle of the floor, tears running down her cheeks. She had known for several days that something was blowing in the wind regarding the tea ships. Now she was certain that Jason was mixed up in it.

Lola came back into the kitchen while Clarice was still pondering the note from Jason. She said to the shivering girl, "Clarice, I'm on your side whatever it is."

Clarice said to Lola, "Someone is playing a trick on Jason and me. Will you put that brown cape that you wear to market on a chair by this door?" She pointed to the kitchen door that opened into the garden. "I want to borrow it later this evening for a few hours."

The Eleanor and the Beaver were also docked at Griffin's Wharf. The Eleanor had arrived December second and intended docking at Rowe's Wharf as John Rowe owned the ship. It so happened that some members of the Committee of Correspondence met the vessel and ordered its Captain Bruce to proceed to Griffin's Wharf. The order also specified that the Eleanor was not to unload any of its cargo of tea but could unload all other cargo and also take on freight that was waiting there, boxes of baled paper, and many kegs of rum. Then it was to set sail for a return trip to England.

The Beaver had arrived early that same morning. It was late in the arriving because it had been quarantined at an island off Cape Cod. Many of its crewmen were sick abed with smallpox. It was held up for ten days there before it could leave. The fumigation that had been necessary before the ship could reach port had penetrated the bales of tea and also the ship's sails. The smell of sulfur was sickening to everyone in the area of the Beaver's mooring.

The Committee of Correspondence, with the help of the Club Nine, had successfully recruited approximately one hundred and fifty of Boston's most daring, courageous, liberty-loving rascals for a brash, lawbreaking escapade to take place that evening.

The one hundred and fifty men were divided into five groups, four of twenty-five each and one group of fifty. They were directed to five secret locations to be disguised and then to meet together at Fort Hill and wait for the signal.

Not one of the men knew when Captain Rotch would return with a message from Governor Hutchinson. If he brought back a negative reply, then the tea party would take place.

The group of fifty had congregated and were quietly waiting, seated on kegs in a barn in back of Joseph Montford's Cooper's Shop. They were hidden from the door, in case anyone should look in, by large stacks of empty barrels. Not a word was being spoken, but momentarily one after another would leave his seat and go over to a small cart where his face would be painted and long feathers attached to his head with a beaded band. Every third or fourth person being painted had a long horse's tail attached to his head dress.

The signal to take off in a run toward Griffin's Wharf would come soon after Captain Rotch returned from the governor's home in Milton, where he had volunteered to go to try to persuade the governor to sign the permits for the tea ships to pass through the customs without paying the charges. The signal would be given only if the reply from the governor was a negative one, which it was.

Thousands of people were gathered in and around Old South Church waiting for Captain Rotch's return.

The makeup man and his helper were waiting at the door of the barn; they would lead the disguised runners to the dock if the message brought back by Rotch was no.

At six o'clock P.M. Captain Rotch returned on his galloping horse and called out as he hastily dismounted, "I have returned from the governor.

"His excellency told me he was willing to grant anything within the law and his duty to the king, that he could not give a pass unless the vessel was properly certified and all customs paid. He said he would make no distinction between my vessel, the Dartmouth, and any other."

When Captain Rotch finished saying this the people became angry and someone in the crowd yelled out, "Tea mingles well with sea water."

Within the next moment someone opened the barn door behind Montford's Cooper's Shop, and a herd of wild Indians began running down Milk Street toward Griffin's Wharf, howling and screeching.

Someone was heard to say, "Boston Harbor is a boiling teapot tonight."

The meeting, still in assembly, in Old South Church was adjourned, and the people rushed out into the street.

John Andrews was standing on his front porch watching the running mob. Mr. Bainbridge had joined him.

Some of the people were shouting insults; others were clapping hands and singing. Mr. Proffitt said to the two men standing there with him, "This is the beginning of a revolutionary war."

There were a dozen large canoes and several sloops tied up at the loading dock. When and how they were left there, no one could say. With haste and without noise, for by this time fear had overtaken most of the participants and onlookers, the Indians climbed into the waiting boats and rowed out to the Dartmouth, Eleanor, and Beaver, climbing hurriedly over the sides. Almost immediately bales of tea began flying over heads and canoes into the sea.

The constables, guards, and soldiers began shoving those who were watching from the dock and threatening arrest to anyone who would fish out any of the tea. This was almost an impossibility, for those who were left to man the canoes were using the oars to bash and burst open the bales, leaving the tea floating out with the tide.

By nine o'clock the raucous episode was over, and only a few were left standing around, watching. The tea was now history, and the Indians had all disappeared.

An old-timer was heard to say, "Ye'll ne'r catch one of 'em; they're slyer than swamp foxes."

At twelve-thirty A.M., Clarice put Lola's cape around her and went out to the gazebo. She had not packed a bag, because it would have been impossible to keep Robin from knowing. She had on her blue silk nightgown and her leather boots that she wore in winter weather.

Jason was waiting in the gazebo. He looked exhausted and scared. He was wet and had smears of red paint on his coat sleeve.

He took Clarice by the hand; he didn't take time to kiss her or say anything except, "Come on, honey, hurry; Henry is holding my chaise for me down on Marlborough. There are so many vehicles there, I hope mine won't be recognized."

Clarice could not have been told from Lola if anyone had seen the running couple.

The first ferry crossed at four A.M. Jason wanted to be the first carriage to drive on, so he would be the farthest from the south shore and first off on the north side of the Charles. He was thinking the constables, guards, and soldiers might be chasing around Boston looking for him.

Clarice had not said a word; she was trying to see where they were. She was in a completely strange place. She wondered what Maggie and Robin would think when they discovered her absence.

Lola had an inkling of what was going on. She kept up her vigil at the back door, watching for Henry to come home. She wanted to question him. Henry did not come home. He left at daylight December seventeenth with John Slade to a meeting with the Sons of Liberty in New York.

Lord Anthony returned to Province House after a short time at his home where he ate a meal and took a nap.

Lady Anthony noticed his exhaustion and was upset with him when he left the house for the second time. He returned again at six o'clock and muttered as he went into the parlor that he hoped he wasn't late for the rehearsal.

Lady Anthony scornfully assured him that the rehearsal had been postponed until eight o'clock next morning. She barked at him that none of the participants showed up, "The governor, Jason, Henry, or you." She added, "Why are you always so adamant to my plans and pleasures?"

"Florence, you know damn well that I am involved in the government of this colony, and sometimes I have to perform my duties. Please let's not argue now; I am a complete wreck."

He went into the bedroom, undressed, and got into bed, saying to himself, "Maybe I can rest until tomorrow."

This was not to be, for his lordship was wakened from his sleep while it was still very dark. It couldn't have been more than five o'clock A.M. when Jackson came and knocked at his door and called out, "There's a messenger here to see you, sir."

His lordship jumped out of bed and went very fast toward the hall, hopping along trying to get his pants on. He had already sensed what it was the messenger had to tell him.

Lady Anthony also had been disturbed from her sleep. She got out of bed and lit a candle. She felt a chill; she took the top blanket from the bed and wrapped herself in it. Her husband was getting into his shirt while running after Jackson, who was about twenty feet in front of him.

Jackson turned to look at his lordship and said, "Lord, sir, you have forgotten your shoes."

Anthony looked down at his bare feet and motioned Jackson on and yelled at him to, "Put the two grays to the laundelet while I go back for my boots."

As her husband entered the bedroom looking for his boots, Florence said, "Maurice, what are you doing? You have only been home a few hours; why are you going back to town at this hour?" She had heard him telling Jackson to put the grays to the laundelet.

Lord Anthony was in such a hurry he mumbled as he left the bed chamber for the third trip to town in twelve hours, "Don't know for sure, Florence, but I'll be back soon, I hope."

In spite of an icy drizzle coming down and a cold wind whipping coat tails and hats around, the streets and alleys were crowded with excited people. Everyone seemed to be headed toward Griffin's Wharf.

Lord Anthony could see that Jackson was having difficulty getting the carriage safely through the bedlam. "Halt here, Jackson. I will walk the rest of the way, it is only a short distance from here to the Green Dragon Tavern. That's where I will be. You find a hitching post wherever you can and wait for me."

His lordship left the carriage and walked down Atkinson's Street. He sidestepped a melee taking place right in front of the popular gathering place for the rebels and wharf workers of Boston.

A hullabaloo was in evidence all around the place. The people were in a jubilant mood. Anthony noticed that the celebrants were of the middle class. He heard some profane and slanderous phrases being shouted about.

As he entered the smoky, crowded room he recognized two members of the Committee of Safety standing by the window. He assumed they were waiting for him. He walked over to a table in the corner already occupied by three young men. He tossed a handful of shillings on to the table and said to them, "Take this and go find another place to sit." He wanted to be in the most inconspicuous place in the tavern. They snatched up the coins and immediately left.

With a crook of his forefinger he motioned for the Safety Members to join him. They came to the table at once. The three men leaned forward and put their heads together and began talking in low tones.

Lord Anthony learned that Indians of unidentified nation, or white men disguised as Indians, in numbers of more than a hundred had boarded the three ships, Dartmouth, Eleanor, and Beaver, and had dumped their cargoes of more than three hundred and forty bales of tea into the harbor.

The deed had been accomplished in darkness between seven and ten o'clock P.M. with stealthiness and rapidity. There had been no rioting or violence. No one had been injured. The guards had gathered in a bunch on the dock and had made no arrests or attempt to stop them.

A few curiosity seekers who had followed the running Indians to the wharf attempted to retrieve some of the floating tea chests but had been stopped. One poor devil stuffing his pockets with some of the wet stuff was pushed into the water, but due to his advanced age he was pulled out and taken to a warm house.

While his lordship and the two men were still at the table talking, John Andrews, who had attended the public meeting the day before, came over and joined them.

"This will be a morning recorded in history, aye sir?" were the words he said as he sat down looking straight into Lord Anthony's eyes.

Anthony's eyes were filled with anger. "This dastardly act will no doubt cause great suffering to the people of this rebel rooted colony," was his reply to Andrews. He softened his voice a bit and said, "If we can corner the actual culprits and give them proper punishment, maybe the rebel faction in this town will come to its senses. As it is, I am sure and I hope, the king will demand restitution for this brazen disregard of Parliament's law. This harbor as well as all the king's harbors should be closed at least until this tax matter is resolved."

When Anthony said that, Andrews got up and angrily left the tavern.

Lord Anthony, after a moment of shaking his head, said to the two Safety men, "He was invited to a wedding at my house this afternoon; I guess he won't be there, seems like I got his dander up."

One of the men spoke up, "He came in here to tell you something, sir. He couldn't get it out. He was afraid you would think he was lying."

"What was it? Do you know?"

"I hate to tell you, your lordship. He could be wrong."

"What was it? For God's sake, this is no time to be standing on principal. If you know something, out with it."

"It's that wedding you mentioned; the groom was one of the Indians. It is thought that he was the ring leader."

"Who told him that? What proof do they have?" Anthony's face was getting redder by the minute.

"He was seen washing paint off his face at a rain barrel behind Joe Thomas's stable a little before midnight."

His lordship was silent. He made no more comment, but he was restless; he crossed and uncrossed his legs, and he squirmed around in his chair. He kept looking over his shoulder, and his eyes were roaming all over the room. After a moment or two he began to question the man who had told him what Andrews knew, "Are you absolutely sure that McKenzie was the one seen at the rain barrel? It could have been someone else. Do you have any other proof?"

"Well, yes, his horse was tied up outside Monfort's Cooper Shop at the time of the tea party."

"That's proof enough," said his lordship. "I don't care to hear anymore; I will look into it."

He remembered that he had been told that the wedding rehearsal would take place at eight A.M. that morning.

He pushed himself back from the table and got up, leaving his two friends sitting there. He stomped out of the Green Dragon, walking very fast along the street looking for his carriage.

Maggie was sweeping the hearth in the library when Lord Anthony arrived at the front door, banging the knocker with angry vigor. He came in, slammed the door behind him, and shouted at Maggie to, "Go and tell you mistress to come to the library at once."

"Sir, she is busy at the moment having her hair dressed."

"You heard what I ordered you to do. Now go and tell my wife I want her here in five minutes. Do you understand?"

Maggie jammed the broom into the corner so fast she knocked over a Chinese Temple Urn that was decorating the corner. Without turning to see what she had done, she bounded up the stair steps as fast as her feet would carry her to her ladyship's dressing room.

When Lady Anthony saw Maggie entering the room breathless and looking scared, she said, "Maggie, what is it?"

"Lord Anthony demands your presence in his library, ma'am, immediately."

She took a lace mantel from a nearby chair and wrapped it around her naked shoulders and breasts. She said to the hairdresser, "Madam Pompadier, I will be back in a few minutes." She followed Maggie down the stairs.

When Maggie began her sweeping again, Lady Anthony told her to leave the room. She then said to her husband, "What do you want, Maurice? I was right in the middle of getting my hair done up into one of those beehives, ridiculous as they are. I swore I would never subject myself to looking like a stack of hay, but I changed my mind when I saw Charlotte Prescott wearing one."

Lord Anthony whirled around to face her, "Good God, Florence, the whole damn colony of Massachusetts is messing with hell and you're idling away your time having your hair combed. Sit down," he commanded her.

Florence was beginning to feel the dong of doom, and curtly she said, "Maurice, have you forgotten that we're having a wedding here this afternoon and I still have much to do?"

Stormingly he replied, "There's not going to be any wedding, Florence. I want that goddamned rebel arrested."

'What do you mean? No wedding?" Florence was absolutely shocked at what her husband said.

At that moment, Maggie knocked loudly on the door. It was swung wide open, and she stepped inside the room and blurted out in a very excited voice, "Clarice is gone; Lola said she left with Jason about midnight."

"How does Lola know that?" asked Lady Anthony.

His lordship was already rushing past Maggie and hurrying out of the room, swearing under his breath. Lady Anthony dashed after him but changed her mind, suddenly, and ran up the stairs to Clarice's room.

Robin was standing by the window, still in her nightgown. She heard her mother enter the room, but she did not turn around to greet her.

Lady Anthony saw that Clarice's bed had not been slept in. She looked in the closet and saw that the governess had not taken any clothes. She picked up the little brass clock and held it to her ear. She said to herself, but out loud, "Well she won't be gone long; everything is still here. Perhaps we are all jumping to conclusions too soon."

When she put her arm around Robin and pulled her up close, the little girl began to sob.

"Robin, we believe that Clarice and Jason have eloped, but I believe she will come back for her things and we will talk to her and maybe we can make some sense out of this."

Robin, rubbing her eyes with her fist and holding on to her mother, said, "I don't see how she could run away from all the pretty wedding parties we worked so hard to have."

Maggie walked into the room, and Lady Anthony spoke to her, "Maggie, will you be Robin's companion for awhile until Clarice returns?"

Maggie reached for Robin's hand and said, "Come Robin, let's you and I and Bo Tay go and see the wedding cake that was just delivered."

Chapter Twenty-Two

It was seven o'clock a.m. when Parson Smith answered a knock at his door. He opened it a crack to see who it was, then he swung it wide and thrust out his hand, "Jason, Jason, come in. What are you doing in Lynn this early in the morning?"

Jason looked a bit sheepish, "I have brought my girl; we want you to marry us."

"When?" asked the Parson.

"Right now, if you please."

"What's the rush, Jason? Is she in trouble?"

"No. No, I'm in trouble. I'm trying to escape to some place where it will take a little longer to find me." The Parson did not know about the tea party.

"What kind of trouble are you in, son?" the bewildered man asked as he stepped outside to join Jason, closing the door behind him.

Clarice leaned forward to look out of the curtained chaise, "Jason," she called out, "how long is it going to take? I am cold." The parson walked out to the chaise. He extended his hand to Clarice and invited her to "Come in where it is warm."

The parson reluctantly married the couple. His wife "stood up" with them. They signed the parson's wedding book, and when the words "I now pronounce you husband and wife" were said, Jason took five pounds from his pocket and handed it to the parson.

He picked Clarice up into his arms and began kissing her mouth, her cheeks, her neck, and breathlessly he said, "Thank God, now you are mine."

He turned toward the door to leave, and Mrs. Smith put her hand on his shoulder to halt him and said, "I believe every marriage should begin with prayer."

"Oh yes, I do too," said Clarice, and she and Jason and the parson bowed their heads and the parson began to pray. Jason was still holding Clarice across his arms. When the parson had prayed for fifteen minutes Jason called out "Amen," and the parson closed his prayer.

Mrs. Smith held the door open while Jason carried Clarice to the waiting chaise. He tucked her in and wrapped her feet into the chaise robe and got in beside her.

"My darling," he said, "can you believe we are married?"

Clarice gave him a very sweet smile as she said, "Jason, I love you."

It was eight o'clock A.M. when Jason, with Clarice in his arms, kicked open the door to his home in Lynn, Massachusetts. He carried her to a large rocking chair in front of the fireplace and sat her in it. He then turned to the hearth and lit the fire that was already laid with fresh cedar shavings and a big oak log.

When the fire was roaring, Jason turned and pulled the rocking chair closer to the warmth, then he tilted Clarice's chin, kissed her, and said, "Darling, I am going to put Charlie in the barn; make yourself at home for this is your home and everything that's in it," and jokingly he added, "including me."

When he left the room, Clarice took a look around. She saw the huge grandfather clock in the corner and a very large chest of drawers and wondered what was in the drawers. She saw a table with a drawer and on it a glass ink pot and several quills.

Through the wide door she could see the kitchen; the hearth with cooking spits and hooks was at least ten feet wide and five feet deep. She saw a dozen or more pewter spoons in a spoon holder on the wall.

As she sat in the rocking chair and began to feel very cozy, she thought, I am going to make this home so happy for Jason and me that he will never want to leave my side.

When Jason came back from the barn he found his bride sleeping soundly in the chair. He tiptoed past her to put on another log, but he awoke her and she said, "Jason, dear, are you cold? We could go to bed until the house warms up."

The smile on Jason's face was from ear to ear. He didn't answer her; he just hurriedly picked her up and carried her upstairs, taking the steps two at a time.

No one in Lynn saw Jason or Clarice for several days, but the next morning, after the wedding, Jason opened the door a crack to see what the weather was like and found a large basket of food on his front step. In it was pumpkin pie, jam, potatoes, ham, apples, cheese, onions, cider, tea, rum, homemade bread, cake, and nuts. He knew Parson Smith had left it there but had too much consideration for the newlyweds to knock or let himself be seen.

Jason brought the basket inside and called to Clarice, who was still hidden way down in the big feather bed, "Come, dear, and see what the parson has brought—and not a minute too soon; I'm raving mad with hunger."

Clarice came down the stairs barefooted and with Lola's cape wrapped around her. She got a package of tea out of the basket and went into the kitchen. She put some water on to boil as Jason stood beside her punching up the hot ashes on the hearth.

"I'm going to make us some tea," she said, "then I will explore the basket further to see what I can find for our breakfast." She was shivering; the house was cold.

Jason took her into his arms, and, after kissing her over and over, he said, "I must tell you all about what happened Thursday night, but first I must tell you, we won't be drinking tea anymore until the tea situation is settled."

"Jason," she said, "I don't understand the tea situation, but I am cold and hungry and I'm going to have some tea right now."

Jason smiled and kissed her again, and he said, "We'll pretend it never happened; if anyone asks us any questions we will pretend that we are ignorant of any facts. All we know is hearsay."

After a day or two Jason took a job in the Lynn shipyard. He left early in the morning and did not return until after dark. Clarice was alone all day, except for Mrs. Smith, who came often to help her with all the new experiences she found herself involved in.

To keep herself and her house warm she had to carry wood and keep poking the fire, to keep the doors and window cracks chinked to keep out the cold air. She had never been exposed to such cold weather. Clarice had never known how to build fires, chop wood, clean house, do laundry, make candles, or go to market.

At her home in Birmingham, the boys who worked at her father's foundry did all the chores. She spent her time tutoring children or reading and writing. This she did for the poor citizens of Birmingham who had no schooling but desired to send letters to their children or relatives in faraway places.

Jason came home the fifth night from his job and announced that he had to go out right after supper because he had joined a drill team and would spend two hours every night learning to shoot a musket and to march to the beat of a drum. Clarice became angry and stormed at him that it was only the beginning of their marriage and she thought he was starting it off very badly. He was neglecting his duties of teaching her how to cope with running a home.

The loving husband took his bride in his arms and kissed her and said, as he stroked her hair and neck, "It does seem that way, dear, but I have to work at a job since I no longer have the bakery shop, and the drill thing is necessary because this colony has to protect itself."

"Protect from whom or what?" asked the astonished Clarice.

"From the British soldiers. You know that," Jason answered her as he released his arm from around her waist.

"Jason, I'm British; are you afraid of me?"

"Of course not, dear, but the soldiers are unpredictable."

"Why are they here? Will they always be watching us like we are about to steal something from them? Are they our dangerous enemies?"

"No, Clarice. It's politics and greed. It's not for you to worry about. Suppose we change the subject and go for a walk. There is something I want to show you." He was thinking of the rock. "Get your wraps and boots. It is way back on the farm, and it is very special."

"The only wrap I have is Lola's cape."

"Then wrap a blanket around you; there is one in the chest." He pointed to the blanket chest in the corner.

"What day is this, Jason? I have forgotten to keep up with the time."

"This is December twenty-fifth, dear—Christmas—too bad we didn't remember to hang our stockings last night."

Clarice laughed and said, "Wouldn't have done any good anyway, but I have the best Christmas present of all: I have you."

Her expression changed to one of sadness when she thought of Robin. "Do you know, Jason, I can't help thinking of Robin. I made her some clay ornaments and a dried flower arrangement. I hope Maggie will remember to give them to her."

Jason saw the pain on his wife's face and he asked, "Are you homesick for the Anthonys?"

"Maybe just a little bit, for Robin. Her parents have been cross with her most of the time lately, and Maggie is not used to coping with her problems like I am. It was because of the frustrations over the tea situation, I am sure, Robin didn't understand the change in her parents."

Jason held the cape while Clarice swirled it around her, then the blanket, but she soon decided the blanket was too much. She couldn't walk with so much weight on her back.

The two left the house with their arms around each other and headed toward Jason's favorite place, the Shiny Squatt.

Jason carried the blanket, and when they reached the rock, he spread it on the ground on the sunny side and they sat on it. He told her the stories about his father and mother and the fishing trip when his father was out in the storm. They stayed at the rock for an hour or more until it got late and colder and the snow flurries began to dim their vision.

"Jason, it is good to be back by the warm fire," Clarice said as she went into the kitchen to prepare something for them to eat.

Jason followed her and heaped wood onto the hearth. He put his arms around her and kissed her and said, "I have something for you, dear," and he took six shillings from his pocket and took her hand and put the coins into it. "Here is my first pay for my first three days of work at the yard. Merry Christmas, darling."

"Jason, what will I do with it?" she asked.

"Whatever you want to do with it. Spending it for a coat would be a good beginning."

Clarice took a sugar bowl from the shelf and dropped the coins into it.

"There," she said, "is where it will be when we need it. I have a coat in my closet at the Anthonys; if we ever go back I will get it. Until then I have Lola's cape."

Jason realized at that moment he had married a woman of wisdom, a frugal, conscientious, caring person.

It got dark and the two lovers, husband and wife, sat in the big rocking chair by the fire and talked and laughed and rubbed noses, for Clarice was cuddled in Jason's arms. They did not light a candle, for the glow of the flickering flames from the dry cedar made light enough. When Clarice fell asleep on Jason's shoulder, he quietly carried her upstairs and put her to bed.

The twenty-eighth of December a packet of letters arrived, delivered by messenger. The outside wrapper was addressed to Mrs. Jason McKenzie. It was the first time Clarice had seen her new name written out. It thrilled her. As she ran her finger back and forth over it, she said, "I love that name."

She untied the string, and three letters were enclosed, one from Robin, one from her parents, and one from Tom Fellows.

She read Robin's letter first.

> Dear Cee Cee,
> We can never tell you how much we love you and miss you. Please come and spend New Year's day with us and tell us all about your new home and let us tell you about us. We are going home to England very soon, much sooner than we expected. Maggie is going with us to be my governess.
> We will have a farewell party on January first. Please come.
> I love you,
> Robin

Next she read the letter from her parents.

> Our Dear Precious Daughter:
> We received Jason's letter, asking for your hand. You are married by now, according to Jason's letter. We hope you will be very happy.
> We answered at once giving our permission. You are so young to be married. Write to us as soon as you are settled. We want to hear from you. We love you and miss you very much. Your Papa and Mama.
>
> P.S. We are sending you your grandmother's silver spoons. They are now being engraved with the initials "McK." You will receive them in about six months.

Clarice opened Tom's letter and read:

> My Dearest:
> I heard from your mother that you are to be married. Congratulations and good wishes for you and Jason. I am very sad that you couldn't wait for me. I love you very much and always will love you.
> Tom

Clarice read Robin's letter again. She could hardly believe what she was reading. Evidently they did not hate her for running away with Jason. She was trembling and tears were falling onto the letter as she kissed it and rolled and tied it up again.

"I wouldn't give up Jason and my marriage for anything in the world," she said to herself, "but I would like to go and see them before they leave."

She was laughing with happiness as she ran down the road later to meet Jason coming home from the shipyard.

She handed him the letter from Robin, then she put her arm around his waist and reached up and kissed his cheek.

They stood in the road while Jason read the letter. He smiled when he finished it; he rolled it and stuck it in his shirt. He then lifted Clarice into his arms and carried her, kissing her all the way, back to the house.

As he put her down at the door, she asked him, "May we go? Please?"

He answered, "Maybe we will go. I need to get some things from my shop."

"And I need some clothes," said Clarice, as she tightened Lola's cape around her. For ten days she had been wearing her nightgown under the cape, taking it off only to launder it. Jason and Clarice drove the chaise, with Charlie hitched to it, to Boston on a cold blustery December thirtieth. They went straight to Jason's Charles Street Bakery shop, where they spent the night in Jason's room. Charlie was happy to be in his old stall.

After spending some time looking around, Jason felt sure that someone had been there, probably searching the place. He said nothing to Clarice about his suspicions.

Next afternoon at about four o'clock Jason helped Clarice out of the carriage at the Anthony garden gate. He kissed her and held her and wished her a Happy New Year.

He told her before they left his shop that he would not be visiting the Anthonys with her. He said he had important work to attend to. He told her to be at the gate waiting for him next afternoon at the same time.

The first person Clarice saw on entering the house was Lola. She came up behind her and put her hands over Lola's eyes and said, "Guess who?"

Lola screamed out, "Cee Cee, my dear, how good to have you back. Have you heard about the tea party?"

Clarice exuberantly said, "Happy New Year, Lola, I'm glad to be back. No, I have not heard about the tea party. The first thing I have to do is go to my room and get some clothes on. I've been wearing my nightgown and your cape for two weeks." She added, "I'm glad I had your cape. Thanks very much."

As Clarice headed toward the stairs, Lola asked, "Are you married?"

"Of course, Lola, didn't Henry tell you?"

"He ain't been here since you left; nobody knows where he's at."

"Doesn't anyone here know that Jason and I are married?"

"I think his lordship and Lady Anthony know, but I don't know how they found out."

Parson Smith had sent the record of the marriage to the Gazette on the eighteenth of December. Lola could not read the paper, so as to understand it, so she did not know.

On entering her room Clarice met Robin, and the child became almost hysterical with joy. She flew into Clarice's arms, while loudly calling for Maggie to "Come and see who is here."

Maggie came into the room, smiling and full of enthusiasm and questions. She asked, "Where's Jason?"

Clarice hated to say he wasn't coming. She said, "He has some urgent business to attend to and won't be able to come."

Both Maggie and Robin looked disappointed. Maggie said "Too bad, I expect he will hear lots of exciting news while in Boston."

Clarice said, "I hope he will hear all about the tea party, of which I have only heard smithereens. If you know anything, please tell me."

At dinner that evening the Anthonys were icy cool and hardly had anything to say to Clarice.

Lord Anthony, when first entering the dining room and seeing Clarice, said, "Well, I see the wayward child has returned."

Clarice answered him, "No, sir, I have not returned—that is, for good. I am the happiest woman alive. Also I have not come as a 'wayward child.' I came because Robin invited me and I wanted to see her very much."

Lord Anthony spoke again without looking at her, "May I ask, if I dare, where is your rebel husband?"

Clarice hesitated for a moment before answering, then she said, "I don't exactly know, sir, but I think he is taking care of some important business."

"Like flunking for the Club Nine?" asked Anthony.

"What, sir? I don't understand," said the puzzled Clarice.

Florence spoke up, "Maurice, you're being cruel. Can't you see Clarice knows nothing about the Club Nine?"

Lord Anthony's face was red. It meant he was slowly trying to depress his anger. Lady Anthony gave her husband a surly look and began to talk.

"Clarice, we are all very glad you came. Robin is doing quite well with Maggie, and we are so pleased. You may stay here as long as you like, but if you do stay you will be taking Maggie's old job. Also, I hope you will be well entertained tomorrow by Lola and Maggie. We are invited to the Hawleys' for a New Year celebration, and we are taking Robin with us. I suppose Robin told you that we are leaving Boston for England as soon as we can get passage. If you have decided by that time that you wish to return, please let us know in time to reserve passage for you. Your husband, also, if he desires to go."

"Thank you ever so much, you ladyship, but Jason and I are happy and he would never leave his home and I won't ever leave him; I love him dearly."

New Year's Day was gloomy outside and gloomy inside. A soft snow came down during the night and made a cold dampness, even in the house, because the fires were not being stoked and replenished. Since Michael was no longer there to do the work, fires were no longer cheerful. The kitchen wood box was more often empty than full, and the wood was not dry and easily flammable.

Lola usually wore a grumpy expression. The poor woman was overworked. She also had bad teeth and ingrown toenails causing her much pain.

Very early on the morning of January first, Clarice went to the kitchen to make herself some tea. She didn't expect Lola to be up, but she couldn't sleep either, so she came very soon and joined Clarice.

The two of them sat at the trestle table and talked while sipping their tea. Clarice spoke reluctantly, "I suppose I should not be having this tea; Jason told me to avoid it and drink coffee or sassafras instead. He says it is going to be very scarce. We may not be able to get tea of any kind from any source."

Lola was gulping big swallows; she caught her breath and replied, "Them big Whigs like Hancock and Adams ain't going to be short of tea. They got plenty in their store rooms."

"Oh no, Lola, they have destroyed what they had stored. Jason says no patriotic American who wants to be free from England is going to drink Tory tea."

Lola asked, "Why do you call it Tory Tea?"

"Because the tea coming into Boston is going to no one except Tory merchants, like the Clarkes and the sons of the governor, Benjamine Faneuil and Joshua Winslow. They will then put a price on it; add a tax; which is fixed by Parliament, and sell it to their customers, who most likely can't afford the cost."

"How do you know all this?" asked Lola.

Clarice sighed and fiddled with her spoon, tapping it against her saucer. "I didn't know it until last night. As I was on my way to my room I noticed a stack of the Gazette on the hall table. I took a few copies with me, and I stayed up reading them almost all night. It opened my eyes to what's been going on. I feel guilty because I know Jason didn't want me to know. He doesn't want me to worry about him. How can I help it?"

Clarice continued to talk but as if talking to herself; Lola wasn't taking it in. "Now I know why he didn't tell me. He was most likely one of the mob, maybe the ring leader, dumping the tea." She laid her hand on Lola's arm to get her attention. "I think Henry was probably one of them too, and that is the reason why he has disappeared."

Clarice jumped up from her seat at the table and turned around as if going out of the room, then she sat down again beside Lola and asked very earnestly, "Lola, don't you have any idea where Henry is and when he is coming back?" Lola usually knew all of Henry's secrets and what he was doing and where he was spending his time. "I want to talk to him."

"No, I don't," answered Lola; her expression was as if she was in a trance or trying to remember if she knew something. She said, "He ain't been here since you left; I already told you that."

"Good Lord! Lola, do you realize that if they are caught they will be hung?"

"Oh my God!" exclaimed Lola in an excited voice.

Robin came into the kitchen, followed by Maggie. She went straight to Clarice and put her arms around Clarice and hugged her neck. "Cee Cee I love you. Won't you please come home to England with us?"

"I can't leave Jason, Robin, and he won't come. He has too much here to take care of. I love you too, and I will write you long letters telling you wonderful stories about my life. I'm going to be living so close to the ocean that I can take my skiff out on calm days and dip my net for small fish and shells.

"I know you are going to have happy times with Maggie. She has had some wonderful experiences to tell you."

January 1, 1774

It was eleven o'clock when Jackson picked up the reins and drove the chaise away carrying Lord and Lady Anthony, Robin, and Maggie to the Hawleys. Robin had put up such a torrent of objection to going that Lady Anthony decided Maggie would have to go to keep her comforted.

Clarice stood on the stoop sheltering her head with the same blue velvet hood she had worn the first time she ever set foot on that doorway.

She and Robin were throwing kisses and waving goodbye.

While lingering there for a few moments she had a longing for Jason. She wished she had not asked him to come to Boston for New Year's Day. If they had stayed at home they would not have the long trip in the cold back to Lynn that was facing them now. As she went into the house she thought of how cold the Anthonys had been to her. She felt the cold chill of the house and thought of the cold weather outside.

She looked around for something to read. She found the new almanac and entertained herself with it for awhile. She went to her room and gathered up her things. The first things she put into her satchel were her blue chamois slippers and her little brass clock.

She did not pack any of the clothes the Anthonys bought for her. When she had filled her little cloth satchel with only the things she had brought from her home, she closed it and carried it down to the kitchen. She sat in a chair by the window where she could see the street. She was eagerly waiting for Jason.

Bo Tay came over by her chair, and she picked him up and held him on her lap and cuddled him and kissed him. She said to the little dog, "I am going to miss you very much." He licked her face, she tickled him, he licked her neck, and she laughed. Then she said, "I'm going to miss robin more than I can say, but I think you and she will have a very happy life under Maggie's teaching."

Lola had left earlier to attend one of her meetings. She had said to Clarice, "You ought to be glad that you have better things to do than flunky around here for an eight-year-old child and be bossed by her parents. This has been one unsettled household since that tea dumping, and I am so confused. I am happy that you got out in time."

Clarice realized that Lola was worried and tired. She was probably wondering what she would do next.

Jason came an hour early. He had hoped to see Jackson or Henry to ask some questions. He had a big smile when Clarice ran down the garden walk to meet him, carrying her things gathered up in her arms. She had seen his chaise when it turned the corner onto Beacon Street. She flew into his outstretched arms, dropping her belongings into the snow, "Oh! Darling, I am so glad to see you. This day has been awful."

Jason held her and kissed her and told her how much he had missed her. He tilted her chin and said to her, "Take a good look at the broken post, my dear. We will never need it again because I am never going to be so far from you that we have to write letters. I'm always going to be in kissing distance."

He picked up her things, brushed the snow off, and put them into the chaise. He lifted her onto the seat and got in and buttoned down the curtains. He took her hand and squeezed it and kissed it. He said, "We will be a little late, my sweet; you just lie back and sleep. We'll be home before midnight."

Clarice closed her eyes. Her mind said to her, Don't tell him about how awful today was and don't tell him that I found out about the tea party. She lay her head on his shoulder and mumbled, "This is Heaven."

Chapter Twenty-Three

January, February, March, 1774

Clarice Creighton McKenzie was trying to be brave, but these months were very hard to get through. The weather was very bad, and it was hard to keep the house warm. Many days were dark as if it were night twenty-four hours a day. Sister Smith did not come often; she said she was getting too old to plow snow.

Jason left the house at daybreak every morning to walk two miles to the shipyard. He could have ridden Charlie, but the horse was getting old and he didn't want to expose him to the cold wind, so he stood in the barn all day with Panzy in her stall next to him.

Clarice enjoyed caring for the horses, she learned to curry and brush them down; she learned to shell corn and pitch hay. Jason spent every Sunday chopping wood and carrying it to the house, enough for a week.

Five evenings each week, Monday through Friday, Jason left the house immediately after supper to go to John Trumbull's farm where he met fifty or sixty other men, all neighbors and friends, where practicing the art of riflery and other war-like activities were studied and discussed. These men spent four to six hours each evening loading and shooting rifles, cleaning and repairing rifles, and learning to form ranks and march. In each man's mind was the premonition that very soon these tactics would be put to use.

Clarice became irritated at any conversation that included the mention of a revolutionary war. The anxious young wife would wait up for her husband to come home. She would sit near the fire and do hand sewing, which she could do to perfection, or knitting, which Sister Smith had taught her. Most of the time Sister Smith taught Clarice the fundamentals of the Bible, going into tiresome, or so Clarice thought, details of the powers of the Holy Ghost. Sometimes Clarice would fake a nap, only to have Sister Smith give her a vigorous shake and call out, "Wake up, child, and listen."

The one thing that brought joyful stimulus to a downhearted Clarice was the newspaper Jason brought home three times a week, the Boston Gazette. The eager young wife would absorb every printed word.

Late in February she turned to the notice of Ships Sailings, which she always studied carefully to learn who was either going, or coming, from England. In this particular issue she read, Sailing for Liverpool, March 1, 1774, Brigantine Clementine, of Royal British Line, Captain, Sir Ancel Helmsley, Grace Lane Devonshire.

Heading the passenger list, she read: Lord Maurice Anthony, Lady Florence Anthony, nine-year-old Robinette Anthony, Governess Marguerite Jeaneau, Valet and Housekeeper Tomas and Marie Straight. Baggage, two hundred pounds. One small dog.

Clarice ran to Jason with the news. "March first is only four days away. Don't you think we should be at the wharf to wish them bon voyage?"

"No, I do not think we should be at the wharf to wish them bon voyage. It would only make it harder for you and them, too. Besides, I cannot afford to lose a day's pay to make a trip to Boston."

"I know you are right, Jason. I will write a note to send to Robin by the stage. Will you deliver it tomorrow morning to the stage station?"

Clarice wrote a very sweet note wishing Robin smooth sailing and a happy return to her English country manor home. She put it on the table by the door and reminded Jason not to forget it.

Next morning Jason left by the back door, so as to look in on Panzy and Charlie; therefore, he forgot the letter.

When Clarice discovered that the letter had not been taken, she vowed she would take it to the stage station herself. She put on her coat and opened the door to see a downpour like she had never seen before.

There was nothing else to do but give up the idea of the note reaching Robin before sailing time. She sat in the rocking chair and tried to envision the huge sailing ship and her family boarding it without her.

She looked at the letter still in her hand and tossed it into the fire, "No use making myself remorseful; I will get busy doing the chores."

She changed the furniture around and sharpened the wicks of all the candles; she stirred up some tea cakes and sliced enough ham to last a week.

When Jason came home, she scolded him for forgetting the letter. He asked her where it was; he would put it in his pocket and take it tomorrow.

"I burned it. No use trying to reach Robin now, it is too late."

Jason apologized for forgetting to take the letter. He put his arms around Clarice, and she gazed into his eyes and said, "I forgive you, dear, but if it hadn't been raining so hard, I would have walked to the station with it myself."

"My darling, that would not have been a wise thing to do. It is dangerous out there; you could have run into guards who would have questioned you. There are spies everywhere."

"What kind of spies?" asked the wide-eyed Clarice.

"British spies," Jason answered gruffly.

"Oh bosh! Jason, they have nothing to spy on as far as I am concerned."

"They could question you about me."

"What kind of questions?" she asked.

"Cee Cee," it was the first time he had called her Cee Cee since their marriage, "the authorities are still hoping to find the participants of the Tea Party, the episode of dumping tea, on December sixteenth. They could confuse you to no end and might even cause you to lie and admit that I was one of the Indians."

Clarice looked him in the eye. "I am not so sure it would be a lie."

Her remark startled him. He never suspected she had any reserved feelings about his whereabouts the night of December sixteenth.

He thought to himself, My God, did I take her for an imbecile? Of course she knows.

He reached for her hand and drew her up to him. "Please don't go out walking without me or Sister Smith."

"I promise, Jason, but there are a lot of facts I believe you could tell me."

"My dear wife," he said, "women do not need to know about every wheel that turns in a man's mind. There is no place in politics for a beautiful girl like you."

"There will be some day, Jason; you just wait and see."

For the last few days in February Clarice fantasized about living at the Anthonys. She was busy helping Maggie and Lola get things together and packed. She was giving Robin last minute instructions and helping her decide which books to take along to read while on the ship. This imagination of hers was making her nervous and she became almost ill. At one point she wished very much that she was also going home to England. She sighed and opened the door to breathe in deeply some salty air.

When she looked at the hand-drawn calendar that Jason had made and noticed every day marked off through February, she sighed and said, "Dear me, it is March first; today is March first." She excitedly ran to the kitchen to look at her little brass clock on the kitchen mantel and discovered it was half past nine. She caught her breath as she ran to the bedroom up stairs and opened the bottom drawer of the big walnut bureau and took out a huge brass spyglass. It was heavy, and she held it across her shoulder as she climbed the dark, narrow stairway to the roof.

There was a two-foot-wide balcony across the east side of the sloping roof. She knew it was called a widow's walk," but she did not wish to use that distinction, so she called it the "lookout."

She opened a shutter from the inside of the attic and stepped out onto the lookout, which looked rotten and she wondered if it would hold her weight.

She put the glass to her eye and adjusted it. She knew how to do this since a seaman had taught her during their sailing to America.

"Perhaps," she said, "I can see the Clementine from here."

There were at least a dozen sailing ships near the Lynn shore, and she realized it would be difficult to see a ship much father out. It would be especially hard to recognize the Clementine, since she had never seen it. She put down the spy glass and leaned against the shingles of the roof. I will rest a while, she thought.

Standing there on the lookout, but leaning against the roof, she felt the warm morning sun shining on her face. She closed her eyes and wondered what was taking place at this time with Robin and Maggie.

If Clarice could have seen what went on that morning. The Anthony landaulet was waiting at the front stile, Jackson perched on his driver's seat with his head hanging down, Henry bustling with bags and bundles while loading them between the seats of the carriage.

Maggie and Robin were the first to leave the house. Robin looking very unhappy and worried. She asked Maggie if there would be any hurricanes. The child was dreading the long, tiresome voyage. Maggie assured her that hurricanes came only in the fall and, as this was springtime, they could expect only blue skies.

Next to come out of the house was Tomas and Marie, quarreling, as usual. Both were wearing expressions of doom. Marie was carrying a pot of roses that she vowed would thrive during the journey. Tomas was trying to take it from her. He said, "You know damn well that the salty air will kill it."

She angrily answered him, "I hope it kills you, you old fool."

As Lord and Lady Anthony came out of the house they were smiling and holding hands. They turned and looked at the house, then got into the carriage. They were joyful and glad to be going home to England.

Henry rode on the back of the carriage to the wharf and helped Jackson unload the baggage. Neither of the black men said a word.

Lola was waiting near the boarding ramp. As Mr. Straight came near her, he reached out for her and she ran into his arms, sobbing pitifully. He held her and kissed the top of her head.

Marie brushed by them and haughtily said, "I'm glad to be going four thousand miles away from this hellish land. You've been trying to steal my husband ever since we arrived here."

"I almost did," answered Lola.

Lord and Lady Anthony at first ignored Lola. Then Lady Anthony turned back and gave the faithful cook a cool kiss on her cheek and pressed a small package into her hand.

When Tomas reached the railing of the stern, he leaned out and called to Lola, "Lola, someday I'll be back to get you."

Robin and Maggie were the last to go up the gangplank, Robin was still hugging Bo Tay in her arms and crying, wiping the tears on Bo Tay's back. The two who cared the most had lingered behind, hoping that Clarice and Jason might show up at the last minute to bid them farewell and watch the Clementine put out to sea. Maggie was trying to comfort Robin by hugging her and kissing her, but the child was sincerely hurting.

The ship was carrying more passengers than it usually did. Lord Anthony remarked, "Everyone who loves England will soon be leaving, and as you can see some are smart enough to leave early." He hesitated a moment and added, "Before the shooting starts."

Lady Anthony took his arm as they walked toward their state room. She raised her eyes to heaven and said, "Oh, thank God."

On the way back to the house, Henry seated himself in the plush seat of the carriage where Lord Anthony had just sat. Grinning widely, he said to Jackson, "Home, Jackson, and let me off at the front stile; I'm goin' in the front door."

Clarice didn't know just how long she leaned against the roof, resting. The warm sun on her had caused her to rest longer than she thought. She aroused herself and lifted the glass to her eyes. "Just one more look," she said.

"There it is," she exuberantly called out. "Behold the Clementine."

She straightened her shoulders and lifted the spy glass a bit higher. There was a large ship on the horizon. She counted five large white sails. She said, "It must already be three or four miles on its way."

She watched through the glass until the last sail slipped out of sight.

When she stepped inside and closed the shutter, she said, "Goodbye, dear ones, may God keep you safe."

Although it was twenty degrees and the ground was frozen hard, Clarice and Sister Smith were stepping off a plot of ground and making calculations and suggestions to each other, planning a vegetable patch in back of the McKenzie barn, when Clarice saw that the man running on the road toward her house was Jason.

She paused and rested on her rake. She wondered why he was coming home in the middle of the afternoon.

"Oh, dear God," she whispered, "please don't let it be bad news." She was thinking about the Anthonys, far out on the sea.

She placed her rake against the side of the barn and ran to meet him, calling out to Sister Smith, "Wait here, I will be right back."

Sister Smith was much too concerned to wait; she ran right behind Clarice.

As Jason entered the yard he realized that he had excited the women.

"What's the matter?" Clarice asked Jason. She was breathing heavily and her eyes were wide open with wonder.

"I have to go to Boston, dear, right away."

"Why? Why do you have to go to Boston?"

"The lieutenant governor has passed away, and the troop of Hancock's cadets are going to march behind the casket bearers."

"But you're not a cadet, Jason. Are you?"

"No, I'm not. I'm going to try to get their participation stopped. It's not doing the cause of liberty any good for the cadets to be showing so much respect to the Tories."

"I can't see how it would hurt the cause of liberty," said Clarice as she followed Jason into their bedroom where he began taking his dress clothes out of the closet.

"Because Hutchinson ordered Hancock to bring out the cadets. I think Hancock should have declined because some of those boys might get shot."

"Jason, who would shoot into a funeral procession?"

"These rebels are so riled up they wouldn't care if it was a funeral. Also, Andrew Oliver's death will delay Hutchinson's departure. The Sons of Liberty want him out of here."

"I'm going with you, Jason. It will take me only a minute to get dressed."

"Oh no you're not. I'm riding horseback. I can make it much quicker."

Clarice stamped her foot, and her expression changed to frustration and anger. "Are you sure you and your Club Nine are not up to some more dirty mischief?" she asked.

"No, no, my darling, I'll be back; let's see," he counted on his fingers, "this is Monday; the funeral is Wednesday, the eighth; I'll be back Thursday."

Clarice ran after him as he hurriedly walked out to the gate where parson Smith was holding Charlie, all saddled and ready to go. She was throwing out questions fast and furiously, but Jason mounted and rode away in a gallop without answering any of them.

She spoke to Parson Smith who had been left standing at the gate. "Parson, what do you think of that? Jason's acting like a lunatic. I'm surprised at his actions, so adamant and evasive."

"Someday we might find out," answered the parson as he sat down beside his wife, who was resting on a bench by the back door.

Clarice went into the house, seeming to be quite upset.

"John," said Sister Smith, "don't you think that you should attend Oliver's funeral?"

"No Missy, I don't, but I do think someone should be looking after Jason. He's acting too hotheaded for his own good. He's about to stir up trouble."

Sister Smith replied, "Now I am confused. Let's go into the house and see what Clarice is doing."

When Jason reached the ferry he saw that there wasn't room for one more carriage and he was glad he was riding horseback. He squeezed Charlie onto the very edge, and when the gate closed the horse's tail hung over the planks.

On approaching the south side of the Charles, Jason and the other ferry passengers observed how brilliantly Boston was lit up. Many street lamps were flickering, and there were torches glowing from many yards and storefronts.

As he rode to his shop on Charles Street, Jason noticed that the many people milling around were mostly farmers from out in the province, the rural areas. As he rode slowly along, he waved at a few people he recognized or nodded as they did. There were many walkers just strolling.

His shop windows and doors were still boarded up. He had taken great precaution he was there New Year's Day to see that the place was safely secured.

He rode around to his barn and installed Charlie. He found some mildewed hay and a few nubbins of corn which would have to sustain the horse until he had time to climb into the hayloft to look for something else.

As he walked toward his back door, he saw that one of the windows in the back of the house had been unboarded, and he knew someone had broken in.

At the moment he gave it no serious thought. "Some young 'un," he said to himself, "looking for cookies."

He opened the door with his key and on entering he felt the warmth and saw a fire burning on the hearth, a hat was hanging on the chair post and then he knew someone was still there.

"Hello, hello, who's here? You have no right to be in this house. Hello, come down here." He guessed they were sleeping in his bed.

At that moment Henry came to the top of the stairs and called out, "Jason, you old curmudgeon, where have you been for so long?"

"Henry, you devil, is that really you? Did you break into my house?"

"The winder was broken in when I got here and I just climbed in. I knew you wouldn't mind."

Jason bounded up the stairs and embraced his dear friend. Henry, in his long red flannel underwear, returned the greeting with hugging and laughter.

"You're the last damn devil I expected to see," said Jason, all wiggly with emotion and smiles.

"I ain't seen you either since I helped you steal Miss Clarice from the Anthonys, right after the big party."

"Shh, don't say that out loud, even the wood worms have ears. Come on downstairs and I'll make us some coffee."

"Ain't none," said Henry. "I looked every place."

"Well I know I left some here," said Jason. "I guess somebody stole it."

"The winder was open when I got here and I climbed in and made a fire and thought I would make some coffee, but I couldn't find one grain."

"When did you get here?" asked Jason.

"Just this morning, I been riding all night with Slade. He decided he would rest a few days and obtain some fresh horses, so I come on over here while he went out to Chelsey.

"We've just got to have some fresh horses; we've about wore out Sam and Dam. We've made four round trips to New York since Christmas." Henry continued to talk, Jason leaned on the door facing, listening. "News is hot in New York; the people there are all fired up. They dumped all the tea that arrived there after out party here in Boston. I hear Charleston done the same. I ain't going near Charleston even if Slade is assigned to go there."

"I don't blame you for that," said Jason.

"People sure do ask Slade a lot of questions. He never says nuthin', neither do I, to the men who are not afraid to speak to me. Black men in New York are mostly slaves. They's skeered to death of everybody."

"Why did you come to Boston today?" Henry asked Jason.

"You have heard that Lieutenant Governor Andrew Oliver is dead and his funeral is going to be tomorrow."

"Yes, I heard he's dead. Slade said he wouldn't disgrace himself by going to his funeral. Are you going to his funeral?"

After thinking for a moment, Jason answered Henry, "My presence will be in evidence, I suppose."

Water Under the Bridge

The two men decided that if they were to nourish themselves they would have to go to a public eating establishment. Arm in arm they paced rather rapidly along the Boston streets, among carriages and people, to the Merry Mermaid Tavern.

The place was crowded and it appeared to Jason that most of the patrons were completely inebriated. The noise was deafening. Gambling was going on in the great room as the back room, the regular gambling room, was crowded to overflowing.

Catching a glimpse of Tom Moore and Joe Mumford, he said to Henry, "Find us a table and order us some grub while I go over and speak to Tom and Joe."

As Jason pushed through the tables, he felt a hand on his shoulder. He turned to see Phinas Alcott, whom he knew only slightly. Alcott was only fourteen years old; he was one of Hancock's cadets and was already earning his own living by delivering messages.

"Mr. McKenzie," the boy said, "will you stake me to a little something to eat? I came in from Lynn early this morning and I haven't et all day. I'm expecting to earn a little money tomorrow, but if I don't eat I won't be much good for marching."

Jason understood what the boy was telling him, but he couldn't remember where he had seen him before.

Henry called out above the noise and commotion, "Come on J, I found us a table and we better take it right now before someone else sits down here."

Jason said to the kid, "Come on, I'll feed you tonight, but don't expect it again tomorrow." Jason took the boy by the shoulder and steered him to the table where Henry was already seated.

Tom Moore had seen Jason and his nodding head indicating him to join them. He was headed for the door but turned and motioned to Joe Mumford, and the two men joined Jason, Henry, and Phinas. The five sat at the table gulping down food and rum. Now and then a word or two would be spoken or a laugh would emerge from one or another. Jason finally stopped eating for a moment, wiped his mouth with his napkin, and spoke directly to Tom.

"I have to see Hancock as early as possible tomorrow morning. Do you think he will be at his warehouse by seven a.m.?" Tom worked at the warehouse.

"Yes, I am pretty sure he will be there, very early. He is bringing out the cadets for Oliver's funeral."

"If I get there, do you think I will be able to talk with him?"

"You'll just have to take your chance. He's very evasive these days. Some people say he wants to be the new provincial governor."

"Governor! Good God! Parliament will never appoint him as governor, he being a Son of Liberty," exclaimed Jason.

"Oh well," said Tom, "if he had prospects of being appointed governor, he would resign form the Sons."

"Do you think Hutchinson will go on his extended leave now that Oliver is dead?"

"That remains to be seen," said Tom.

The boy had been very quiet; he now and then raised his eyebrows at some statement that surprised him. When he finished eating and sopping his plate with the last crumb of bread, he got up from his chair and said, "Thank you very much, Mr. McKenzie," and left the room.

A year would pass before Jason would see him again.

Henry was also very quiet. He was a good listener and later would review with Jason what he had heard when they were alone. He went to the bar and ordered two bottles of rum which he put into his inside coat pocket.

Tom Moore and Joe Mumford thanked Jason for the food; he had paid for everyone's meal. They wished him success with his mission to Hancock and left the room.

A contingent of British soldiers rushed into the tavern, blowing whistles.

The officer in charge called out, "Everyone leave this place immediately, without comment, no noise please, no questions. Just leave; return to your homes."

To the proprietor he said, "Lock your doors; don't open again until Friday, the tenth of March. This is an order from the governor of Massachusetts."

Jason and Henry returned to Jason's room around midnight, both barely able to stand on their feet. It was the first time since his marriage that Jason had had any intoxicating refreshment, and he felt good, like he was single again, not that he wanted to be.

When the two men had gotten into bed and were lying there talking, Henry asked, "Jason, old boy, what's it like to be married?"

Jason thought for a moment, then said, "Well, I guess it's the closest I'll ever be to Heaven until I actually get there."

"Do you do it every night?" asked Henry.

This blunt question fired into Jason like a gunshot. "That's none of your business, you impudent cuss. Get out of my bed and sleep on the floor and don't talk to me any more tonight; I'm tired and want to sleep." Jason was very drunk, he began to sing.

Henry rolled out of the bed and stretched out in front of the fireplace.

Jason, in a blubbering, slurred voice said, "Henry, old pal, you had no right to ask me a personal question like that, but I'll answer it because I want you to know. My wife is the most generous, lovingest, warmest woman in the whole world. I wish she were here beside me."

"Do you ever wish for Truly?" asked Henry.

"Truly was always enticing me, actually inviting me, but I always put her off. I never once made love to Truly."

"God, man, how could you? I would have killed for her, but she always put me off. I sure hope that sweet thing is happy with that one-legged man."

He continued, "I'm going to see Tablow and Duncan tomorrow to see if they have heard from her."

Soon both men were snoring. At six A.M. Jason was up and tiptoeing down the stairs on his way to the barn to saddle his horse.

When he saw the barn door open, his heart jumped into his throat. He suspected Charlie would be missing, which he was.

"That rascal," said Jason. "He opened the barn door and wandered off. No, that's not it; someone has stolen him or maybe just borrowed him."

"I suppose I'll walk to Hancock's warehouse. I haven't time to look for Charlie. Maybe I can hitch a ride."

He walked around his building to the street and saw a carriage coming toward him, going toward town. He stepped out on to the brick road and waved his arms up and down.

The driver yelled to his horse, "Whoa" in an excited voice.

Jason asked, Will you be so kind as to give me a ride to town?"

"Whereabouts in town?" asked the elderly country man.

"I'm on my way to Hancock's Wharf. I have to see John and try to persuade him to stop the cadets from marching in the funeral procession."

"Why in the hell would you do that?"

Jason was seated beside the old man, and the carriage was moving along toward town at a speedy pace. The old man was wearing his white powdered wig and his red velvet waistcoat and his silver buckled shoes. Jason surmised that he was going to town on business of a royal motive or maybe he was dressed for the funeral.

"Because if Hancock is a dedicated Son of Liberty he ought not to be lending aid to the Tories."

Before he could catch his breath, Jason found himself getting up off the wet bricks of Charles Street where he had landed after being shoved off the seat of the carriage.

He felt the wet seat of his white breeches and knew they must be badly soiled with the red brick dust. He thought, Where is my hat? It was in the ditch about ten feet away.

"Uhm," he said to himself, "that old shit ass must be a Tory." He looked himself over and concluded that he certainly couldn't go to see Hancock looking like that. He knew of a haberdashery about five blocks away. He began walking toward the place thinking about buying a new outfit.

When he reached the store, which was displaying the very clothes he wanted in its large paned window, he stopped to reflect his battered and soiled condition and to imagine himself regaled with the elegant new outfit in the show window.

His countenance fell when he read the calligraphic sign on the door. "Closed until Friday, due to the death of the lieutenant governor. By order of the Provincial Council and Governor Hutchinson."

"Now what?" Jason was bewildered, but he vowed to fulfill the mission he had come all the way from Lynn to attempt.

He headed for the warehouse. "I will apologize for my appearance," he said, as he hastened his stride. It was ten minutes until seven A.M.

He saw John Hancock dismount his beautiful bay stallion and tie him to the hitching post. As the handsomely dressed man was unlocking the door, Jason called out to him (Jason was about one hundred feet away).

"Oh, there, Mr. Hancock, I would like a word with you." Jason did a hop-skip-and-jump to reach the door.

"Come in, Mr. McKenzie. I haven't seen you for quite a long time. Where have you been?" After a moment of inquisitiveness, Mr. Hancock asked, "What is it about, that you wish to have a word with me?"

When he found out that Jason wanted to call off the participation of the cadets in the funeral of Andrew Oliver, he informed him that it was not for the man but respect for the office.

"Are you going to attend the funeral, Mr. McKenzie?" Hancock was eyeing Jason's dirty clothes.

"Only as a looker-on. I knew Mr. Oliver, but we were barely on speaking acquaintance. I served his household with my bakery goods. He still owes me for the last big party he held. I catered it and was out several pounds for cakes and sweet buns." He added, "These rich office holders are mighty slow pay."

He hoped John Hancock would pick up on that for he also owed Jason a goodly sum for his last party and for cookies delivered to Hancock's workers at Christmas over a year ago.

Jason left the warehouse right after Mr. Hancock stood up and announced that it was too late to call off the cadets. They were already dressed and assembled, waiting to march.

He walked out into the street, stopped under a large tree and spit-shined his boots, and brushed his hat with his coat sleeve while gathering his thoughts for his next move. God how he hated to be outdone.

Actually his thoughts were not on the funeral of the lieutenant governor but on Clarice. He felt her presence near him. "I wonder how she got along without me last night," he said to himself. He had an urge to go home that moment, then he remembered he had to look for Charlie first. He began to walk toward his shop.

The streets were crowded with walkers, horseback riders, and vehicles of all kinds. Jason met a few people he knew; he nodded and touched the brim of his hat in greeting.

Everyone has changed, he thought. They look so solemn. Could it be they are sorry for the death of Oliver, or are they thinking what is inevitably going to happen here in this colony?

When he got to his door he found it locked from the inside. He thought Henry was still there sleeping—maybe. He fumbled in his pocket for his key. He did not have it. After banging on the door and calling Henry, who was not there, he realized that he would have to go around back and climb in through the window.

In his back yard he saw that the barn door was closed, "Good," he said, "Charlie came home." He knew he had left it open just in case that would happen. His feelings soared; now he wouldn't have to go out looking for him.

Jason climbed through the window and noticed that Henry was gone. Now who locked that door from the inside? he wondered. He presumed that Henry had gone to the wharf as he had mentioned he wanted to do.

Jason stepped in front of the long mirror and was looking himself over when he saw someone in the adjoining room pass in front of the door. It was a man wearing a red coat and short black hair. Jason watched in the mirror for a moment, then tiptoed to the door, peering around the door facing.

Chapter Twenty-Four

As the stranger turned and came back, Jason jumped him. Snarling an oath under his breath, he caught the red coat by the shoulder and began yelling, "Who are you? Why are you in my house?"

He was choking the fellow as he called out, "Speak fast, before I kill you."

The stranger's eyes looked wild with surprise as he struggled to pry Jason's hands from his neck.

When he realized that he might be killing the man, Jason loosened his grip and pushed him backwards to the floor. He straddled him, and, holding his outstretched arms, he began jumping up and down on the poor man's stomach while beating the floor with his hands.

"Now you better speak for yourself, you red-coated thief." He didn't give the culprit time to speak; he continued his bouncing.

Gulping for breath, the man, in a weakened voice, finally said, "I am Tom Fellows from Birmingham, England. I came here to your shop hoping to find Clarice Creighton."

Jason released the stranger's arms and stood up, lending the frightened man his hand to assist him to his feet.

"Well, why didn't you say so?" demanded Jason.

"How could I? I was helpless in your grasp." He continued, "I'm sorry to be intruding on your premises. I feel guilty. I should have waited outside for your return. There was a slave here. I saw him leave, then I climbed in through the window. I was surprised to see a slave locking the door."

Jason spoke sternly, "Henry is not a slave; he's a free man and my friend. He works for me occasionally and gets paid for it. Did he take a horse out of the barn?"

"No, I didn't see a horse. He walked east on Charles Street."

After being quiet for a few seconds, Jason looked at Fellows and asked, "Do you know that Clarice is my wife? We were married in December."

"Yes I know. I went to the Anthonys' house on Beacon Street. I encountered a sassy woman there. She told me about the marriage and said I might find you here. She also told me the Anthonys had gone back to England; seems I just missed them. I was disappointed because I expected to be quartered with them while I am here in Boston in the British Regular Army."

Jason again looked down at his rumpled, muddy, torn clothes. He apologized for looking so shabby, but angrily he growled out, "It was one of your damned British sympathizers that caused me to be in this disarray...looking like this."

Tom made no reply to those remarks, but he said as he walked toward the window, "Where is Cee Cee now?"

In his mind Jason sneered, Oh, he calls her 'Cee Cee,' does he? He knows her well enough for her nickname.

"She's at home in Lynn," and in a loud, rude voice he added, "waiting for me. I'm going home to her as soon as Oliver's funeral is over."

He did not invite Tom Fellows to accompany him to Lynn. The two men stood facing each other, jittery and confused. Neither knew what to say.

Jason was still angry because of the break-in into his house. He said, "I suppose, if you have to be quartered in Boston, you could stay in the house the Anthonys vacated. Lola will be there to take care of your meals and laundry."

"No, she won't. She told me she was leaving as soon as she could collect her wages."

"Do you know where she is going?" asked Jason.

"No, she said she will be glad to get away. She remarked that she hates all Tories. She said they were all snobs and won't pay their servants."

Jason was pacing back and forth across the room with his hands clasped behind his back while thinking, Should I offer Tom Fellows this place? The downstairs storeroom is dusty and bare; maybe he could look after it, keep it swept and aired once in awhile, to keep it from falling to ruin.

"Under the circumstances," he spoke in a calm quiet voice, "you better settle in here for awhile." He caught his breath and lifted his voice, "But when Henry is here he will also stay here. That will be about once a month, maybe."

"Who is Henry?" asked Tom.

"He is the man you thought was a slave."

"Oh, a Negro?" exclaimed Tom.

"Yes, and a good one, too."

"Will he polish my boots and iron my shirts?"

"No, he won't. He has plenty to do with his regular job." Jason added, "Henry is nobody's flunky." He didn't tell Tom that Henry worked with the Committee of Correspondence. He was thinking, Maybe Henry can pick up some valuable information when he is here with Tom Fellows. He also knew that Henry would never breathe one word of anything he knew. Jason remembered that Clarice had once told him that Lola told her Henry was "closemouthed."

In a few moments, Tom sighed and said he had better be joining the rest of his squad who were waiting for him over on the Common.

Jason asked, "What is a squad of regulars doing on the Common?"

"We are going to scatter out around the town to keep the peace during the funeral," answered Tom.

"I hope you can do it," replied Jason.

Fellows and McKenzie went downstairs. Fellows straightened his coat and put on his hat; bowed slightly to Jason, who was holding the door open; and walked down the street.

As Fellows walked down Charles Street, Jason called out to him, "I'm not going to tell Clarice that you are here, so don't show up in Lynn. Don't come near the place or make any attempt to see her. She doesn't want to see you."

Tom turned to face Jason, "Are you sure she doesn't want to see me?"

Jason didn't answer that question because he wasn't quite sure. Jason went to his barn; he sensed in a second that his horse was not there. He noticed that the saddle and bridle were also missing. Under his breath with an oath he yelled out, "Some son of a bitch has stolen my horse!"

He stomped out of the barn and around his shop to Charles Street, removing his hat to scratch his head. He whispered to himself, "Perhaps someone saw someone taking my horse." He knew all the shops on Charles Street were closed for the funeral, but he peered through the window of the saddlery and tapped on the window.

Mr. Harvey opened the door and let Jason in. After hearing Jason tell about his missing horse, he vowed he had seen no one near Jason's barn. Jason got the same response at the chandler's shop; Winkler didn't know anything, didn't even know Jason was in town.

While standing in front of his empty baker shop, Jason was contemplating his next move when he heard the fife and drum and could see the British Union Jack held high leading the funeral procession. He moved a few feet away from his door to lean against a large tree to have a better view.

The Sons of Liberty were represented by only a few men. They were draggin their feet and wearing sullen expressions. Probably because of their jobs, they had been forced to march.

The governor's carriage was in full regalia of flags and rose garlands. Oliver's family carriage had crepe of purple and gold. After a few carriages of parliament government officials came the cadets, stepping high and performing their rifle drill exercises.

Someone of the bystanders yelled out an oath calling Hancock's cadets "traitors to the cause of Liberty." This caused someone else to begin swearing and shoving. A melee broke out along the sidewalk, and a few people were knocked down and kicked about.

Jason suspected the ruckus was deliberately started. He ran to the angry scufflers and tried to pull two of the ring leaders apart. His coat tail was grabbed and the back seam ripped open. Jason looked like a ragged bum when the disturbance subsided.

The funeral procession passed on down the street and entered the church yard. The mourners entered the church, and the sexton locked the doors.

Jason went back into his shop, sat down, and put his head in his hands. "Good God," he said, "what am I going to do now?"

He thought of Clarice and how much he wanted to be with her in Lynn. His thoughts of Tom Fellows being in Boston irritated him. He wondered if he should tell her that he was there.

"This trip has been a complete farce," he said to himself. "I've failed and been humiliated." He remembered that Charlie was missing and went to check the barn once more. He decided to walk around some more and went toward the river, whistling the horse call that Charlie knew so well. He asked almost everyone he met, but no one had seen the horse.

After several hours he realized it was late in the day. He hadn't eaten, he had walked miles, and his face was sore from a blow he had taken and from whistling and calling. He had not one shilling, and Henry had not returned. "All in all," he said, "this is a bad ending to a mission that began so eagerly."

Jason sat in his chair by the window wondering how he was going to get home. Walking ten miles seemed the only solution.

It was midnight when Henry came back from his visit to Tablow and Duncan. He had found Lola there enjoying herself. The comforts of the schooner Gospel Truth and being waited on by the two black men lifted her ego, he told Jason.

Duncan read a letter to her and him, which he had received from Don Carlos, instructing them to bring Lola to Cuba as soon as the weather in Boston was favorable for them to leave.

Jason and Henry talked the rest of the night. The news Henry brought to Jason was music to his ears. He was happy for Lola and Truly. He asked Henry if he learned anything about Jackson.

Jackson was still at the house on Beacon Hill, still caring for the two horses, Stomper and Shoe Fly. He was feeding himself with whatever was left in the Anthony larder.

Henry said, "He's been told by the governor that he could stay there and serve the next occupants of the house."

Friday morning the sun broke through the clouds over the harbor and a golden glow tinted the windowpanes of the buildings along Charles Street. Jason and Henry walked along together, hoping Cindy Waters's Little Fritters shop was open for business. Both men were hungry and tired.

Little Fritters was a small coffee and tea shop in a room off the kitchen of Cindy Waters's house. Cindy only served breakfast, which was a variety of flapjacks with molasses or honey and coffee or tea, which was in scarce supply at this time. Cindy Waters was a young widow, age twenty-five, whose husband had been lost in a ship wreck. Jason seldom patronized her establishment because he had his own source of breakfast. Henry had agreed to meet John Slade there that morning to hear the order from the Committee as to their next assignment. Two horses were tied to the hitching rail.

Henry said, "Them's the two fresh horses John got for us, I suppose."

On entering The Fritters, they noticed only one customer seated at a table in the corner. It was John Slade.

"Morning Henry, morning McKenzie. You two look tuckered out. Been painting the town?" Slade was in jovial mood.

"Not quite," said Jason as the two sat down with Slade.

Slade asked, "Henry, you ready to ride? We gotta go out to Salem first, then switch back to Lexington, and from there on to Providence."

"Good God," replied Henry. "How long that gonna take us?"

"Only a couple of days to Lexington, but we'll be in Providence in a week and stay there another week. That's about three weeks, all told."

Jason's eyes brightened when he heard Slade say they were going to Salem. He asked if he could ride behind Henry as far as Lynn.

"Why?" asked Slade.

Then Jason and Henry—both in the throes of excited conversation—related in detail their activities of the last forty-eight hours, in special emphasis, the disappearance of Charlie.

All the time the three men were eating their fritters and talking, Cindy Waters was busy around their table, as close as possible without being conspicuous, to hear what they were talking about.

Cindy was not a rebel, a patriot, or a Yankee. She was one individual, strictly for herself. She would take on any scheme if it would put a few shillings into her pocket. A new and exciting venture she recently got into was buying and selling horses, rifles, hunting knives, etc., be it stolen or not. She sold as soon as possible whatever she bought if she could turn a small profit.

Only the day before, she had purchased a horse with saddle and bridle from a man she took to be half Indian, who told her he had to sell his horse because he was going into the wilderness and needed money to buy provisions. Cindy did not care what he needed the money for and she did not care if he told the truth.

After hearing Jason's tale of woe, she came closer to his chair and said, "I have a horse and saddle for sale. If you would like to see, I will accompany you to the stable."

Jason seemed stunned by the woman's offer. He knew he didn't have money to buy a horse; however, he agreed to take a look.

All three of the men followed Cindy to the stable in back of her house. They heard the horse neigh before Cindy opened the door. As the men stepped inside, Jason and Henry simultaneously said, "It's Charlie."

Then Jason sternly said, "Woman, you've bought stolen property. This is my horse." He added, "There is a fine and punishment for buying stolen property."

"Makes no difference to me," she replied. "I buy whatever is for sale." She seemed self-assured when she said, "I buy firearms, muskets, knives. Seems like all my customers are rebels. I think they are taking these items to some place and hiding them. They're hiding them somewhere near Concord. I have customers from that part of the country who come back time and time again. They don't talk, and I don't ask. I just buy and sell. I know, though, if they tell me they lost the last one or they gave it away, I know they are lying."

She caught her breath as she took the bridle from the tack rack, put it on Charlie, and handed the reins to Jason. "If you want him, pay me only what I paid for him."

"How much?" asked Jason.

"Twenty pounds."

"You paid twenty pounds for this old horse?" It was Slade, the professional horse trader. He added, "This horse is old."

Jason spoke despairingly, "Miss Cindy, I haven't got any money. Will you trust me to send it to you in a few days?"

"No, I can't do that. I have merchandise on the way that I have to pay for. Besides I do not do business on credit."

Henry spoke out, "If ye'll take ten pounds, I'll pay for the horse."

Jason turned to Henry, "I will pay you back, Henry."

Cindy pulled the bridle off Charlie, and, as she hung it back on its hook, she scornfully said, "Not one pence less than twenty pounds."

Jason looked discouraged as he stroked Charlie's forelock.

"I'll put up the other ten pounds," said John Slade.

"Thanks, John, I'll repay you in one month." In his innermost conscience, Jason was wondering where he would get ten pounds in one month to pay Slade. Henry could wait a little longer.

"That will be all right with me," said the woman. "I'll throw in the bridle, but the saddle is five pounds extra."

Jason answered quickly, "Forget the saddle; I'll ride bareback."

As the little bunch of horse traders left the stable, Jason was lovingly leading Charlie. The horse seemed to be expressing his joy by nuzzling Jason's shoulder.

It was mid-afternoon when the three horseback riders reached the outskirts of Lynn. Jason motioned and they halted. "You fellows linger behind me for a spell. I'm going to go galloping toward my house, waving my hat and hollering so Clarice will think I'm in a big hurry to take her in my arms, which I am."

When Clarice heard the galloping hoofs and Jason's hollering, she ran out to the road to meet him.

She was quite abashed at his appearance, and he had no saddle under him. When he slid off the horse and took her in his arms he could hardly stand up. As he squeezed her tightly and kissed her again and again, she felt he had been in a fight.

"Jason, Jason," she said as she pushed herself away from his embrace. "What on earth has disheveled you so? Look at your clothes and a big bruise on your cheek. Have you been fighting? I can tell you've been drinking."

Jason didn't answer her questions; he just picked her up off her feet and began kissing her again.

She said, "Stop it, Jason, your whiskers are rough and your hair is not combed. You look like the buzzards have been at you. What have you been doing?"

He held her back from him and said, "I haven't got time to tell you all that happened to me in Boston, but I will later." He continued, "Henry and John Slade are right behind me; they will be here in a minute. They are on their way to Salem but want to stop here to see you. Will you make us some tea?"

"Jason, I dumped all the tea we had into the slop that I save for Parson Smith's pigs. We don't have one tea leaf in this house. I do have some dried berries mixed with spices which makes a very fine brew, if you think they will like it."

"That will have to do then, if it's all you have."

When Henry and Slade arrived a few moments later, they found a dainty tea table and plenty of delicious tea cakes and a hot steaming beverage made with dried blueberries and spices.

John and Henry didn't tarry long; John said their mission was urgent. Clarice and Jason stood by the yard gate, waving until the riders were out of sight.

"Now, my darling, how did you get along without me?"

"I was thinking of you every minute," she said.

"In what way?" he asked.

"Well, to begin with—the bed was too cold without your warm body. The food I cooked didn't taste good when I ate alone. Panzy whinnied all night for three nights. The rooster flew up into the barn loft and wouldn't come down, and the hens drove me crazy squawking and clucking. I was worried about you and kept watching for you all day yesterday. You promised to be home by Thursday. What happened? I want to know."

"Cee Cee, dear, you mustn't ever worry about me. I can take care of myself very well. I love you too much to bore you with all the frivolous hodgepodge of my trip to Boston."

Clarice answered that statement with, "Huh? Never mind, I'll find out. I'll ask Parson Smith to make you confess. I'll ask him to threaten you with the danger of going to hell." She laughed and squeezed Jason's hand.

They entered the house, and Clarice made straight for the stairs, taking them two at a time. Jason was right behind her, holding onto the tail of her dress. They went into their bedroom and slammed the door. No one saw Clarice or Jason until next day.

In the meantime, Sister Smith was calling on a few families who had small children. She had conjured an idea that small children, especially those of her husband's congregation who did not have any discipline, needed some instruction in singing, drawing, and recitation. She was making an effort to get such a class started in Lynn.

Knowing most of her husband's congregation very well, she felt all the mothers would welcome the idea. The only problem would be getting the children to the classroom.

She got the notion that Clarice McKenzie would make a perfect teacher, and she could also pick up the children in the McKenzie chaise and transport them to her house where she would set up a schoolroom.

Sister Smith bounded into the McKenzie back door with, "Hello there, Clarice dear, I have the most wonderful idea! I know you are going to like it."

She drew Clarice by her hand into the large front room, and, while gesturing with her arms and eyes, she related her plan. "Just think, dear, how much fun you will have with the children."

Clarice did like the idea, but after thinking about it a moment or two she replied, "It will take so much of my time, and I have to cook and sew and go to market and feed the cow and horses."

"Don't think of the other chores; I'll help you." Sister Smith looked wishful as she said, "The children are so obstreperous at meeting. They are learning nothing at home but roughnecking. You could charge their parents a small tuition. I'm sure they would welcome such a school."

"How much?" asked Clarice, as her expression turned to eagerness.

"Oh, maybe three or four shillings a month," answered Sister.

"Would I have to teach every day?"

"No, I think three days a week would be sufficient."

"Good," exclaimed Clarice, "I do love children. I will discuss it with Jason and ask his permission. He may object to my taking his chaise, and he says I'm a poor driver. I know he will object to driving Charlie. He is very protective of that horse."

"Then use Panzy; she is well rested and very gentle."

That evening Jason did not go to drill with the minutemen. It was plowing and planting time, and the drilling was only on weekends for awhile. The nights were cool for plowing.

After supper, when Clarice was washing the dishes and Jason was drying them and putting them in the cupboard, he asked, "Was Sister Smith here today?"

"Yes," Clarice answered, "and I want to talk to you about a plan she has for me to teach school."

"There is already a school teacher in Lynn," he answered.

"But this will be a school for very young children; I will start it. It will be private, and I will charge tuition. Let's go and sit on the bench by the back door and talk about it."

It was almost midnight when the couple quit talking and decided to go to bed.

Jason said, "If you want to do it, Cee Cee, I will support your effort all the way."

Clarice was very busy for the next few days setting up her school room. She placed a table, which she dragged down from the attic, into one corner of the great room. She blistered her fingers sawing off the legs so the table would be just the right height for four- or five-year-olds.

With her quill she printed a notice on parchment for Jason to take to the shipyard to post up in a conspicuous place where papa's of small children would read it. She asked Parson Smith to round up for her four or five milking stools, they would be just right, to place at the table.

When Jason came home he brought several thin, small boards, scrap from the ship boards, for the children to use in their painting.

Something was on Jason's mind; Clarice could tell. She hoped it was not the school venture. Jason had not told his wife that Tom Fellows was in Boston. He didn't want to tell her, but knew he had to before he showed up at their house unexpectedly.

How was that going to affect everything? he thought.

In about a week, John Jolly came up to the McKenzie yard gate with his twin daughters, age four, riding behind him. John Jolly was the son of the Mrs. Jolly who used to work for Jason in his bakery shop in Boston. He now lived about two miles away in Saugus and worked at the shipyard in Lynn.

"Good morning, Mrs. McKenzie. I've brought you two pupils. They're such a handful, my wife is threatening to lock them away somewhere."

Clarice was a little abashed at such characterization of her first pupils. She lifted Molly down from the horse while John lifted Polly. The four-year-old twins began to cry and scream for their papa as he rode away toward the shipyard.

Clarice stooped and gathered the girls into her arms and carried them into the house. She was thinking she had forgotten to tell their papa to come back for them in four hours. That, four hours, was the duration of the class. As she set the twins down by the window she wondered how she was going to get them to stop crying.

Before she could get their bonnets and sweaters off, she heard someone calling, "Mrs. McKenzie, Mrs. McKenzie." Through the window she saw Sally Melville holding a small child by the hand on each side of her.

Clarice didn't know Sally Melville, a very young woman about her own age, although Sister Smith had once remarked, "Poor Sally Melville is so young to have to take in her dead sister's children. That mean husband of hers beats on them all the time, and now she is pregnant herself." Sally was seventeen.

"Good morning, Mrs. McKenzie," said Sally as Clarice opened the door to greet her. The children were Sally, her namesake, age five, and Matthew, age three. "Here are my niece and nephew I've brung you to learn them their ABCs. They're pretty good, that is, when Clinton is around. Clinton is my husband, and he sure makes these two toe and mark."

Clarice knew at once that Sally Melville was a very shy country girl.

She smiled at the Melvilles and said, "Come in, Sally; come in, Matthew. There are two friends here to meet you."

She turned toward the two Jolly children and said, "Come here, Polly. You too, Molly, and shake hands with Sally and Matthew."

All four children began to cry and yell and scream and hold their breath. Sally Melville ran out the gate and down the road. She called back to Clarice, who was looking quite bewildered, "God bless ye."

Clarice said to herself, "Oh me, I forgot to tell her that she should come back for the children in four hours." She turned to face the crying foursome.

A memory suddenly entered her mind of the first moment of her meeting with Robin, who also had thrown one of her famous tantrums.

Clarice closed the door behind her, and, moving close to the four, she bent over and placed her hands flat on the floor. She called out quickly each child's name, "Polly, Molly, Sally, Matt." The crying got louder. "Come on, let's play like we're cats."

She stuck her thumbs in her ears and wiggled her fingers. She stuck out her tongue and made funny noises. She said, "Meow, meow, fizz, fizz!" She stood on her toes and whirled around and jumped up and down. She began to sing while carrying on many different antics.

The children's crying soon stopped, and they began to laugh, that is, everyone except Matt. He walked over to the door and began kicking it very hard.

Clarice then went over to the door and began kicking it very hard. She said to the three girls, "Come on girls; let's all kick the door."

They hurried over and crowded into place and began kicking the door. They were still laughing.

"Now," said Clarice, "let's all clap hands, but keep on kicking the door. Now that we're kicking and clapping, suppose we sing. Here are the words; everyone sing them after me."

"Hello everybody, how do you do?" Clarice was making up the words and also the catchy tune. "I'm here at school, I like it, too. Hello everybody, come help me sing. I love to be here, ding-a-ling ding."

After a moment of singing, kicking and clapping Clarice plopped down to the floor and spread out her skirt. She motioned and the children plopped down and sat on her skirt. She pulled the skirt up around their shoulders and with a big smile she said, "I love children. I have fun with children. Children keep me laughing. You are children, and I love you. We are going to learn lots of good things together. So now let's go over to the table and look at some pictures."

Parson Smith had obtained six small milking stools which were placed at the table. Each child had a place.

Sister Smith had helped Clarice make several sketches of animals, trees, birds, and such to have ready for use at school. Clarice gave each child a picture; such subjects as a dog burying a bone, a cow eating grass, a cat climbing a tree, a frog jumping on a lily pad.

Clarice said to the children, "We will take turns talking about the pictures. Now look at your picture for awhile, and tell me what animal you have and what it is doing. Take your time, no hurrying. I will call your name when we are ready."

Each child showed much enthusiasm, and each was eager for more as no one of them ever had so much entertaining attention.

The parents began to show up to collect their children after six or seven hours.

Clarice was exhausted, but she had pinned a note to each one's garment: Class begins at 8:00 A.M. Class is over at twelve noon.

Jason came home and wanted to know how the first day went.

"The children cried when they got here, and they cried when they left. The crying when they got here was for fear. The crying when they left was because they didn't want to leave. I am almost sure that is the end of the crying. It is going to be a lot of work."

Jason pulled her onto his lap and hugged her tightly. "There's no one in this world that can do a better job of it than you, my love."

Clarice laid her head on his shoulder and fell asleep.

Clarice taught six children, three days a week, all summer. Two more squirming little boys, Johnny Sears and Paul Phillips, called Puppy, joined the others a little later. They were five years old.

The school and home chores kept Clarice quite busy. Sister Smith had coaxed her and Jason into attending the Sunday meetings and that kept Jason from chopping wood for the fireplace, which he had been doing on Sunday. Sister Smith taught Clarice the Anglican prayers, and, on the mornings that school was not in session, she appeared on Clarice's threshold for two hours of prayer. The Sister insisted that Clarice open each school session with a prayer.

Each night Clarice related, in detail, her day's activities to Jason, and sometimes when he was at militia drill and didn't get home until midnight.

Jason was becoming an expert marksman with his flintlock musket. Now and then he practiced at home, shooting at rocks on a fence post or nails driven in the side of the barn. Hitting the nail heads and driving them in was his favorite target practice.

One morning in early May, after Jason had gone to work, Clarice answered a knock at her door.

It was a messenger with a rolled up parchment in his hand and another sticking from his pocket.

"Are you Mrs. Jason McKenzie?" he asked.

"Yes, I am," answered Clarice.

"I was told to hand this message into you hand only and to get your signature on this." He drew the paper from his pocket and held it out for her to sign.

She took a charcoal from her pocket and signed the one and began unrolling the other.

"Wait," she said, "there may be an answer."

She read:

> My Dear Cee Cee:
> I am taking the liberty to write you this warning. There is a terrible storm brewing in this province. I wish you safety and health.
> Because of this pending storm, I am leaving for England June first. I pray that you will give thought to also leaving.

I will be happy to take you under my wing until you are safe at home in England.

Before leaving, the Anthonys urged me to get in touch with you and persuade you to come home.

Your husband also is urged to come, or to follow, as soon as his business is dissolved.

I will arrange your passage on the Minerva as soon as I get your word.

I wish for you all the best of whatever it is you desire to do.

Please know that I regard you most highly.

Yours,

Governor Thomas Hutchinson

Clarice felt the tears roll down her cheeks, but she smiled at the messenger as she took her charcoal again from her pocket and wrote on the bottom of the page:

My Dear Friend:

Thank you and God bless you. God bless your journey and your stay in England.

Part of my heart is in England and part of it is here. And I love the part that is here best of all. I will not leave it.

Give my love to the Anthonys, especially Robin.

Yours ever, respectfully,

Clarice Creighton McKenzie

She rolled the parchment and tied it with the ribbon. She handed it to the messenger and thanked him.

He put the parchment roll in his satchel, mounted his horse, and rode down the pike toward Boston.

Clarice laid her head against the door facing and whispered to herself, "He was so kind to me; why is it that the people hate him so much?"

She wiped her eyes with her kerchief and went back to the kitchen. She thought about telling Jason, then she changed her mind. He may insist that I go for awhile. He also knows of a pending storm. He will, of course, want me to be safe. I just won't tell him.

Now it was factual. She and Jason each had a secret. To reveal it or not reveal it, that was their question.

Every day Jason asked questions of his fellow workers. "Have you heard of any resolutions made by Parliament regarding the 'tea dumping'? There have been many vessels coming in from England, and there has been plenty of time for the old beards to have made decisions." He asked, "Do you suppose anyone who went over has given names of suspected participants to the lords or anyone who would have proposed punishment measures, say, for instance, North or Dartmouth?"

None of his fellow workers knew more than he. They were all just as dumbfounded as Jason that no word had come. There was feeling amongst the lot of them that some retaliation was sure to be invested upon them.

It was only a few days before the news of the Boston Port Bill reached the shipyard. A horrendous uproar immediately began. The workers realized that their jobs would be in jeopardy.

The news of the Boston Tea Party reached London in mid February. Several Americans arrived there at the same time. They were people who could give accurate details of the riotous activities that took place at Griffin's Wharf on the night of December sixteenth. The Privy Council was immediately called into session.

To say that the lords of both houses were angry would be putting it mildly. There were a few, however, who sat quietly smirking at the others. They were those who had predicted that the Americans would take drastic measures at the new policies of the East India Tea Company, appointing a few favorite merchants as consignees.

The king was irritable and showed his anger by shaking his fist at any of his assistants, or ministers, who mentioned the tea dumping. Especially after February nineteenth, on hearing and reading of testimony before the Privy Council, that the attorney general and solicitor general were embarrassed when they agreed that there was not sufficient evidence to press charges of treason against any of the suspects whose names were on the list.

May tenth, at home, Jason was so subdued that Clarice thought best to ask no questions. She knew his mind was on some serious problem. When Sister Smith came, she immediately noticed Jason's unusual sullen expression. He barely spoke to her as he slowly went upstairs.

"What's the matter with Jason?" she asked of Clarice. "I can tell he's bothered about something."

Clarice was bent over removing ashes from the fireplace. Without looking at Sister Smith, she answered, "I didn't ask him. It's best to let him stew it out when he's like this."

A little later, two men from the shipyard came to the door. Clarice met them with friendly greeting, but she didn't know who they were.

The burly one inquired, "Is the Mr. at home? We would like a word with him."

Jason had seen them through the window. He came down the steps and went to the door, pushing Clarice aside and saying, "Excuse us," as he stepped outside between them and pulled the door shut behind him.

Clarice turned toward Sister Smith, who was rocking vigorously while flipping the pages of her New Testament, which she had taken from her pocket. She asked, "Did you know who those two men were?"

"No," Sister answered, "they're not from around here."

For a moment or two Clarice showed her fright, thinking maybe they had come to arrest Jason. Sister Smith saw the anxiety on Clarice's face. She wanted to comfort her, to reassure her. She quit her rocking and went to the kitchen, calling back, "Do you have any cider, dear? I'll heat some up for us. A hot cider drink will still your nerves."

Clarice went to the cupboard and brought out a jug. It was only half full. She said, "We are almost out. This is all we have." She handed the jug to Sister, who poured the contents out into an iron kettle and set it on the hearth to warm.

She and Clarice sat at the table drinking warm sweet cider and discussing "John, Chapter Two, where Jesus turned the water into wine at the wedding in Cana, in Galilee."

Jason and the two strangers walked down the road toward Lynn. Clarice got up from the table and went to the front yard gate to look down the road after the men. They were not in sight.

Sister Smith came out to Clarice, put her arm around her shoulder, and said, "Don't worry, honey. Jason is not being arrested; he will be back shortly."

"How do you know that? Why didn't he tell me what the men wanted? He knows I am worried all the time. Sister, do you know that Jason was one of the men who dumped the tea?"

The parson's wife stepped back, gasping for breath. "Oh, my Lord," she exclaimed. "maybe they were arresting him."

It was hard for Clarice to keep her mind off Jason and what he might be doing. He had not returned home. Several hours passed. Sister Smith left to go home, "to tend to her own chores."

The old clock in the great room and the little brass clock in the kitchen seemed to be talking to each other about the late hour and the darkness which came early. It was still not summer.

Clarice saw Parson Smith putting away the cow and the horses for the night. She was glad he was close by, and she appreciated his help. She called to him from the back door.

"Parson, please come in...I want someone to talk to."

"In a few minutes, Mrs. Clarice, but I can't stay. Sister will be needin' me and supper will be ready. Besides, I got to walk home."

The parsonage was about a mile away. It was a clapboard cottage attached by a breezeway to the red brick Anglican church. Parson Smith had been rector there for almost ten years.

When the parson came into the kitchen, Clarice poured some of the cider into a cup and held it out to him as she said, "I am worried about Jason. He didn't say where he was going or when he would return. I know he was uneasy about something because he was so glum this morning. He did not go to work but didn't say why. He didn't eat his breakfast!"

The parson was gulping down the cider and looking over the edge of the cup at Clarice. "I don't know why Jason was acting like that or what caused his solemn mood, but I will try to find out if it is a serious concern or just a flip in the pan. Don't take it on yourself to get sick over it. Jason is a solid rock. He will tell you what you need to know when the time is ripe."

Clarice flopped into a chair and pulled up the tail of her apron and buried her face in it.

Parson Smith went out the back door, not bothering to close it. Clarice heard him say, "Weeping, worrying women, Lord help them."

She jumped up and ran to the door calling after him.

"Parson Smith, I'm not a weeping, worrying woman. I'm a woman in love with my man and I don't want to be without him."

The parson heard her. He removed his hate and scratched his head thinking as he hurried along, "Not many women would admit to being in love; it would be too embarrassing, but this one is shouting it out so anyone can hear it."

As the parson reached his house, he noticed the church door was ajar. He went over to close it and saw men and heard voices. He opened the door wider and stepped inside but remained standing in the back of the church to listen to the men who were seated in the two front pews. Someone was standing in front of them reading from a parchment scroll by the dim light of a barn lantern.

One of the men turned his head around and called over his shoulder, "Come on down, Parson, and sit with us, and listen to the outcome of our conviction."

As he walked down the aisle he could see that several of the men were reading from pages of the Gazette. He knew at once that the meeting was about the Boston Port Bill, the news of which had just reached Boston the day before.

"Good evening, gentlemen. I see you are all taking stock of the punishment we are about to endure, all because of a few cranky hardheads and a few foolish pranksters."

No one answered the parson's remark. He took a seat near the rostrum, took his spectacles from his vest pocket, and adjusted them to his eyes. He picked up a page of the paper from the floor. It was badly crumpled; someone had stomped on it and spit on it.

"Now," said the parson, "this colony can expect hard times. It's bound to happen. I pray the Lord every day that He will be merciful."

One of the men loudly replied, "Mercy, merciful, we're going to need more than mercy. We're going to need muskets and swords and a fighting spirit."

"Guts and brains," shouted out another. "That's what we're going to need."

Then another shouted out, "I expect our guts and brains will soon be scattered where seed-corn should be planted."

The parson held up his hand to quiet the squirming men, "We can escape the misery if we will pay the East India Company for the tea. Listen, men, up till now the company has been fair. We should not ruin their business or run down their new policies which are not bad. Everything changes in time. It was a dastardly act to dump their tea. That company lost more than seventy-five thousand pounds."

Parson Smith was "het-up." Now he was the speaker. He read aloud from the page (he knew that some of the men could not read), "Boston Harbor will be closed June first. No foreign shipping will be allowed to enter port. No vessel that is now in port will be allowed to leave after June fifteenth.

"The custom house will be moved to Salem. Only coastal lighters will be allowed to enter and only after careful inspection. The lighters must be fuel and supply vessels only.

"This punishment will continue until the cost of the tea has been paid and the Royal Officers compensated."

"Never, never," shouted the men in unison. "We won't pay one pence, not one."

The parson walked out, beating his hat against his hand and mumbling angry words under his breath.

Jason McKenzie stood up and faced the men. "Men," he said, "we now know what is going to be demanded of us. Let us vow to stand pat and stand together to preserve our rights."

"Yea, Yea," was the resounding response.

A dozen or so of the men who had assembled there were residents of neighboring towns: Salem, Marblehead, Saugus, Cambridge. It was too late and too dark to travel to their homes. Each one, including Jason McKenzie, stretched out on a church pew and slept there until morning.

Clarice climbed the stairs around eleven P.M., carrying her flickering little candle. She had waited for Jason and tried to keep his supper warm, thinking every moment she would hear his footsteps. Although she was in bed, she could not sleep. She imagined Jason locked in the village gaol or workhouse. She mulled over in her mind her life at the Anthonys. She had no anxieties there.

She got up and wrote a note to Governor Hutchinson, telling she had changed her mind and did wish to go home, asking him to reserve passage for her. She still had more than two weeks to get ready.

She went to the bureau drawer and took out her blue chamois slippers. She held them up to her face, caressing the. She said, "You darlings, you know I am in the wrong place. I belong in England; I want to go home."

At that moment her thoughts turned to Jason as she thought she heard him enter the house. She ran downstairs, the slippers still in her hands.

"Jason," she called out, "I was worried." Then she suddenly stopped and sat down in the rocking chair. She had been mistaken. It wasn't Jason, just the wind banging against the door.

Returning to the bedroom, she put the slippers back into the bureau drawer. She tore up the note she had started to the governor and dropped the pieces into a pitcher of water that was standing on the night table. She remembered that she had done that once before.

She got back into bed and repeated over and over The Lords Prayer, which Sister Smith had made her learn. She fell asleep.

Just before dawn Clarice was awakened by a bristling, cracking noise. She got out of bed and went to the front window. There was a red glow in the sky. She ran to the back window and saw huge flames and black smoke billowing up from the barn.

She didn't take time to put on her robe or shoes. She ran down the stairs and out the back door, grabbing a pail and filling it with water from the horse trough by the barn door. Her only thought was to get Charlie and Panzy and Bessie, the cow, out of the barn.

The fire seemed to be in the hayloft only. It was hard for her to lift the bar that crossed the double doors. Parson Smith had shoved it down hard. She tugged at it; finally she lifted it up and off, and the doors swung open.

The smoke was heavy and strong smelling. She went into the barn under the burning hay. A big ball of the smoking burning stuff fell. It hit the floor of the barn right in front of her. She saw a pair of boots in the burning bail, she grabbed at them and retrieved them from the fire. She threw them out the door and proceeded to Charlie first, then Panzy, then Bessie. Just as she led the last frightened animal to safety, the roof fell in and a big burst of flame shot toward the sky. She stood by and watched the barn disintegrate very fast and saw the three animals escaping to the pasture.

She saw in the distance, at the turn of the road, a fleeing horse with a bareback rider. That is when she had a feeling that the fire had been set.

Before she went into the house, she remembered the boots she had thrown out the door. She walked to where they were laying, still smoldering. She poured the water from the pail onto them and turned each one over with her bare foot.

"Oh my God, these are Truly's boots...then she did sleep here. I wonder what Jason knows about this."

As he was walking on the road toward home, Jason saw the smoke and flames. He knew at once that it was his house or barn. He began to run.

Clarice went to the yard gate to look down the road, hoping to see him coming. He saw Clarice at the gate and ran faster. She ran to meet him in a state of hysteria, her arms outstretched to him.

"Oh darling, where have you been? This has been a terrible night. Are you in danger?"

"No, no, my sweet, everything is fine." He lifted her into his arms and carried her.

She tried to tell him how she saved the animals, but her sobs were choking her.

He put his hand over her mouth, "Hush dear, you can tell me later," he said.

They sat in the rocking chair, she on his lap.

"My dear," he said, "you are the bravest, dearest person in all the world. Thank you for saving our horses and cow. I love you and am thankful you were not hurt."

"Jason," she said, now in a positive mood and she had stopped crying, "there is something else bothering me."

"What is it, Cee Cee?"

Clarice sternly said, "Truly has slept in our barn. Did you sleep there with her?"

"Of course not. What makes you think Truly slept in our barn?"

"I found her boots; they were burning with the hay."

Jason's eyes filled with surprise. "That's where she was when we all thought someone had killed her." He began to rock and laugh. He said, "She was sure some tricky kid and she outsmarted all of us."

"She didn't outsmart me," said the smiling Clarice. "She had to settle for Don Carlos, a one-legged man."

Jason pinched her on the butt and said, "It's not the legs that matter, my darling."

Jason and Clarice drove to Boston for the celebration of the arrival of Governor Gage. He had been appointed by Parliament to act as governor of Massachusetts while Governor Hutchinson took his leave in England. Gage was also commander-in-chief of all North American forces in New England.

There was a lively parade, and again Hancock's cadets marched. The Club Nine bitterly opposed their participation but did nothing to stop it.

There was also a banquet in Gage's honor held in Faneuil Hall, where British officers, prominent Patriots, and rich Tories sat down together toasting, laughing, and drinking until drunk.

Jason told Clarice that he didn't drive all the way to Boston to celebrate the arrival of Gage but to celebrate the departure of Hutchinson. He added, "I hope he never comes back."

He never did.

There was a large crowd at the wharf on June first to bid bon voyage to the governor. Clarice and Jason stood way back in the crowd. Every time Clarice made an attempt to move a little closer, Jason held on to her arm and held her back.

Some of the people were crying. Some children pushing through gave him a bouquet of flowers or a gift. Two of his house servants were helping him along, as well as a few government officials.

A very fine ketch was waiting to take him to the Castle William where the Minerva was waiting. As the ketch left the wharf, the governor removed his hat and waved it toward the crowd, then bowed low, swooping his hat back and forth in front of him until the craft was quite far out in the sea.

Jason hugged Clarice up close to his side and kissed the top of her head. He said, "I understand, dear, why you are crying; I just can't feel the way you do. Please forgive me."

She raised her face to his and whispered, "I'm so glad you understand. I'm very proud of the way you feel, darling. I love this country and our home. I also want it to be free, but I also love England."

General Thomas Gage was now the acting governor of Massachusetts, also the commanding general of the British Army in America.

He had been accompanied to Boston by five thousand British troops purposely to see that the Boston Port Bill was put into effect and strictly obeyed. There were British camps set up all over the town. Every vacant lot and every vacant building accommodated at least a squadron and many were quartered in private homes.

Johnny Burgoyne emptied out the Old South Church and set up a training school therein. Three thousand were staying at the outpost Castle William but going and coming to and from hourly.

On the way home Jason was very quiet. Clarice could see by his twitching lips and shifting eyes that he didn't like seeing a red-coated, pistol-carrying sentry on every corner. He turned his head away at each one, only to face Clarice smiling sweetly, bowing, and waving her little Union Jack in greeting.

Finally in anger, Jason yelled at her, "Clarice, for God's sake, put that damn flag down and stop bowing at these goddamn soldiers."

This outburst made Clarice mad. She yelled back at him, "You know I'm British. I'll always be British."

He yelled louder, "Not in my house you won't. You'll be an American Patriot Rebel or you can leave." He paused a moment and slapped the reins against Charlie's rump so hard the horse bounded into a gallop. He stormed out again, "Why didn't you go with Hutchinson? He invited you, didn't he?"

Clarice showed her astonishment at his knowing about that. "How did you find out about that? Who told you that he invited me?"

Jason didn't answer her.

"Ah," said Clarice, "the messenger. He must be the one who told you. Tell me, was it the messenger?"

Jason still didn't answer, but in a moment he did scornfully say, "I've known ever since that week you spent in Milton that he had designs on you. I watched him the night of your arrival. At the reception, he watched every move you made. I knew then he was attracted to you."

Clarice was now very angry. She said, "Jason, you are crazy. He was the governor; I was a servant of the Anthonys. This is too foolish to talk about. Why are you acting like this?"

He picked up the whip and gave Charlie a whack across his backside, taking his anger out on the horse.

"Why the hell are you bowing and smiling and waving your flag at the goddamn British solders? And why, for God's sake, were you crying at Hutchinson's leaving? It was a good riddance if you ask me."

She wiped her eyes and sneezed, then she said, "Jason, let's stop this; we are being mean to each other." Then she began to cry again, and with her quivering voice, she said, "I still have my doubts about you and Truly."

"For God's sake, Clarice, I've told you that Truly and I were only friends. She was like my little sister; I felt a responsibility toward her. I have known Lola for years. Truly was a baby when I first met her."

A moment of silence passed, then he let out a burst of loud anger. "I don't want to hear any more about it; forget it, I'm tired of your suspicions. We'll probably never see her again. Do you hear me? No more about Truly—ever—never. I hate her."

Clarice wiped her tears away and wiped her nose, and between sniffles, she whined out, "Why do you hate her? She loved you. Maggie told me that Truly was in love with you."

Charlie stopped at the yard gate and bobbed his head up and down. Clarice threw the duster back from her lap and started to climb down out of the chaise without waiting for Jason to come around and help her.

Neither of them had said a word for the last few miles, but now Jason laid his hand on her arm to hold her back.

"Sweetheart," he said, "I'm sorry I said hateful words to you. I love you more than anything or anybody in this world. I think you love me, too. Let's forgive each other and never bicker at each other again. Please."

Clarice gave him a half smile and replied, "Oh, all right, Jason."

He leaned forward to kiss her, but she jumped from the chaise before his lips reached her. She ran into the house.

After unhitching Charlie and covering the chaise with an old ship's sail, Jason walked around the charred rubbish that used to be the barn.

He said to himself, "I've got to do something about this." He began kicking over burnt boards, looking for bits and pieces that could be used again, picking them up and stacking them in a pile. "I'm going to ask some of the fellows at the yard to help me rebuild this barn."

He felt so good with his brainstorm that he went into his house, singing a little ditty:

> Swing your ax, son
> Swing it jolly
> Swing you ax up high, son
> Swing it hard by golly.
> Swing you ax, son
> Swing 'til the tree rips
> You can tell a workman, son
> By his pile of chips.

He hoped he would find Clarice in a friendly mood. He did. She was busy at the children's table, putting out new pieces of charcoal and colored paste which she had previously made from flour, water, and berry juice. She turned to face Jason and said, "Come here, dear, and see the different colors I have made for the children's painting class."

Jason went over to her and dipped his finger into the jar she was holding. While squeezing her up against him he painted her nose a bright red. He held her back and laughed, then kissed her nose and made his mouth red. They stood looking into each other's eyes in ecstasy. He took her hand and led her upstairs.

June was a happy month for the McKenzies. They tried to keep the Boston Port Bill and other political issues out of their minds.

Clarice enjoyed the teaching and playing with the six small children. By the middle of the month, they each knew their ABCs. They each could name the royal officials of Massachusetts. They could sing and keep time. They could tell time and count to a hundred.

Sister Smith was as happy as a mother hen. She came every school day, always bringing apples or cookies for recess.

Clarice reminisced when cutting out patterns and making plans. She had fond memories of herself and Robin getting ready for the king's birthday party, which never took place, or of her own birthday party, when Jason never showed up with the cake.

"Ah," she sighed, "those were happy but frustrating times. I was so deeply in love then...I still am. Now I have some bigger occasions to plan," she said to Sister Smith.

"We're going to have a barn-raising. You and I have been designated to take charge of the food and entertainment. We are also to notify all our neighbors and friends. July fourth will be the day, and that will be on Monday." Clarice was looking Sister Smith right in the eye, hoping for some expression of approval. "I have never been to a barn-raising; I don't know what to do. Will you take charge?"

Sister Smith liked very much to be in the center of all confusion so she readily accepted.

Each day for the rest of June someone from the shipyard brought something: lumber, logs, stones, nails, tools. It seemed that every time Clarice went outside she saw something being unloaded near the site of the old barn where the new barn was going to be.

The shipyard was closing down. Since the Port Bill there had been very little business activity. The company was letting their inventory go out on credit, and Jason was taking advantage of it.

He often was seen jotting down figures on a piece of parchment which he carried in his pocket. He realized that he was going deep into debt, remembering also that he owed John Slade ten pounds and Henry ten pounds. But he had to have a barn; winter was just around the corner.

Jason and Parson Smith shared a secret. Panzy was with foal. The parson said to Jason, "I watched it kicking her sides out. I was surprised because I never knew when she was in season. I thought she was too old."

Jason beamed with delight when he patted Charlie's shoulder and called him a 'sly old rascal' and added, "I didn't suspect you had it in you."

The morning of the barn-raising, several of the men showed up at daylight. They raked the space and measured it off by stepping back and forth and driving stakes at the corners.

About seven A.M. Clarice came out of the kitchen with a large platter of ham, fried eggs, and biscuits and hominy. A large table had been improvised with large wooden sawhorses. She spread a long patchwork quilt over it and set it with her pewter plates and mugs. These had been left to Jason by his mother, and this was the first time she had had a chance to use them.

She tapped on a mug with a spoon and the men hurried to their breakfast. A large urn belonging to Sister Smith held gallons of rich coffee.

Not long after Clarice cleared away the breakfast things, another half dozen men came bringing their wives and children.

Jason, a few days earlier, had circled off a place under a large oak tree, quite a distance away from the building site. He had made a seesaw and put up a swing. He brought out the school table and chairs. In a basket he put building blocks, small stones, pieces of white bark, and small pieces of fresh charcoal. This basket of play tools he placed on the table. His intention was to keep the children away from the busy workmen, where there might be danger, as they erected the barn.

The wives soon began their work making the noonday meal. There was so much to eat and so much punch to drink made from grapes, plums, gooseberries, cranberries, and mint leaves. Laughing, talking, singing, and finally dancing to the music of fiddle, French harp, and fife, continued until dark. At eight o'clock everyone formed a circle and skipped around the new barn which was completely finished.

As the neighbors and friends began to gather up their sleepy children and think of home, Clarice suggested that Parson Smith christen the barn. He walked to the table and picked up the keg with the remaining punch. He carried it over to within five feet of the barn and tossed the punch all over the door. His voice rang out as he said, "I christen this barn, McKenzie Barn. Long may it stand!"

A big "hooray!" went up from the crowd.

Jason lifted Clarice into his arms and jumped up onto the table. He held up his arm with her hand clasped into his own.

"Dear friends and neighbors, children, countrymen, and Americans. My wife and I are very grateful to you for your help and your friendship. Long may it last, forever and always."

They both waved and bowed, like performers at the end of a play, as the barn builders all departed.

"Gee Whiz, darling, it's been a great day," Jason said as he and Clarice held hands and went into their house.

The men of Lynn gathered almost every day at the village store to discuss the Justice Bill, which happened to be the follow-up of the Port Bill.

"This should be the In-Justice Bill," said one old farmer. "I don't believe any honest to goodness American born man will stand for it."

"Ah," said the storekeeper, "it's going to make a lot of us real mad. Just think how long it will take for a man accused of a crime to be bound in chains, shipped to England to stand trial, and serve his punishment—for a crime he may not have committed—while his family suffers in agony to learn what became of him."

"Sounds confusing," said a Lynn lawyer, "and what about our people not being able to elect our judges or ministers or the governor?"

"Well, I'll say," said James Trumphill. "Parliament is going to hear from a good many American sympathizers." He continued, "It is not too late to get quickly to the task of filling up some storehouses with muskets and shells. I know of a place we might get; it's out near Concord."

"You are a little behind time," said John Jolly. "We have been doing that for several months! Oh, we don't have nearly enough to stop a British brigade, but we will continue to stock up as long as we feel the need. Frankly, I am in doubt that any aggressive attack will come about. However, I am pretty sure that Gage has his informers and is aware of our drilling and storing arms."

Jason McKenzie spoke up, "I have a copy of the Port Bill and its segments right here in my pocket. If you so desire, I will read it to you."

Heads all nodded in the affirmative as "Aye, aye, aye" was heard from every mouth.

The Boston Port Bill went into effect June first, 1774, the same day that Governor Hutchinson left for England and Governor Gage, appointed by the king, took over the governorship of Massachusetts.

The Port Bill became the Justice Bill and the segments became the Coercive Acts. The acts were Parliament's punitive measures against the colony of Massachusetts as punishment for the Boston Tea Party.

Jason pulled a rumpled piece of paper from his pocket and began to read:

> First...No vessel from abroad will be allowed to enter Boston Harbor. All foreign vessels already here will be required to leave before June fifteenth.
>
> Second...Custom House will be moved to Salem.
>
> Third...The Massachusetts Charter will be amended and by August first the Governor's Council will no longer be elected by the General Court but will be appointed by the king. The governor will hereafter appoint, and remove, all judges and officers of the law.
>
> Fourth...No more town meetings will be held unless the king gives permission.
>
> Fifth...Freeholders will no longer be allowed to select juries after September first, 1774.

Sixth...This is called the "Regulating Bill." It gives the royal governor the power to shift trials to England if he thinks impartiality is a factor in trying a soldier of the king who has been roughly handled while trying to enforce the Justice Bill. In other words, if the soldier has met with revenge and hostile treatment.

Jason said in closing, "If you ask me, this is martial law taking the place of civil law." Jason did not sit down after that statement. He asked, "Men, I would like your opinion. Are you in favor of a vote?"

"Aye," was the unanimous reply.

"Here is the question," said the inquisitive Jason, "in order to get these overbearing Coercive Acts rescinded, are you willing to contribute any pecuniary restitution toward paying to the East India Company compensation for the tea they lost?"

Twenty-five men were present, all freeholders. The result of the vote: twenty-four "nays." Now who was the person who voted "yea"?

Everyone was surprised. It was Parson Smith.

The parents of Clarice's pupils called on her and asked her to continue the school through the summer. They needed lots of freedom to do the heavy summer work such as canning, spinning, weaving, gardening, making cheese, drying apples and peaches, and hay making, etc. Clarice was happy to have school in summer.

Clarice added that she would like to continue the school year through the fall months but shut down when the cold weather set in.

On one particular day in July, the six pupils with Clarice and Sister Smith went for an outing.

Each child had a shoulder satchel; a biscuit with ham, an apple, and a cookie; a piece of parchment; and a piece of charcoal. They walked in pairs with Clarice in front and Sister Smith following.

The Saugus Road was a quiet lane with hardly any traffic. The river ran close by, and along the bank of the river there was a wonderful place to watch frogs and butterflies and spiders, where one could hear and distinguish the birds and locusts.

Clarice led the children to a shady spot and spread out a large linen sheet and motioned the children to sit on it.

"Now," she said, "take out your paper and charcoal and draw something that you see or whatever you like."

Matthew, of course, rebelled. "I want to fish," he yelled out at his teacher.

"But we didn't bring our fishing pole," said Clarice.

"Then I want to wade in the water," said the boy.

Clarice knew then that he was going to be difficult.

"Matthew, let's you and I take a walk along the river bank and see if we can find something that no one has ever seen."

The purpose of the walk was to talk to the child about being obstinate. She realized that scolding him, or taking a stand against his wishes in the presence of others, would probably cause more stubbornness and detract the others from their pleasurable activity.

She nodded to Sister Smith who knew the purpose of the proposed walk and that she was to be in charge while Clarice and the boy were gone. "I want to wade," Matthew said sternly as he jerked his teacher's hand.

"Matthew, the water is too deep to wade," she answered.

As the two walked along the river bank, Matthew, at last became reconciled to other matters and gave up on fishing and wading. They discovered a large fungus growth on a log which Clarice loosened and held high over her head, laughing and telling Matthew that it was her umbrella.

Matthew had never seen an umbrella and didn't know what she meant. Clarice sat down on a log and pulled the boy up onto her lap. She told him about her home in England and how it rained almost every day, and when it was raining and she carried her father's lunch to him at his factory, she carried her little umbrella that her father made for her.

"Like this," she said, as she held the fungus over her head.

Matthew was full of questions and was eager to find another fungus.

"Sometimes," said Clarice, "frogs use these as shelters, and sometimes they use them as podiums to sit on and sing. That is why people call them toadstools."

Matthew ran ahead of Clarice for a while looking for another treasure. He saw a large black heap. It looked to the boy like a pile of rotten leaves. He went closer and saw a raccoon run from it and disappear into the woods. He picked up a stick, which was about four feet long and began to punch into the heap.

Clarice came closer to see what it was. She had already surmised that it was not a pile of leaves. She saw at once that it was a pile of dark feathers. Matthew had moved the object with the stick until it was in a more horizontal position. They both saw hands and feet.

"Oh, my Lord," cried out Clarice in a very frightened voice. "Get away, Matthew, run back to the others. I'm right behind you."

Matthew and Clarice made it back to where the sheet was spread and the others were busily drawing. Sister sensed something strange and said to Clarice, while trying to be unperturbed, "What is it Clarice? Did you find something interesting?"

Matthew blurted out, "Yeah, a dead man. He was all covered in tar and feathers."

"Can we go and see it too?" almost simultaneously the children's voices called out. Paper and charcoal were thrown right and left. Children scrambled to their feet and gathered around Matthew.

"What did he look like?"

"How do you know he was dead?"

"Who done it?"

Matthew was swelling with pride. He was the big wheel in this commotion. He knew the answers but not "Who done it."

Clarice was leaning against Sister Smith, with her head on Sister's shoulder. She was bewildered and scared. She whispered, "What are we going to do? We have to tell someone. Jason is not at home."

"Neither is the Parson at home," said Sister Smith. She added, "Seems like men are always somewhere else when their help is needed."

Clarice turned to the children and said, "Let's all sit down and eat our lunch, then we will go home."

"Can't we go and see the dead man?" asked Molly Jolly.

"Why is he dead?" asked Johnny Sears.

"I'm scared," said Puppy Phillips.

When they got back to the McKenzie house, they were a very quiet bunch of pupils and teachers. Clarice had shushed them so many times because she couldn't bear talking about the tarred and feathered dead man who had apparently also been in the river. He had either been thrown in the river and died there and later washed up onto the bank or had been thrown into the river while still alive and had crawled up onto the bank and died there.

She said to the children when they were seated at their table, "We must forget about the dead man. Someone will take care of him as soon as they can. All we can do is believe he was a good man and has gone to heaven."

Sister Smith came into the room with an arm full of flowers she had gathered from the yard and garden. She placed them in a pile in the center of the table.

She said to the group, "When I call your name, pick out a flower from the pile, call out its name, and place it in this vase of water."

She placed a vase near the pile of blossoms. She called Molly's name first. The child reached for a long-stemmed flower and said, "I like blue; I thinks this is blueberry."

"No," said Sister Smith. "That is a very pretty name, but the real name is larkspur. Puppy Phillips, it's your turn."

Puppy chose a black-eyed Susan. He held it up high and said, "I think this is named black button."

"That's a good guess," said Sister, "but its name is black-eyed Susan."

"Is it a girl?" asked Puppy.

"Maybe it is," said Sister.

"Flowers ain't girls and boys," said Matthew.

Clarice spoke softly, hardly loud enough to be heard, for she was still feeling distraught over finding the victim of such an ugly act. "Flowers are girls and boys who do not do mean things to each other," she said. "They bloom because of their love."

After each child had added a flower to the vase and learned its name, Sister Smith arranged the rest of the flowers into a pretty bouquet.

She said to the children, "When you come to school next Monday, we will take a walk to the graveyard and put this bouquet on the grave of the dead man. He will be buried by then."

Clarice then said to the children, "Now we must say 'Thank you, Sister Smith.'"

Their childish voices in unison called out, "Thank you, Sister Smith."

Later that day, after Sister Smith had spread the news of the tarred and feathered corpse, the Lynn constable called on Clarice to get information of all she knew about what she had found on the river bank. It was very little she could tell him, for she only saw his hands and feet, which were bare.

Jason came home while the constable was still there. He had heard about Clarice and Matthew discovering the dead body.

Sister Smith had been watching for him to pass by the rectory. When she saw him coming, she went to the road and hailed him. She was a great news spreader. To be able to report some exciting happening lifted her ego to enormous heights.

"I've already heard," said Jason to Clarice when she began saying, "Jason, I'm sick of this day. It has been very disturbing. The children expected a fun-filled adventure, but I'm afraid that our unfortunate discovery will stay on their little minds forever."

The constable thanked Clarice and gathered up his note pad and his billy stick. He was about to leave when he said directly to Jason, "I think that eventually all of the culprits who dumped the tea will get what they deserve."

Jason's eyes immediately filled with anger. He bragged at the constable's coat sleeve to halt his departure. "Wait a minute, officer, are you implying that the corpse is one of the patriots who dumped the tea?"

"Well...Mr. McKenzie, I know those lawbreakers are being sought and since no legal orders have been issued for their arrest, the loyal citizens who have been so drastically harmed and deprived have to take matters of punishment into their own hands."

"How do you know if the corpse was a loyalist or patriot?" asked Jason.

The constable seemed confused by the question. "Oh, I have no proof of his politics, but that will soon be established. We are calling in a good many citizens to try to identify him as soon as we get him cleaned up. You know it takes time to get all that tar off his face.

"Good day, Ma'am." He tipped his hat to Clarice as he left.

"Jason, dear, please talk to me about something else...something nice. I want to get that poor fellow off my mind."

Jason hugged her and kissed her and smoothed her hair back from her forehead as he looked into her eyes. "You are so precious to me, darling. Whenever something troubles you, remember our love. By the way, I do know something very nice to tell you. Panzy is with foal. We must take good care of her. She is a twenty-year-old mare."

Clarice asked, "Do you think Charlie is the father?"

"Of course, dear. Panzy hasn't been near any other stallion. The funny thing is...neither I nor Parson Smith know when she was in season."

Clarice, now sitting on Jason's lap and holding his hand, said, "I think I know. It was when you got back from Oliver's funeral. She had been so lonesome, whinnying all the time while Charlie was away for three days."

"To think I almost lost him. Thank God for Cindy Waters's Little Fritters and for John Slade and Henry who redeemed him for me."

"Jason, we do have some good friends. I wonder where John and Henry are now."

Clarice and Jason went into the kitchen together and set out some supper. Earlier that morning when preparing lunch for the children's outing, she had made a big batch of cookies. There was some baked ham and applesauce.

It was now dark and Jason lit the candles, and Clarice put a bouquet, which she plucked from the children's bouquet, in the center of the table. She and Jason sat, slowly eating while gazing into each other's eyes. The ham; applesauce; cookies; and fresh milk from Bessie, which Parson Smith had just left on the back bench, made a delicious meal.

Jason got up and walked to a shelf and removed a book. He came back to the table, and as he sat down, he said, "I want to read something to you, dear; will you listen?"

"Of course. I love to hear you read. Your voice is like music to my ears."

He took a piece of paper from the book. It was brown with age and quite worn.

"This," he said, "my mother wrote for me when my father died. She saw me sitting on the stair step," he pointed, "there...crying. She said, 'Jason, my son, you and I have to continue our lives just as we have been doing. Your papa would want us to enjoy our work and home. I have written a poem for you. Here it is.'

"It was in late summer," said Jason. He unfolded the paper and read:

"Sorrow in Summer
by
Anne McKenzie

If sorrow comes on a summer day
Weep, but little, it will pass away
Enjoy summer, it is so brief
There's always sorrow, always grief.
If it be summer, smile and sing
Gather flowers, watch birds on the wing
Taste the raindrops, smell the hay.
Skies are bluer on a summer day.

If it be summer, when leaves are green
And snow and ice are never seen

Walk in the woods and talk to the trees
Wade in cool water and hum with the bees
If it be summer and work is real
When spiders spin their gossamer wheel
Take hold of the task with brawn and brain
Summer may never come again.

Weep no more at sorrow's door
Nor think of times to be no more
But think of summer's sweet repose
Let sorry settle in the rose."

Clarice was sitting quietly at the table. Jason folded the paper and returned it to the book. He got up and placed the book back on the shelf.

He then took Clarice's hand and led her to the door and pointed to the big, bright, full moon. Moonbeams were bounding all over the new barn.

"What a beautiful evening," he said.

"Jason?"

"Yes dear."

"What would you like Panzy to have? A colt or a filly?"

"Doesn't matter."

"I wonder what Charlie would like."

"Let's take a walk out through the pasture and ask him," said Jason as he put his arm around Clarice's waist.

Chapter Twenty-Five

The moon made so much light it was like daylight. The pasture was lush in green grass four inches high.

Charlie and Panzy were standing close together under an oak tree. The small pond was glistening with moonbeams; the dragonflies and lunar moths were busy at their flying over the water and diving at the fireflies.

"Must be because it is so light," said Jason.

A long, moving, flashing stream of pink and green hurried across the northern sky in five or ten minute intervals.

"Look at that," said Clarice, "the Aurora Borealis."

"Time to kiss and make a wish," said Jason as he moved himself squarely in front of Clarice, facing her smile. He lifted her into his arms and carried her to the remains of last winter's hay stack. Their haybed was very soft and sweet smelling. The ecstatic sweethearts enjoyed their delicious lovemaking, there in the moonlight, serenaded by a whippoorwill and spotlighted by the Northern lights.

"My darling," said Jason to Clarice, when they were walking hand in hand back to their house (it was daylight now; the sun was big and golden over the treetops), "we forgot to ask Charlie what he would wish Panzy to have."

"Then we will have to take this walk again tomorrow night," said Clarice.

The tarred and feathered body that Clarice and Matthew discovered turned out to be a British soldier. His muddy uniform was found a few days later. It was hidden under an overturned canoe. A letter addressed to Corporal Edward Channing was found in a pocket.

Why he was on the Saugus River in a canoe was a mystery that baffled the constables of Saugus and Lynn for several days. It took three weeks to unravel the facts, then a few people were skeptical.

When Clarice heard the reports, she couldn't hold back the tears. She knew Corporal Edward Channing. He was one of the guards that Lord Anthony had stationed at the house on Beacon Hill to keep intruders out. She said to herself, "And to keep Jason away."

She had spoken to him frequently and Robin had had conversations with him. He had always been kind and seemed loyal to his duties.

Parson Smith said to Clarice, "Word of the drilling and storing of arms must have gotten to Gage and he sent Channing to spy it out. Anyway, I'm glad it was not a Royalist who did the dirty work."

The parson continued, "I'll tell you, girl, these hotheaded rebels are bringing a lot of trouble and disgrace on themselves. If they get us into a war, they will suffer the most. It will be impossible for a measly bunch of ragged hungry boys to whip the king's elegant layout of prepared, handsome men of the British Brigades."

Clarice had suspected Parson Smith of being a loyalist; now she was sure of it.

After the parson left, Clarice sat down to rest from her ironing and also to consider herself. Meditatively, she said, "Who am I? How can I be any other than a believer in the king's authority and Parliament's laws? But I am so much in love with Jason, who is one of the strongest patriots. He drills, he attends secret meetings, he plots and plans. He is a dedicated Son of Liberty; a member of Club Nine; a good friend of Samuel Adams, John Hancock, John Adams, Judge Otis, Paul Revere, and so many others who are pushing for independence. They call it freedom.

"I wish I understood what it is that they call liberty; I wish I could get Jason to talk about it. He seems to want to keep it from me. Must be because he is afraid for my safety. It is also because of his love of his parents and his property. He is adamant on breaking loose from England."

Sister Smith led the school children, single file, to the cemetery. Each child carried a bunch of flowers. Clarice walked behind the children carrying a bundle of pieces of sail cloth to use as covers in case of rain. The morning sky had shown prospects of thunder showers.

The grave had been covered with the sandy loam of Potter's Field. The flowers placed by the children gave it a more respectable appearance. As the little group stood by the grave, Sister Smith repeated an Angelican prayer. Clarice tried to hold back her tears, but when Matthew's sobs were heard, she let her tears flow down her cheeks.

It did not rain; the walk back to the house was pleasant. They stopped by the public pump and had a drink of cool water. They sang one of the songs Clarice had taught them. They changed places in line, twice. That gave them more chances to be friendly with different chums and less pugnacious, for Matthew loved starting an argument.

When the parents came to pick up their children, they found them to be more gentle and subdued than usual.

In late June one morning, a messenger knocked on the McKenzie door. Clarice was at home alone; Jason was in Salem on business, and she did not know on what business.

Parson Smith was staying in his church office many more hours of late for some unknown reason. If Sister knew, she was not telling Clarice. She was also not coming to see Clarice and was missing school more often. Her excuse was that she was not well.

Clarice opened the door to the messenger.

He said, "I have a message here," he patted his pocket, "for Mr. McKenzie."

"I'm sorry, he is not at home. I will take the message." Clarice was eager to know what it was.

"Sorry, Ma'am, but I've got orders to deliver it into his hands only. I'll just wait for his return."

"All right," said Clarice, "but it might be late today or it might be tomorrow. He did not say when he would return." She said to him, "Would you like to let your horse out into our pasture? We have a mare there who is with foal. Is your horse friendly?'

He answered her, "No, he might not be friendly. I think he will be satisfied just standing here by the gate. He can chomp on the grass here."

He sat down on the ground, his back against the fence.

Clarice went back into the house. She sat in a chair which was in front of the window. She intended to keep an eye on him. She was glad it was not a school day.

"Now what can that message be?" she said to herself. "It has been six months since the tea dumping. Why are they still searching for the people who did it?" She lived in constant fear of Jason being arrested.

It was late, nearly midnight, when Clarice heard Jason talking to the messenger, who had patiently waited for thirteen hours so he could deliver the message into Mr. McKenzie's hand only.

"Have you had anything to eat or been to the privy in all that time?" Jason asked him.

"No," answered the messenger. Jason could see the fellow was very young and timid. He knew being hungry wouldn't hurt him, but not relieving himself was a dangerous neglect.

The messenger softly said, "I would like to go to the privy while you're reading this message," he handed the scroll to Jason. "I would like you to keep an eye on my horse. So many horses are being stolen; I'm afraid to leave him for a minute."

Jason said, "Yes, my own was stolen in Boston, but I got him back. I don't think there is any horse-stealing going on out here in Lynn."

While the young man went around the house and hurried along to the outhouse about a hundred feet from the back door, Jason opened the scroll. He knew Clarice was right near the door where she could hear and see it all. It was like her to be that nosy; Sister Smith had rubbed off on her.

He called out, "Bring a lighted candle out here, Cee Cee; I can't read in the dark."

She was ready with the candle, just waiting, just as Jason had thought. She went out to the yard gate, sheltering the lighted candle from the breeze with her hand. She smiled at her husband and said, "I'm so glad to see you. Where were you for so long? I asked the messenger to give me the message, but he wouldn't do it. He was so loyal to his mission."

Jason was reading, and she was holding the light to the paper. "Well, what does it say?" she asked.

He looked pleased, but he didn't answer his wife. He said, "Stay here and watch the man's horse, I have to go inside to answer this." He went into the house almost in a run.

"Well at least he's not being arrested," she said as she blew out the candle.

Clarice waited there; when the messenger came back, he asked, "Ma'am, where is your husband?"

She answered, "He's inside writing an answer to the message. Will you tell me who sent the message?"

"Guess that won't do any harm," he said. "It was Mr. Samuel Adams."

Clarice let out a long breath. "Good gracious," she said, "wonder what he wants?" She continued, "Now that you're back, I'm going in the house and make you a tote of biscuits and jam to eat as you ride. My husband is taking such a long time. Don't get impatient, and be sure to wait for the tote."

"I sure will," Clarice heard him say, but she didn't hear him say, "God, I'm hungry."

She saw Jason sitting at the desk, quill in hand, writing. She hated to interrupt him. She quietly stood beside him trying to read over his shoulder. He covered the page with his arm. It was then impossible for her to see what he was so vigorously putting down on the paper.

When he began to roll the scroll, Clarice moved back from him so as not to be in the way when he pushed back his chair to get up. He hurriedly crossed the room and went out the door carrying the answer to the waiting messenger.

"Hey there, you trusty one, do be careful with this letter; it is very important. Don't drop it into the river or anything like that."

The messenger laughed as he put the scroll safely in his saddlebag. He said, "Don't worry, Mr. McKenzie; I'm going north. Mr. Adams is in Salem. I'll be very careful." He climbed aboard his saddle but did not ride away.

Jason called back to him from the door, "What are you waiting for?"

Clarice brushed by Jason waving a small sack. "He's waiting for this," she said, "his biscuits."

The McKenzies watched as the messenger rode off toward town.

"Now," said Clarice to her elated husband, "what did Sam Adams have to say? I'm dying to know."

"It will take a while to explain it to you, my dear. When the sun comes up, let's take a walk to Shiny Squatt. That's my lucky spot. I always feel good about the answers I get when I go there to think. I will tell you the whole story when we are there."

The sunrise was glorious. Pink and gold clouds were like hues from angel's wings drifting over the wedded lovers as they hopped, skipped, and chased each other through the dew-covered meadow. When they reached the pond, where the ripples were playing, Jason bent over and picked up a pebble and skipped it across the water, causing frightened frogs to suddenly leap into the water from their sunning spots on the muddy bank.

Clarice tucked her head in laughter as she squeezed Jason's arm. "Those frogs brought back my memory to me," she said, "of Robin. When we were on our weekend visit to Milton Hill, at lunch, she helped herself to a large portion of fried frog legs. She thought it was fried chicken, and when the governor's grandsons told her what she had eaten and that she would have warts, she threw one of her tantrums and refused to have anything to do with the boys."

Jason laughed with her as she related the story, then he asked, "Did she ever make up with them?"

"Yes, when you sent the petits-fours. She was so proud of the fancy little cakes, she wanted to show them off. It lifted her spirits to have something so luxurious to offer them, but she never did become friendly enough to play games with them."

When they came within sight of the big blue boulder, they began to run to it, Clarice holding up her skirt to keep from tripping over it. As they reached the stone, Jason spread both his palms against it and said, "My dear rock of ages, see whom I've brought." He drew Clarice up closer. "We need your help in a decision we have to make."

The two sat on the ground, their backs against the rock as they had done once before. Jason took the folded paper from his pocket. He turned to his wife and said, "Cee Cee, please don't let this upset you."

She felt an alarm going off in her bosom, but she smiled and said, "Read it, Jason."

"Dear Mr. McKenzie,

I hear you are looking for work. I know what a hard working man you are. I feel like I know you very well. Your trustworthiness was proven in December, and you were a dedicated patriot when called upon.

I thank you as do other members of The Sons, also Club Nine.

Now a much riskier opportunity arises, and I am in need of an aide. I am offering you the chance to become a very great man, that is, unless you end up at the noose of a rope.

In doing the work I am offering you, you will have to spend several months in Philadelphia, beginning September first, 1774.

If you can meet me in Boston in Hancock's warehouse office Monday, July eighteen, at ten o'clock A.M., I will lay out to you all of the details.

Please send an answer if you will be available for the July meeting.

I will remain in Salem as long as the General Court is in session here. I will be adjourned, I hope, by July first.

Yours,
Samuel Adams, Esq."

Clarice sighed, and she reached for Jason's hand. "What answer did you give him?" she asked.

He hesitated a few seconds before saying, "I gave him an affirmative answer, or course. I can't afford to miss an opportunity like the one he is going to offer me. His aide, Lord, he is a big, big man." He meant important.

Clarice jumped to her feet. "It makes me shudder," she said.

"Shudder...how?" Jason asked. "With joy or with fear?"

"Both," she answered.

They laid their heads back against the rock, closed their eyes, and were silent for at least half an hour. Then Jason raised his head, looked around, and put his hand over on Clarice's hand, "Are you asleep, Cee Cee?"

"Not now," she said, "since I felt your touch."

"Do you want to hear what I sent as an answer? I made a copy to have for my record."

"Yes, dear, if you want me to know."

Jason pulled a folded paper from his inside pocket, opened it, and read:

"Mr. Adams,
Honorable Sir:
I have read your message with excited pleasure. It will be a great honor to help you in any way I can.

It is true, I am looking for work, but I did not hope to find anything as rewarding as you are indicating.

I will be at Mr. Hancock's warehouse office July eighteen at ten o'clock A.M.

Respectfully, Jason McKenzie"

Clarice was very still; she didn't say a word, but Jason leaned forward to look at her and saw that her eyes were full of tears. She then broke into sobs. "Jason, dear, what will I do if you go to Philadelphia?"

"We will have to work something out," he said tenderly. He took her hand, and they got to their feet and began the walk home.

Chapter Twenty-Six

Clarice found much consolation in her little pupils. Their eagerness to learn, their laughter, and their sparkling eyes brought back memories of other children she had taught.

Every hour, though, something reminded her of the fact that Jason would soon be off, first to Boston, for she did not know how long, then to Philadelphia, for probably several months.

The children sometimes asked her what she was thinking about because she often answered their questions with words that didn't make sense.

Jason got very busy for the time between June thirtieth and July eighteenth. He quit looking for work, knowing he had a good prospect in mind. He helped Clarice gather the ripe garden vegetables and do the canning. He said that it might be a month too soon, but everything would keep with enough salt added.

Clarice knew nothing about canning, and at this time she didn't care to learn. She assured Jason that she wouldn't starve.

One morning while the two were preparing beans for drying, Jason said, "Honey, I'm going to tell you something that you just have to know. I should have told you two months ago, but I'm a coward, afraid of losing you."

"What is it, you silly goose? You know you're not going to lose me." He sighed after a pause. She said, "I know you've been gambling with your shipyard mates; I missed the Christmas shillings from the sugar bowl some time ago. I didn't say anything. It was your money, anyway."

"No, dear, that's not what I'm talking about. I did take the six shillings to buy a saddle. I needed one after mine was stolen.

"What I have kept from telling you is something more important, and I should not have been so afraid of your reaction." He ducked his head as he said, "Tom Fellows is in Boston. He has been there since early March. He is a British Regular, and he is quartered in my apartment."

Clarice jumped up from her chair, spilling her lap full of beans to the floor. "Jason, how could you let him into your apartment? That place is our own."

Jason was completely surprised at the way she reacted. He thought she would be thrilled and exuberant.

Her face reddened, and she was quite irritated. She was not glad to hear of Tom's presence in Boston. She asked Jason to ask him to vacate the apartment. She had already had thoughts of going to Boston and staying in the apartment while Jason was in Philadelphia.

Clarice did not return, after her sudden outburst of the news about Tom, to her bean snapping. Jason finished the job. He did not talk again until he stood to hang the strings of beans against the outside wall, where they would be in direct sunlight and would soon dry. As his clumsy hands did this "woman's work," he called out, "Cee Cee, come here and see if this is satisfactory."

She answered, "I don't care beans about beans. All I care about is you."

He answered, "Then come here anyway."

"Why?" she called out.

"Because I want to give you a kiss."

"Why?" she called out again.

"Because I love you," he said.

She went to where he was hanging the beans. "Jason, I thought you hated all British soldiers; why are you giving shelter to a British soldier?"

"Because he is your friend. That is the only reason I can think of," he answered.

"I don't consider him that much of a friend, not since I married you. I love you, Jason. If you are a patriot, then I am a patriot also. Tom Fellows is my enemy."

"Maybe you better wait, my dearest, to make your decision about being a patriot. Pretty soon you will have eyewitness occasions to pass judgment on each side. There are going to be some positive actions taking place right here, maybe even in this neighborhood, to sway your loyalty to one or the other direction."

Jason did not want his wife to be on his side just because she was his wife. He knew she held on to her homeland with great affection. He said to her, "Freedom means the right to choose."

She went to the doorway where she stood looking out at the yard, the road, and the rosebushes full of beautiful pink roses. She took several deep sniffs to inhale their luscious fragrance. After a few minutes she turned to face her husband who had come up behind her.

She said, "Jason, I love this house; I love everything about America. I want it to be my home forever." She put her arms around his neck, drew his face to hers, and kissed him.

July seventeenth, 1774, the chaise was loaded as Jason drove away to attend the important meeting in Boston. A bale of hay for Charlie was tied on the footman's board. Two valises were anchored on top. A large basket with bread, apples, potatoes, honey, ham, and condiments was sitting on the seat beside him. He had anticipated all the markets in Boston would be closed. His valises were crammed with clean clothes. All his linen shirts and drawers had been freshly washed, starched, and ironed.

On arrival at his Charles Street property, he put Charlie and the chaise in the barn. He took the valises and basket of grub to his apartment.

As he looked around it didn't appear to him that anyone was living there. This surprised him because he had expected to find Tom Fellows, or Henry, or both. The place was full of cobwebs and dust.

Jason said to himself, "I wonder where Henry is right now?"

Then he examined the bed. It was made, the sheets were clean. A copy of the Boston Gazette was spread open on top of the counterpane. He looked at the date, June third, 1774.

"Then no one has been here since June third or fourth," he said. "Clarice and I were here June first and second. Maybe I will find a solution to this puzzle tomorrow. After I attend the meeting, I will comb the wharf."

He took an apple from the basket, then lit a candle and sat down to read the Gazette and eat his apple.

Next morning he met with a small group of men in Hancock's office. He learned that Samuel Adams, John Adams, Charles Cushing, and Robert Paine had been chosen as delegates from Massachusetts to represent that colony at a Congress which was held in Philadelphia. He learned that there would be delegates from the other colonies as well. He heard the Committees of Correspondence praised for the work they had done in bringing these colonies together.

The topics of discourse between these men excited and thrilled Jason. He was eager to be a part of it; even though he was to be Mr. Adams's secretary and valet, he knew he would learn much and would have access to Mr. Adams's books to read. He knew he would be part of the social life in Philadelphia, but he wished his charming wife could enjoy it with him.

Jason returned to Lynn after three days in Boston. Clarice sat on his lap as he related all he had learned about what his new situation would require of him.

She asked him if he learned what this Congress expected to achieve. He said he did not know; the purpose was to reconcile conditions and differences, he thought

"Do you know how long you will be gone?" she asked.

"No, probably a month, but I will write to you every day. Are you sure you will be all right?" he asked.

"Of course, the parson and Sister will be close by. They will help with the chores. They will take over as soon as you leave. I am going to ask them to stay here with me. The sexton will look after their property."

Jason thought Clarice sounded skeptical but was trying very hard to make him feel less weary of leaving her.

"The school will keep me busy," she said. "The time will fly. I also have weaving to do and lots of letters to write. I will be busy, but I will miss you."

August dragged by, hot and humid. Jason rode to Boston twice more for instruction from Mr. Adams. These two meetings required his being there for a few hours only; therefore, he returned home at night.

On one of his days at home, he decided to call on John Jolly. His purpose in doing so was to ask John and his wife to look in on Clarice now and then while he would be away. "Just for company and conversation," he said.

He knew Clarice sometimes got bored with Sister Smith. He had noticed that the parson and his wife were acting peculiar of late, and their visits were less frequent. The news Jason got from John Jolly was not good. He was glad he had learned it though because Clarice ought to know about it.

"How am I going to tell her?" he said to himself. He was whistling to bolster his courage as he entered the kitchen door.

Clarice was cutting vegetables at the table. She looked up with a smiling face and said, "Good afternoon, Mr. McKenzie, have you been somewhere chumming?"

His answer was stern. "I've been to call on John Jolly. I have news for you. It's sad news. John and his wife are separating, that is, for a while anyway. They will be taking the twins out of your school."

"Oh no," sighed Clarice, "why?"

"Well, John has no employment; his farming is a failure, and his wife's parents are ill. She wants to go there, to Provincetown, and care for them."

"Since the Port Bill went into effect John has been despondent, but try and try everywhere he can't find work. Seems they argue and spat at each other all the time. She wants to leave. He wants to stay and care for their animals, although he has already sold two of his cows and a horse just to make ends meet."

Clarice was almost in tears when she said, "Dear little Molly and Polly, they will miss their school and their playmates." She asked, "When are they leaving?"

"Very soon, I think, and they will stay there all winter."

"I do hope I will see the children before they go. May we invite them, the whole family, for supper?"

"Sure, my dear, but do we have any decent food to offer them?" Jason knew there wasn't much in the way of meat.

"I will make roast chicken and corn pudding. For dessert I will make gingerbread and applesauce."

Clarice was elated at the prospects of a supper party. The Jollys came and the supper was scrumptious. The children were delightful, at least Clarice thought so, but their mother was haughty, and scolded them too often.

It was the last time Clarice saw the Jolly twins, although at the departing from the McKenzie home that evening, they each promised to get together again in the spring.

At the next school session, Puppy Philips handed Clarice a note as she came in.

She read: Dear Mrs. McKenzie, Puppy will be dropping out at the end of this week. We are moving into Boston where it is safe. You ought to move also. Thank you for your friendship. Puppy will miss you. Sincerely, Jane Philips.

Clarice asked Jason later, when all the children had gone, "What is this fear that's taking over everyone's minds? I'm not afraid of anything, are you?"

He sat down and removed his shoes. He held them up to face level and said, "See this mud? It's from drilling. There are now more than a hundred men drilling and musket practicing every day in a field very close to here. They're not doing it for play. Isn't that enough to scare you?"

He continued, "It's only the Tory families that are running to Boston. They think they will be safer there with all the troops that are there to protect them. Maybe you also ought to go into Boston. You can live in the apartment."

Clarice's eyes filled with fire. "Do you think I would leave Panzy, in her condition, and Bessie? Never!"

Jason pulled her down onto his lap. "You are one brave woman, my darling. I'm going to leave you a gun. I am also going to teach you how to shoot it."

Clarice looked at him and said, "Jason, are you crazy? I'm not going to shoot anyone."

"Never can tell," he said. "Won't hurt to learn how. You might even want to shoot a rabbit or a squirrel if you get hungry enough."

"Never! Never! I wouldn't hurt a little defenseless animal."

Jason was now in a teasing mood. "If you should go to live in the apartment in Boston, you might encounter Tom Fellows living there. I wouldn't want you living with him, for then I would have to shoot someone."

Clarice jumped from his lap and kicked him on the shin. As she did this he, in his sock feet, began the chase after her to the bedroom.

Chapter Twenty-Seven

Jason left for Boston August fifteenth. There he would pick up his valises from his apartment and take them to the stage station to be taken to Philadelphia. There would be a rest period of one day, which also was a day for more planning.

The Committee of Correspondence representatives met with the delegates and their aides in John Adams's Boston office to map out the overnight stops and other places of refreshment and to rendezvous with committee members.

Just before the departure, a small crowd of well wishers congregated on the door steps of the office: Mr. Hancock, Mr. Bainbridge, Mr. Revere, and other friends and relatives kissing and waving.

Jason felt quite lonely; no one was there to wish him well. The four delegates rode together in one carriage. The aides rode postillion, two in front, two in back.

Clarice closed her front door after watching until the faintest vision of Jason and Charlie faded out of sight. She wiped her eyes with the lace cuff of her shirtwaist. She had purposely dressed herself in her prettiest frock and had let her hair fall over her shoulders. She knew Jason loved her hair when she wore it loose and long.

She thought she had better get ready for the children. She was glad it was a school day, even though she now had but three pupils.

Sally Melville would be bringing little Sally and Matthew very soon. Maybe she could persuade her to sit and talk for a few minutes. Being alone for even a short time, knowing Jason would be gone for a month or more, caused her to tremble. In a moment or two, Parson and Sister Smith came in through the back door.

The parson, before saying, "Good morning," asked, "Has Jason left?"

"Yes," Clarice answered, "about ten minutes ago."

"I'm sorry he's gone; we have news we wanted him to hear."

Clarice thought nothing of this announcement; she was used to news from either the parson or his wife.

She asked, "Will it keep? He will be back in a month."

"Nope," said Sister Smith, "it won't keep."

"Sit then," said Clarice, "and tell me what it is."

She removed some books from two chairs and turned them to face the rocking chair which she sat in.

Sister Smith saw her kiss the back of the rocker. She asked, "What are you doing, child? Pretending that Jason is sitting here and I'm going to sit on his lap? Grow up!" scolded Sister. "You will learn to do without your man if a Revolution breaks out."

Clarice flashed an angry look at Sister, then at the parson. "You are always predicting revolution. Well, I don't believe there is going to be one, and if there is one, I will take up my musket and run around shooting all who are against whichever side Jason is on." Clarice knew very little about what was going on in Massachusetts.

Parson Smith crossed his legs and moved his chair. He got up and walked to the window and stood, gazing out toward the road. He sat down again and cleared his throat.

Sister seemed fidgety also. She said, "Go ahead, tell her."

The parson looked at his wife despairingly and said, "You tell her."

Sister moved her chair closer to Clarice and reached for her hand, "We're moving to Connecticut," she said as she burst out crying. She released Clarice's hand and immediately went into the kitchen.

"Why?" Clarice called after her. "Why?"

The parson answered her, "It's the bishop's orders. The bishop says we're not getting enough money in the collection plate to buy even the wine. My wife makes the bread, but that is not much help. I haven't had one pence in wages in many months. Connecticut has a much bigger and richer parish."

Clarice sighed, and tears filled her eyes as she said, "I was getting ready to ask you to move in here with me while Jason is away. Now what will I do?"

While she was talking, Sister was edging back into the great room. Parson was staring out the window while twiddling his thumbs.

Clarice went on talking, "I can't leave Panzy in her condition. I can't leave Bessie, but I don't know how to milk her."

The parson began to talk, still facing outside, with his back to Clarice and Sister. "Hire a woman to come here and help you," he said.

"Good idea," said Clarice, "but who would it be? I couldn't pay a woman's wages."

She asked, "Do you know that the Philipses are moving, also? They sent a note withdrawing Puppy from school. They mentioned that they thought I should move into Boston to be safe."

Sister said, "Might be the best thing to do, but where would you stay?"

After a moment of thinking, Clarice said sternly, "I'm not going anywhere. This is my home, and I don't feel afraid of anyone. No British soldier is going to harm me. See," she pointed, "there I have my Union Jack boldly displayed on the mantle." She nodded her head in affirmation and frankness.

"You are one brave woman," said Sister. "We will be here for you until we leave. I doubt the parson will be able to reserve a passage on any vessel before a month or two...maybe Jason will be back by then."

"Thank you," said Clarice. "You have been such good friends."

She went over to Sister Smith and put her arms around her and kissed her cheek, then Clarice put her arm across her eyes and rushed up stairs and closed her bedroom door.

Sister said to her husband, "I'm going into the kitchen to stir up a cake or gingerbread or something sweet. You better see if Jason left a pile of logs sawed up for cooking."

It wasn't many minutes before Sally Melville came, bringing Sally and Matthew. Sister greeted them and asked Sally, the grown one, to sit awhile and talk. She told her that Clarice would not be down for a little while; she was resting after seeing Jason off to Philadelphia.

Clarice heard them talking and she came down; she had changed her dress and tucked her hair up into a bun.

She greeted the children with a hug and laid some sketches on the table. She had made sketches of buildings in Boston. The lesson for the first hour was about the buildings. She explained the purpose of the buildings: Province House, the Old North Church, the Old South Church. Then she told them about the three tea ships and how the Indians had thrown the tea into the ocean and made King George III mad. For punishment he had closed down the Port of Boston, and this made the people of Boston mad. And now everybody, in some way, was upset about it, and that is the reason for Molly and Polly and Puppy being taken out of school and why they had moved away.

Sister Smith came from the kitchen bringing a tray of slices of cake. Sally was still there; she had enjoyed the stories Clarice had related. She was not educated enough to have understood the tale of the tea party from anyone else as clearly as she now understood it.

The parson stuck his head in the back door and called to his wife, "Sister, we had better be on our way home; we have much to do and many letters to write. Everything here is in good supply, wood, water, hay...Jason has done his homework well, I would say."

Soon everyone was gone, and Clarice was alone. She sat at the desk and wrote a letter to Jason, although he had not reached Boston yet. She laid it aside, saying, "I will post it in a couple of days."

The nights were dark and the foghorns, sounding mournful, kept Clarice awake. She would get up from her bed, light a candle, and search the rooms downstairs trying to find causes of strange noises. Usually she scolded herself for being such a willy-nilly as she described her fears.

One late evening, almost one week after Jason had left, as she passed her window in her bedroom, she noticed a red glow in the sky with black clouds flowing swiftly in front of it. She drew the curtains to one side to take a closer look. She blew out the candle behind her and shaded her eyes with her hands as she pressed her face against the glass. She had no doubt that it was another barn fire, but she knew she could do nothing about it, so she got back into bed and pulled the sheet over her head. Sleeping was impossible, as was not thinking about the fire, even thought it was at least five miles away.

After tussling with her fears and nervousness, she got up again. She remembered the spyglass in the bureau drawer and the widow's walk around the roof of the house. Within the next five minutes Clarice was adjusting the glass to her eyes as she stood in the smoky wind that was about to whip her off the narrow balcony.

She could see the fire plainly, although it was now flat on the ground, having consumed all the timbers. She knew it was a barn, because she could also see a large house standing nearby.

"Oh, Lord," she said, "another barn. I wonder whose it is? I hope it wasn't deliberately set."

She went back inside and down the tiny narrow stairway to her bedroom. She put the spyglass back into the bureau drawer and got back into bed.

Just as she began to repeat the Lord's Prayer for the third time that night, she was startled by fast hoof beats against the road in front of her house.

Again she jumped out of bed and went to the window. Passing her front gate at that moment was a bareback, barefooted rider on a dark horse. He was kicking the horse's sides to make him gallop faster.

Clarice snatched her robe from the bedpost, wrapping it around her as she hurriedly went downstairs, running across the great room and out the front door to the yard gate. By this time the rider was far in the distance toward town, but when Clarice saw him turn his horse around and head back, she went behind the rose bush and stooped low, covering herself with her robe. As the rider approached her house, he slowed his horse's gait to a walk.

Clarice was thankful that she had not left a candle burning and thankful that Panzy was near the house in the pasture and that the chaise was standing near by. This, she thought, will make him think that Jason is at home.

As the rider walked his horse on past the house, Clarice crawled to the front door and went inside. She reached up over the door to the gun rack and took down the long rifle Jason had bought for her and taught her to shoot.

She saw the shadow of the rider as he was coming back and she stepped just outside the door and fired two loads of powder into the air. The shots made such a loud noise. She saw the horse lurch sideways and the rider fall off onto the road.

She stepped back inside her house and as fast as she had ever moved in her entire life, she began shoving furniture against the door.

She waited with the gun loaded and positioned, "ready to blow him away," but all became silent and the bareback rider got away while Clarice was getting ready to kill him.

She didn't move from her staunch position, inside her house, for half an hour or more. Finally, she seated herself in her rocker with the flint lock across her knees until morning.

When Sally Melville brought the children to school next day she told Clarice that her husband, Clinton, had left on a schooner for Nova Scotia to take command of a ship and he wouldn't be back in Lynn for several weeks.

Immediately, Clarice became aware of Sally being alone during the final days of her pregnancy, so she took advantage of that moment to propose to her that she and the two children come and stay with her.

At first Sally was hesitant, saying that she had chickens and a cow to take care of. With much conversation pro and con, Sally finally agreed to give the proposition some consideration.

Clarice suggested that she bring the cow and ask a neighbor to look after the chickens for the eggs and one hen each week for Sunday dinner.

Clarice asked Parson Smith to hitch Panzy to the chaise and go to Sally's place and bring back whatever Sally would need to bring and to tie the cow on behind and bring her also. All was soon accomplished.

Now Clarice was no longer alone and she had a family to share with her and help her. She asked Matthew to be the head of the family and laid out his chores for him. Feeding chickens and the horse, bringing in the eggs, and many other chores she thought a young boy could do. It gave Matthew a sense of importance.

Parson Smith met with John Jolly and mentioned that Clarice McKenzie and Sally Melville were without their menfolk, and, since he was without a wife, he probably could be of some help to the women and maybe they could be of some help to him.

John asked the parson if he didn't think this would cause talk around the town.

The parson said, "Not if there isn't anything to arouse suspicion."

John was a tall, handsome, stevedore, strong as an ox. He was a ship-builder also and a progressive farmer up until then.

The opportunity to be of service to two beautiful young women pleased him very much, if he could persuade them to allow it. He didn't doubt that Jason McKenzie would approve, but Clinton Melville was a horse of another color. He was grinning from ear to ear as he walked away from the parson, headed toward the McKenzie house.

It was five-year-old Sally who opened the door to John Jolly.

"Good afternoon, miss, is your mama at home?"

Sally looked at him quizzically but did not answer him. She knew who he was, but he didn't have the children with him and she ignored his question.

He asked, "Or is Mrs. McKenzie at home? Will you please go and get her?"

While Sally was still standing, staring at him, Clarice came to greet him. "Good day, John. Come in. I sure do miss the twins...have you heard from them?"

"No. So far I haven't gotten one word from them."

Little Sally blurted out, "Polly is my friend, but Molly don't like me."

Clarice, looking straight at the child, said, "Sally, the word is doesn't, not don't."

Now John had a chance to speak, "Your school teachings were a great help to all of us."

"Is this just a friendly visit?" asked Clarice, "or have you come to pay me for the last week of your daughter's schooling?" Ordinarily, Clarice would never have mentioned the debt, but she was in dire straights monetarily. It might have been the times and the circumstances, but something was changing Clarice's attitude about everything. Or was it that she was "growing up," as Sister Smith had advised her to do?

"No," said John, "I will pay you the six shillings soon, but I have come now to offer you help if you need it."

"What kind of help, John?" asked Clarice.

"Anything you need done: cut wood, milk, clean stables and stalls." He waited for a reply.

Clarice nodded her head at him and offered him a chair. He continued to stand. She said, "I'll make us some coffee. Talk to Sally while I brew it."

Sally asked, "When's Polly coming back?"

"I don't think she will be back until winter is over."

"Why not?" asked the child.

"Her grandma and grandpa are both sick, and she has to stay there to help them."

Sally Melville came wobbling down the stair steps. She was the color of wood ashes.

John called out to her, "Hold on to the rail, Mrs. Melville, don't fall." He was rushing toward the stairs to help her. His arm was outstretched toward her, but he was too late. She lost her footing and came tumbling down to the floor with a thud.

Clarice, hearing the fall, came running in from the kitchen. She saw John bent over Sally working her arms up and down.

She called out, "John, don't do that! She may have a broken arm."

Both the children began to cry and scream.

Clarice was crying out, "Sally, Sally! Are you all right?" Sally rolled her eyeballs around, but did not say anything; she gave out a few whimpers and soft sighs.

"Go quickly," said Clarice to John. "Hitch Panzy to the chaise; we have to get her to the doctor in Lynn."

In less than fifteen minutes, Panzy was clop-clopping down the road, almost out of breath, trotting as fast as she could, white steam coming from her nostrils, pulling the loaded chaise toward Lynn to Doctor Miller's office.

Sally was unconscious in the back seat, enfolded in Clarice's arms. Clarice was trying to keep the tears out of her eyes by wiping them with her shoulder.

John Jolly was on the driver's seat with the children beside him. They were still crying loudly. He was slapping the reins against Panzy's hips, urging her to go faster. The pregnant mare was doing the best she could. If anything, she was slowing down.

The shingle read: Doctor E. Miller, M.D. Graduate of Harvard. Infirmary and Lying-In care. The small medical center was in part of the doctor's residence.

John pulled the carriage up to the side of the building. He jumped from his seat and lifted Sally from Clarice's arms and carried her into the office. There was a couch in the infirmary. He gently laid Sally down on it and straightened her clothing.

The doctor took his time getting out of his dinner clothes and into his long white physician's coat. He was entertaining a bunch of his Harvard alumni associates when the patient arrived.

When the doctor came into the room, he saw Clarice down on her knees in front of the couch, rubbing Sally's head, chest, and arms and calling her name, "Sally, Sally, wake up, speak to me."

The doctor looked the patient over and took her temperature. He took Clarice's hand and lifted her to her feet.

"This lady is definitely in labor," he said. "She will have the baby within the hour."

"But she is unconscious," said Clarice.

"Fine," replied the doctor, "we won't have to give her morphine."

The doctor told John to leave the room and take the children with him. He then went over to the door opening to his residence. He called, "Phoebe, come here." When she came to answer his call, he said to her, "Carry on with my guests and send Jenny in here to help me."

He said to Clarice, "That was my wife, Phoebe, and Jenny is my sixteen-year-old daughter." He busied himself, as he continued talking, with wiping his instruments with alcohol. He poured water from a pitcher into a tea kettle. He put the tea kettle on a trivet and placed it on the hearth, raking hot coals under it.

The doctor laid out some towels and other things on a small table. Clarice was watching him when he said, "I don't believe Jenny and I will need your help, Mrs. McKenzie. You can join Mr. Jolly outside." He went on, "Jenny is quite good at this. She has helped me deliver more than fifty babies since she was twelve years old."

Clarice wanted to stay and be a comfort to Sally, but she was scared and nervous. She left the room and joined John on a bench under a maple tree.

Leaves were coming down all around. The children were running to catch the leaves and piling them up at John's feet.

Squirrels were chattering overhead, and a flock of wild geese flying south were honking their loudest. Now and then Clarice heard a scream coming from Doctor Miller's "Lying-In" room. She thought Sally had regained consciousness. She said to John, "Do you think I ought to go back in there and see how Sally is doing?"

"No, not yet, give her some more time. It took my wife ten hours to have the twins."

John walked over to the hitching post and rubbed Panzy's nose. He said to her, "Your time is coming, old girl, but you will be brave, and maybe by then Charlie will be back to stand beside you. You see, Mrs. Melville's man is not with her and that is sad."

Clarice was walking toward the door, but she turned and came back, undecided whether to go and ask or to remain outside and try to stay calm and assured.

She called Matthew and Sally to come and sit beside her and listen to a story. They came and sat through half of the story, then they ran off to chase more leaves.

She asked John, "Do you suppose Sally is up to this? It is her first, you know?"

At that moment Clarice heard a loud scream. She jumped from the bench and ran to the infirmary.

Sally had been undressed, a sheet was covering her breasts and stomach, but her lower parts were naked. Her legs were spread wide apart and tied to a rod, swinging horizontally from the ceiling. Jenny was poking at her pelvis with an iron instrument that looked like tongs about a foot long.

Clarice heard Doctor Miller shout out at Jenny, "Use the forceps, Jenny!"

Jenny jabbed again at Sally's pelvis, propping her foot against the foot of the couch to give her more pulling strength.

Clarice screamed and threw her hand over her mouth and coughed. She staggered backward, and, as if she had watched a horrible murder, she collapsed to the floor.

John Jolly had followed her into the infirmary; he saw her collapse and ran to her. He gathered her up into his arms and carried her to the chaise. He laid her on the back seat and covered her with the duster. He called the children from their play, lifted them to the driver's seat, mounted himself beside them, and said, "I'm taking you folks home."

He turned to see that Clarice was arousing herself, and he was glad that she was all right. He said to her, "Mrs. McKenzie, I will come back and stay until it is over, then I will bring you the news. For now, you belong at home."

She said, "You are so kind, John Jolly, but I prefer to be let off at the parson's house. I must let them know about Sally."

"As you wish. I think that is a good idea," he said.

Parson and Sister were having supper on the porch. They saw the chaise approaching and ran out to the road to meet it.

Clarice began to cry as she got out of the carriage and ran to them. Both children were crying; of course, they didn't know why.

John looked bewildered as he spoke, "Good day to both of you. We are coming from Doctor Miller's infirmary where Mrs. Melville is having her baby."

Sister said, "Why are you crying, Clarice?" That is good news."

"Because I can't help it. It is a brutal thing, and Sally brought it on too soon by falling down stairs."

Matthew was fighting with Sally, pulling her hair and shoving her about. "I wish it was you," he said, "instead of Mama."

Sally Melville was the children's aunt, but they called her mama.

Sister took Matthew's hand and drew him aside. "Now listen here, young man, you ought to behave like a gentleman. You are soon going to have a little brother or sister. You won't fight a little baby, will you? You must set a good example."

The parson led Clarice into the parsonage. John was following, leading Sally. Sister and Matthew went in a little later, after Matthew had promised to behave himself.

Sister said, "Now, tell me about the fall Sally M. had." Sister had decided that since there were two Sallys, she would distinguish them by calling them Sally M. and Sally C., M for Melville, C for child.

Clarice explained, "She fell down about six steps. She landed on her stomach, but she hit her head against the wall. She was unconscious when we got to her and did not regain consciousness as long as we were at the infirmary."

Sister helped Clarice to lie down on the bed. Parson and John went outside. The children were each sitting on a chair, quiet as mice. Sally C. was beginning to doze; Matthew was eyeing everything in the room.

John said to the parson, "I'm going back to the infirmary and will stay until it is over. I will come back here to pick up Mrs. McKenzie and the children in a few hours."

Sister came out and informed John that Clarice and the children would spend the night.

The parsonage had three bedrooms. Sister thought Clarice would rest better if she had one bedroom to herself, but Clarice asked that the children sleep with her. She needed their warmth. They were soon sound asleep, but she lay there thinking: of Jason, wondering how far he was from Lynn, how close he was to Philadelphia. She couldn't sleep, she kept seeing Sally on that couch. She said, out loud to herself, "A sweet little baby will make it all worthwhile."

It was after midnight when John returned. Clarice heard Panzy's hoof beats, so she climbed out of bed, over Sally, and went to the window. She saw the beam of the chaise's lantern. She put on the robe that Sister had laid out for her. She crept down the stairs, holding very tightly to the rail.

John did not come toward the house joyfully; his head was bowed and his steps were slow. He saw Clarice waiting at the edge of the porch.

"Mrs. McKenzie," he said, "the baby was, was, was...stillborn." He had such a hard time getting the words out.

"Oh no!" gasped Clarice. "Poor Sally...how is she?"

John looked away for a moment, then he reached out for Clarice, put his arms around her, and whispered, "She's dead."

By the time the parson and Sister had joined John and Clarice, they had already sensed that something bad had happened.

Clarice was mournfully sobbing. She pulled away from John and ran into the house and up the stairs to the bedroom where the children were sleeping.

She went from side to side of the bed to kiss each child, "You darlings," she said, "no mother, no father, no aunt."

She stopped crying, wiped her eyes, lifted Sally from the bed, and carried her to the rocking chair where she sat rocking and singing softly, holding the child on her lap. She repeated the Lord's Prayer and a few lines from Shakespeare that she knew. "'The quality of Mercy is not strained, it droppeth as the gentle rain, from Heaven upon a place beneath.' Oh God," she pleaded, "be Merciful to these children."

John Jolly drove the chaise home to the McKenzie place. Clarice and the children and Parson and Sister Smith walked behind. The grownups were carrying baskets of food; the children were carrying armloads of autumn leaves and goldenrod that they were gathering along the roadside.

When Clarice entered her house, she saw a folded paper that someone had pushed under the door. She picked it up quickly and read it. It was written by John Slade. He and Henry had stopped by on their way to Salem with messages for the Committee of Correspondence.

> Dear Cee Cee, We met the delegates and aides in New York, and are happy to report that they are progressing toward Philadelphia with vigor and enthusiasm. They are resting and dining every night at some fine ordinary along their route. Signed, J.S. and Henry (x).

Clarice read the note to the Parson and Sister. Jason had enclosed a note:

> My Dearest, I miss you so much. I'm trying hard to endure the loneliness, especially at night. Please know that every minute you are in my heart, and I love you. J.

Clarice asked Sister Smith to stay overnight. Sister accepted the invitation with the parson's approval. He had already told his wife to stay with Clarice to protect her reputation in case John Jolly also stayed. John Jolly went on to his own place after helping to carry in baskets of food and supplies that the parson had put into the carriage.

The children were a joyful tonic to a sorrowful atmosphere. Their questions had to be answered realistically, and adult conversations had to be guarded.

Clarice was careful in explaining to them that the baby they had expected would not be coming, nor would their aunt be coming back, that they had chosen to go and live in heaven. After she saw their expressions change—from sorrow to wonder—she explained to them the miracle of birth and death.

Next day, Sister Smith was still with Clarice when she saw Doctor Miller's chaise pulling up at the front gate. She called Clarice from the kitchen to come and open the door.

"Good day, Doctor, come in."

He removed his hat and stepped inside the great room. "I will make this call very brief," he said. "I am sorry we couldn't save Mrs. Melville and the baby, but you must know, it wasn't the birthing that caused the demise. It was a concussion of the brain. She had had a bad fall, but the baby had been dead several days. That is why it didn't move out of the birth canal as it should have.

"I hate to tell you this, but Mrs. Melville had bruises all over her torso, as if she had been kicked or beaten. Did the children talk about any fighting between their aunt and uncle?"

"No," Clarice answered, "but Matthew is mean to Sally at times. He seems to think it is the right way to behave. Maybe he is following an example set by his uncle."

"So sad, so sad," said the doctor. "Now I have another matter to discuss with you, Mrs. McKenzie, since you seem to be the one in charge. That is the matter of my pay."

"Oh," replied Clarice, "Mr. Melville will be back in a week or two. You will have to take that up with him."

The doctor fumbled around in his pockets and drew out a folded piece of paper which he handed to Clarice. He said, "Here is a note from Mr. Melville, written, I suppose, the day he left, to his wife."

He handed the paper to Clarice, she read:

> Monday...I won't be here for your confinement. Go to Doctor Miller's Infirmary. I don't have any money to pay him. If he can't wait for awhile, give him the cow and any pieces of your furniture he will accept for payment.
> Signed, Clinton Melville

After reading the note, Clarice asked, "Where did you get this?"

"It was tacked up on her kitchen door facing."

"Then you've been in her house?"

"Yes, the door was not locked. I went in to look over the furniture, as I didn't expect any real money."

After shifting his weight and jacking up his trousers and eyeing the McKenzie mantel and everything else in the great room, he cleared his throat and said, "There was one piece in Melville's house I admired. It was a fiddle that was on a shelf over the kitchen door. I will accept that fiddle and the cow as full payment for my services."

Clarice asked Sister Smith what she thought about that kind of agreement.

"Well," said Sister, "no one knows when Clinton Melville will be back. You can't afford to feed the cow and you can't play the fiddle, so why not just go ahead and settle the account.

Clarice replied, "I too think it is a good way to get the doctor's charges off our minds." She smiled and felt relieved as she took the paper from the doctor's hand and went over to her desk, where she wrote on the bottom of the paper this acknowledgment:

> Received this day, September eighteenth, Seventeen Hundred Seventy-Four, one milk cow, and one fiddle (property of Mrs. Sally Melville) for payment in full for services rendered for her own confinement, delivery, and demise of herself and her baby.
> Signed by _____
> Witnessed by _____

Clarice asked Sister to sign as a witness, then she signed it herself. She never let go of it while the doctor read and signed.

The doctor gave Clarice a look of admiration. She supposed that he had not expected her to agree to his demands but found that she was capable of conducting business, even though he had seen her faint and collapse in his delivery room.

As the doctor folded the paper and put it in his pocket, Clarice said, "I will go and bring the cow around to your chaise and tie her on behind." She also said, "I would like to go with you into Sally's house when you go to get the fiddle."

Sister spoke out, "You stay here with the children. I will go with him to get the fiddle."

Clarice thought about Sister's suggestion only for a minute before she said, "No, you stay here with the children. I'll go with him."

She went out to the barn, tied a rope around the cow's neck, and led her through the front yard to the chaise. The doctor was already seated. She tied the cow on behind and patted her neck and said, "Be a good girl; Sally was fond of you."

She climbed onto the seat beside the doctor and called to Sister and the children, who were waving from the front door, "I'll be back soon."

Clarice entered the Melville house before the doctor. She noticed it was neat and clean. There was a cradle, with a new blanket and a small blue pillow, in one corner of the room. When Clarice saw it, tears filled her eyes. She realized that Sally had been busy preparing for her baby. She turned her eyes to the fiddle in its case on the shelf over the kitchen door. She watched as Doctor Miller lifted it down.

"Have to be careful with this," he said. "It is so old the strings might pop."

Clarice asked, "Where do you suppose Sally got it, or did it belong to Clinton?"

"I know all about this fiddle," said the doctor. "It belonged once to Mrs. Melville's grandfather. His name was Danzeo. He and my father came over from Italy in seventeen hundred and thirty-five to start a shoe manufacturing business, right here in Lynn. Mr. Danzeo, Mrs. Melville's grandfather, was a violinist as well as a shoemaker, but he was also a drunkard and soon lost all his money. He married a young girl from somewhere up in the Maine woods and moved in with her family to fight Indians and to farm. It is said he was lazy and sat around in taverns playing his fiddle, too much of a coward to fight Indians and he hated farming."

The doctor opened the case and took out a beautiful instrument. He handed it to Clarice to look at.

She rubbed her hand over the satiny amber finish and lifted it closer to her eyes as she read the inscription, Cremona, Italy, Seventeen Hundred Ten. By Antonio Stradivari.

She said to the doctor, "This is something to treasure; can you play it?"

"Just a little bit," he answered, "but Phoebe and Jenny can play it."

As she handed the instrument back to the doctor and watched him carefully lay it in its case, she said, "I think I will be going, as I don't see anything of much value that will be worth worrying about. I hope Clinton will be back soon."

The doctor asked if he should drive her back.

She said, "No, I think the walk will do me good and give me time to consider the children."

As she turned to go out the door, he laid his hand on her shoulder to halt her for a few more words. "Do you need anything?" he asked.

"No," she answered sarcastically, as she gave him a look of complete resentment and whisked out the door.

As she went past the cow, waiting at the gate and tied behind the doctor's chaise, Clarice bent over and kissed her on the nose.

The doctor came out of the house carrying the violin case under his arm. He got into his vehicle as he watched Clarice swinging down the road toward home.

Chapter Twenty-Eight

There were ruts in the road. Clarice stumbled, and a rock caught in the sole of her ragged boot. "I will have to remove it," she said.
She sat down on a grassy bank and tugged at her boot. It was difficult to get it off. She noticed the sky, as it was getting dark, and storm clouds loomed in the distance. She thought she had better hurry along; she still had two miles to go. She tugged harder at her boot. Finally it slipped over her heel and came off. She shook out the rock and began tugging to get the boot back on.
She lingered there, lying back on the grass. "I think I'm very tired," she said. "I wish Jason was here to lie beside me and talk to me. I wonder what he is doing at this moment."

At that moment, if there had been a magic spirit at work and had transplanted Clarice to Philadelphia and to the meeting room in the building where fifty-six men were seated around a table, she would have seen her beloved, sitting in a high-back chair directly in back of a seated Samuel Adams who was handing parchment paper with important words written on it over his shoulder to his secretary, Jason McKenzie. She would have noticed that a mahogany lap desk was across Jason's knees and that he was writing with a quill and ink, copying every word of the paper that passed over Adams's shoulder.
She would have supposed that the original was to be sent to England and the copy retained in Adams's possession for future reference. She would have seen the men around the table become very noisy at times, discussing the petitions and pleas for dissolving grievances and reasons for rescinding the Boston Port Bill.
She would have seen, in the background, a long table set with a silver urn of coffee, a baked ham, and loaves of bread. She would not have known that her husband had arisen at four o'clock in the morning to comb the markets of Philadelphia to acquire the goodies so daintily displayed. She would not have known that after the marketing he had prepared the table in the meeting room so that the busy, tired, homesick delegates could nourish their bodies and brains for the tedious arguments and decisions each day. She would not have seen him rushing, after preparing the food, to his boarding house to change

into his white buckskin trousers and blue velvet coat, to brush his queue and ruff his ruffles to get ready for his secretarial duties, perhaps sitting for hours behind Samuel Adams's chair and copying his written words.

Clarice aroused herself from her wool gathering and stood up. She had been stirred from her imagery by a loud clap of thunder. She realized that the storm was not passing over but was immediately coming toward her. She looked around for a barn or a church or a house to run to for shelter. Not one such place could she see.

She was not familiar with the surroundings because she had done no walking alone since moving to Lynn. She had heard of the woods and the flats which she had not seen.

She had walked on a different road when she and Sister took the children to the cemetery, but Sister had known the way, and she, Clarice, had paid very little attention. Now she wished that she had taken more walks, but Sister and Jason were always warning her of dangerous things that could happen to a woman alone. Thoughts came to her of the bareback horse rider. She shivered, for the rain was coming down hard and she was getting wet.

She began to run, but now there was a rock in her other boot. She was feeling much pain, and she knew she was getting a horrible blister. "Good Lord," she said, "help me to get home."

A feeling of complete exhaustion caused her to slow her pace. She saw a tree stump and in a hopping-skipping sort of motion she went to it and sat down. She pulled at her clothes, realizing that she was soaked clear through to her skin.

She pulled off her boots and hurled them aside, "I will ask Sister if she has an extra pair that I may borrow," she said to herself. Her feet were like lumps of ice. She wiped them on the hem of her skirt.

The storm was passing over. She heard a horse's snort and the wheels of a carriage coming toward her. There was so much rain on her face and in her eyes, it was hard for her to tell who it was.

She heard a loud "Whoa" and a voice calling out, "Mrs. McKenzie!" She saw Doctor Miller getting out of his carriage and coming to her.

He reached out his hand to her, "My dear woman," he said, "I wanted to drive you home, but you preferred walking. Now look at you, you are in danger of a cold or maybe pneumonia. Here let me help you."

She was truly glad to see him; she went with him to his carriage, and he helped her to climb in. Clarice had not said a word up to this point.

The doctor tucked the lap robe around her and wrapped her feet with a sheepskin blanket he took from under his seat. He smiled at her and said, "I always go prepared for cold, wet weather."

Clarice was shivering when she asked, "Why did you come after me? Did you think I couldn't make it to my house on my own?"

"Yes, that is exactly what I thought, especially since it began to storm. I knew it would take you about an hour and a half. I waited forty-five minutes before I started out to overtake you."

"I stopped to rest for awhile," said Clarice, "and that delayed my progress."

The doctor laid his hand over on Clarice's lap. She felt a sudden surge of gratitude because she knew if he hadn't come along she probably would have not gone much further before falling in the wet road.

For a few moments neither said anything but sat smiling at each other. Then the doctor spoke softly, "Mrs. McKenzie, I admire your loyalty to your friend," referring to Sally, "and I also admire your generosity to the Melville children, but what do you think will happen to them now?"

Clarice had already made up her mind to keep them and take care of them. She had not, however, thought of how she could manage financially. She answered the doctor's question. "I will take care of them, of course. When Jason comes home we will decide what we can do." She heaved a big sigh, "Unless Clinton comes home and takes them away."

The doctor said, "He is not their father."

"I know that," said Clarice, "but he is their legal guardian. That gives him the right to take them. If Jason is here when Clinton comes (if he comes) the judge may decide that Jason will make the best father. We will just have to wait and see, but for now they are mine."

The doctor was looking into Clarice's eyes with tenderness. "I hope I can be of help to you, Mrs. McKenzie. I can see that you are willing to do more than you can possibly do, alone. I hear the parson and his wife are leaving this area. You won't have them to help you. John Jolly is a good and willing neighbor, but I can do more than he, so please call on me."

Clarice thought, Now what did he mean by that?

"Do more?" she said. "Thank you, I'm going to try to manage by myself, but I will remember your offer."

They arrived at the McKenzie gate, and Clarice began to unwrap herself from the lap robe and kick her feet out of the sheepskin. The doctor bounded around to her side and lifted her down. He squeezed her up close to him and whispered, "Now I feel that...that beautiful body is alive and warm."

Clarice gave him a look of disdain as she sharply said, "Let me go!"

He held on to her hand. "May I come in for a moment to see the children?" he asked.

"I suppose so," she replied, thinking Sister Smith was there. "It is their bedtime; they may be asleep."

Clarice opened the door. No one was in sight. She called out, "Sister, I'm home." No one answered. She ran up the stairs and saw that no one was there. Realizing that Sister and the children were gone, she slowly returned to the great room where the doctor was warming his hands at the fire place.

"No one is here," she said. "I suppose Sister took the children to the parsonage when she saw the storm brewing."

"Good," said the doctor. "We can talk about them some more."

"I will make us some coffee," said Clarice.

"Do you have any tea?" asked the doctor. "I think tea will do us more good."

"No, Jason doesn't allow it in this house. I do have some cider; I can heat it up."

"The coffee will do if you have no tea. It is so stupid to do without your tea."

Clarice noticed his facial expression for a second. It was not as friendly as it was a few moments ago. Had the mention of tea infuriated his thinking? She made the coffee and brought it in on a tray with sugar and cream and a few tea cakes.

She said, "When we finish our coffee, I will ask you to drive me over to the parsonage."

Clarice had not found a note Sister had left for her under the bootjack at the front door (she hadn't had need of a bootjack).

The note said: Clarice, John Jolly came in his carriage and invited us to supper at his house, which he claims is a real feast that he prepared all by himself. The parson, the children, and I are all gone with him. He will bring us back soon after supper...Sister.

When the doctor and Clarice had finished the coffee and Clarice had gone back upstairs and changed her clothes and put on the boots that she had retrieved from the fire, and had once belonged to Truly. She found out that Jason had resoled the boots and polished them, it seemed to her like he had done the repairing with tender, loving care and she wondered about this.

As she came down the stairs, she said to the doctor, "I'm ready to see my children," emphasizing my.

He smiled at her and said, "Let's go."

The doctor hesitated at the door and asked, "May I call you Clarice?"

"Yes," she answered, "but I don't see any reason for it because I won't be seeing much of you."

"That calls for another question," he said.

"What is it?" asked Clarice.

"May I kiss you? Please...just once."

Clarice almost tripped as she hurried out the door. She remembered Governor Hutchinson asking her that same question a year ago with that same longing look in his eyes.

As she approached the doctor's chaise and began to climb in, he laid his hand on her shoulder. He had come up behind her. She turned to face him. He threw his right arm around her waist and drew her up to him. With his left hand he pushed her head up to his mouth. He kissed her lips long and hard and rubbed his cheek against her cheek.

Clarice was squirming in his grip and pushing him away from her. She finally got out of his arms and stood back a few inches. Then all at once she grabbed the doctor in her arms, pushing his hat off his head. She began kissing him on the lips, on the cheeks, on the forehead, then she picked up his right hand and kissed it.

She stepped back from him and said in any angry voice, "There, you old fool, that ought to be enough kisses to last you the rest of your life, and if your wife finds out about it, send her to me for the details."

She and the doctor rode along without any conversation, both stiffly sitting on the carriage seat, Clarice as far to the right of the doctor as possible without falling off.

They halted in front of the parsonage. Clarice said, "Thank you, please don't get out. I can make it into the house by myself."

The doctor tipped his hat to her and said, "As you wish, you spunky one."

As Clarice ran to the parsonage, she thought, What will I do if he comes to my house again? Oh, I do hope Jason comes home soon.

It was a very cool night, and Clarice sat on the parsonage porch, waiting and wondering where everyone could be. She began to sneeze and had no kerchief. She tried a window, but couldn't get it open. She thought she had better go into the church, where it might be warm. The church door was locked, a most unusual thing, but since there had been reports of violence in the town and the parson's transfer to Connecticut, caution had been implemented, thus the locked doors and windows.

Clarice was becoming weary; the day had been so long. Trying to decide what to do, she at last went around to the back of the church. She hoped the sexton had left the back door unlocked. She tried the heavy iron latch. "Thank you, Lord!" she said as it slipped out of its bracket and the door opened with ease. She stepped inside. There was a candle burning on the altar. It gave a dim light to the aisles and pews.

She stood there very still for a moment after closing the door. She thought, I will lie down on a pew and take a little nap. Maybe the parson will come to check on the candle and discover me.

Just as she was settling herself down, she saw two bare feet sticking out from an old coat. Someone was asleep on the front pew across the nave on the other side of the church.

Clarice thought of clearing out of there in a hurry but was afraid of waking the sleeping man; she assumed it was a man because his feet were quite large.

Instead of stretching out on the pew, she hunkered down then straightened out on the pew and kept rolling under several more pews until she was way back in the middle of the church. She covered herself, as best she could, with the shawl she was wearing.

Almost in tears she was thinking, How did I ever get myself into this situation?

After lying there on the floor under the bench, Clarice got over her fright and began to conjure up something to do. She repeated the Lord's Prayer and the Ten Commandments. She was glad Sister had made her learn the commandments. Sister would have been glad to know that her teachings were now a comfort to Clarice.

Everything was so quiet; she tried to turn over, but it was hard to do. She finally said, "This is ridiculous, I'm getting out of this church."

She wiggled out to the aisle and stood up. She walked over to the sleeping man and shook him vigorously, waking him. He looked like a scrounger with his matted beard and dirty face. He picked up a battered tricorn hat and jammed it on his head. He said nothing.

Clarice scolded at him, "Who are you? Why are you in this church? You are trespassing. Get up and get out."

The man began to look around, he reached under the pew and brought out a dirty bundle. It was tied with a piece of rope.

Clarice asked, "What's in that bundle?" She thought it looked like something hard, not clothes, she was sure.

The man remained quiet.

She stood in front of him, again she asked, "What's in that bundle?" As if it were any of her business.

He looked hungry. Clarice remembered the thief in the Anthonys' kitchen. I was in no danger then, and I'm in no danger now, she thought.

She wished the parson would show up—or someone, anyone.

She saw the man fumbling in his pocket, and he drew out a folded piece of paper. It was so worn, it hardly held together where it was creased.

She took it from his hand and read, "I'm deaf and dumb."

In a split second Clarice went out the door. She ran around the church to the parsonage porch. She tried the door again, but it seemed to be more tightly locked than before. She tried to think of a way to get inside when she realized that the barefoot man was right at her elbow. She said nothing; she knew now that saying anything was useless.

She left the porch and went to the church steps and sat down, looking right and left, up and down the road, hoping someone would come along. She saw a horse tied to a tree about a hundred yards away. The horse had no saddle. She looked back at the man who was now hunkering down behind a bush on the parsonage lawn. She assumed the horse was his.

She said under her breath, "I think that is the same horse that was ripping up and down the road the night I fired the rifle to scare him."

At that moment she heard the sound of hoof beats and wheels. The dust was heavy so as to block out her view of who was coming. She silently prayed that it would be the parson.

Suddenly the thought came to her that the stranger would attempt an escape as soon as he saw someone coming. She ran to him and pointed to the back of the church, trying to turn his attention away from the approaching carriage.

It was John Jolly and the parson in John's chaise. The two men jumped from the carriage at the same time and ran to Clarice. They had seen her distracting the stranger's attention away from the arrival of the carriage.

John called out, "Mrs. McKenzie we were worried about you."

"And I was worried about you," she answered. "Where were you and the children?"

The parson was unlocking the door to his house. He pushed it open and stepped aside while Clarice led the stranger by the hand into the parson's parlor.

The parson was sizing the stranger up and down from head to foot. Seemingly he had seen him before or knew who he was. He motioned with his head toward chairs, indicating everyone should sit down. All did, except Clarice.

She went across the room to a desk and picked up a piece of paper and a stick of charcoal. She wrote on it, "What is you name? What is in the bundle?"

Then she noticed that he did not have the bundle. She handed the note to the deaf man. He refused to take it, holding his hand in front of his eyes and turning his head back and forth, negatively, telling Clarice that he could not read.

The parson saw that Clarice had much compassion for him. She patted his back and rubbed her hand down his arm.

John Jolly said to the parson, "What is the answer to this man's indigence?"

The parson shook his head as he said, "If we could get some information from him we might be able to help him."

Clarice said, "He had a bundle with him when he was in the church. He has left it somewhere, but I didn't see him hide it."

The parson asked, rather sternly, "What was he doing in the church, and why were you in the church?"

Clarice then explained to the parson and John all that had happened to her since she left her house to go with Dr. Miller to Sally Melville's house to get the fiddle.

A few seconds later she said, "Lord'a mercy, it's been a long day and I'm very hungry." She turned and spoke directly to John, "Will you take me home?"

Then to the parson she said, "You're the Holy One; you're God's representative. I leave this poor man to your discretion."

Clarice began walking toward John's chaise. She turned as she reached the carriage and called out, "I do believe he is the one who set the barn fires."

As John's carriage pulled away, Clarice saw Parson Smith leading the deaf mute out of the house and down the road toward his horse.

Soon she was dismounting the carriage at her front gate. John tried to get around the chaise to assist her, but she was too quick for him. She ran toward the children who were on their way to meet her.

Clarice, with outstretched arms, enfolded Sally and Matthew close to her breast and kissed first one and then the other on top of their heads. She said to them, "I've missed you both today. We will make up for today tomorrow."

Sister was standing in the doorway, witnessing the happy greetings. She said, as children and Clarice came through the door, "We carried some supper for you home from John's. I see you did not find the note I left for you under the boot jack."

"No," said Clarice, "If I had it would have saved me a lot of fear. I will eat the supper you brought, then I will tell you about my harrowing experience."

John Jolly came to the back door and looked in. He said, "I've taken care of the chores. Here is the milk." He set a pail of milk on the table and said, "I am going back to see about the parson."

Clarice thanked him.

He turned to say something else before he left, "Mrs. McKenzie, I have to go into Boston in a couple of days; would you and the children like to go along for the ride?" Clarice's mouth popped open in awe. She would love to go. John continued to talk, "You have been through a lot of grief and maybe you should have a bit of recreation. Think about it and let me know tomorrow."

Clarice said, "I will think about it." To herself, she said, I wonder if Jason would approve. She knew that Sister Smith did not approve; she showed it by her negative expression and wagging head.

Sister said to John, "If you are going back to see about the parson, may I ride with you? I need to see about the parson also."

John replied, "You are most welcome."

As John and Sister drove away, he looked back and nodded his head at Clarice.

Clarice sat in front of the fire, in her rocking chair, holding a child on each knee. She sang softly to them as they placed their heads on her shoulders. Soon they were showing drowsiness, and Clarice was also sleepy. She suggested to the children that all important matters be postponed until tomorrow and that they should all go to bed.

The big feather bed was quite full and puffy when Clarice and Sally and Matthew were all tucked under the old, worn crazy quilt.

Soon the children were soundly sleeping, but Clarice was smiling as she fantasized in sweet solace of her peaceful, secure, and happy embrace while lying in Jason's arms. She hoped she wouldn't go to sleep and end the beautiful feelings, but if she should fall asleep, she prayed that God would send her delightful dreams of Jason.

The house grew cold and dark as the night crept slowly to dawn. The candle burned down and flickered out. Somewhere a cow lowed with a lonesome sound and a little later a rooster crowed and woke Clarice, who thought she hadn't been asleep more than an hour. She sat up in bed and wondered how she was going to get out over Matthew, or over Sally, without waking them. She then thought she would try butt-scooting to the foot of the bed and slide out over the blanket roll.

The bed was a large cherry four-poster with a blanket roll post at the foot. It wouldn't be hard to do, she thought. She began the maneuver, and just as she placed herself on the blanket roll, it quickly rolled her out of the bed and onto the floor with a loud bump. Both children awoke with a start and saw Clarice lying spread-eagled on the floor at the foot of the bed.

They began to squeal with laughter as Clarice tried to untangle herself from her long ruffled nightgown. Someone was clapping the knocker on the front door vigorously. She called out from the top of the stairs, "In one minute please; I was not up yet. I will be there in a minute."

The children scrambled out of bed, ran past her and down stairs to the door, and opened it. There stood the deaf man. The children saw his dirty hands as he handed a note to Matthew and pointed to the stairway and up. Matthew understood that he was to take the note to Clarice. He ran fast to the top of the stairs.

Sally backed off from the open door. She backed to where she could reach the door latch. She slammed the door and bolted it, leaving the deaf-mute outside.

Matthew rushed into the bedroom where Clarice was getting into her clothes. He handed the note to her, she took it and began to shake as she read it.

It was from Parson Smith. It said: This vagrant has tied up Sister and left her locked in a closet. He has tied me up and is demanding money. I have none to give him. Maybe you can convince him that he will have to go into Boston to the Alms House. I don't know how to tell him since he can't read. I can't get to a constable since I'm tied up to a chair and chained to the hooks in the chimney. I think he is bluffing and will soon go away. The bundle that he was carrying was a load of flints he probably used to start fires. He has no gun; I don't think he is dangerous. The note was signed, Parson Smith.

Clarice called to Sally to come upstairs. She put the children in bed and covered them and told them to stay there and keep quiet. She told them that she had to go and see what the deaf man wanted and that she would return to them in a few minutes.

She said as she left the room, "When he is gone we will eat breakfast and then go for a nice walk."

She closed the door behind her and went downstairs. She opened the door and saw the man sitting on her steps. He smiled at her, but it was such a curious smile Clarice felt a shiver run down her spine.

To herself she said, "Be brave; he is too pitiful to scorn. Be gentle; he is hungry. Offer him friendship, and look at him with trust; he is scared, too."

"Good morning," she said; she knew he couldn't hear, but maybe he could read her lips. She extended her hand to him and stepped outside to stand beside him. She looked into his eyes with pity. She pointed to his mouth, touching his lips, then his stomach, and then to her own mouth and pretended chewing. He understood.

She hurried back into the house and into the kitchen where she took some food from the basket of food brought from John Jolly's. She returned momentarily with roast beef, bread, and apples.

He grabbed at the plate and began eating greedily, cramming food into his mouth with his hand. He licked the plate when all the food was gone. He handed the plate to Clarice and bowed low, Chinese fashion, over and over to thank her.

Clarice heard horses coming, she heard whoops from wild riders. She stood on her toes and craned her neck to see who it was. She saw two Indians approaching, their horses galloping as fast as they could under tight reins.

She took the deaf mute by his arm and pushed him inside the house; she followed and bolted the door. She motioned him to a chair. He sat down, but his head was turning swiftly from side to side surveying everything in the room.

Knocking began at the door. Clarice called out, "Who's there?"

A voice gruffly answered, "Big Moo Goo."

Clarice had heard of "Big Moo Goo," chief of a tribe of Algonquins who lived near Penobscot, Maine. She loudly asked, "What do you want?"

The Indian answered her, "We're looking for Firebug. We're told by the parson to come here and ask if you've seen him."

Clarice was thinking, as she leaned her back against the closed door. Should I lie and say I haven't seen him or should I turn him over to the Indians? She was studying the deaf-mute with sympathy when she saw two brown hands placed against the window glass and shading two wild-looking eyes, peering into the great room.

She said to herself, Those eyes are looking straight at the poor man; they know he is here, no use in lying to save him.

"What do you want with Firebug?" she called out as she opened the door just a crack.

"He is lost; we are his brothers. He will not be punished for running away. We must care for him."

Clarice opened the door and Firebug jumped into the arms of Big Moo Goo.

There was much rubbing cheek to cheek and laughter and back-slapping. Then Firebug turned to Clarice and gave her a tremendous hug and bowed from his waist, over and over again. He reached for Big Moo Goo's hand and Clarice's hand and placed them together and covered them with his own two big hands. He was smiling with happiness and bowing his head.

Soon the two Indians and the deaf-mute rode away with Firebug riding behind Big Moo Goo. Clarice watched as they rode out of sight toward the hills. She waved goodbye as long as she could see them. She wondered what Firebug had done with his horse.

Heaving a sigh of relief, Clarice went into the house, straight to her rocking chair and plopped into it. She laid her head back and ran her fingers through her hair. "Thank you, God," she said, "for getting me out of that situation. Please speed them on their way—far away—I never want to see them again."

She suddenly remembered the children and very quickly left the rocking chair and bounded upstairs. Both were in bed where she left them, and both had gone back to sleep. Well, it was only six A.M. and barely daylight. She considered going back to bed herself, but she was already dressed. She brushed her hair, then sat down in her chair and picked up her Bible and opened it to the Twenty-third Psalm. "I think I will memorize this," she said. "I find it most comforting when I'm scared or sad.

"The Lord is my shepherd, I shall not want...."

Clarice heard Parson Smith calling her. He was at the back door. He usually knocked and entered, but she had bolted it and put a chair against it before going upstairs.

"I'm coming," she answered. "I'm so glad it's you."

She opened the door and gave him a big hug. "Thank God you're all right."

The parson was calm and returned her hug. He began to talk as the two proceeded to the great room. They sat down in chairs in front of the fire, and he told her how the sexton found him and Sister tied up and how he released them and how he had written the note and also drawn a sketch of her house and the road to follow. And how fast the mute had grabbed the note and sketch and was last seen running down the road.

Clarice said, "I did not see any sketch; he only gave me the note."

The parson said, "There were three Indians when they arrived shortly after the mute left, but one of them took the bundle of flints and the horse and rode north. I directed the other two to you. They seemed civil enough to be trusted. Tell me they found him."

"They did," she answered. "I found that they had raised him and named him Firebug. They said he got lost as they rode through the woods...I doubt that. I have a queer feeling that he steals for them and they sell his loot to someone. The one who called himself Big Moo Goo had a guilty look about him." After a pause, Clarice asked, "What about Sister, how is she feeling?"

"She's fine, laughing about how she slapped him as he was tying her up and he didn't slap back." She said, "There's something likable about that deaf-mute."

The parson and Clarice sat still and quiet for a short while. Then Clarice asked, "Have you heard anything from your schooner?"

"Yes," he answered, "I was getting around to telling you. It will be here to pick us up day after tomorrow."

Clarice's expression changed to despair, "Oh how I hate to see you go," she said.

With his eyes lowered, the parson said, "Sister is taking it very hard also; it is tearing her heart out."

"If you could stay only until Jason comes home, I need you both so much."

The parson sighed and reached for Clarice's hand. He patted it with his other hand as he told her that word had been sent to Clinton Melville about his wife's and baby's deaths and about her taking the children until he returns.

He said, "It was sent by a fishing boat and no telling when he will receive it. Those boats are so slow. Doctor Miller wrote the letter."

Clarice got up from her chair and poked at the fire, Matthew and Sally came downstairs, still in their nightgowns, each asking for something to eat.

"I'm going to fix breakfast now for all of us. Sit here and talk to Parson Smith." She lifted Sally into the rocking chair. Matthew sat down on the floor near the fireplace.

They were eager to hear more about the Indians, and Sally asked the Parson, "Please tell us some more about the Indians." They had not seen the Indians but had heard Clarice and the parson talking about them.

They got a big laugh out of the name Big Moo Goo.

Clarice soon called the parson and the children to come and sit at the trestle table on which she had put fried apples, hominy, fried ham, biscuits, and big cups of coffee for herself and the parson and mugs of milk for the children.

While they were still at the table, John Jolly came. He said, "Good morning," but nothing else. Clarice thought he looked perturbed, as he picked up the milk pail and went to the barn.

The parson, after eating like a hungry dog, wiped his mouth with the edge of the tablecloth. He winked at the children, who were watching him do everything that Clarice had taught them not to do, and told them to be grateful that they had a place to live.

He said, "You are orphans and must do what you are told to do and be humble and obedient."

Clarice gave the parson a most objectionable stare and said to Matthew and Sally, "Don't be worried, my darlings. I will be a loving mother and teacher. But for now I think it would be nice if you went upstairs and took some of your clothes out of the basket that your mama brought with you and dressed yourselves in something pretty and hung the rest in your closet."

To the parson she said, "I'm going to follow the instructions I got from Lady Anthony. Sally will grow up to be a proper English lady, and Matthew someday might be a lord."

The parson sneered and shrugged his shoulders. He got up from the table and walked over to Clarice and lifted her hand from her side and held on to it. She almost jerked it from him but suddenly remembered all his and Sister's kindnesses. She let him hold on.

"My dear," said the parson, "within a few full moons this province will be spattered with blood. Those idiots in Philadelphia are now laying the ground for a serious confrontation with England."

Clarice pulled her hand from his and turned her back on him. He put on his hat and started toward the door to leave. Just then John came to the door with the milk.

"Thank you, John. Please sit down. I will pour you some coffee." She poured the coffee into a pewter mug and the aroma caused John and the parson to sniff with pleasure.

The parson sat down beside John. "I will have another cup too, if you please," said the parson. "I have something I want to talk to John about," he added, "alone, if you don't mind."

"I will go upstairs and help the children," she said. She left the two men sitting at the table, the parson leaning toward John, speaking in a low voice. Clarice paused at the top of the stairs. She was filled with curiosity about the conversation taking place at her kitchen table.

"You know," said the parson, "that is one beautiful woman, both in body and spirit. I hate to leave and leave her alone here. Her husband will be in Philadelphia for no telling how long. My wife tells me that you have invited her to go with you to Boston. Now, we don't think she should go."

John Jolly looked surprised. "Why not?" he asked in an angry voice. "She has been through a lot of grief and frustration in the last few weeks and needs some recreation. I hope you are not thinking that something other than being a good friend to a neighbor is in my mind. By the way, just what are you thinking?"

"It is only your big heart I am sure, but what will others think? The absence of your presence along with the absence of her presence I know your intentions are respectful and your heart is big and that nothing wrong will take place, but I think her reputation will be jeopardized."

Clarice saw the children digging into the basket of fresh, clean clothes. She felt a tear sliding down her cheek as she thought of Sally Melville ironing and folding the clothes and gently laying them in the basket. "Be careful with your clothes; don't muss them into wrinkles," she said, as she watched them tumble the shirts over the skirts and jab at the stockings and drawers while tossing them about.

Sally yelled out, "I can't find my white pinafore. I want to wear it now."

"Oh well," said Clarice, "we will come across it somewhere. Don't worry, it's not lost."

She noticed Matthew was wearing his very best waistcoat, his blue knee breeches, and his white stockings. She put her hand over her mouth to hold back the laughter.

"Matthew, why did you choose your very best waistcoat? We are not going anywhere today; this is not Sunday."

Matthew looked down at his clothes and smoothed his lapels. "You said to put on something pretty. I haven't got anything that's any prettier than these clothes."

When Clarice heard the back door slam shut, she returned to the kitchen. John Jolly was still sitting at the table. The parson had left. Probably in anger, thought Clarice, judging by the sound of the slamming door.

"What some more coffee, John?" Clarice pretended not to notice the tapping of John's fingers on the table by the side of his plate.

"No thank you, I must be going."

"Before you leave, may we talk about the trip to Boston?"

"Oh, that...well I've decided to ride horseback; it will be quicker."

Clarice dropped her head, "John, I'm disappointed. I was looking forward to getting my mind on something else. The Smiths' leaving is saddening me terribly. The children's questions are hard to answer. Jason's absence keeps my heart breaking into bits. Do you realize how much I need a change?"

"Yes, I do, and damn it, I don't care what the parson says, I will drive the carriage and take you and the children."

"But," said Clarice hesitatingly, "let's not go until the parson and Sister have left. That way they won't know that I went with you."

"Good, that will be Thursday, September twenty-ninth."

John was going out the door, Clarice reached for his hand and held it. "Thank you, thank you," she said, "you have been so kind."

Chapter Twenty-Nine

Before the day was halfway through the afternoon, and while Clarice and the children were taking a nap, Sister Smith came calling. She stood on the sixth stair step and called out, "Clarice."

Clarice heard her and got out of bed and went to meet her, saying to her, "I was very tired. The worry and excitement and then all this after yesterday's hullabaloo, I think I'm about done in."

"I, too," said Sister, "but I just had to spend some time with you and the children. Parson told you that we're leaving tomorrow?"

"Yes," Clarice softly laid her head on Sister's shoulder and whispered in her ear, "I love you and will miss you. I hope we," meaning herself and the children, "can be at the dock to see you off."

"No, please don't come to the dock. I can't bear to leave you standing there and knowing you are trying to hang onto these children alone. Have you heard from Jason? When will he be coming home?"

"I hope it will be soon," Clarice answered. "But since John Slade and Henry Cook passed through here and left me a note, I have not heard another word."

"That reminds me," exclaimed Sister. "Our sexton was in Salem last Saturday and happened to run into John Slade. Mister Slade told him to get the word to you that he and Henry Cook will be stopping by your place September twenty-ninth. If you have a letter ready they will take it to Jason in Philadelphia."

Clarice immediately acquired a startled expression. The mention of September twenty-ninth reminded her of the expected trip to Boston.

"That is good news," Clarice said. "I will be sure to write a letter." Then she asked, "Are you sure you don't want us to come to the dock?"

"Yes, I am very sure. Because we will be too busy bidding 'farewell' to a good many of our congregation who will be there. I would have to ignore you and the children for the most part because you have not attended the meetings enough for them to know who you are."

"Sister, dear, I understand. We will not be there, but I do have something for you to remember me by."

Clarice went upstairs to her bureau drawer and got out a tiny box. In it was a small pin cushion. She had made it while still living in Boston. It was made from a scrap of the wedding dress Maggie made for her.

She then opened another drawer and took out a knitted scarf. It was bright red. Jason's mother had made it for him with home spun yarn and dyed it herself. He didn't like it. He didn't like red. He wouldn't care if she gave it away.

Sister was sitting in front of the fire peeling an apple, cutting off chunks of it and eating, when Clarice returned with the pin cushion and scarf. She held out the presents to Sister and said, "These, I want you and the parson to have. I wish I could give you something more valuable, but I am also giving you my love and promise to write to you often and to read my Bible and pray."

"Clarice," said Sister, "those are the sweetest parting words anyone could wish for. These gifts we will treasure," she said as she hugged the little box and scarf up close to her heart. "I will be going now, and by noon tomorrow we will be gone."

With quavering voice and choking words, Clarice cried out, "God speed and safe sailing," as she stood at her threshold and watched Sister Smith hurriedly walk down the road. She went into her house to see what the children were doing. She closed the door, closed her eyes, and wiped the tears away that were running down her cheeks.

The children were busy at the school table, so she headed toward the kitchen. She wondered why Sister had not said goodbye to them. They had not noticed, or pretended not to notice, when she was leaving. Maybe it was because their hands were deep into a bowl of mud Clarice had put on the table for them to mold into models.

She paused a moment at Matthew's back. He was shaping into form a schooner. Clarice asked, "Is that the schooner that's taking Parson and Sister Smith to Connecticut?"

"No, It's the Gobbel Truth."

Clarice was surprised and she wondered where he ever heard that name and what else was in his smart little head.

Next morning, trying not to think about the Smiths leaving, Clarice kept busy gathering together clothes and other things, spreading them out on the bed in readiness for putting into the old sea chest to take to Boston. The sea chest could hold everything they would need and could be tied onto the back of John's chaise.

Getting tired after a while of sorting and packing, she plopped down in her rocking chair. She glanced out the window and saw John Jolly ride up to the front gate. There was a young boy riding behind him. They dismounted and she saw John pointing toward the barn. The boy took off in that direction.

John came in through the great room. He spoke to the children and asked if Clarice was at home.

"Upstairs," said the two in unison.

John tiptoed very quietly, but one creaky step let Clarice know that he was coming. She laid her head on the chair back and pretended to be asleep. He came up behind her chair and placed his hands over her eyes. She reached up and placed her hands over his and pressed gently.

"Are you very tired?" he asked.

They released their hands and John moved around in front of her and squatted down at her knees. He gave her a warm smile and took hold of the chair arms, fencing her in.

"Clarice," he said, "you are so pretty and sweet and good. How can Jason stay away from you?"

She blushed and turned her head away, but she felt a hot rush of blood flowing through her body. She said nothing, but was thinking, It has been a long time—six weeks.

She removed John's hand from the chair arm, stood up, and walked across the room to the top of the stairs. She called down, "Matthew, what are you and Sally doing?" She got no answer. She went to the window and saw them standing by the gate feeding nubbins to John's horse.

John had seated himself in her chair and was holding his bowed head between his palms.

"John, why are you sitting here like this?" she asked.

"Damnit," he answered, "I've made a complete fool of myself."

"Don't feel that way, John; I rather enjoyed being told that I am pretty, sweet, and good. Although, sometimes I'm unkempt, pushy, and demanding."

John got up from the chair and walked over to her. He put his arms around her and kissed her on the mouth long and hard, while holding her close. She did not resist or pull away from him. His hands moved slowly up over her shoulders and slid softly down her arms to her hands which he held tenderly.

John went outside and met Phinas at the barn. Clarice watched from the upstairs window. She saw John pointing up at the hayloft where the boy would sleep.

Matthew, followed by his sister, stomped up the stair steps and joined Clarice.

The children had never seen or been told about Clarice's magic blue chamois slippers. When Sally saw them on the bed by the folded clothing that Clarice had laid out for the sea chest, she picked them up and put her hands down inside them and walked them across the edge of the bed.

The children were now calling Clarice Cee Cee as she had told them to do. "Cee Cee," said Sally, "are these pretty shoes yours?"

"Yes, they are, Sally; they are my good luck shoes. I wear them when I'm going on a trip or to a party, and sometimes I wear them just around the house when I'm expecting something wonderful to happen."

"Are you expecting something wonderful to happen now?" asked the child.

"Never can tell. I am taking them with me to Boston. I hope something wonderful will happen while we are there."

Sally continued to fondle the slippers. She held them out for Matthew to feel. He ran his fingers over the smooth silk and remarked, "Feels like taffy we used to pull when we had butter all over our hands."

John came back into the house to let Clarice know that he was going home and to tell her that Phinas was all set up in the barn and that he had plenty to eat, for he had brought bread, honey, apples, and jerky in his satchel.

Clarice came to the top of the stairs. John was at the bottom step starting up. She said sweetly, "Do not come up, John; I will see you tomorrow. What time will you be here to pick us up?"

He answered her on his way out, "Probably around noon. We will get to my mother's about four o'clock."

Clarice said, "That is good. Maybe John Slade and Henry will get here before we leave."

Matthew was digging a hole in the front yard when he saw the two riders stopping at the gate. The men didn't know about the children living with Clarice, but they did know about Clarice's school. Jason had told them.

John Slade called out to Matthew, "Hey there, son, why aren't you in the house getting some learning?"

Matthew scowled at him and jabbed harder at the hole. He didn't answer John. Henry lifted his leg and swung it over Matthew's head. "Oh, my gosh," he said to the boy, "I thought you were a big bullfrog sitting there, but I see you are a full-fledged dirt digger."

Matthew threw down the trowel he was using, sprang to his feet, and ran past John and Henry to announce their arrival.

"Cee Cee," he yelled out, since he didn't see her, "these men are here."

Clarice was tugging at the heavy sea chest at the top of the stairs. She heard Matthew and at the same instant saw John Slade and Henry standing in the great room.

She called to them as she hurried down to them, "John...Henry, I'm so glad you have arrived." She hugged first one and then the other, then she asked, "Do you have any news, some news a news-hungry woman wants to hear?"

"Well," said John, "nothing good. There's lots of talk about the gathering and storing of arms, not only rifles and pistols, but also shovels, poles, hoes, kettles, and barrels."

Clarice interrupted him, "What in the world for?" she asked.

Clarice had heard some talk about this. Jason had mentioned it more than once. She had always changed the subject, as she did now. She asked, "When do you expect to be in Philadelphia?"

She took the letter she had written to Jason from the desk and handed it to Henry as she noticed he was wearing a large leather satchel strapped to his back. He put the letter into the satchel.

"Probably in two weeks," answered Slade. "That is, if we are assigned to Philadelphia from New York."

"I won't worry about it," meaning the letter, "not reaching Jason. There is nothing in it about arms or war or politics. It assures him that I love him and miss him and wish he was home."

The committee men didn't tarry long. They could see that something was in progress and Sally had informed them as soon as they arrived that they "were going to Boston for a visit. That Mister Jolly was taking them in his carriage."

Henry knew John Jolly, but John Slade did not recall having met the man. As Clarice walked with them out to the gate where their horses were waiting, she made sure that they knew she and the children would be staying with John Jolly's mother.

She explained that the few days in Boston were mostly for the children's educational benefit. She wanted them to know that there was another side of life.

"I intend to take them into every shop on Charles Street and to the wharf and to the market and Faneuil Hall," said Clarice.

"Jason sure married a smart woman," Henry remarked as they rode away. John Slade slapped his reins, shaking his head. He was thinking of something else.

Almost as soon as the riders were out of sight John Jolly drove up to the gate. His chaise was polished to a brilliant shine, his horse was curried, and the harness oiled and fresh looking.

The two children and Clarice were still standing at the front gate where they had said goodbye to John Slade and Henry when John Jolly drove up. He got out of his chaise, came around to Clarice, and extended his hand to her, squeezing it lovingly and placing his other hand over it. "Good morning," he said.

He bent to hug Sally and laid his arm across Matthew's shoulder. "I see you are not quite ready, so I will step out to the barn and see what Phinas is doing." He walked away toward the barn as the two girls and Matthew hurried into the house and upstairs to get dressed.

The traveling clothes were already laid out on the bed. She had selected a brown linen to wear, but she changed her mind in a flash and put on her blue dimity shirt waist and lavender cotton skirt. She swished around the chair and viewed herself in the mirror. "What am I thinking about?" she asked herself. "I am being too coquettish. I will wear the brown dress."

She called Sally to her assistance. While in her petticoat, she asked the little girl, "Which dress should I wear?"

Sally thought about it for a minute and surprised Clarice with her answer. "Do you want Mister Jolly to think you are beautiful?"

"Good heavens," said Clarice, "that is exactly what I wanted." She snatched the brown linen and began pulling it over her head. She knew that some strange and delightful feeling was creeping over her. She did want John

Jolly to think she was beautiful. Sally had already left the room and was sitting on the bottom stair step. In a moment Clarice appeared at the top of the stairs.

Sally looked up to see her and saw that she was wearing the brown dress. She asked, "Why didn't you want Mister Jolly to think you are beautiful?"

Clarice was being a bit childish when she answered, "Sally, your eyes are too sharp and see too much. Let us drop the subject, dear."

Sally asked, not heeding the order to drop the subject, "Do you like Mister Jolly like you like Jason?"

Clarice was completely awed. "No," she answered harshly.

John came into the house and carried the sea chest to the chaise and secured it firmly to the luggage rack.

The children climbed in and John fastened the lap straps across their laps. Clarice mounted beside John, and they were off to Boston in gleeful moods.

The day was warm and hazy. Leaves were breaking loose from their branches and swirling down in diving motions. The road was ankle deep in oak, spruce, maple, hemlock, and sycamore leaves.

The children grabbed at those that drifted through the carriage. Bittersweet berries and wild grapes getting ripe on the vine gave off pungent odors. A walnut dropped and hit the top of the carriage causing eyes to roll upward to see if it made a hole.

The ferry was crowded, as usual—Harvard students, mostly, going home for the weekend or just to town for a frolicking noisy bash in some tavern.

Matthew and Sally got out of the carriage and stood by the rail, hanging their heads over to watch the wake.

Clarice saw Matthew take a marble from his pocket and toss it overboard. "Matthew, what are you doing?" she asked him as she stood between him and Sally.

"I'm trying to hit that fish that's following us," he said.

There were hundreds of small fish following the wake and grabbing the crumbs the passengers were throwing to them. The ferry captain told the children, as he helped them back into the carriage, that no one ever caught the ferry fish, but feeding them was a great amusement while they were tugging along from shore to shore.

John's mother was pleasantly surprised when she opened the door after John stood knocking for at least five minutes.

"Lordy me," she said, after hugging and kissing him, "I never expected to see you again until Christmas."

"Well, Ma, I have business in Boston and I just wanted to see you. We ought to visit each other more often."

"Did you bring the twins?" she asked, as she looked around to see.

"The twins and their mother are in Provincetown. I expect they will stay there until spring." His eyes were scanning the great room while his mother was craning her neck to see who was in the chaise.

He said, "I've brought Jason's wife and the two children she is caring for since their mother died. I guess you know Jason is in Philadelphia; he is Sam Adams's aide at the Congress. You must have read about the Congress in the Gazette."

"Well, go and help Mrs. McKenzie out of the chaise and bring her in." John did as his mother told him.

After introductions and other first words of greeting, Clarice said, "I do hope we won't be intruding if we stay a day or two."

"No, of course not. I have plenty of room, but I do have a British soldier quartered here. It is not of my choosing, but as I was ordered to do after my house was inspected for extra room. A survey was taken because rooms were needed to shelter the extra five thousand soldiers that came with Gage. I am glad you are here with the children; that will excuse me from having to take in another mercenary."

Clarice thought about the situation for a moment. She sighed as she said, "The children and I can stay in Jason's apartment over the bakery, if our being here might cause trouble."

Mrs. Jolly knew about the apartment as she had worked for Jason in the bakery. She said, "Oh, I think it is occupied with two or three soldiers." She took Sally by the hand and said, "I'll show you to your room. Follow me."

She led them to a large airy room with two double-poster beds and a large bureau, plenty of windows with starched cotton curtains, and a huge rocking chair.

"This is simply wonderful," said Clarice. John came in carrying the sea chest and a basket of apples.

Matthew and Sally had been very quiet up to this moment. Matthew suddenly pulled on John's hand and asked, "Where you going to sleep, Mister Jolly?"

He smiled at the boy. The childish suspicion had penetrated his own brain. "I have a room off the kitchen where I will sleep," said John. He continued, "It is the room we call the beggar's room. When I sleep there I will be close enough to hear someone knocking on the back door as beggars always do."

"Are we going to have any beggars?" asked Sally. "Well, I've heard that Boston is thriving in beggars, so many people are out of work." By the time John had answered Sally's question, she was occupied with a bowl of shells sitting on the credenza. She didn't see John as he went over to Clarice, lifted her hand, and kissed the back of it, saying jokingly, "Is that all, madame?"

Clarice blushed and moved away but was smiling at John.

Mother Jolly had already left the room. She was talking as she went hurriedly about. "I have to go over to School Street, I have a midwifery job to take care of. Supper is all ready on the table; it is not much. We are scarce of everything except what we have harvested from our own garden. There is stewed pumpkin, roast chicken, and blueberry pie. Also plenty of milk and cider."

Clarice and the children and John were following Mrs. Jolly single file downstairs. Clarice said, "Sounds delicious to me."

Mrs. Jolly kept talking, "It's been delivery time for four days, and each day I've walked three miles each way, back and forth, to a false alarm. If it doesn't happen tonight, I'm going to bring Ellen here to wait. I can't be wearing myself out like this. Ellen is eighteen years old and has had one baby already. I can't see what's taking this one so long."

Clarice was standing at the door, watching Mrs. Jolly hurrying down the street, but she was thinking of Sally Melville. She called out, "I pray that there won't be any trouble, that someone won't die."

When Clarice saw Matthew's head falling forward as he sat quite still on a chair, she knew he was getting sleepy. John, who was close by, picked the boy up and carried him upstairs and laid him on the bed.

Sally followed him and went straight to the bowl of shells again. She asked John, as she twiddled the shells, "Is my brother going to bed without his supper?"

John put his finger across his lips, indicating to Sally to be quiet. "Oh, he will have his supper. We will wake him when it's ready. He needs a little nap now, and he will enjoy his food more if he has rested. We all have had a busy day. Wouldn't you like to take a little nap while I fix our supper?"

The child said, "No, I want to stay with Cee Cee." She ran past John, calling for Cee Cee as she went.

Clarice stood at the front door looking out at the street. She wondered why people were in such a hurry, seemingly headed toward some excitement. She heard drum beats and marching feet. Sally came to her and asked her what she was looking at.

"The street is an interesting thoroughfare," she answered the little girl. "Do you hear anything like a band?"

"Yes, I think it is a parade."

At that minute a large brigade of marching redcoats came into view. They were carrying rifles and high stepping to the commands of two flag bearers carrying Union Jacks.

"Oh, goodie," said Sally, "there is a parade."

"I think it is a practice drill," said Clarice.

John stepped up behind the two girls and saw what was entertaining them. "I have heard that this goes on day and night, disturbing the citizens terribly. Some merchants won't open their businesses. Children are sitting in the school rooms scared to death."

"Seems like everyone is in a big hurry, like they were running from something, trying to get somewhere to hide. Do you think that the people are afraid of the soldiers?" she asked John.

"Yes, I do think they are afraid of the soldiers, but there is no immediate danger of war breaking out, but it will eventually."

"I've heard that the Old South Church is being used as an equestrian school, that the British soldiers threw the church pews out into the trash and ripped up the floor and spread sawdust, that their horses are stabled there and every day they teach their cavalry tactics there. What a shame."

Clarice had a disturbed expression on her face. She said, "I suppose I had better go tomorrow and see about Jason's building."

John led her away from the door. He said, "I'll go with you. You are apt to run into mercenaries there."

The two sat down in chairs opposite each other, and John pointed out the portraits hanging on the wall and explained each one's place in his family history.

Sally came close to Clarice, and she lifted the child onto her lap. John kept looking at Clarice in an affectionate way as she rocked the child. Her eyes met his, and there was definitely a surge of passion.

Sally squirmed out of Clarice's lap and went upstairs. "I'm going to wake Matthew up so we can eat," she said.

As soon as Sally was out of sight, John went over to Clarice and took her hand. He held it as she walked with him to the table.

She at one end, he at the other, lifted the table cover from the food and began arranging the places. They noticed that one place was set and a place card read, Tom. This had to be the soldier-roomer. After all, Mother Jolly had not expected anyone else. The food was in scarce supply. Clarice realized that she must pretend that she was not hungry, so there would be enough for John, the children, and the roomer.

While they were taking plates from the cupboard and silverware from the sideboard drawer, someone came into the room behind them. A reflection in a silver platter standing on its side on the sideboard showed a red-coated soldier ready to sit at the place assigned to Tom.

Clarice gasped for breath and dropped a china plate, then grabbed at the edge of the sideboard to steady herself. She could not speak; she recognized the face in the platter. It was Tom Fellows.

"Great God, have mercy," she whispered to herself. She did not want to turn around to face him.

John noticed her weakness. How could he miss it? She was shaking like a leaf. He reached out and took her arm.

John asked her, "What's the matter? Are you ill?"

"No, I'm quite all right; I've seen a ghost."

She knew she had to face Tom. She quickly turned around and stood looking at Tom for a second. Then she called out, "Tom, darling," as she ran into his outstretched arms while John Jolly stood abashedly looking on.

Clarice did not have to pretend that she was not hungry. She could not eat one bite, and she could not say one word. She was about to choke.

The children were seated in their places, one on each side of Clarice. John was at the end of the table acting as host in his mother's absence.

Tom was helping himself but was very unconcerned with his food. He seemed quite embarrassed.

It was Matthew who broke the silence. He looked Tom Fellows straight in the eye and boldly asked, "Are you a Tory?"

"Yes, I suppose I am," answered Tom.

"Then why are you living at Mrs. Jolly's house? She is a Patriot."

"Because I was assigned to this house." Tom was smiling at Clarice. Clarice was watching Sally but listening to Tom and Matthew.

John was gulping his food. His uptightness was showing. He dropped his knife heavily onto his plate as he said, "Tell me, Tom—I presume that is your name; Clarice didn't bother to introduce us—why do you unwelcome British soldiers settle yourselves in private homes of patriotic Americans?"

The talk was becoming raucous when Tom gruffly said, "It's the king's business. The British must do what they must to protect what's theirs. Billeting soldiers in private homes is a protection for that home and family."

Sally spoke, "Jason says we're going to chase all the redcoats back to England."

Tom smiled, "Oh yeah?"

Clarice finally got her bearings; she said, "I'm sorry, John; I was so overwhelmed at seeing Tom I forgot my manners." She raised her hand to John. "John Jolly, this handsome soldier is Tom Fellows, a friend—a very dear friend—from Birmingham, England, a former fiancé of mine." She continued, "He is now, and always will be, a very dear friend."

John had a sour expression on his face. He said as he left the table, "I need some fresh air and a drink. I'm going to ride over to the Merry Mermaid."

Chapter Thirty

When John Jolly entered the Merry Mermaid, he saw that the place was crowded with drunken riffraff and British Regulars. There was no kind of order. Just as he walked up to the bar a mug of cold beer was dashed into his face and the one who threw it called him a "filthy rebel."

John snatched an empty mug from a table and hurled it at the bar, hitting the bartender in the shoulder, knocking him backward into a barrel of beer which overturned, pouring beer out onto the floor and causing patrons of the establishment to slip and slide into each other.

Quicker than the eye can wink, a roughhouse was in progress and bloody noses were gushing all over the place.

John felt a big, tough hand gripping his arm. He had just gotten to his feet after being shoved down into the slithering stream of beer and sawdust. He looked over his shoulder to see the constable of the tavern about to hit him with his billy stick.

"Hey, wait a minute. I haven't done anything, but I'm about to, as soon as I find out who threw that beer into my face and called me a filthy rebel. I am a rebel, but I'm not filthy."

The constable gave him a jerk and said, "I'm throwing you into the hoosegow anyway." He manhandled John out the door and into the paddy wagon. The handcuffs had already begun to hurt.

John screamed at the driver, "Stop this thing; let me out of here. I'll go straight home and behave like a saint. I am not to blame for that fracas. I didn't even get my drink; I wasn't in the place five minutes."

"Shut up, you rabble-rouser; you are a menace to humanity." It was the driver of the wagon yelling at John.

John was getting mad and crazy. He stood up from the long bench and with his handcuffed fists he hit the driver in the back of his head, knocking him out. He shoved the driver and the constable out into the street. He took over the reins, although it was hard to do.

John managed to guide the horse to the barn in back of his mother's house. He immediately went to the grindstone and cut the handcuffs off his wrists. He pushed the wagon into a different stall and threw a few forks of hay over it. He closed the barn door and put the bar across it.

It was a dark night, and he was sure no one was aware of his activities. It was too far for the wagon driver and the constable to walk there and it would take time. John remembered he had left his horse at the hitching post at Merry Mermaid. He had to go back there and get him. As he walked he began to think about all the things that had happened since that afternoon. He felt like he needed a drink more than ever. He walked faster.

He was afraid he might run headlong into the constable, but that didn't happen. He wondered if that S.O.B. went back to the tavern and might still be there. John said, "Thank God he didn't get my name and address."

The tavern patronage had thinned out considerably as John saw when he looked through the window before going in. He didn't see the constable.

He went in, walking with a stride of importance as if he had never been in the place before. He walked up to the bar, threw one leg over a stool and sat down. With one elbow on the counter, he ordered, "A large flip, make it with rum and don't be stingy with the rum."

After two large flips John was reeling and his eyes crossed. He began babbling away, pounding the bar with his palms. He was in a maze of thoughts. First he talked of his wife and twins, how they didn't care if he was alone and lonesome. He rambled off and talked about Clarice, how cruel Jason was to go away and leave her. He kept pounding the bar and calling for more flip.

He was in a very drunken state when he began to cry. Tears were rolling down his face. He cried out, "I can't help it. I love that woman, but she is another man's wife—a friend's wife. She needed me; I went to her. She let me do what she needed. I think we are good for each other." He wept out loud in an inebriated condition, "She loves me and I love her."

Several patrons heard John Jolly weeping into his flip, talking to himself. He had really flipped. He had given those people plenty to talk about. He had not made it clear he was so drunk he didn't know what he was saying. When he said, "She loves me and I love her," he was alluding to his wife. Clarice's reputation was now painted red, especially those who were in the tavern and who knew Jason McKenzie.

The bartender realized that John would not be able to ride his horse. He helped him from the stool, just as he was passing out, and partly carried and partly dragged him into the back room. He put him down on a stack of sacks of sand, which were used when the place was flooded, where he became the fifth drunk stretched out there.

While John Jolly was sobering up on the sand bags in the back room of the Merry Mermaid tavern, Clarice and Tom Fellows were having a great conversation in Mother Jolly's great room. Several lighted candles were flickering here and there, making a light that was soft and endearing to the two (once upon a time) sweethearts.

Clarice was most anxious to hear news of her parents, their business, and old friends.

Tom was thrilled and delighted to be near her again. He asked, pausing frequently between his words, "Cee Cee, do you really love Jason? How could you fall in love so quickly after you left me, professing your love and promises to me? Are you a happy woman?"

"Yes, yes I am, to all of your questions. I nearly lost my mind worrying about Jason before we married."

"Why?" asked Tom.

"The mobs here in Boston were ruthless...still are. All that rumpus about the Boston Tea Party. I believe he was mixed up in it in some way. I know he attended meetings where Sam Adams and John Adams were making speeches. After we moved to Lynn he still attended meetings."

Tom asked, "What were the meetings about?"

Clarice was telling the truth when she said, "I don't know; he wouldn't tell me. He would say to me, 'Don't worry your pretty head about the meetings, just concentrate on how much I love you.' I know you will like him."

"Oh, I already do like him, Cee Cee, but he swings a mean fist. After knocking me down, he apologized and offered me quarters in his apartment. For some reason, the quartermaster told me to find another place to live. I found Mrs. Jolly's address in Jason's time book which was on his desk. I knew she had worked for him. I asked my quartermaster to send me here and here I am."

There was a few minutes of absolute quiet. The air was fragrant with autumn. It was warm enough to have the door standing open. The night was full of sounds.

Clarice, after clearing her throat said, "Tom, I never stopped loving you, but you must understand, it was a different love that I acquired for Jason. He was devilish, which you were not. He was independent, which you were not. He was flirtatious and unpredictable. I never knew when he would show up, and I was lonely for something of my own. Jason was well liked by the Anthonys until they found out he and I were attracted to each other, then they forbade me to see him and banished him from their house. Lord Anthony went so far as to order sentinels stationed at our house."

Tom was listening with interest, and finally said, "I still love you, Cee Cee, very much. I can't help it. I couldn't get to America fast enough. The only way I could do it was to join the regular army. My request was granted to be sent to Massachusetts. I was on a list for Charleston, but I think it was your father's influence that got me here. I wanted to be near you, even though you belong to another man."

"Tom, that is sweet, but I do hope you will find someone else soon. I cannot be too near you either. I do love Jason with all the love I have to give. He gets it all."

Tom said, "I understand, my dear; I wish you blessings beyond belief. I will always love you." He stood up and pulled Clarice up to her feet. He put his arms around her and kissed her lovingly. "There, my darling, that was our last kiss." He went out of the room.

Clarice sat down again on the settee where they had been sitting. She folded her hands and prayed, "Oh, dear God, please send Jason home to me."

Mother Jolly came home around nine o'clock the next morning. The night for her had been successful: Ellen Cabot had delivered a nine-pound boy at midnight. All was well, and mother and child were both sleeping soundly when Mother Jolly left them. A day nurse had been called, and she, with Mister Cabot, would stand by. Mother Jolly hoped she would not be needed again.

Tom had left to join his company. The children were fed and dressed, ready to go with Clarice to town. John had not returned or been heard from since he stalked out from the supper table the night before. Clarice was wondering if she and the children were going to have to walk. It was a long way for their little short legs, Mother Jolly informed Clarice. Mrs. Jolly's house was on Hanover Street. Clarice was thinking of Charles Street where there were plenty of interesting shops and also Jason's apartment.

As they went out the door Mother Jolly called out to them, "Bear to the northeast and you will come to Charles Street."

"Thank you," Clarice called back; however, she was looking toward southwest. She remembered Boston Common and wondered if the clowns were still performing there as they were in June. She did not remember that June was a celebration month for the new governor.

She took each child by the hand and began walking toward what she remembered as a happy place; that is, it was for a few days in June.

People stared at Clarice and the children, "Who was that woman out on the street with her children without a male escort?"

An old man with a push cart stopped them, "Good day to ye, ma'am. Where might ye be going to taking these young'uns? Do ye know the redcoats is a looking for to question strangers? I guess ye are strangers, ain't ye? I never seed ye before, and I peddle up and down this street every day."

Matthew and Sally were trying to see what was in the push cart. They had dropped Clarice's hands and were feeling around under the tarpaulin cover.

Clarice smiled at the old peddler. She observed him closely before replying to his inquisition.

"What are you selling, sir?" she asked.

"Just junk, only junk," he answered.

Matthew piped up, "Why would anyone buy junk?"

"Well, because them redcoats is anxious to get their hands on anything outs a rebel's house."

Clarice reached for the hand of each child; she said curtly, "We must be on our way, no more dilly-dallying, goodbye." She briskly led the children on toward the Common.

Approaching the place where she and Jason had watched people picnicking, dancing, and singing, she was appalled at what she saw.

There were small tents set up in rows, pig pens here and there, a stockade, cows were tethered to trees, barrels of water in front of almost every tent, muddy messes all around the barrels. A contingent of British soldiers were drilling nearby.

"Good heavens, children, I didn't expect this. We have to go back; we won't be allowed in the park. We might even be arrested."

"Will they put us in jail?" Matthew was rather thrilled at the prospect.

Sally began to quiver. She clasped Clarice's hand tighter, then she began to cry. "Cee Cee, I have to pee," she whimpered.

"Go ahead, wet your drawers. I don't see a privy anywhere." Then she saw a small square building on the edge of the Common. "Oh, there it is," she ran to it pulling the children into it. There was a big wooden bolt; she fastened it, then helped Sally onto the seat.

Someone began pounding on the door.

"Go away," she called out. "We will only be a minute."

She heard a man's voice. "My God, it's a woman."

She kicked the door; her hands were too busy to knock. She yelled, "Yes, it is a woman and two children. We were desperate; we appreciate the use of this facility."

Whether the soldier (must have been a soldier) who pounded the door deliberately bolted it on the outside, or bolted it from habit is not known, but Clarice and the children were locked inside the privy.

Clarice began pushing the door to open it. It would not budge. She threw her weight against it, a mere 110 pounds. That didn't shake the bolt loose as she hoped. She looked around for something to pry it with. She saw the frightened expressions on the children's faces. "Don't be afraid," she said. "We will soon have this problem solved. Let's all holler for help as loud as we can, all at the same time."

The two children became excited and thrilled to yell and stomp. "Help, help," the three of them hollered out. They tried the same alarm tactic over and over, but no one came.

There was a stack of old Gazettes in one corner. Clarice looked at the stack. "Must be some way this paper can help us," she said to herself, "unless the troops have all left the camp and gone off on their maneuvers. If they have done that, they won't be back before twilight." She gave a sigh of wonderment.

She reached for the stack and tore off a page which she pushed through a crack above the door (without tearing it or wadding it). She held on to the edge of it, but wiggled it around. She said to the children, "Let's all yell for help again while pounding on the side of the building."

Within a few seconds two large dogs were scratching at the privy door and barking furiously. They went from one side to the other. Their yelping was scary. At one instant Clarice thought the small building was going to topple over, the lunging dogs were throwing themselves against it with full force.

The children were clinging to Clarice's skirt. "Cee Cee, what are we going to do?" asked Matthew.

"We're going to be out of here very soon, I can assure you. These dogs will bring someone to our rescue."

A few more minutes and Clarice heard someone running toward the privy. Two sentinels were yelling at the dogs to "Hush up."

First they leashed the dogs, calling their names. "Bruno, be quiet; Buster, cut it out." Then they unbolted the door. They couldn't believe what they saw. A woman and two frightened children.

"Well, I never!" exclaimed the soldier, as he looked upon the three who were scaring the dogs.

The other soldier had moved off a little ways with the dogs, who were now calm.

The one who had unbolted the door said, "What's a woman doing here with two children? Spying, I suppose and the children are cover-ups?"

"No, I am not a spy. We will gladly be on our way. We thank you and wish you well," said Clarice. Her face was red as she held tightly to the children's hands trying to keep them from petting the dogs. They left the Common almost in a run, heading back to Hanover Street.

When they reached Mother Jolly's, they went to their room and changed their clothes. Clarice gathered up the ones they took off into a bundle and hurried out to the back yard clothesline where she hung them out to air. She met Mother Jolly coming from the barn.

"There's a strange horse and a paddy wagon in my barn. I feel like I have to ask John some questions," she said as she walked with a gallant pace into her house.

Clarice did not know that John had come home. She hadn't thought of him. Her mind was on the predicament she had just gotten out of. She still wanted to get to town and show it to the children, but most of the day was over. There was little time left of daylight. What she should do was her mind's occupation.

When she passed through the great room on the way to her room, she saw John and his mother sitting on the settee, talking in low tones. She did hear Mother say, "What will your neighbors think? And what lies will they multiply and spread? John, I don't approve."

Clarice heard nothing more, but she had her suspicions that Mother Jolly was talking about her and John coming to Boston together.

She said to herself, Maybe I did the wrong thing, but I don't feel guilty. Jason asked John to look after me, and I am in control. Having the children near me all the time is a big help, like a bodyguard. By the way, where are the little rascals? She called for them as she opened the door to their room.

The two were standing at the window watching a squadron of redcoats going through their drill exercises. They were stooping and shifting arms and turning about-face. Matthew and Sally were laughing and clapping.

"That's enough of that, children. Those soldiers are getting in shape for fighting. I don't believe in fighting." She enticed them away from the window.

As Matthew took Clarice's hand, he said, "One day when we were in school and Jason ate lunch with us he said, 'to fight for our rights is honorable and someday, all us men are going to fight.'"

"Oh, is that so?" Clarice responded to Matthew. "Well, I'll speak to Jason about that. My son is not going to fight other men. You are going to grow up to be a doctor or teacher. I won't have you fighting."

Sally spoke up, "Matthew already fights. He fights me, he kicks me and pushes me and pinches me and pulls my hair."

Clarice smiled at Sally and squeezed her hand. "That's play fighting. He loves you, don't you, Matthew?"

"No, but I do love her sometimes."

Mother Jolly was calling Clarice. "Do you and the children want some pie? I made a big old spiced cushaw cobbler."

"Yes, we do; I am starving for cushaw. Thank you so much."

Later Clarice encountered John. He acted aloof. She said to him, "We wondered what happened to you. Tom and I were still talking at ten o'clock. You had not returned."

He waited a moment, then said, "Did you get your talking over with? Because I forbid you to spend time alone with him again."

Clarice drew up her shoulders and took a deep breath. "John Jolly, are you aware of what you just said? You cannot forbid me anything. I am my own person."

"But I am looking out for you while Jason is away."

"Well, you don't have to look out for me any longer. I can take care of myself."

"What about the children?" John asked.

"I will take good care of the children. Just go about your business and forget about us."

Clarice nor John knew that Tom Fellows was in his room. When he opened his door and heard them talking he hesitated before going on, not intentionally eavesdropping but unable to get past them without interrupting their conversation.

He surmised that John was either overprotective or jealous or both. He was not surprised at his feelings. He was also desirous of looking after Clarice. He thought, I have the first right to her love. She was my dearest one before she came here. If Jason does not return I will pursue her absolutely.

"Hello," Tom said, as he pretended to look surprised at seeing them and walked very fast as he passed them and left the house.

Clarice turned away from John and attempted to walk away, but he reached out and put his arm around her and drew her up to him. He tilted her head and kissed her forehead, then her lips, then her mouth.

"Don't you understand me, Clarice? I've fallen in love with you."

"John, you can't," she answered. "I belong to Jason. I belong to Jason," she repeated it.

"But how can I help it?" he asked.

"What about your wife and twins?"

"I don't know. I don't think Dora loves me. She said when she left that if either of her parents die she will continue to live in Provincetown. I don't love her; she is not pretty like you."

As Clarice twisted out of John's arms, she said, "John, please don't try this again. I'm not going to allow it to happen. I love Jason." But she did not move away from him; she picked up his hand and held on to it. She said, "It is a wonderful feeling, this thing called love. You are so worthy of love...you will have a different feeling about Dora when you see her again." She looked John in his pathetic eyes and said, "If there's a schooner going to Provincetown, why don't you catch it and visit Dora and the twins? I will wait here at your mother's until you get back."

"I don't want to see her now. She would see that my mind was somewhere else. I wouldn't be able to get you off my mind and out of my heart. Even if I was holding Dora and kissing her, I would be pretending it was you."

Clarice turned on her heel and shook her finger at him. "Shame on you, John, try to forget out little embraces, and I will, too. It must not happen again. Now I must get started to town; the children have my promise and the day is going fast." She gathered her skirt up in her hand and took the stairs, two steps at a time."

"Matthew...Sally, are you ready to go?" Both children rushed past her, not only ready to go but also dashing ahead of her out to the street where they waited.

Soon the three were on their way to Charles Street leaving Boston Common away off in the rear and Mother Jolly waving from her front door. John had gone to the beggar's room and was writing a letter to Dora.

Clarice was an observing person. She noticed as she walked along that picket fences needed paint; some were broken down in places. House shutters were also dingy looking, and some were hanging on one hinge. There were chips off mounting blocks and now and then a cracked or broken window. Why is this town in such disrepair? she wondered. People she met were angry-looking and did not speak.

She thought, This is the result of that awful Tea Party. Maybe in a year or two they will have forgotten about it and King George III will open the port again and everyone will be back to normal.

Clarice was quiet, not talking to the children as they walked along. Her thoughts were for awhile on John Jolly. He is so kind and helpful to me and so sweet to the children and kind to his mother.

Matthew noticed she had stopped talking to him and Sally. "Cee Cee," he said, "you're s'posed to tell us about Boston. What is that over there?" He pointed to a small shelter house, with a bench all around its three sides. It had been built recently for the benefit of the soldiers in case of rain.

Clarice said, "That is a place to go when it's raining."

As they came closer they saw the same old man they had met earlier that morning when they were on their way to the Common. His cart was parked in back of the shelter and he was asleep, stretched out on the bench. He was snoring loudly.

Clarice held Matthew's hand tighter to restrain him. He was going to wake him, but Clarice said, "Don't disturb him; he must be very tired."

On reaching Charles Street, Clarice wasn't sure she knew which door was Jason's building. She decided to go into the chandler's shop and ask Mister Winkler. She saw that he was open. There was a sign on his window.

She said to the children, "Rest here a minute while I go in and inquire." She pointed to the steps.

She was gone only a few minutes. The chandler, Mister Winkler, came out with her. Jason's building was next door. The door was not locked and was sagging, the bottom hinge was missing. Clarice asked Mister Winkler if he ever saw anyone going in or out of the building.

"All the time," he answered. "It's a regular hangout for riffraff. Soldiers sometimes peek in the door but never go in. I think the door should be boarded up or the storeroom leased out. When will your husband be coming back? We miss him from this neighborhood."

The children followed the chandler around as he looked into cabinet drawers. There was nothing in them but dirty flour and ants wading in spilled sugar.

Matthew stuck his finger in a small pile of sugar, flipped out the ants, and sucked the finger. Sally watched her brother and said, "Yuk," while screwing her face into distortion.

Clarice and Mister Winkler were surprised by loud knocking on the door. It was John Jolly; he had followed them there. "I felt very guilty after you left, Mrs. McKenzie." He called Clarice Mrs. McKenzie for the benefit of Chandler. To have called her Clarice would have sounded too intimate. "I should have offered to drive you here. The streets of Boston are no place for a woman."

"Oh that's all right, Mister Jolly. I appreciate your concern. "Mister Jolly" was for the same reason he had addressed her as Mrs. McKenzie.

Matthew and Sally looked at John and Clarice with lowered eye brows and protruding lower lips. They were puzzled but said nothing.

Clarice said, "I'll take a run upstairs and see what kind of shape Jason's apartment is in. We may have to sleep here." She soon returned.

"Well?" questioned Mister Winkler.

"It is not so bad. A little cleaning would make it livable, but I'll not bother with it now. I think someone has been sleeping there."

Mister Winkler said, "That black boy that used to hang around with Jason shows up here about once a month. I'm a bit leery of him. He doesn't talk to anyone. He takes good care of his horse. He seems like a good fellow, but you never can tell. I don't think he is owned by Jason. I think he is a free man. That is why I'm worried for his safety."

"Don't be worried," said Clarice. "He can take care of himself. He is our friend."

Sally was turning pages in a book she picked up from the floor. She looked at Mister Winkler and said, "That's Henry."

John stood quietly off to one side. Clarice walked over to him. She introduced him to Mister Winkler.

She said to John, "I would like to show the children where I used to live. Will you take us there?"

They said, "Good day," to Mister Winkler and thanked him for his help and they left.

John helped them into the chaise and said, "I am so happy to be of help to you."

Very soon they were getting out of the chaise at the garden gate in back of the large house on Beacon Street. Clarice had told John to drive to the back because it would seem more reminiscent to go there than to the front stile which she rarely ever saw while living there. She looked for the broken post, it was gone. A new post had replaced it.

She passed the gazebo and pointed it out to Sally and Matthew and said, "Robin and I had lots of fun, really good times, in the gazebo."

"Better than with Jason in Lynn?" asked Matthew.

"No, not better than in Lynn, but Jason was a part of all the good times here until the Boston Tea Party."

"Is that why you moved to Lynn?" asked Sally.

"No, dear, we got married is the reason we moved to Lynn."

As Clarice came near the stable, she saw Jackson, nodding in his chair at the stable door. She ran to him and he squinted up at her, not recognizing her at first. Then he stood up on wobbly legs and reached out to her. "Why it's Miss Cee Cee. How is you?" he asked. "And what brings you here?"

"Jackson, my dear friend, I'm so glad to see you. Are you well?"

"Well, no I isn't well zactly. I'z still got this big ball on the back of my neck. It's purty bothersome sometimes."

Clarice said, "Tell me, how do you live?"

"Well, Henry Cook comes by here once in a while. He brungs me food and gives me a few shillings. I manages very well."

"Bless Henry," said Clarice. She told Jackson that Henry should take him to a doctor.

"Oh, Henry tried to take me already. I just don't want to go to a doctor. They won't waste their time with an old Negro lak me. They is so busy now tooking care of the soldiers. Lots of people got the small pox. Purty soon I'll be out of my misery and out of the way. I ain't been happy since you and Maggie and Lola and Robin and Lord Anthony left."

Clarice hugged him and told him that she was still in love with Jason and would come back to see him when Jason comes home from Philadelphia. She asked about Shoo Fly and Stomper.

"Old Stomper died about two months ago. Shoo Fly is my old standby. I hitches him up to Lord Anthony's fine new chaise and go driving about, just to see what's going on. But nowadays there is too much traffic for me; I gotta let up some."

Clarice said, "Keep well," as she walked away.

John shook Jackson's hand and said, "Don't catch cold, keep warm."

Clarice stopped on the garden walk and took a long look back at the big brick house. No one was living there at that time. "It looks so lonesome," she said.

She called to the children who were climbing around in the gazebo, "Get into the carriage," she said to them. She must have forgotten to be elusive, as she had vowed to be, for she took John's hand as they walked along.

She smiled at him and said, "Now, will you drive us to the Long Wharf? I want the children to see it." She said, "I will never forget the day we went to the Long Wharf to bid bon voyage to the Cordelia on its return trip to England."

She remembered the chills that ran down her spine when she saw Truly and Don Pedro and found out that they were married.

John thought she was having a chill when he saw how she was shaking. He asked, "Do you need a wrap? I have a cape under the seat in the chaise."

"No, I don't need a cape. I just remembered something and it gave me a chill."

She looked at the children and pointed out to them the big ships that were anchored there.

"Where is the Gobbel Truth? asked Matthew.

"It isn't here, Matthew; it sailed away before the port was closed. Tell me," she said, "who told you about the Gobbel Truth?"

"Jason did," he answered.

"I thought so, but when?"

"One day at school."

"Where was I, and what did he tell you?"

"You went outside for a minute. He said someday he was going to own a schooner like the Gobbel Truth."

Clarice thought about Truly and Don Pedro and how pretty and rich Truly looked that day. She spoke again to Matthew, "Jason has plenty of dreams all right."

She noticed John's expression of horror. He said, "My God, I can't believe the changes." He seemed nervous.

"This wharf is a hoodlum's harem. Do you suppose Hancocks' and Rowe's is like this?"

"Let's get out of here, John, before some hoodlums attacks this beautiful carriage." She remembered Lord Anthony's chaise.

"Yes, these rabble-rousers might think we are Royalists. Some of them are mean." He turned around and headed for the main road back to his mother's house.

The children were enjoying every minute of the dash along the wharf. An old peddler was selling singing birds made from paper attached to long limber sticks. John stopped long enough to buy each one of the children one. Sally chose a bright red cardinal. Matthew chose a blue jay.

Clarice was very quiet but smiling at the children. Their joy cheered her up. She glanced sideways at John and thanked him for his kindness and generosity. They went straight on to Mother Jolly's, not stopping again. It was almost dark, a very cool Friday evening.

Clarice sat in front of the fire, a child leaning on each chair arm. She put her arms around them and kissed each one tenderly.

Mother Jolly came into the room and saw Clarice caressing the children. She said, "Clarice, let me give you some advice. Do not spoil these children. Do not show too much affection; give them chores to do, and speak to them sternly."

Clarice said, "Thank you, Mother Jolly. I will need much advice; I will try hard not to spoil them."

The children left the chair's side and occupied themselves somewhere else. Their laughter and their singing birds could be heard. They were not too far away from Clarice's side.

Mother Jolly seated herself near Clarice and began a conversation. "Have you ever thought you might move back to town?" she asked. Then she continued, "When I worked for Jason in the bakery I did a lot of his bread making and cookie making. I enjoyed the work. He was easy to work for. If you would like to open up the shop for business to pick up some income, I will help you. I can teach you the baking process and also the selling part of it."

Clarice didn't answer Mother for several minutes.

Mother finally asked, "Well, what about it?"

Clarice forced a cough, then said, "I don't think I would like making bread, commercially, that is. And I'm not good at talking to people. I wouldn't make a good clerk.

"The Anthonys did not allow me to have friends or to go shopping. I don't have any Boston connections outside of Jason's. Jason likes living in the country. I know he will never live in town again. I don't want to live in Boston either."

Mother Jolly saw that Clarice was not interested.

Clarice said, "I do have an idea also. Mister Winkler suggested that we should lease the building out to someone, just for the sake of keeping vandals from ruining it. Would you like to lease it and open up a bakery?"

Mother Jolly frowned at Clarice. She hastily got up from her chair and brushed herself off. She said, "Well, I'll study on it." She went to her kitchen, humming as she went.

John came in and sat down where his mother had been sitting. He asked, "Would you like to go home tomorrow?"

"Yes, I think we should go home. I have not accomplished what I came to Boston to accomplish…I don't believe this is the right time for shop browsing and history lessons. Maybe next spring when people are not so uneasy and so angry."

Clarice had a sad look on her face. "Lord Anthony was supposed to reunite this colony and appease their discontent. He failed miserably and returned to England a year before his assignment ran out. I truly believe he had much sympathy and understanding for the Rebel Cause."

Saturday morning was cold and overcast. It looked as if it would snow. John had hitched his horse to the chaise and was ready to go.

Two burly constables drove up to Mother Jolly's front gate. One sat in the patrol wagon while the other came to the door. Mother Jolly opened to him and he said to her, "We're looking for John Jolly; is he here?"

Mother was apprehensive; she hesitated, then asked, "What do you want with him?"

John stepped up behind his mother. He reached out to shake hands as he said, "I'm John Jolly; what is it you want?"

The constable did not extend his hand but said gruffly, "You're under arrest, mister. You must come with me. You have some explaining to do about the assault on an officer, the theft of a paddy wagon, and the inciting of a riot—also the destruction of property at the Merry Mermaid Tavern."

Mother Jolly spoke up. "That is why a strange horse and paddy wagon are in my barn."

John acted as if it were all a joke. He said, "Oh, that? Well, it won't be hard to explain. Let's go; I have to be back here shortly. I'm on my way home to Lynn."

The constable said, "You may have to postpone your trip 'home to Lynn,'" as he gripped John's arm and ushered him out to the waiting wagon.

Both the women were shocked at what they were watching; John being shoved into a restraining vehicle and putting up no resistance at all. Resisting arrest the night before was part of the reason for this subjection. Mother Jolly now knew the reason for the horse and paddy wagon that were stashed away in her barn. She turned to Clarice and said, "We have to do something. He must not be confined in jail; he has a farm to tend to."

Clarice was thinking about getting home. She answered Mother Jolly, "I think we had better follow them to wherever they're taking him and listen to what he has to say."

"Yes, let's go."

Clarice ran to her room for a bonnet, and Mother grabbed a shawl from a peg near the door. The children were called to "come quickly." The four of them climbed into John's chaise, which was waiting at the side of the house where he had been loading Clarice's sea chest.

Mother was driving; she was not used to driving. The traffic was heavy, and there seemed to be much pedestrian conglomeration.

Not a word was spoken until Sally began to cry. She reached for Clarice's hand, "Cee Cee, I forgot my bird."

Matthew looked at his sister and said, "Don't cry; he won't fly away."

Clarice said, "Don't worry, precious, we'll be going back to the house soon. We have to go and help John get away from the men who arrested him."

Mother slowed to keep from running over people who were crazily rushing back and forth across the street. It being Saturday, there were stands set up with goods for sale.

It was a busy day for farmers who had come to town with their produce and fowls. They no longer depended on the wharf locations but would set up their stands anywhere the patrolling soldiers would allow.

They soon lost sight of the patrol wagon, but Mother vowed she knew where it was going. "To the Town Hall of course," the court house. She soon was "whoaing" the horse, stopping him suddenly, and crying out "There it is" while pointing it out to Clarice.

She and Clarice jumped out and began to run toward the building, then Clarice remembered the children. She ran back to the chaise and lifted each one down and said to them, "Follow me." She ran after Mother Jolly, who was already inside the building.

An officer halted her and told her to wait in the anteroom. She and the children waited an hour or more without seeing or hearing anything from the courtroom where John was being arraigned. At last Clarice heard Mother Jolly's voice. She was talking to the judge who was escorting her and John out of the courtroom. Clarice walked to the anteroom door, the children at her heels. She saw that the judge was James Otis. She had a great feeling of relief; the judge was their friend. She soon learned that John had been the victim of mistaken identity and was not responsible for his actions, so his case was dismissed. She followed them outside and said nothing.

After Judge Otis bade "good day" to Mother and John, he spoke to Clarice and shook her hand. He spoke to the children and patted their heads.

He said to Clarice, "I am very proud of your husband, doing such a good job for Mister Adams and the Sons of Liberty. I trust you are praying for his safety."

"That I am," she answered.

The drive back to Hanover Street was just about as wild as it was driving into town while trying to keep sight of the patrol wagon.

On reaching the Jolly house John said, "If everything and everybody is ready, we might as well head on home. We will be there about supper time. It is now three o'clock."

Clarice looked around and did not see the sea chest. "Wait a minute," she excitedly called out, "we have to put my sea chest on the back."

"I already have it on," John said, as he walked around to the back of the chaise. It was not there, but a couple of loose straps were dangling where it had been.

Everyone, especially the children, became hysterical at once. Clarice began to cry out loud, "We have to go back; we have to find it." She was running down the street. "Oh I hope I will find it. I must find it." She ran until she was out of breath.

Mother Jolly ran after Clarice. She tripped and fell.

John ran to her, "Ma, are you hurt?" He helped her to her feet.

She was trembling and pale. She said, "I believe I've broken my arm. Help me into the house. You may have to go for the doctor."

John was bewildered. He had to go catch up with Clarice, and he had to go down Cold Lane for the doctor in the opposite direction. John could hardly bear to see his mother hurt and moaning with pain. The children were hanging on the front gate looking down the street for Clarice, who was now out of sight.

Clarice ran up to a constable on the corner of Hanover and Brattle Streets. She interrupted his conversation with a soldier.

"Pardon me, sir. I'm looking for my sea chest that fell off the back of our chaise. Sir, please, have you seen it?"

He didn't answer her until he had sized her up and down. "No, but don't you think someone has found it by this time? What time of day was it that you missed it?"

"I missed it only moments ago, but it was lost off our chaise several hours ago." She went into details of their chase after the patrol wagon and the drive back home.

The constable made no further inquiries, and he said, "You'll find it. Be on your way; this soldier and I have much more pressing problems than your missing sea chest."

Clarice was becoming more distraught than ever. She wondered why John hadn't come to help her.

At the shelter house she saw the old man with his cart. He was just pulling out going north on Hanover. She went to him and asked, "Mister...Oh I don't know your name, but it seems we meet each other every day."

He smiled. No one ever spoke to him in a friendly way. He said, "Good day to ye, madam. Where be ye children?"

"They're at home, sir. I'm trying to find my sea chest which fell off the back of our chaise this morning. We didn't miss it until we got home about half an hour ago. Have you seen it?" She measured the size of it by extending her arms. "I do hope I can find it."

"Well now, ye just may be in luck." He threw back the tarpaulin from his cart. There it was, sitting on its end amongst the dirtiest pile of old rags, papers, broken mugs, old shoes, and a half rotten pumpkin.

Clarice's eyes were dancing with happiness. She threw her arms around the old man and kissed his cheek, then she kissed the sea chest. She said, "You darling man, you've saved me from complete collapse. My good luck slippers are in that chest." She clasped his arm and began to talk as they walked back toward Mother Jolly's. "You must have supper with us and I will pay you a reward." She was thinking she would have to borrow a couple of shillings from John.

"Ye don't owe me a reward, I'm jist happy that I wus right there to pick it up when it bounced off the chaise. Some other folks tried to capture it but found out it was too bundlesome to carry. So's I got it 'cause I had a cart to haul it. I's alas got my cart with me. Never can tell what mout fall off a vehicle."

Mother Jolly had dozed off under her dose of morphine that John gave her. He got it from her midwife's satchel. Clarice was stricken with sad surprise. She could see Mother's pale face and quivering body.

Sally said, "Mrs. Jolly fell down, and John's gone to get the doctor."

The old man called from the great room where he had seated himself to rest for "jest a minit." He called, "Can I hep ye any?"

Clarice had forgotten about him being there. Matthew was hanging around the old man and had told him about Mother Jolly's fall.

Clarice, seeing that Mother was resting, came back into the great room. John and Doctor Thatcher came in at the same time.

John spoke to Clarice, "I guess you know that Ma fell down and may have a broken arm or shoulder. Mrs. McKenzie, this is Doctor Thatcher."

Clarice smiled at the doctor and reached out to shake his hand, "Yes, I know Doctor Thatcher. He came to Governor Hutchinson's house to care for all the measles patients last year."

The doctor smiled a big broad smile and said, "Yes I did, and I put all of you under quarantine for ten days."

Mother Jolly was quite sound asleep as the doctor examined her arm and declared that it was fractured. He worked more than an hour putting on the splints. John and Matthew stood nearby and watched and Matthew vowed to be a doctor when he grew up.

Clarice sat down and talked to Sally and the old man. Finally, she went to the kitchen and brought out a tray with bread and ham and leftover cushaw pie and apples. The old man ate heartily. Matthew and Sally ate only apples and biscuits. John couldn't eat anything; Clarice at a little of the bread.

As the old man left Clarice put two shillings into his pocket and said to him, "I will remember you when I pray."

"Thank ye, thank ye," he said.

Chapter Thirty-One

Tom Fellows came in to find everyone pretty much distressed at Mother Jolly's accident. He said to Clarice and John, "You two look all tuckered out." He went on up to his room but returned shortly to the great room and sat down, facing Clarice and John who were sitting together on the settee.

He said, "I'm going to a jubilee tonight at Connie Cooper's house. It's in honor of our new adjutant general, who is her cousin. I can invite several guests. I would like you two to come with me." He waited for their answer, then he said, "I will go next door and ask Mrs. Moody to come and spend the night to watch over Mrs. Jolly and the children."

John knew Mrs. Moody. He said, "My God, Tom, she must be ninety years old. Do you think she is capable, or able, to take that responsibility?"

"Well, she is capable and able to go here and there. She walks at a pace equal to a racehorse. She sweeps her sidewalk every morning and hollers at everyone passing by, whether they are walking or riding. Yes, I believe she is able."

John said, "Ma probably won't wake up all night. What about Matthew and Sally...Clarice?"

Clarice got the indication that John would like to go. She said, "I will explain to them about it before I put them to bed, which will be within a few minutes after they meet Mrs. Moody. Tom, do you think she will come?"

Tom said, "I'll go right now and ask her." He seemed pleased that Clarice and John wanted to go with him to the jubilee.

In twenty minutes John was paying Mrs. Moody five shillings, in advance, for one night's watch care for his mother and Clarice's children.

Soon the three of them were in John's chaise, lanterns all aglow, and on the way to the far west end of Cambridge Street to Connie Cooper's house to the jubilee.

What John and Tom did not know was that Clarice was carrying a neat little shoe bag with a pair of blue chamois slippers tucked inside.

While John was securing his horse to a hitching post, Clarice and Tom were looking around at many other horses and carriages hitched to various posts and trees. Tom took Clarice's hand to assist her over the rough walkway to the house. She felt his affectionate grip and squeezed his hand in response.

They walked so close together their sides touched. John, walking behind them, noticed their happy byplay. He didn't like it but decided not to spoil the anticipation of a happy evening by saying anything.

On entering Connie Cooper's house, Clarice looked around at the people, the furnishings, the long table spread with many kinds of food and punch. She saw at each end of the entrance hall a door; one was the wig room, the other the coat room. She excused herself from Tom and John and went to the coat room. She quickly changed her shoes. Putting her high button black shoes into the shoe bag and putting the blue chamois slippers onto her feet. She removed her long brown cape and hung it on a peg, the shoe bag concealed under it. She removed her hood and let her hair fall down around her shoulders.

When she joined Tom and John, she smiled at them and spread wide her blue dimity skirt as she bowed. She said, "Now I'm ready for the jubilee."

Both of the men were reaching for her hand, and each was feeling chills running down his spine. They were thinking, She is the most beautiful and refined woman in this room.

Connie Cooper approached them with greetings, the adjutant general on her arm. Introductions were exchanged. She handed Clarice a small folded piece of paper with blue and red ribbons attached to it. She said, "Here is your dance card."

Clarice took it and thanked her.

Connie said, "There will be only four dances: the Highland Fling, the Minuet, the Rocking Reel, and the Hornpipe. The musicians will leave at eleven o'clock. You may stay as long as you like. Breakfast will be served at six o'clock. After that, everyone is supposed to leave for church."

Tom took the card from Clarice's hand. He wrote his name after Rocking Reel, Minuet, and Hornpipe. He handed the card to John and said, "I hated to leave one dance for you, but I am a British gentleman. I know your appetite for beauty and dancing."

"How do you know that?" John asked.

"Because your mother constantly brags about your many graces."

John wrote his name after Highland Fling.

They moved along into the mixture of guests. Tom did the introductions to the various officers and others.

The women, for the most part, were older than Clarice. They had their hair done up in beehives and chignons. Clarice was a bit conspicuous with her hair hanging around her shoulders, but it seemed to be attracting quite a number of admirers.

Clarice could not help remembering Lady Anthony, and the day she called in the hairdresser to put her hair up into "one of those damnable beehives." Lady Anthony was being groomed for the wedding, which never took place.

Each dance seemed to bring Clarice closer to Tom. Her eyes met his with passionate longing each time she twirled into his arms.

They whispered to each other when they were close, "Remember the rocks above the river bank where we use to sit and talk about 'some day when'? Do you remember the picnic we had, just the two of us, when the wind blew our blanket and our lunch into the river?"

"Yes, dear, I remember it all. That day we had to walk home through a hard rain."

Tom was aching with heart throbs and longing. He suggested they meander for awhile and get some air. "I'm smothering, how about you?"

Clarice understood. She answered, "A cool drink might help; I think there's lemonade. Want some?"

While standing by the table dipping into the lemonade, a woman Clarice slightly knew came up to her.

"Hello, Mrs. McKenzie, remember me? I'm Josephine Hawley. I met you at the reception the night of your arrival. You were in the Anthonys' service as a governess."

"Yes, Mrs. Hawley, I remember you. It's good to see you again." Clarice was as gracious as one could be, but Mrs. Hawley was haughty when she said, "You must be enjoying your husband's absence with delight and the discovery of new friends."

Clarice got the implication immediately. She motioned to Tom and John to join her. She said to Mrs. Hawley, "Mrs. Hawley, I want you to meet a very near and dear friend of mine since childhood, from Birmingham. You can tell by his uniform that he is a British soldier. We met again only two days ago. And this gentleman is John Jolly, a close neighbor of mine in Lynn, whom my husband asked to kindly escort me around wherever I might wish to go during his absence. It truly is a delight to have such handsome and gallant men at my side."

Mrs. Hawley swished away. Clarice thought she saw her lift her nose and shrug her shoulders. She could have been mistaken. She sipped her lemonade and pondered the impression she might be making. Tom and John were also sipping lemonade.

John said to Clarice, "I believe the next dance is the Highland Fling; I've waited all evening for it."

She hated to turn him down, but after Mrs. Hawley's snide remarks, she felt like leaving "this Royalist's bash" and returning to her two children.

She said, "Yes, I know it is your dance, but I'm so tired I would like to go home. Do you mind too much?"

"Of course not, I'll be glad to get home to see about Ma."

After she changed her shoes and gathered her wraps, she joined Tom and John who were waiting for her near the door. She said to them, "I will write a note to Mrs. Cooper. She's too involved with the general to be disturbed now with my respects."

They left. The jubilee had been a fair diversion from Clarice's humdrum life, she concluded.

The house was very quiet and dark. The only sound they heard was Mrs. Moody's snoring.

John soon realized that his mother had been up from her bed and had eaten something. He put his horse and chaise in the barn and discovered that the paddy wagon and patrol horse had been taken away. He was glad for that. He sincerely hoped that he could take Clarice home to Lynn on Sunday morning. He actually wanted to get her away from Tom Fellows.

On seventeenth of October, about midday, Clarice was in her front yard covering the roots of her rose bushes with the manure which Phinas brought to her from Panzy's stall.

She thought she heard hoof beats that sounded familiar. She put her hand over her eyes and looked down the road. It was not a bright sunny day; the distance she could see was only about two hundred yards. She went to the split rail fence and stepped up on the second tier to see better.

She saw a horse and rider coming in a gallop. She recognized Jason and Charlie. She ran so fast down the road to meet them she lost her bonnet, causing her hair to come loose and fall around her face and neck.

Jason saw her running toward him. He slowed his horse and when directly along side her he swooped her up and seated her on his saddle in front of him.

The kissing and caressing began. They were laughing and cooing and hugging and squirming. Jason kissed her lips, her forehead, her arms, her neck. She kept saying over and over, "Oh darling, thank God you're home! Oh my sweetheart, you're home!" while Jason ran his fingers through her hair and said, "I've missed you terribly. I almost lost my mind I needed you so much. I love you and I will never leave you again."

They rode up to the gate. Phinas was standing there gawking. Jason slid off Charlie over his rump. He lifted Clarice down and held her in his arms as he said to the boy, "Take my horse and give him some water and corn."

He carried Clarice to the door, kicked it open, and carried her upstairs. He saw the children, through the door, playing in their room.

He yelled at them, "You two little tadpoles, scamper downstairs this minute. Go to the barn. Help the boy feed Charlie."

Matthew and Sally gave Jason and Clarice quizzical looks but did as he told them. They ran fast to the barn.

Jason kicked backwards to close the bedroom door. Only laughter and moans of satisfaction could be heard but by no one except them.

Phinas was a pretty good cook, so at five o'clock, when Clarice had not left her bedroom, he calculated it was time to get some grub ready for the children and himself. Humming into a tune his thoughts, "Maybe them two can survive on love, but I ain't got nobody to love me, so I gotta survive on grub."

He put some hominy on to boil and scrambled six eggs to fry in ham fat. He peeled a few apples, then sliced them and dipped each slice in melted butter, then in honey, then in crushed walnuts.

He told Matthew to put enough logs on the fire to make a big blaze. He told Sally to put the blue checked cloth on the table, to get out the pewter plates and cups, and to light the candles. Sally did a super job; the table was shining bright and beautiful and inviting.

He made fresh coffee and wrapped a bottle of brandy in a cold wet cloth and placed it in a large urn at the end of the table.

Phinas told Matthew to go and knock on the bedroom door and call out to Clarice and Jason that they "are invited to supper."

Matthew hurriedly went to do as he was told. He was so shy, he was trembling. "You all better come out now, we know you're in there," is what he said, instead of saying what Phinas told him to say. His little head was full of suspicion, and he couldn't straighten it out.

Jason had many questions for the fourteen-year-old lad, whom he had last seen at a Boston tavern several months ago. Jason remembered paying for his supper.

"Hey, boy, I remember you. I expected to see you again in Boston after Oliver's funeral, but you disappeared. Where you been all this time?"

He did not answer, just grinned. Phinas was filling up a plate to carry to the barn, where he was used to eating.

Clarice said, "Sit down here, let's talk," she pointed to an empty chair. "We want you to live here with us, if you have no permanent place now."

Phinas was thrilled; that is what he had been hoping for. His face showed his happiness as he replied, "Well, all right."

Before Clarice was awake next morning, Jason was up and off to Salem, where the Committee was meeting. He had written messages and reports to deliver to the Salem members that he had carried from Philadelphia. He left Clarice a note, which he placed on her desk, telling her he would be gone only until early evening.

When she awoke and found the note, she began to feel depressed. She remembered that he had promised never to leave her again. She retrieved her realistic mind and said to herself, He will have to leave me at times for moments or days or weeks or maybe longer. Life is full of broken promises. She remembered an old saying, "Promises are like pie crust, easily broken."

John Jolly came by to see if she needed anything from the market as he was on his way there. When he learned that Jason had returned, his expression changed rapidly from one of hope to one of despair. He asked Clarice, "Is he home for good?"

"Oh, I hope so," she replied.

"Where is he now?" John asked. He had moved over to the window and was looking out toward the barn.

"Gone to Salem," she answered, "to deliver some messages."

John saw Phinas going in and out of the barn. "What will become of that boy?" he asked. "Did Jason ask him to leave?"

"No, no. We asked him to live here with us. He is a wonderful boy. Did you know that he can cook?"

301

"No, I didn't know that he can cook." He was smiling at Clarice and inching a little closer to her. "Did he say he will stay?"

Clarice noticed John's movement toward her, so she stepped back. "He didn't give us a positive answer, but I think he was delighted at our invitation."

"Well, if he doesn't want to live here, I will offer him a place with me. I'm going over to Provincetown next week, and I may stay all winter. He could look after my place for me."

John Jolly hadn't thought of going to Provincetown before he learned that Jason was at home. When he left the McKenzie house tears were in his eyes. He reached for Clarice's hand, pulled her a little closer, gave her a short kiss on her cheek, and whispered into her ear, "I love you."

She held on to his hand and walked to the gate with him. As he rode away she waved. Going back into the house she was praying, "Dear and good Lord, please make it possible for John to fall in love again with Dora and to forget about me."

For the next few days, Clarice and Jason spent their time making love, planning for the winter ahead, and talking about Philadelphia. Clarice was eager to hear about the petitions sent to the king, the speeches that were made, and the important men who were delegates from other colonies.

Jason was not willing to reveal all he knew, but he did tell her that a regular army would soon be in the making; that the militia was to be immediately organized into companies; that the drilling would be stepped up to four nights a week; and companies formed, called minutemen, who would have arms at hand and be ready on a moment's notice to meet the enemy in battle if such aggressiveness occurred.

She told him about the trip to Boston but not about John's very affectionate attention to her needs. She left out altogether the encounter and conversations with Tom Fellows. She also did not tell him about the jubilee. She told him about going to see his shop and finding it in run-down condition. She told him about seeing Jackson and about the old man. She did not tell him about John's arrest or her being locked in the privy.

The weather began to change rapidly. The trees were bare by the end of October, and the children were in the house all day. The rain was cold and the wind whistled under the eaves of the house. Clarice spent many hours at the spinning wheel or at the fireplace cooking. She had begun to love her housekeeping chores. As she sat at the spinning wheel, her mind turned to thoughts of reopening her school. Jason tried to dissuade her from thinking about it. He knew there was much conflict in the area. It would be risky to have children away from their homes and their parents, even for a few hours a week. Hardly any schools had opened for the fall sessions. Clarice was disturbed about Jason's attitude toward her idea.

He said to her, "Forget about opening your school. Get busy melting down your pewter spoons and mugs to make bullets."

Scorn was showing on Clarice's face. "Jason, I refuse to make bullets."

"Then make bandages and swabs."

"How can I do that?"

"Tear up some of your sheets and pillow shams. Tear pieces into strips and wadding."

"You must be crazy, our linens are all new. Sister Smith spent hours hemming sheets and other linens. I will not tear them up. You are making me very angry, Jason."

"Angry or not, Cee Cee, the British are making camps on the banks of every hidden creek in Suffolk County."

At that moment, there was a loud pounding on the door. Jason opened it to see a British scout standing there. Two other scouts were waiting at the gate mounted on their horses and holding the horse belonging to the scout at the door.

"Good morning." Jason was being polite. He would rather have slammed the door.

"We have come to search your house. Orders from headquarters."

"What are you searching for?" asked Jason.

"Weapons," answered the scout.

"Well, you won't find any. We are peace-loving people, and we don't keep weapons."

Clarice could not believe what she was hearing; Jason standing there telling a lie. She took the little Union Jack from its stand on the mantle. She walked to Jason's side and said to the scout, who had brushed past Jason, stepped over the threshold, and was now inside the great room, "See, sir, we keep our flag flying all the time. We are the king's loyal subjects. Would you like some coffee, sir, while I tell you about my home in Birmingham?"

Jason was so dumbfounded, he just stood there.

"No, thank you, ma'am," said the scout, "we have many houses to search today. We will be on our way." As he left, he turned, raised his hand in salute, and said, "God save the King."

Jason gathered his wits, slammed the door, snatched the little Union Jack from Clarice's hand, and threw it into the fire.

"There," he yelled, "that's the end of George III in this house. Do you understand...Clarice?"

"Yes, dear, I was just about to do what you just did, burn the British flag. From this day forward, for the rest of my life...I am an American Patriot."

"You are?" Jason had a broad smile on his face. "Hooray," he yelled.

Matthew and Sally jumped to their feet from the floor where they had been playing. They hugged Clarice around her hips and repeated Jason's "Hooray."

November second was Clarice's nineteenth birthday. She thought about it a couple of days beforehand and wondered if Jason would remember. She got the urge to celebrate. She baked a ginger cake and made herself a new dress.

Well, not really. She made over an old dress by taking the sleeves out and dying them a different color and sewing them back in the original arm holes. She lowered the neck and embroidered silk flowers around it. She dipped some new candles and decorated them with wild berries and ribbons.

When the second rolled around Clarice put on a happy face. She put on her old, new dress and did her hair up into a bun. She took her blue chamois slippers from the bureau and put them on her feet.

She called the children to ask them how she looked. They giggled and said, "Cee Cee, you are pretty." They asked her if she was going to make birthday wishes. She said, "I already have."

She was all decked out for her birthday and singing when Jason and Phinas came in from the barn. Jason announced that it was going to snow, and he pretended not to notice Clarice.

She said, "Let it snow, let it snow. Maybe it will keep you at home for a few hours."

Jason winked at the children. He saw Clarice in a jovial mood. He bowed low in front of her and said, "Happy Birthday, darling," as he took a small package from his pocket. He took her hand and clasped her fingers around the package.

Clarice looked at it and said, "Jason, you didn't forget." She began to open the package as she asked, "What is it?" She was shaking as she fumbled with the blue silk handkerchief that it was wrapped in, tied with pink ribbon. Nested in goose down was a sterling silver thimble, engraved with her name. "Oh, I love it," she said. "How did you know the right size?"

"I guessed at it," he answered, "but I have kissed your fingers so many times I had a pretty good idea of the size."

Clarice put the thimble on her finger and kissed it, then held it out for Jason to kiss. "Thank you, dear, I will cherish it always." As she placed it back into its box, she asked, "When did you get it?"

"Before I left for Philadelphia, while in Boston, I stopped in at Paul Revere's shop and ordered it."

"You are a dear. Shall we eat some cake?"

The children rushed to the table. Clarice allowed each child to hold a lighted splinter from the fireplace to light a candle.

Jason sat at the end of the table. He said, "There's no place in the world as friendly and cozy as at home with a wife and children."

This statement from Jason caused Clarice's heart to jump and then to beat faster. She felt flushed and dizzy. She had anxiety feelings that any day now Clinton Melville would show up and take the children away.

She said to Jason, "Dear, don't you think we had better go to the judge and talk about adopting Matthew and Sally?"

"Yes, we had better do that. I will go to see Judge Otis in Boston and set a date."

"Please don't delay it, Jason. I am afraid of what might happen to them if Mister Melville gets custody."

Jason announced a few days later that he was going to Walden Pond to cut ice to store in the new ice cellar he had made in back of the barn.

He said to Clarice, "Everyone is laying in their ice; that is something we cannot put off. If it rains or the weather turns warmer, the ice will be ruined."

Clarice didn't care about the ice. She haughtily asked, "When are you going to see Judge Otis about the children? It is very important to me that we get negotiations under way."

"I will take care of it, Cee Cee, as soon as I get the ice laid in." But Jason was so busy with ice and wood for the fireplace that several days went by.

One morning he caught Clarice crying; her eyes were red, and she was shaking with chills.

"Cee Cee, are you ill?" he asked her, as he put his arms around her.

"Jason, I had such a bad dream. A big giant with green eyes was pulling Matthew through a muddy lake, and Sally was floating away, sitting on a big block of ice. I was standing on a hill too far away to reach them, and Judge Otis was circling around way over my head, screaming, 'It's too late; it's too late.'"

Jason picked her up and carried her to the great room. He kissed her and stroked her hair as he sat in the rocker, holding her on his lap. He said, "It's not too late. I will go to Boston tomorrow to see the judge."

Clarice laid her head on his shoulder. She lifted the hem of her apron and wiped her eyes. She said, "That will make me very happy. I cannot give them up to Mister Melville."

In Boston Jason found much to disturb his mind. His store building was in much need of repair. He began to search out workmen to help him put it in order. He hired a plasterer, a carpenter, a glazier. Then he put an ad in the Gazette that the apartment and the storeroom were for lease. He had not been to see the judge.

Three days went by. Clarice, at home, was anxiously waiting for Jason's return. She was worried that the judge would not decide in their favor.

Jason, in Boston, was busy seeing to the work going on at his building. He found a boot maker who leased the storeroom. The repair of boots was a thriving business now, especially to British army boots. The money he received for six months' lease was like manna from Heaven.

He finally went to call on Judge Otis. He told him the story of Sally Melville and her sister's children, how Clarice had loved them and taught them and now was wanting to adopt them.

Judge Otis was understanding and sympathetic of the McKenzies' situation. He folded his arms across his chest as he leaned back in his chair. "Jason," he said, "law is law and I cannot, alone, change it. Mister and Mrs. Melville have already legally adopted the children. The legal paper does not say that if one parent dies the adoption will be voided. You understand that, do you not? Mister Melville is their legal father. All you can hope for is that

Clinton Melville will willingly relinquish his fatherhood and turn the adoption over to you."

Jason's reply was, "My God, how can I tell Clarice? I hope he never returns unless he is willing to give them up."

When Jason left Judge Otis, he wanted to talk to someone. He went to the Green Dragon Tavern, hoping to find an old friend. He was curious to see if anything had changed. He sat down at a table overlooking the wharf where he had done a brazen thing almost a year ago. As he sat alone sipping his beer, he wondered, "How much harm, how much sorrow, that episode had caused."

He silently prayed, "God, please make it a just and rewarding thing."

It seemed strange to Jason that he didn't see one familiar face. He missed the tall ships and the activity of a busy wharf such as it was a year ago. The tavern was crowded with redcoats.

He didn't stay long. When he mounted Charlie he didn't know that the horse had been thoroughly evaluated and his feet examined, as well as his teeth and eyes. Horses were badly needed by the British at this time.

Jason rode back to his store on Charles Street with the note to Clarice from Judge Otis in his pocket. After he called on Mister Winkler and asked him to keep an eye out for his building, he headed for home.

"What took you so long?" Clarice asked him as he entered the house.

"There were many things I had to attend to. It was better to take care of everything while I was there than to have to go back real soon."

"Jason, I'm so eager to hear what Judge Otis said."

He took the note from his pocket and handed it to her.

> Dear Clarice: The adoption of the children by the Melvilles was clear and complete and law is law, and I alone cannot change it. The legal paper does not say that if one parent dies the other has to relinquish parenthood. Therefore the only chance you have to adopt is if Mister Melville is willing to void his legal right and give the children back to the court to decide. Then you could make application to adopt. Respectfully, James Otis.

After reading the note, Clarice began to quiver and cry.

Jason took her into his arms to comfort her. He said, "We'll do something to get custody. Maybe Clinton will give them up, at least until they are several years older."

Matthew and Sally came running out of the house to meet Jason. He lifted them up, one on each hip, and began galloping around the yard singing, "Get up, old boy, get up and go; take these children to see a show."

Clarice's tears turned to smiles. Later, after supper, Clarice told Jason that she was feeling queasy and her nose was running. "I think I'm going to be sick," she said.

"Then go to bed," he advised her. "I will read to the children until they are sleepy. Then I will tuck them into bed."

"Thank you, dear." She climbed the stairs, but halfway up she stopped to rest a moment. She called back to Jason, "The steps are moving."

He watched her as she went on up to their bedroom. Jason held the children on his lap and read to them from the Bible, the story of Joseph and his coat of many colors and the story of Jonah and the big fish. When they dozed off, he carried them upstairs to their beds. He returned to the chair in front of the fire. Many thoughts were going through his head.

A loud knock at the door startled him. He opened it to a man holding a lantern up to his eye level to see better for it was now quite dark.

"Good evening," said Jason.

The stranger asked, "Might you be Mister Jason McKenzie?"

"That I am. What do you want?"

"I've come bringing a message from Mister Clinton Melville."

Jason hesitated a second or two before taking the scroll from the messenger's hand. "I wonder what it is about," he said. He unrolled the paper and read:

> Dear Mister McKenzie:
> I will be calling for my children in a couple of days. Please have them ready to go.
> I will send a trunk for their clothes. My schooner is being made ready for the return trip to Nova Scotia.
> I have enrolled them in a convent school on Prince Edward. I appreciate very much what you have done for them.
> Signed, Clinton Melville

Jason asked the messenger to step inside while he penned a reply to the note. He asked Phinas to bring the messenger some coffee. Phinas did as he was told.

Jason wrote this reply:

> Mister Melville:
> I have received your message. We do not wish to part with the children. To do so will sadden my wife almost to death. She loves them very much. We wish to adopt them. She is a splendid teacher. I will come to your ship day after tomorrow to talk to you.
> Respectfully, Jason McKenzie

The talk that Jason had with Clinton Melville did no good. Melville said, "I will not relinquish my parenthood. Those children are my wife's kin. She would not want me to give them up. I'm selling her house that she inherited from her parents to…to pay for their schooling in the convent."

"But," said Jason, "we will see that they are educated."

Melville said sternly, "You are not practicing your Christianity, are you? Are you attending any church?"

Jason answered him. "No, we are not—that is, at the present time. We do worship God in our own way. We do read the Bible and pray. We are generous and loving."

"That is not enough," answered Melville. "We want them taught to worship in a church. My wife had plans for Matthew and Sally to learn Latin and French and music. That's why I enrolled them in the convent school. They are to be there by January first."

Jason looked at Melville long and hard. He said nothing for several minutes. Was this man selling his wife's property for his own self-indulgence or was he telling the truth? The man seemed to Jason to be a kind and compassionate man. His countenance was one of honesty.

When Jason said, "I'll be going," Melville stood up and extended his hand and said, "The children will be fine; they will enjoy the sailing. They will adapt quickly to the change. You will soon be over your grief." Then his voice changed to gruffness as he said, "You ought to be busy getting some issue of your own."

Jason left the ship twisting his hat and feeling angered. "Sally and Matthew are not his issue," he said.

Clarice ran to her bed and put the pillow over her face. She did not want the children to see her crying. For several hours she stayed there, leaving Phinas in charge of the children. Jason left to go to Walden Pond for some more ice.

Panzy was getting heavier and broader every day. Phinas thought she did not get enough exercise. He saddled the mare, lifted Sally and Matthew to her back, then he mounted and laughed as he said, "Now we are three on a horse." He patted Panzy's neck and said to her, "Carry us to Shiny Squatt."

Phinas had learned about the boulder from Clarice, who loved to relate the stories Jason had told her. Phinas did not know if the children had heard of the magic rock.

The whole afternoon was spent there. Phinas had brought bread and cheese in small packages in the saddle bag. They had a picnic, then it began to snow. Panzy snorted and shook her head. It was a warning that they had better get back to the house. A blizzard was on the way.

The children ran ahead part of the way, then Phinas lifted them on to the mare's back. He said, "We must hurry." He ran on foot, leading the horse through a blinding blizzard.

They reached the barn and the children were lifted off and told to "hurry into the house." Phinas put Panzy into her stable and gave her some hay and apples. Charlie was not there. Jason had not returned from Walden Pond. Phinas, on entering the kitchen, saw that Clarice was not there. He called up the stairs, "Cee Cee?" She had told him to call her by her nickname. "Cee Cee, where are you?"

The boy wondered if he should prepare a meal; the children could help. He asked Sally to go upstairs and check on Cee Cee. He said to the child, "See if she is sleeping. Ask her if we should prepare supper."

Sally went to Clarice's bedroom and discovered she was not there.

Chapter Thirty-Two

While the children and Phinas were picnicking at Shiny Squatt, Clarice had left the house to take a walk. She had felt the need to clear her mind of the children leaving. She wished for Sister Smith, another woman to talk with and to pray with.

She walked west on the road, and she thought of John Jolly. "He will understand," she said to herself. She wondered if he had left for Provincetown. She was getting cold, but she could see John's house in the distance. It was more than a mile away. She thought she could make it, although she was very tired. She wondered if Jason might come along. He wasn't expected until tomorrow. Maybe he had to return the rented wagon earlier or something. She thought Jason was not at home much of the time anymore. Always something to do somewhere else.

She was walking rapidly and talking to herself. "I will run away and take Matthew and Sally. How can I do it? I couldn't carry our luggage. I don't drive very well. We could go while Jason is away, but then we wouldn't have Charlie to pull the chaise."

Clarice noticed the dark clouds rolling in over her head. "Those clouds are snow clouds," she said. Soon she was walking faster through the blizzard. "John, dear John, please be at home. I need you. You were so kind to me. Please be kind again."

She felt tears turning to ice, and snow was collecting on her face. She shivered, then stopped for a moment, saying to herself, "If John is not there and his house is locked up and I can't get in, I may be left out in the cold. I may freeze to death."

She turned around and began to run toward home. She thought, If Phinas and the children have missed me, they may be out in the cold looking for me. Oh dear, they may be out in this blizzard. She ran faster, but the snow was deeply covering everything. She had to lift her feet higher, and she was out of breath.

When in sight of her house, she heard a wagon coming. It was approaching her wen she turned around to see Charlie bobbing his snow-covered head up and down. The driver she knew was Jason, but he was tented under a blanket and didn't see her.

She began to call out, "Jason, Jason. Jason, stop. Let me ride with you."

Charlie stopped suddenly. Jason heard her at last. "What in the hell are you doing out here on the road in this blizzard?" He jumped from the wagon seat and covered her with the blanket he pulled from around himself. Clarice began to cry, sobbing loudly. As Jason lifted her on to the wagon seat, he asked, "Well, tell me, why are you out here in this snowstorm?"

"Jason, I was very sick this morning; I needed someone. I...I was on my way to John Jolly's to ask him to drive me to Doctor Miller or to go for Doctor Miller and bring him to me. It began to snow and I thought I had better go back home. I never reached John's house."

He asked, "Why didn't you send Phinas for Doctor Miller?"

"Because I needed him to stay and care for the children."

"I am sorry, dear, that I was not here. I will never leave you again."

"Jason, don't say that. You know it isn't so."

"Clarice, you have to pull yourself together. The children are leaving, and we can't do anything about it. You are making yourself sick. Please don't ruin your health over it."

"I am a nervous wreck and nauseous most of the time."

"Think positive, Clarice. They will be better off in a convent school. We are not sure of the future here in Massachusetts. Looks like the British intend to cause us many hardships in the coming year."

"Yes, Jason. And it's because of the damned Tea Party." She continued, "You just don't understand my heart. I am trying to become a dedicated Patriot, but it is hard for me. I have given up so much."

"I know, Cee Cee, and now you have to give up the children you love, but I know you are strong enough to endure it."

He put his arm around her and drew her up close to him. He said, "I will not go away again overnight until you are feeling much better. Then I have to go back to Boston on business."

"I knew it; I knew it. I almost hate Boston," she replied.

They rode the rest of the way in silence. When they reached their house, Jason jumped from the wagon seat and lifted her down.

"I feel much better now, she said as she waded through the snow.

"I think this cold, fresh air helped your sickness to go away," said her kind husband.

She looked at him and smiled, "No, it was your coming along and rescuing me from the cold. From now on, I will be brave about giving up the children."

Jason came in. He stood in front of the fire with her to warm his hands. The silence was broken when he cleared his throat and said, "Cee Cee, there is another thing. I don't want you running to John Jolly for help. Especially when I'm away."

She answered, "Jason, that is the only time I need his help." She secretly hoped that her friendship with John Jolly would never end.

Nothing was heard from Clinton Melville until December tenth, then a note by messenger came saying that he would be at the McKenzie house on

December twelfth to pick up the children. The messenger carried a brand new sea chest which he said Mister Melville sent to hold their clothes.

Clarice had washed and ironed all their clothes and polished their shoes. She finished a dress for Sally which Sister Smith had started before she left. She packed all their things into the sea chest, and she added some pictures they had used in school and some books they had acquired while living with her and Jason.

When they all sat in front of the fire in a friendly farewell chat, Clarice held a stern face as she said, "Now children, everyone loves an ocean voyage. You will love your papa's schooner." She wasn't sure if she should call Clinton Melville their papa or their uncle, but she was sure they knew who she meant.

"In the convent, you will have lots of children to play with and teachers who will make you wise and who will love you and care for your needs. And best of all, someday I will come to visit you."

"Will you come to visit us when Jason gets a schooner like the Gobble Truth?" asked Matthew.

"Absolutely, for sure when he gets his schooner. But in the meantime I will write letters to you."

Matthew nor Sally shed a tear. They had already learned to be brave.

Clarice later said to Jason, "I believe they are going to be all right. I think they are looking forward to it."

"Of course they are, Cee Cee. It is sort of dull here in Lynn, nothing for them to do that they don't originate. They need other children. They have already been through enough to make them strong. They lost their own parents, then their aunt. The baby they hoped for never arrived. Their uncle coming back for them probably gave them a feeling of security. But I would say, some of their best and happiest times have been while living here with you."

The twelfth arrived. The children were kissed and hugged by their uncle as he lifted each child into the chaise he had hired to take them to his schooner.

Clarice and Jason, with their arms around each other, smiled and waved and threw kisses as long as they could see the chaise going down the road.

Jason said, "Melville seems like a compassionate man. I think everything will be just fine."

Clarice was very quiet for several days. She stayed in her bedroom, reading or sewing. She even wrote a few letters to her parents and to Sister Smith, although she had no address as yet. She wrote a letter to her sister, Julia, the third letter in a year, but she had had no answers. She darned all of Jason's socks and mended his underwear.

Her hands were busy, but her heart was heavy. She would touch and kiss everything that reminded her of Matthew or Sally. She put away a memory box their torn and ragged shoelaces; a half-eaten muffin she found under Sally's bed; the contents of a pocket from Matthew's old coat: a dead and dried bug, an acorn, a piece of string.

"I need these mementos," she said, "to take the place of their laughter."

Jason saw her sad face and knew her grief was profound. He suggested that they go for a drive. He knew about an ordinary in Salem where they could have a meal and watch a theatrical, a once a year performance, by a troupe of thespians from New York.

He asked, "Have you forgotten that tomorrow is the seventeenth of December?"

"No, dear, I have not forgotten, but I have no present for you. That is why I didn't mention it."

"You always have a ready-made and most wonderful present for me. One of your smiles and about a thousand kisses will be most welcome."

She hugged him tightly and held his face between her palms and kissed and kissed and kissed him. She said, "Jason, you need a shave." She added, "I will be glad to go with you, but what if the weather turns bad? What will we do then?"

"We will stay overnight at the ordinary. We may even stay for a week. We will stay in bed the whole time."

She began to laugh. "Jason, you idiot. I love you. When will be go?" she asked.

"Will tomorrow be too soon? We will be celebrating our anniversary."

"Oh no, tomorrow will be just right."

Jason sent Phinas on Charlie to John Jolly's house to borrow his sleigh. He said to the boy as he left, "If there is enough snow by tomorrow, we will enjoy a sleigh ride." He said to himself, I wonder if Cee Cee has ever ridden in a sleigh.

Jason said to Clarice, as he assisted her in getting out of the sleigh in front of the ordinary, "I will take Charlie and the sleigh to the livery stable. You go on in to the great room and wait for me. I will be there in a few minutes.

Clarice lifted her skirt and waded through the snow into the ordinary. It was brimming with patrons, all dressed in elegant and expensive clothes.

She thought, This is a more fashionable gathering than at Connie Cooper's jubilee. Of which Jason had not heard.

As she entered the room, heads turned toward her and some whispering began. There were some people there who had been at Connie Cooper's and remembered that on that occasion Mrs. McKenzie had been accompanied by two men—one a British soldier.

At first glance around the room Clarice recognized two faces. She wanted to run out the door and follow Jason to the livery stable and beg him to take her home. It was too late. Connie, leading Tom Fellows by the hand, was hastily approaching her.

"Clarice, Clarice McKenzie, how wonderful to see you. Come, let me introduce you to some of these adorable patrons of the theatre."

Clarice was shrinking fast, down into her remodeled clothing, feeling very insecure and embarrassed. She wished Jason would hurry and show up.

Tom Fellows was smiling at Clarice but not saying anything. Connie was beaming and overindulging her enthusiasm.

Clarice looked over her shoulder toward the door. She said, "I am waiting for my husband. He went to the stable to put the horse and sleigh away. He will be here momentarily."

Connie took Clarice by the arm and ushered her into the midst of the mingling crowd. Clarice was not being as bubbly as Connie wanted her to be. She whispered to Clarice, "Don't be shy. Here's Captain Lucas; I believe he is from Birmingham."

The captain was astonished when Clarice said, "Excuse me, there is my husband." She rushed to Jason's side.

Jason sensed immediately that Clarice was trying to avoid someone or something. Then he saw Tom Fellows and the babbling lady that was leading him around.

Clarice said, "Jason, I want to go home; I feel faint. I don't want to stay here with all these people."

"Cee Cee, we just got here, and we haven't had our supper. I'm hungry. It's beginning to snow…hard. I have already engaged our lodging for the night. We can't leave now. Are you sure it's not because of someone you've seen?" He nodded his head and smiled at Tom, who was watching them.

Tom nodded and smiled back. Jason clasped Clarice's hand and led her across the room, through the people to Tom Fellows. She was trying to avoid this encounter by jerking on Jason's hand. But before she could sway him in a different direction, they were side by side, face to face with Tom and Connie.

"I've already spoken to Tom," she said, while looking sternly at Jason. "Mrs. Cooper brought him over to see me as soon as I entered the room."

Jason looked surprised, "How did Mrs. Cooper know who you were?" he asked. "And how did she connect you with Tom Fellows?"

"Jason, I can't explain everything here and now. But remember, you were away for ten weeks."

People were laughing and talking. Clarice and Jason were in the center of the hubbub. She said, "You said you were hungry; I'm hungry, too." She pulled him away from the crowd into the annex where tables were set up in front of a stage. The large fireplace was aglow with burning logs. Three violinists, making sweet music, made the atmosphere very pleasant.

A barmaid ushered Jason and Clarice to a table set for four. Clarice laid her hand on the maid's arm and said, "We would like a table for two and on the far side of the room."

Jason frowned at his wife and said to the maid, "This table is fine. My wife is shy; she must get over it."

They sat down. Jason said, "I hope you will forgive me, dear; I could see you were trying to avoid Tom Fellows. Now, I want you to tell me how you came to know Mrs. Cooper. When did you meet her?"

"Jason," answered Clarice, "you have hurt my feelings. I am trying to avoid Tom Fellows and also Mrs. Cooper. I'm not going to tell you how I happen to know Connie Cooper. Not here at this time, and this is the third time I've told you so."

Before Jason said anything more, he realized that Clarice was hiding something. "All right, my dear, I'll be waiting for your explanation soon, but I won't spoil our anniversary by insisting on it tonight."

Clarice curtly replied to that statement, "Thank you very much."

At that instant Tom and Connie came to their table. Jason stood up. He could see that they wanted to be invited to join them. "Please join us."

Clarice gave Jason a swift kick under the table, but Tom and Connie were already sitting down.

"How good it is to see you again, Clarice," said the giddy Connie.

Clarice didn't answer her.

Jason asked Tom, "Where are you quartered now? I know you are not staying at my place."

"I thought Cee Cee would have told you. I'm at Mrs. Jolly's on Hanover."

Jason said, "Cee Cee has been too busy getting the Melville children ready for their departure to Nova Scotia. I have been away from home much too much lately, but when duty calls, I go."

Tom reached for Clarice's hand. She drew it back and put it in her lap. He said to Jason, "We had a short conversation while she was in Boston, and we danced a couple of dances at Connie's jubilee."

"Well, seems like there's a pretty good bit of news Cee Cee has to tell me."

Connie asked Clarice, "Did you enjoy yourself at the jubilee?"

"I suppose so, to a small degree, but I was so worried about Mother Jolly and my children, I just had to leave early."

Tom spoke up, "But they were fine and John missed his dance with you."

Jason gave him a look of disgust. He said, "Was John Jolly also at that shindig?"

"Yes," answered Tom," very much so."

"I think I need another mug of rum; this is a big pill to swallow. Anyone else want more rum?" He motioned for the barmaid. "Another round, all around, make it bottles instead of mugs."

Clarice said, "Excuse me, I'm going to our room." She headed for the stairs. Jason jumped up from his chair, turning it over. He caught her just as she set her foot on the bottom step.

He picked her up. He said, "Oh, no you don't. You're not running out on me. You're going to sit here with the rest of us and listen to what they have to say about you."

"Jason, you are acting like a fool. Put me down." She bit Jason on the back of the neck. He dropped her to the floor. She was lying at his feet. She bit him on his leg. He picked her up and placed her in her chair, "Eat your supper," he said.

Connie and Tom were completely awed but pretending to be ignoring Jason and Clarice. However, they were beginning to feel as if they had intruded on the McKenzies, which they had.

Tom wiped his mouth with his napkin, then reached for Connie's hand. "There's some of my officer friends coming in. We had better go and greet them."

"Sure," said Connie.

Jason stood up, looking after them, "You better come back; your supper will get cold," he said.

Tom looked at him with disgust. He and Connie went across the room and began a hearty greeting to some loudmouthed redcoats.

Clarice sat silently eating.

"Well, say something," Jason said to her.

She said, "I'm listening to the music," as she gave him a most disconcerted stare.

The barmaid came to the table, carrying a tray with four bottles of rum. She seemed uncertain when she saw there were only two people at the table. She asked, "Shall I leave all four bottles?"

"Of course," snarled Jason, "I ordered four bottles, didn't I?"

"One bottle will be enough to leave," said Clarice, looking up at the maid, "Our friends have joined some other people. You may take the other three bottles to their table with our compliments."

"Hell no, you won't," Jason scornfully yelled, "I'm not setting up drinks for a bunch of damned lobster-backs."

The barmaid set one bottle down in front of Jason, and with an oath slipping from her lips, she hastily left the McKenzie table. Neither Jason nor Clarice spoke again for a long while. They silently ate their oysters and crabs.

The players gave an excellent performance, but Clarice paid no attention. She absorbed only the setting and the costumes. At the end when everyone was clapping and whistling and calling for another curtain call, Clarice said to Jason, "I don't believe I enjoyed it. You spoiled it for me by acting the way you did."

"Well, I'm sorry you didn't enjoy it. My curiosity about your activities in Boston got the better of me."

"Are you sure it was not your suspicions and jealousy? May I ask you what you did for recreation while you were in Philadelphia?"

He answered her, "Let's get out of here, Cee Cee. Our room is number four, upstairs."

Snuggling down in a huge feather bed, Clarice and Jason lay staring at the ceiling. Their hands folded across their chests. Their bodies as far apart as they could get for two people in the same bed.

Clarice said, "Jason, while you were in Philadelphia, John Jolly was a godsend to me. Especially when Sally Melville fell downstairs and we had to take her to Doctor Miller. Her death was very hard for me. Parson and Sister Smith left right after that, and if John hadn't been there to do the outside chores I couldn't have managed. He realized that I was at the breaking point and he offered to take me and the children to Boston. We were very happy to have the change."

She heard Jason snoring and stopped talking. She said to herself, "The rum got to him." She blew out the candle and lay there in the dark listening to the wind howling around the building.

The next day they went home.

Christmas was sad without the children. Phinas left for a few days. The McKenzies thought he went to Concord to visit his mother, but they had no assurance of it because Phinas was the silent type. He felt independent and kept his thoughts tightly concealed in his mind.

Clarice made a nut cake and cooked a squirrel that Jason brought in, already skinned and quartered. The bells in the church belfry rang out at Midnight. The sexton was faithful to his duties.

Jason said to Clarice, "You haven't told me about the Boston trip."

She answered, "I did, but you feel asleep, which I couldn't prevent. Now, you can't expect me to go over all that again. Really, it is so boring I couldn't blame you for falling asleep."

Chapter Thirty-Three

A couple of days after Christmas, Jason brought to Clarice a packet of letters that he picked up at the stage station. The stage had brought the packet out from Boston. Clarice's eyes popped with surprise and joy when she untied the roll and found letters from her parents; Robin; Sister Smith; and Julia, of all people, after all this time.

She read her parents' letter first. It was already seven months old, as it had arrived in Boston before the port was closed. They, her parents, had not learned that the Anthonys had returned to England. Robin's letter was second, Maggie was being courted by a count. Clarice wondered if Lord and Lady Anthony approved. If Maggie should marry a count, would she be a countess? Sister Smith reported that the church they were pastoring was too drafty, the people of the congregation were all old people, the young people were rowdy and full of meanness. The parson does not have enough to do. He misses helping out at the McKenzies. Her sister's letter brought a sad bit of news. Her children, a boy and girl, ages five and four, were down with measles. Clarice said, "That was three months ago; they are well by now." She, Julia, had been tested for consumption and found positive. She, Julia, was not able to properly care for them, her children. Her husband, John Hopkins, was hardly ever at home. He was kept busy at his apothecary shop. New York was a sweltering, swampy, mosquito-ridden, bedlam of foreign people.

Clarice held the letters in her lap, as she contemplated each one. She also tried to solve the mystery of their long delayed arrival into her hands.

She asked Jason, "Can you figure out the puzzle of my letters? My parent's letter was addressed to me here in Lynn. Sister Smith's letter had the most recent date and was addressed to Lynn. Robin's letter was addressed to your Charles Street address and was written in September but was posted from New York to Boston. Julia's letter was written in June and addressed to the Beacon Street address. That means she had not received the letter I sent to her in March."

Jason scratched his head, "Cee Cee, my dear, this whole batch of American colonies is in such confusion there's no telling where your letters have been or who has read them or how they got into one parchment roll and finally reached you. It is a wonder you ever received them. Had the letters been opened?"

"Yes, I believe so. The sealing wax was broken on each one."

Phinas came back in February. Clarice or Jason never asked him why he stayed away so long, and he gave no explanations. He did say he was happy to be returning to the McKenzies.

Clarice said, "We are very happy to have you back."

Jason and Phinas noticed that Panzy was hanging around the barn all day and night. She seldom ever went out into the pasture. They also noticed that whenever one of them finished their chores and went into the house, Panzy stood by the fence and whinnied. She had taken up the habit of biting Charlie if he came close enough. Charlie was learning to stay clear of the mare.

Jason had to go into Boston on most urgent business, or so he told Clarice. As he rode Charlie out onto the road, Panzy followed as far as the fence. It was strange the way she acted, pawing the ground and bobbing her head up and down.

When Jason leaned over from the saddle to kiss Clarice goodbye, Phinas said to him, "You might find a colt or a filly when you get back."

"I hope it's a colt," answered Jason.

As Clarice turned back to go into the house, she heard Panzy whinnying, "I think she is crying after Charlie," she said to Phinas.

"Phinas," she called from the door, "I'm going to write some letters and I want you to take them to the stage station when I'm done with them, so don't get too busy. What are you planning to do today?"

"Oh, I think I will grind up some corn for the chickens and some coffee beans for the kitchen."

"Phinas, you are a poet and don't know it." Clarice and Phinas did a lot of tomfoolery like two children. She was about as young at heart as Phinas was young in age.

After a while, Clarice went to the barn to tell the boy that she was finished with the letters. She suggested to him that he should ride Panzy to town, the exercise and a visit to town might calm her nerves.

Jason had brought three copies of the Boston Gazette and left them on the table. Clarice picked them up and went to a chair by the fireside to read them. The large bold caption that caught her eyes was disturbing: rebel faction under severe scrutiny. Such names as John Hancock, John Adams, Jonas Clark, Samuel Adams, and James Harvey were mentioned.

In a different copy she read: england sending more troops, and still another item not quite so bold, mentioned that Governor Gage had ordered confiscation of commodities stored in Rebel smokehouses.

Clarice sat there pondering the newspaper items. She convinced herself that it was just propaganda. She threw the papers into the fire and set about busying herself in the kitchen. She said to herself, "I think I will put all of our dried beans and dried apples up into the lookout. No one would bother to climb up that narrow stairway nor would they suspect food to be hidden in such a difficult place to get to. I will ask Phinas to help me carry it up there. Now where can I hide Bessie and Panzy? I wish we could bring them into the house, but that wouldn't hide them from the British commissariat."

When Jason returned, Clarice asked him what the urgent business was that sent him so hurriedly to Boston.

He explained, "There was a meeting of the Sons and also a secret meeting of the Club Nine. There had been some replies to a few of the requests and petitions that were sent to Parliament from the Continental Congress. All of the replies were negative, and some of the petitions were ignored. It seems the king is in favor of opening the port, but Lord North says, 'No, not until the East India Company has been paid for the tea they lost'." He added his own summation, "That will never be."

Clarice sighed, "I wish this argument could be settled, I'm really tired of it all, and I'm very tired of being left alone so much of the time while you're there settling nothing."

Jason left the room without further comment.

Clarice followed him as far as the back door where she threw her hands up in adverse sentiment. "He gets more adamant toward the British all the time. How am I ever going to change his mind? Or maybe change my mind?" She sighed.

Later in the month of February, Clarice was still in bed; Jason had gotten up early and gone into town, Lynn. He was quite secretive lately, and she was lying there wondering why. She was conjuring up in her mind many different reasons for his strange behavior. Was he looking for work? God knows he needs to do that. Was he trading something for something? Was he meeting a friend? Or was he seeing a mistress?

This last bit of suspicion caused her to sit up in bed quickly and reach for her robe. As she reached, there was a quickening leap under her breast. She caught her breath and ran her hand over her stomach. There was definitely a lump there.

She went to her bureau and stood in front of the mirror. She pulled her clothes up to her neck and took a long look at her body. It was plumply filled out. She noticed that her nipples were fat and rosy.

Great God have mercy! she exclaimed excitedly to herself, I'm going to have a baby!" She screamed out, "Jason...Jason!" then remembered he had left for town. "Oh dear me, when and how can I tell him? I'm afraid he will be angry with me. Why should he be angry with me? It's his fault. I believe he loves me, although he hasn't told me so for weeks. If I tell him, he might leave me."

Clarice returned to her mirror; she stripped to complete nakedness and examined her body carefully—again. Her breasts were tight and larger than usual. Her hips were wider, her stomach hard and heavier.

"Yes," she said, "I'm pregnant." She had not remembered to jot down the days of the months of her periods since Jason's return from Philadelphia, but now she made a notation. "October the twentieth," then she counted, "November, December, January, February. I'm four months gone, that is why I felt the baby kicking. That means I will have him in July. Him, why did I say 'him'? I might have a girl. I hope Jason will love either a him or a her."

She heard Phinas calling her. She put her clothes on and went downstairs. Phinas said, "Good morning, Cee Cee...God, you are pretty."

"Well, Phinas, I don't feel pretty, but I'm hungry. Let's have some breakfast."

He continued his admiration of her with his eyes. He said, "I've made some coffee and some biscuits. Here, sit down." He pulled her chair out from the table.

"Cee Cee, I wish you was my sister." She didn't answer. Then he said, "No...I wish you was my wife."

Clarice felt the boy's eyes on her. She said, "Phinas, quit your wishing, you are only fourteen years old. You had better be wishing for an education."

"I don't need an education. If a war breaks out I'm joining the militia."

"Hush up, I won't let you join the militia. Anyway, you will need your father's permission. Hope he won't give it to you."

"He's not around anymore. He left just before Christmas. That's why I stayed so long; Ma needed me."

After a moment of thinking about it, Clarice asked, "Why did he leave?"

"Well, I reckon it was because Bill Evans was hanging around our house too much. I left to come back here when he began sleeping with Ma."

"Phinas, are you sure about that? You could be mistaken."

"I'm not mistaken, Cee Cee. Pa should'a left two years ago." He had the expression of a real angry man when he said, "Ma and Bill have been carrying on for a long time."

Clarice, between bites of biscuits, said, "I'm sorry, Phinas, to hear that, but I'm glad you have a home here with us."

After that morning Phinas became very elusive. He stayed near the barn, even sleeping in Panzy's stall, taking particular care of the mare.

Jason told Clarice that Phinas was going to be a midwife for Panzy.

Clarice was standing beside Jason watching him unload the bags of ham and rice from the saddlebags. Charlie was chomping his corn. Phinas was currying the horse's mane.

Jason was talking to them. "There are schooners unloading provisions at both Griffin's and Roew's wharfs. They have brought all kinds of goods to Boston's needy people: medicine, food, clothing, newspapers, and books. I didn't see any arms, but there might have been some hidden amongst the other stuff. The southern colonies are in great sympathy with the Boston Patriots."

"Where were the schooners from?" asked Clarice.

"Most were from Charleston and Savannah."

"That is all very good," she said, "but did you bring us anything besides ham and rice?"

"Well, nothing else. What more do you want?" He went on talking, "Charlie was short of energy. You know he is old. I couldn't load much of anything else on his back."

Clarice was thinking of linen and yarn. She realized she must get busy making some baby clothes. She also was thinking she would soon have to give the news to Jason before she started to show or he would be mad at her for not telling him.

That evening Clarice came to the chair by the fireplace where Jason was dozing. She uncrossed his legs and sat down on his lap. She put her arms around him and laid her head on his shoulder.

"Wake up, darling," she whispered into his ear, "I know a secret and I have to share it. Do you want to hear it?"

"Uh huh," he sleepily mumbled.

"What to guess what it is?" she asked.

"No, I don't guess very well. You tell me."

She laughed and kissed his lips, then placed her forefinger across his mouth. As he kissed her finger and removed it, he said, "Well, what is the big secret? Stop leading me on."

"Darling, I hope you will like it...we're going to have a baby."

She waited for his response, watching him turn a brilliant pink. His smile covered all of his face. He was in a state of complete giddiness. He pushed her off his lap and jumped from his chair, raised his arms high, and yelled out, "Jason Angus McKenzie, the third."

Clarice was beaming, "Jason, I never knew your middle name was Angus."

"Well, it is and...wait a minute, Cee Cee, are you teasing me? Are you really in the family way?"

"You bet I am. Here, feel my stomach."

He felt and patted; his eyes were sparkling. The baby kicked just as he laid his hand on her navel. "Good Lord, the little dickens waved at me...his pa. How far along are you? When will he arrive?"

"Jason, as far as I can determine, it will be the middle of July. Kicking begins about the middle of the fourth month or about half way."

"How do you know that?" Jason asked her.

"Sister Smith knew everything about pregnancy. She was often asking me if I was keeping track of my periods, which I was not. I was so busy and worried about losing the children that I forgot all about myself. You were away and I just wasn't concerned—there was no need to be. When I felt a movement, I began to count back. You came home October seventeen; that must have been the day."

"Oh my darling, you've made me the happiest man in all of Massachusetts. Thank you. Bless you. I love you."

"Jason," she took his hand and held it to her heart, "I'm just as happy as you are, so will you please bring me some linen cloth and some yarn next time you go to Boston? I want to make the little tyke some clothes."

"Yes I will, and I'm going now to begin making him a cradle."

"Never mind, dear, there's a cradle in the attic. Must be the one your papa made for you."

"Then I will make a new one that will fit in the chaise, so we can take him with us wherever we go."

The trips to Boston became more frequent during the month of March. Jason was away two or three days each week. When he was at home the conversations between him and Clarice were more concentrated on his affairs and the people he saw while away rather than on her condition.

Jason brought home plenty of coffee, sugar, meal, molasses, and also newspapers and books, linen cloth, and yarn. Clarice was happy and kept her household running smoothly. Phinas kept the fires going and the wood laid in. March passed quickly and the air began to have the aroma of spring.

April came in with a few snow flurries. Clarice was busy at the spinning wheel. Jason was expected to return on the sixteenth. He was signed up for a meeting of the Committee of Safety and a special gathering of the minutemen, to which Jason had pledged his allegiance. Also he was to oversee the inventory of muskets and shells stored in various places around the neighborhood.

He did not come home on the sixteenth. Clarice began to worry, Where could he be? Why? She called Phinas, "Come into the house and talk to me; I'm lonesome." She said to him as he obeyed her, "Jason knows I get anxious if he doesn't come when he's supposed to."

Phinas sat on the floor near her spinning wheel. He told her that he was also worried...about Panzy. The mare was very quiet, and her head was hanging low. She would not eat her corn and there was much movement in her sides. Her tail was switching constantly, but there were no flies bothering her. "I believe she is ready to have her foal."

Clarice said, "Then you better go back to the barn and stay by her." Phinas left the room in a run.

When Clarice opened the door to test the temperature, she felt the warm sun. She opened the door wide and moved her spinning wheel up into the sunshine, just inside the open door. Now she could see down the road and watch for Charlie to come, bringing her beloved husband home to her. One minute she was singing as she spun, the next minute she was wiping tears.

She prayed, then she scolded herself, "Clarice McKenzie, you are being childish. Jason is busy; he is all right."

While sitting there near the door, Clarice saw four mounted soldiers riding along abreast of each other. They were headed west and were riding in a fast-moving gait. She stood up to watch until they were out of sight.

Phinas came around the corner of the house, also to watch the four horsemen. He saw Clarice at the door. He said, "I wonder where they are headed and what for."

Clarice answered, "Don't worry, Phinas; they are just out scouting, soldiers passing the time. They are probably on their way back to Boston."

When it began to get dark, Panzy began to whinny.

Phinas came to the back door and saw Clarice at the hearth. "I'm going into town to the livery to ask the horse doctor to come out. I believe Panzy is having trouble."

"All right, Phinas, but hurry back. I will be alone here."

She put her wheel away and swept the fuzz and lint off the floor. She thought she would go to the barn and see for herself just how the mare was doing. She took a lump of sugar from the sugar bowl. She said, "Maybe a little treat will make her feel better. Phinas ought to be back by now, he's been gone two hours."

Clarice found Panzy lying on her side on the stable floor. Her eyes were rolled back, and she was breathing very hard. When Clarice held the sugar to her mouth, she took it and snorted quietly.

"Maybe she wants a drink of water." Clarice took a bucket and went to the pump and filled it with fresh water. She found it to be heavier than she ought to be carrying, but she managed to get it to the mare's mouth. Panzy didn't raise her head to take a drink. Clarice took off her apron and doused it into the bucket of water. She bathed Panzy's head and rubbed the wet apron into her mouth. Panzy rolled her eyes.

Clarice could tell the "poor dear" was in great pain. She hugged the mare's head and said to her, "Panzy, you are a wonderful mare. Jason and I love you very much. Phinas has gone for the doctor. You will be just fine."

Clarice went to the house and soon came back with a lighted lantern. She saw the mare twisting and kicking her feet but seemingly having a convulsion.

Where is Phinas? she said to herself. Why isn't he back? Where is Jason when he is needed so badly? She realized that she was becoming very nervous.

She looked out the barn door. She saw Phinas coming running alone toward the barn. She called out before he reached her. "Where is the doctor?"

"He wasn't there. I left word. He may not get back before tomorrow." The boy said in an excited voice, "Cee Cee, I got to go to Concord. Ma sent word to the livery man in Lynn that she needs me. Bill left about a week ago and Ma is sick." Breathlessly he continued, "I also heard that the soldiers are getting ready to march on Concord and capture all the arms that are stored there. Ma's got three or four guns under the bed, and I have to go and get them before the soldiers get them. I've got to go now."

Clarice stood listening to him, shaking with nervousness. "Phinas, you can't leave now, I need you. Panzy needs you."

Phinas gave Clarice a look of regret as he grabbed his few belongings from a hook and crammed them into an old gunny sack, threw it over his shoulder, and took off running down the road.

Clarice began to quiver; she was cold. She said, "That's gratitude for you." She thought she had better go into the house and get a wrap. "I must not take a cold."

She came back instantly and was down on her knees beside Panzy, talking to her and covering her with the wrap she had brought for herself.

She saw two little feet moving slowly out of the birth canal. She moved around, on her knees, the mare's hips until she was facing the little feet. She took hold of the feet, one in each hand, but her hands slipped off. She tore pieces from her skirt and wrapped her hands, then took hold of the feet again. She pulled hard, then pulled some more and pulled and pulled. She paused and wiped the sweat from her face and eyes.

She kept talking to Panzy, "You're doing fine; you're doing everything right. You're going to have a beautiful baby, and so am I. Come on girl...push."

Clarice began to smile and release her pulling to rest and catch her breath. She saw the hips of the foal passing through, then a moment of hard breathing, then the stomach came through. Clarice now knew that it was a filly. She felt a surge of delight.

"Panzy, you have a baby girl. You deserve a baby girl." Then the head came through and a sound of hard breathing and a short snort, then the front legs, long and slender. Clarice looked up and said, "Thank you, Lord."

She went to Panzy's head. The mare had made no sound nor moved. Clarice noticed her eyes. She poured some water over her head and lifted her eyelids. Panzy did not respond. She was very still.

Clarice looked at the baby mare, trying desperately to get up on its legs. She went to the little filly and wiped its face and eyes with the wet apron. She saw the white star under its forelock, exactly like her mother's. She helped the little beauty stand up.

She went back to Panzy's head and patted it. She tried to shake her, "Wake up, wake up, Panzy, and see your beautiful baby." All at once the real sorrow of life hit her, "Oh, my God, she's dead."

Clarice ran to the house and to the front door, opened it, and looked down the road. It was nearly daylight. No sight or sound relieved her broken heart. "What am I going to do?" She sat down in her chair; the fire was going out. "I have to be sensible; I must think what to do. Oh, dear God, help me." She knew she had to get back to the barn to the newborn. She knew from her reading that the first thing a baby horse does is nurse.

"Bessie...oh yes, Bessie. It is morning milking time; she will have plenty of milk. I hope she is not way off in the meadow somewhere." Clarice grabbed a shawl from the peg by the door and went to find the cow.

Bessie had come in from the pasture and was waiting by the gate. Clarice led her to the stall where Panzy was stretched out, dead, and the baby mare was standing over her on very wobbly legs. Bessie seemed to understand. She put up no resistance when Clarice pushed and pulled at the baby to put her mouth near Bessie's udder and squirted milk from a teat all over the foal's face. She grabbed hold and began sucking. Clarice laughed as the foal's tail began to wiggle in complete satisfaction.

When the foal quit nursing and Clarice rinsed off the cow's udder and the foal's face, she led the cow to her own stall and gave her some corn and bran. She then wondered what she should do about Panzy. She went to the house and made herself some coffee and parched corn. She said, "I will rest awhile and think about it."

The moment she relaxed, she fell asleep. Must have been two hours later, someone was shaking her hand while calling her name. She opened her eyes to see John Slade and Henry Cook.

"Oh, good morning to you both. When did you get here? I'm sorry you caught me sleeping. Everything was so quiet and I was so tired. I guess I lost control of myself."

"We wanted a word with Jason, but looks like he's not at home."

Clarice said, "He's been gone longer than he expected. I don't know what's keeping him."

The two men could see that Clarice was quite pregnant.

John reached for her hand to assist her to her feet. "It's good to see you again. Don't worry about Jason, he won't neglect you for long."

Henry was just standing there, not saying anything.

Clarice said, "Mounted soldiers are passing here, riding west. Do you know why they are way out here?"

John Slade answered, "There is much activity among the troops. We saw dozens of canoes and other small craft tied up at shoreline across from Charlestown. I think they must be getting ready for maneuvers on Harvard Yard."

Henry spoke, not with knowledge but with speculation, "I believe they're going to attack. We'll find out when we catch up with Hancock and Adams. They're waiting for our messages in Salem." He then said, "We better get on our way, wouldn't you say, John?"

Clarice stepped in front of the two men. "Don't go," she said. "I am in need of some help. Our horse Panzy died last night while giving birth. She is in the barn and ought to be taken out and buried."

"What about the foal? Was it born or did it die inside of her?"

"Fortunately, it was a perfect delivery. It's a filly and a real beauty. Come with me to the barn and see for yourselves."

Clarice and the two men went to the barn.

As they were crossing the yard, they heard horse's hooves hitting the rocky road. They saw the riders in redcoats riding west. They rode past the McKenzie place but stopped suddenly when about two hundred yards away and had a moment or two of consultation. One of the riders came galloping back, took the reins of John Slade's and Henry Cook's horses off the hitching post and led the horses down the road. When the rider met the other two, who had waited, there was uproarious laughter as the three soldiers and five horses galloped off toward Charlestown.

John said, "Excuse me, Clarice, if I call them sons of bitches. Now how will Henry and I get to Salem?"

Clarice said, "I'm really scared. I wish Jason was here. Now you will have to stay here; you have no horses."

John said, "The awful truth is, our messages from the Committee in Connecticut were in the saddlebags."

"No, John, I got 'em right here," Henry patted his pocket. "You know you told me to always hide 'em in my clothes."

"Thank God, Henry, I can depend on you."

Clarice walked in front of the two men. She pulled the leather thong and the barn door opened. There was the little filly. Her legs had quit wobbling and her eyes were shining brightly. She came and sniffed at Clarice's outstretched hand.

John patted her head and asked Clarice if she had named her.

"Not yet, I'll wait for Jason. I hope he names her Panzy."

The dead mare had stiffened and was as hard as stone. Clarice stooped and rubbed her hand over the head and smoothed the mane. John and Henry were standing over the corpse and wondering what they could do. Clarice was waiting for them to say something while she wiped her tears.

In a moment John said, "Henry, will you walk to the livery in Lynn and rent a block and tackle and a horse and slide and be back here in a couple of hours?"

"Well, maybe in three hours," answered Henry as he started off, running.

Clarice said to John, "I suppose you and I had better start digging a grave. It will have to be a very big hole."

John said, "Clarice," he pointed "out there in the field there used to be a sinkhole, but when it rained it became a pond. Let's go and see if it is still there. We can use that hole for a grave."

"You have been here before?" Clarice questioned John.

"Well, truthfully, I've been a scout almost all of my life. I've walked many miles over this territory. I suppose I can tell you where every creek crosses a path, and where every sinkhole is located or wherever there was an Indian or a bear."

John looked around for some digging implements. He discovered a spade, a shovel, and a pitchfork all in a corner of the barn.

Clarice followed along behind John as they walked about four hundred yards, about one-fourth of a mile, to the old sinkhole. A grove of maple trees bordered it.

John stopped and said, "Here it is, the old pond, deep enough, wide enough, a pretty luscious location. Just right for Panzy's resting place. I will just turn back the top soil now and leave the rest of the digging until tomorrow. I will leave the tools here. Then we should go back to the house and wait for Henry."

While waiting for Henry's return with the equipment they needed, Clarice and John sat by the fire, as it was still quite cool. They talked of the disturbances and confusion taking place all about them.

John told Clarice about several close encounters with danger and narrow escapes from death. "Why it's gotten so bad we have to carry our saddles into our sleeping quarters and put them right by our beds, or they would be gone next morning. Also we have to hire guards for our horses."

Clarice told John of Jason's many absences. How she never knew where he was going. She said, "I wish I could be contented while he is gone, but I am a perpetual worrywart."

John asked if Jason would join the Continental Army. He said, "I am sure one is now in formation."

"Oh, I suppose he will be one of the first to sign up. He is a venturesome man."

While talking, they heard more mounted soldiers passing the house. Their laughing and loud talking led Clarice and John to believe they were on their way to a bivouac somewhere nearby.

It was late afternoon when Henry returned with the horse and sledge and the block and tackle.

John asked Clarice to stay in the house while he and Henry put the mare onto the sledge.

"Yes, I will," she answered, "but will you put the foal to Bessie's milk? She hasn't learned yet where her supper is coming from."

John called back from the barn, "The foal has learned, all right; she's doing fine right now. And Bessie is as pleased as punch."

About an hour later the hardest part of the job was done. John came to the house to ask Clarice if he and Henry could sleep in the barn. He said they were too tired to walk to Lynn's ordinary.

"Yes," she told him, "you may sleep in the house, and I have set out a good supper for the three of us."

John and Henry pushed up their sleeves and scrubbed their hands and arms at the wash basin outside the back door.

They sat down at the table and ate with big appetites.

Clarice said, "I am as hungry as a starved rabbit."

Next morning the cortege to the burial spot began just after daylight. Clarice walked behind the slow-moving, screeching sledge. She plucked wildflowers as they went along and threw them onto Panzy's body. She looked back as they left the barn lot and saw Bessie and the foal standing side by side at the barn door.

The sun was three hours high when Clarice, John, and Henry returned to the house.

Clarice asked, "When your business is over in Salem, will you go to Boston and look into Jason's trouble and his absence?"

"Clarice, we will, but first we have to get some horses. That may be hard to do, but we will try to find him. We may have to walk to Boston." He continued to talk. "Horses seem to be much in demand these days. You see how quick those soldiers were to grab Henry's and mine."

Chapter Thirty-Four

It was the eighteenth of April in 'seventy-five,'
Hardly a man is now alive,
Who remembers that famous day and year,
The midnight ride of Paul Revere.

It was the eighteenth of April. Clarice was alone in her house, and she was feeling many regrets. She wished she had not married. This was not the first time she had felt this way. Thoughts of Governor Hutchinson's bid to see her safely home to England entered her mind. Then her thoughts of Jason and how much she loved him and their happiness when they were together blotted out the negative and the positive took over. She became more reconciled and decided to go for a walk.

She went to the barn to see the little filly. She thought the air was heavy. "No," she said, "it's me that is heavy. My heart is heavy, too." She prayed, "Dear Lord, where is my Jason? Why did Panzy die? Show me a way to live so as to make Jason happy. Help us all to be free of these soldiers and all bad men and their doings."

She stood at the gate. Her eyes were closed, and she heard fast-moving feet coming up behind her. She turned around to see a stranger. He looked like a poor farmer, so she was not afraid of him.

He said, "Good day, Mrs. McKenzie, I've come to see your husband...on business."

"I'm sorry, he is not here. He will be back today...I think."

Clarice didn't want him to know that she was alone. She said, "My farm hand will return from the store momentarily. Maybe he can help you with whatever it is you want." She made up that lie.

He replied, "Well, if he can fire a musket, he may be able to help. I will stop again later today."

Clarice stood by the gate a few more minutes, watching the stranger mount his horse and ride away.

"I'm sorry I told that lie. I suppose I was wishing that Phinas would come back."

She thought about the rifles Jason had hidden in the barn, and before returning to the house she went to see if they were still in the loft under the hay. The awful looking things were still there. She pulled one of them out of its hiding place and carried it into the house and hit it under the bed.

She watched the road all day. Her work was put off because of her nervousness. She began talking to herself, "Well, I think I have enough clothes already made for Jason Angus McKenzie the Third. I will make him some blankets next week. Today I'm going to relax. I am full of anguish over losing Panzy, and I'm very tired from all the work. I'm angry at the British soldiers who stole John and Henry's horses. I'm worried sick about Jason."

Clarice then began to take what she called her relaxation by plopping down in her rocking chair and singing as she rocked. She made up a song:

> Dear Mrs. McKenzie, Life is short,
> Dear Mrs. McKenzie, Life is hard.
> But not for the Anthonys
> Nor for King George
> Dear Mrs. McKenzie, Don't trust to Luck
> Dear Mrs. McKenzie, It takes a lot of Pluck
> Your husband Loves you, You ought to know
> Although he forgot to tell you so,
> Don't be foolish and sit and cry,
> Get up, get busy
> Go make a pie.

Clarice saw a very fine chaise stopping at her front gate. "Now, who can that be?" she asked herself as she went out to meet the man coming toward the house.

"Good day, sir, may I help you?"

"Yes, madam." He handed her a sealed message.

"Who is it for?" she asked. "May I open it."

"No," he answered, "it is for Mister McKenzie. We know he is in jail, but may be released today and return home. The message should be given to him as soon as he arrives."

"In jail? What for?" Clarice became excited.

"He will explain it to you, madam; I cannot."

"Who is in the carriage?" she asked.

"Very important men, madam."

"Where are you going?" she reached for his arm to delay him until he answered her question.

"Our next stop will be in Lexington at the Jonas Clark residence." He hastily climbed onto the driver's seat and tipped his hat to Clarice, who was standing near the gate holding the folded and sealed message with a scowling look of bewilderment on her face.

She returned to her great room and placed the message, unopened, on her mantle where it could be seen from either front or back door.

"Now I will get busy making some pies."

As she was sifting flour, she saw a man running across the yard. She went to the door to see where he went. She saw that he was carrying a rifle and he was taking a shortcut through her yard, not halting at the fence but just jumping over it.

"Good Lord, I do wish I knew what's going on," she said to herself.

The pies turned out deliciously brown and appetizing. Clarice lined them up on the table. One was apple, one was custard, and one was blueberry. "Now when Jason gets here he can have a feast," she thought out loud.

It was a busy day for the worried Clarice, but she kept fighting her anxieties. She stayed with the little filly for an hour, petting her, talking to her, and feeding her crushed corn. She cleaned up the stalls and removed Panzy's saddle and bridle to a different peg across the barn so it wouldn't be so obvious that the mare was not there.

When the shadows began to move around the tress to the east side, Clarice felt tired enough to rest. She went to her bedroom, and, after viewing her body in her mirror, she measured her circumference. She was two inches rounder than last week. She could barely see her feet. She held one foot at a time out in front of her to look at it. Yes, her feet were swollen. She had been on them too much. She brushed her hair, then laid down on her bed. She noticed her little brass clock said three o'clock.

"I will lie here awhile and then go let Bessie into the barn."

She rested but could not sleep. A wagon loaded with something that made a loud rattling noise passed along the road. She said, "This is certainly a busy, noisy day. I wish Jason would get here if he is coming today. I hope I won't spend another night alone."

Before long the shadows disappeared. The sun had gone behind the Berkshires. The house was getting dark inside. Clarice took a few long, new candles from the mold. As she placed the candles in their holders she said, "I think I will leave them burning all night. Then Jason won't have to come into a dark house."

She cut herself a piece of apple pie and made a pot of coffee. She sat in her rocking chair with a tray on her lap. She was not hungry, but she ate the pie anyway. She said, "My little one wants me to eat."

She read some pages of the Bible. Then she read a few pages of Gulliver's Travels but was more interested when she read The Public Spirit of The Whigs. Both books were the works of Jonathan Swift and once belonged to Jason's father, she supposed.

She thought she heard thunder but saw no lightning when she went to the window, pulled back the curtains, and surveyed the sky. There was something strange going on. She bolstered her courage by concluding that the Harvard men were celebrating.

"But what was it that sounded like thunder?"

It seemed to Clarice that midnight came earlier; she was glad the time had passed, but she wanted the night to be over. Hark, hark, she heard horses' hooves sliding to a stop. Someone was in a very big hurry. Then there was a banging at her door. She was frightened, so she opened it only a crack. Two eyes, wide open and expressing great fear, peered through the crack at her.

"Madam, madam, have ye heered? The British are a comin'. There's thousands and thousands of 'em gittin' off the boats and runnin' toward Lexington. Tell ye husban' that the minutemen are 'semblin on Lexinton Green and to hurry up and get there with as much powder as he's got."

Clarice was holding a candle, but the wind blew it out. She shivered; she didn't have time to tell the man that her husband was not at home. He was gone.

"Thousands and thousands of 'em." She repeated what the midnight rider had said.

She re-lit the candle and placed it on the mantle. She whispered, "Thank you, dear God, Jason is in jail."

She put the coffee pot back on the coals and heated up the leftover coffee. She poured herself a cup, picked up her book, and resumed her reading.

When morning finally arrived and Clarice opened her back door she saw smoke rising from six different spots on the western horizon. She wondered what was burning. She found that out later that afternoon from minutemen straggling along going home to Lynn, tired and hungry from fighting, killing, and putting out fires.

The British had burned houses and barns and bridges, but 247 of their Light Infantry Brigade had been put out of service. The minutemen suffered 95 casualties.

Clarice wondered what she could do to help those tired men, some of them wounded and still bleeding.

She boiled a large kettle of water and gathered together some rags, a basin, and towels. She placed them on stools near the front gate. She made a feast of cheese, bread, apples, butter, jam, milk, and cider. She spread a cloth on the ground, like a picnic, and put the food on it. She penned a notice and nailed it to the gate post. "Help yourselves and rest."

There was a lot of running back and forth into the house to replenish that which was soon consumed and to get camphor and lard and asafetida to stall infection.

She saw three men approaching; two were holding up one. The one being carried had a bleeding leg and half his face was gone. She ran to help them. The wounded man was placed on the ground near the basin. Clarice tore a towel in half and made it wet and washed his face. She ripped off his pant leg and bathed the wound. He passed out. She didn't know what to do next. The two men who had carried him were at the spread of food, eating and drinking.

There was very little talking, but Clarice did ask, "Where did this fighting take place, and what was the outcome of it all?"

"Murder," answered one of the men, then he yelled out, "We sent them devils back to Boston and we ain't done with 'em yet. The road from Concord to Boston is red with their blood. We hope Gage will think hard afore he tries to slip up on us again."

When darkness came again to Lynn and Clarice again lit her candles, she realized that she had put out for the minutemen every scrap of food, every bean of coffee, and had used up on their wounds all of the camphor and asafetida that she possessed. She drew back her curtain and looked out at the sky. There was still a smoky haze, but there was no sign of Jason.

She climbed the stairs slowly and went into her bedroom. She undressed and noticed that some of the blood from wounded minutemen had stained her skirt. She cut out the stained spot and pinned it up as a plaque on the wall by the bureau.

"There," she said. "I will always remember this day." She wrote under the piece of stained cloth, April 19th, 1775.

The next day was filled with the constant passing of caravans, the yelling, the crying, the arguments and threats among the walkers and horseback riders, the continuous rapping at her door by travelers wanting something: information, a piece of paper, a drink of water, permission to use the privy.

Clarice, already exhausted from the fury and excitement of the three previous days and the worry about Jason, caused her to throw herself across her bed and give in to hysteria. She cried until her body ached and she became nauseated and weak.

She got up and staggered to the wash basin and pitcher of water near her bed. She had several minutes of hard retching and vomiting. Finally getting her breath back and a little composure she straightened herself and looked in the mirror. Her hair was tousled, her eyes were red, and the circles under her eyes were a dark purple. She said, "I am ashamed of myself for falling apart. I cannot let Jason see me looking like this."

She repeated some lines from Shakespeare to justify her debility. "His composure must be rare indeed, Whom these things cannot blemish." *(Antony and Cleopatra, Act 1 scene IV line 22).

The little filly was a great joy after a tornado of death and destruction. When Clarice entered the barn, the baby kicked up her heels and raised her front legs and shook her head as if in gleeful welcome.

Who knows, thought Clarice, if she was aware of something horrible and unusual taking place. She must have heard the mournful sounds and the yelling.

As Clarice spoke to her very kindly and held out her hand to her, the sweet soft nostril came to the coaxing fingers and nudged with understanding. Understanding that Clarice was a friend and from those fingers she would be fed and petted.

A voice behind her caused Clarice to quake and shiver as she turned around and saw Phinas.

"Oh, Phinas," she called out as she ran to him and hugged him. "I'm so happy to see you. Have you come back to stay or are you leaving again in a few minutes?"

"I'm here to stay if you want me to. Ma ran off to Vermont when the soldiers came to her house. She didn't even take her clothes. The last I saw of her, she was riding as fast as our old horse would go. Right after that the soldiers set fire to the house. That's when I lit out to get away. The only place I had to go to was here. I snuck through the woods. I'm so hungry I'm about starved."

He did look lean. Clarice wondered if his mother had been giving him enough food to sustain him. She thought about herself, how hungry she was, and that there was no food in the house. Phinas was stroking the little filly and telling her how pretty she was.

Clarice said, "Well, Phinas, we haven't got any food, I fed it all to the poor, weary minutemen who passed here going home to Lynn after the battle. I had no one to send to the market. I doubt that it is still operating. The owners probably ran off to fight and it closed down. I don't know what we're going to do."

Phinas sort of grinned. He said, "Quit your worrying, there must be something here; if there is I'll find it."

Clarice looked relieved. She hugged the boy again and said to him, "You are a blessing from heaven; you always look on the bright side."

Phinas's face turned red, and his smile was one of great pleasure. He said, "Please don't hug me no more, Cee Cee; I can't stand up to it."

Clarice caught on; she hadn't forgotten what he once said to her. "All right, Phinas, but I am so grateful for your coming back." She smiled at him and added, "I wish you were my little brother."

He looked disappointed, he said, "Cee Cee, I'm only four years younger than you; I could be your husband."

Clarice kissed the foal and said to her, "Good night, little one," then she went into the house.

Phinas kicked the side of the barn and said, "Damn."

Clarice looked into the cupboard, hoping she had overlooked something when she hastily put together food for the soldiers. But she found nothing.

"Tomorrow I will send Phinas to the market, maybe there will be something. Perhaps a fishing boat has brought some cod or turbo." She looked in her satchel, but could not find a shilling.

"Look, Cee Cee," it was Phinas coming in the back door. He was carrying a small sack in one hand and a bucket in the other hand. There was a dozen or more fresh eggs in the sack. He held it out for Clarice to see. He was in a jovial mood as he said, "Here's a bucket of molasses I found in the barn. I think Jason brought it to mix with Bessie's bran. I'll make us a big ole omelet and we can have a feast. We won't starve as long as we have eggs and molasses."

Clarice was pleased. She said, "Phinas, you are so helpful. I'm so glad you have come back."

There was a pounding on the front door. Clarice opened it enough to see who it was. She didn't know the man who held out a printed page from the

Gazette. "Here, madam, is a list of the men from Lynn who were killed at yesterday's battle. Sure hope your husband's name is not on it."

Clarice trembled as she took the paper.

"My husband is in Boston in jail, and I hope they keep him there until this fighting is over."

The man had a handful of the papers. He hurried away to deliver them.

Clarice stood there, too scared to read the list. Phinas came near her to listen. Her lips quivered as she read, Abednego Ransdell, Daniel Townsend, William Flint, Thomas Hadley, and wounded Joshua Felt and Timothy Monroe.

Phinas had made the omelet and covered it with the Cuban molasses. He said, "Come and sit at the table and fill up. You'll feel better if you eat."

Clarice lifted the hem of her apron and wiped the tears from her cheeks. She asked, "Do I look bad, Phinas? I must pull myself together before Jason gets here."

They both ate and drank milk which Phinas said he filched from the filly. "Nothing works better than grub to make a man willing and able," said Phinas, as he reared back in his chair rocking it back and forth as he straightened his shoulders and hooked his thumbs under the armholes of his vest. He swirled his tongue around his teeth to get every tiny bit of egg, then he picked up his milk and took a big gulp and swiggled it around in his mouth before swallowing.

Then he took a big breath and said, rather positively to Clarice, "Cee Cee, I can see that you are in the family way, and I can see that you are worried about Jason. I don't like to see you so downhearted. I would like to help you. I will do whatever it takes to make you smile."

He waited for her response. She sat still and stared at the boy with loving regard, but as a mother stares at a child when the child is perplexing her. Her thoughts were roaming, but she did not put them into words. He has become a man in the last few days that he was away. His shoulders are broader. He is strong and taller. His eyes have a beckoning look that is quite mature. He is willing to do my bidding. His boyish look has disappeared. He is a man, a good man.

Clarice left the table and went to her desk, "I'm going to write some letters now," she said. She then spoke to Phinas, "As soon as you can, please go to Lynn and round up something for us to eat and gather some more news about the fighting."

He answered her, "I got enough of that stored up in my head already."

Clarice didn't write the letters. She sat at the desk with her pen in her hand trying to think what she should say. Then she decided to wait until Phinas got back with some more news.

She took her paper and pen and went back to the kitchen table where she made a list of their needs. Phinas joined her at the table. "Cee Cee, I'm ready to go to market. It may take me all day; I hate to leave you here all alone. If I wus you, I wouldn't open the door every time somebody knocks."

Clarice looked at Phinas with an expression of a different opinion. "Phinas, the people that are leaving the country for the safety of Boston are the people who should be afraid. I'm not afraid. If I open the door to those who knock I may be able to help in some way. If I refuse to open the door I may be turning my back on a friend."

"Have it your way, Cee Cee," Phinas answered her resolve.

Clarice began enunciating to Phinas, pertaining to the marketing.

"Phinas, you may have to find some work to do to earn some money to pay for the things we need. I've searched every pocket, and I can't find one pence. There will be someone ready to hire you, so many are leaving, you may find work loading wagons. I do hope you can earn enough to buy some food."

Phinas was trying to get a word in edgewise, but it was difficult since Clarice went on and on about her finances being in poor condition.

He could tell she was becoming depressed. He reached for her hand; she drew it back, but he began talking, raising his voice above hers.

"Cee Cee, quit your fretting; I have plenty of money."

A look of sudden surprise flooded her face and her mouth flew open, then shut as a moment of hesitation, then words, "You do? Where did you get it?"

"From Ma," he answered, "but she don't know about it. After I realized that she was gone for good—not coming back, the British had scared her too bad—I went upstairs to her room. I wus looking for Pa's pitcher. I knowed she had it hid somewhere so's Bill wouldn't know she had it. When I opened her bureau drawer I saw one of her long stockings, stuffed full of something. It wus way back under her long underwear. I lifted it out. Gee, it was heavy. It wus full of pound notes rolled up into balls and shillings by the dozen. I found a piece of warp and I wound it around the stocking, then I wrapped it to my leg, like a splint. My pant leg covered it. It sure made running difficult, but I run with that stocking full o' money until I reached the woods. When I realized I wus safe from the soldiers I set down to rest. That's when I saw our house in the distance going up in flames.

"Ma'll never know that money didn't burn up. It's too bad I never found Pa's pitcher. It sure saddens my heart that it burned up."

Clarice now seemed calm and pleased. "Well, Phinas, you are a lucky lad to have come across the money, which should have been yours anyway if it was your pa's in the first place."

Phinas staunched his stand. "Now, gimme that list." He read it out loud for verification. "Meal, lard, camphor, onions, potatoes, apples, salt, sugar, asafetida."

Clarice sat nodding her head affirmatively. She added, "And some meat if you can find any."

The boy said, "I'll be off." He stuffed the list into his satchel and left the house for Lynn.

Chapter Thirty-Five

During the time of the Lexington and Concord episodes, which was a time of conflict, confusion, despair, death, and uprooting, Jason McKenzie was chained to a wall in Boston's detainment quarters near Province House.

All day long April eighteenth, he was aware of preparations being made by the soldiers for some hostile activity. Through the narrow barred window he could see wisps of dust; it was passing horses. He could hear the snorts and whinnies, and he could hear orders being given by their riders. Several times, when it grew quiet for a few minutes, he dozed off and enjoyed sweet dreams of Clarice and his home. Within a short time, however, the outside noises would awaken him.

It was four o'clock in the afternoon, and a bell began to ring furiously and loudly. Jason jumped to his feet from his pallet on the floor and tried to lift himself to the window. He was too weak from hunger to grasp the sill, but he stood still and listened. There was movement of many feet. The bell continued to ring, and other bells began to toll. It was a loud sorrowful sound.

Jason heard a command, from an officer, he presumed. He heard the words, Arsnell, Lexington, boats, rifles, bayonets, satchels, sulphur, water.

"Good God," he cried out, almost in a scream, "they're going to attack the stores at Concord. I've got to get out of here." He pounded on the wall, rattled the chain holding him, kicked the bars, and yelled at the top of his voice. The sounds he made could not be heard above the sounds outside. His voice was like a leaf falling to the ground. He dropped to his knees and began to pray. "Dear God, can you hear me? Can you see me? In the name of freedom and Jesus Christ, get me out of here. How can I help if I don't get out of here?"

During his praying he heard footsteps; they were wearing boots with steel caps on the toes and heels. It was only one pair of boots, that meant only one soldier. He heard someone unlocking the barred door of his cell. Thick walls separated him from the other prisoners. He wondered if someone was coming to let someone out. He didn't care who was let out or who stayed in, just so he got out.

Then Jason saw Tom Fellows; he was taking a key from his coat sleeve. He also noticed that Tom was wearing two coats. He unlocked the handcuffs holding Jason and then removed the outside red coat. He whispered to Jason, "Put it on."

Jason threw his arms around Tom and said, "Tom, God bless you. You are my answered prayer."

Tom said nothing but, "Shush." He took Jason's hand and led him from the dark cell to the waning sunshine of April eighteenth. Tom, in a muffled voice said, "I will see you later; I have to scram. If anyone sees me here letting you loose I will be shot without time to explain that you are my friend. Hurry home to Cee Cee, and give her my love. So long."

Jason began to run on his weak legs toward Charles Street to his barn. He didn't give any thought to why he had been arrested or why Tom Fellows let him out. He did not take off the red coat. All he could think about was getting home.

Tom quickly disappeared out of sight. He was last seen striding along toward the Common.

Jason's building and barn were half a mile away. He made it in less than ten minutes. He saw his barn door standing open. Rushing to it, expecting to bridle Charlie right away, he began to whistle a tune that Charlie would recognize.

Jason did not hear Charlie's nicker. He suspected that Charlie was not there, and his suspicions were right. He hurriedly went to the Common. As he supposed, many horses were corralled there. He began his whistling and immediately he heard Charlie nickering. He spotted him tied to a pole with seven other horses. Jason went to Charlie, untied him, and nonchalantly rode away. The red coat had disguised him.

When he reached the bank of the Charles it was getting dark. Many canoes were filling up with soldiers beginning their crossing. He reached a canoe waiting for one more passenger. He dismounted Charlie but led the horse behind him. Jason had to get his bearings in a hurry. He coughed up his cockney accent and greeted the soldiers already seated. He stepped into the back of a canoe, leading Charlie into the water. The horse swam like a sea horse. Jason turned his back on the others and sat facing Charlie, singing to him in cockney English. He was still wearing the red coat.

His hair was shaggy and dirty from his imprisonment. As soon as they reached the north bank, he and Charlie disappeared into the darkness, and no one had doubts as to his being on his way to Lexington.

In the quietness of the evening Jason encountered John Slade and Henry when he stopped at a tavern to rest. They were purposely delaying their return to Boston because of the expected hostilities. When Jason entered the tavern, looking as he did, like the worst vagabond deserter in the British Army, John Slade's mouth fell open in awe.

The red coat set off an alarm in his mind. He loudly exclaimed, "Oh, my God! He's joined the British. What will happen now?" He cried out, "Jason,

Jason McKenzie, what in hell's name are you up to? Where'd you get that red coat? Have you heard there's real trouble brewing?"

Jason was tired and hungry. He held up his forefinger, shaking it back and forth, to silence John. Henry's eyes were dancing. He knew in his heart that Jason was pulling the wool over someone's eyes. "Let him alone, John. He ain't up to answering questions. He needs some grub."

Jason fell from his chair. The hunger and escape shenanigans had gotten the best of him. Henry picked up the lean, dirty Jason and carried him up the three flights of stairs to the loft where he had a rented bed. (All the black people slept either in the loft or the barn.) He poured some water into a wash bowl and carried it to the bed. He sat on the side of the bed and bathed Jason's face. He pulled the red coat off of Jason, also his pants. He said to the groggy Jason, "There, old pal, you'll be better in a jiffy." He squeezed Jason's trembling hand and said, "I'll bring you some soup after you've slept a little while."

When the kindhearted Henry rejoined John Slade in the great room of the tavern, they watched through the window a contingent of British soldiers tying up their horses at the hitching pole. Like a flash one of the soldiers began to run down the street. The others began yelling at him, "Come back, come back."

John Slade believed that they had spotted Charlie and were looking for Jason. He said to Henry, "They're looking for Jason." Henry's mind worked very fast. He rushed out the door, confronting the soldiers, "If ye're looking for a deserter, he run outta here about ten minutes ago, running toward Saugus. I heered him say he's going into the wilderness 'cause he ain't intended to git kilt." Henry was overdoing his black pronunciation to lead the soldiers into believing he was a low class servant.

John came out of the tavern and joined the soldiers and Henry.

Only a moment elapsed before a rider came galloping by, yelling as he passed, "They're shootin' it up at Lexington. Dead men are falling all over the green."

The soldiers mounted and spurred their horses and rode swiftly toward Lexington. John and Henry went back into the tavern. There wasn't one person to be seen. All had left for some place to hide.

Henry went into the tavern kitchen and found some potatoes. He peeled them and put them into a kettle with some onions to boil to make some soup. He laid aside several onions to make a poultice to put on Jason's chest. Shortly, he was carrying a bowl of soup, a bottle of flip, and an onion poultice up to the loft to Jason.

John Slade, Henry Cook, and Jason McKenzie stayed in the tavern all day, listening to strange and rumbling sounds, watching smoke and scared birds heading out to see.

Jason knew he was coming down with pneumonia. He said to John, "Do you have time to accompany me the rest of the way to Lynn? If I fall off Charlie I may be too weak to get up."

He answered Jason, "Henry can accompany you, I have a meeting here tomorrow. It may not assemble because of the trouble today, but I better wait and see." He continued, "We missed our meeting in Boston because the principal factors had escaped to Salem. God only knows where those men are now."

Jason, with Henry's help, was able to climb onto Charlie's back. The two men rode slowly along the road passing many people walking, mostly women leading small children and livestock. Some were crying, and some were cursing, shaking fists, and slapping at the children.

It was supper time. Henry had filled his pockets with boiled potatoes. He handed Jason a potato, and he ate it ravenously.

Henry said to Jason, "Let's cut through the woods. It'll take a little longer, but there are just too many vehicles on this road. We may be delayed by some fool needing help."

Jason nodded his head yes, then they turned their horses into the leafy paths under the trees. They rode slowly but as close together as possible. They didn't have very far to go, about three miles from Pig's Nose, a little farther through the woods.

Jason began to cough, Henry said, "Don't cough, if you can hep it. We don't want to stir up any varmints in red coats. You can't tell where they might be snooping around."

"I can't help coughing, Henry. I'm filling up with snot in my head and I'm burning up. I can't stay in this saddle very much longer. If we could just go faster." Henry had borrowed the saddle from John Slade's horse.

Henry pulled his reins, "Woah," he said. He was close enough to Jason to reach out from horse to horse and pull Jason from Charlie and place him in front of himself. He said to Charlie as he threw the bridle reins over the horn of the empty saddle; "Follow us, Charlie; stay close." The horse understood.

Jason's head began to drop. Henry lifted it up. He had such a high fever, Henry could feel it, hot, from Jason's body to his.

The going was very slow. The trees were so thick it was difficult to see but only a short distance. Henry wasn't sure he was on the right path. His horse, only recently acquired, was not familiar with the path. Henry halted a moment and said to Charlie, "Get around in front of us, old boy, and lead the way. You probably know every gully and fallen log. It will make it easier for Sam to get a foot hold."

Henry laughed a short quiet laugh as he said to Jason, "I ain't had Sam but three days. I bought him in Salem after some sons o'bitches stole mine and John's from right in front of your house. I never learned his name so I named him Sam."

Henry was still talking. "I named him Sam for Sam Adams, who had escaped to some other place by the time we got to Salem because the British were going to arrest him for treason."

Jason didn't hear what Henry was saying. He had passed out. When Henry realized that Jason was unconscious, he became frightened. He halted the horse and pulled Jason down from the saddle and placed him on the ground. He straightened his legs and arms. He took a bottle of water from the saddlebag and poured some water over Jason's face. He took another bottle from the saddlebag and poured some brandy into Jason's mouth. Jason swallowed it and mumbled something. Henry shook him and pounded on Jason's chest, an old method that Lola used to unlock the congestion in his chest when he was down with pneumonia.

It must have worked because Jason opened his eyes and in a very weak voice said, "Do that some more, Henry."

Henry began the pounding and the rubbing. Jason said, "Now I can breathe."

"Just lay still and don't talk," was Henry's advice. "Here swallow this." He poured some more brandy into Jason's mouth.

Henry thought, God, what will I do if he dies?

But Jason soon began to revive and within a couple of hours he opened his eyes wide and gazed around at the sky, which was a bright blue, and at the trees budding and dropping sap. He didn't see Charlie or Henry, who had moved a few paces away and was sitting with his back to a tree. Sam was standing near Henry with his eyes closed. Charlie, who had been given the freedom to lead the way, had bounded on ahead toward home.

When Henry saw Jason rousing and turning his head, he jumped to his feet and ran to him. "Hell, Jason," he said, with a big smile on his face, "I knowed you wouldn't die. I asked God to hep me git you outta here," meaning the woods. "Can you stand up yet?"

"I think I will have to have a little more time; my legs are jelly."

Henry answered him, "We got all the time in the world. Ain't nobody else here to bother us. Do you want another cold potato?"

"No, I want some of those wild May apples. They are around here somewhere. I can smell them."

Henry went into the woods and soon returned with his hands full of the golden, ripe fruit. Jason said he felt like going on home after he ate three of the luscious forest apples.

In the meantime Charlie had trotted up to the front gate. The saddle in place, but empty. Clarice saw him before he stopped, and she heard his nicker and snort. She put down her knitting and went hurriedly out of the house to the gate.

"Charlie, where is Jason?" She petted the horse as her eyes searched the countryside. She could see two loaded wagons to the west and a crowd of people walking to the east. She knew they were some more escapees on their way to Boston. There was no use to approach them with questions about Jason; he would be somewhere in the opposite direction.

She opened the gate and let Charlie into the yard, but she didn't have time to remove the saddle. He took off around the house to the barn. If Clarice could have kept up with him, she would have seen his surprised expression when he came face to face with the little filly.

After a moment of nuzzling and making friendly acquaintance, he began to nicker loudly and move about the barn. When there was no response to his calling and he had gotten the smell, he dropped to the soft new hay in Panzy's stall as big tears rolled down his nostrils.

Clarice followed Charlie to the barn. She sat on a stool beside him and rubbed his quivering body. Tears were flooding her eyes until she could hardly see. The little filly came to Clarice and nudged her into reality. She noticed that the eyes of the baby were scanning Charlie as he lay there. She placed her palm under the nose of the baby and said to her, "This is your papa, and you must be kind to him."

Clarice left the barn and went around the house to the gate. Looking up and down the road, she decided to walk a ways and meet Jason. She said to herself, "I will not allow myself to think he may be hurt or dead. I think he is walking alone toward home. He must be this side of the Charles. I do hope and pray that he is all right." She was trying to hold on to good thoughts.

She walked about a mile, and there were others on the road. She did not ask anyone any questions. She felt like they would tell her about Jason if they knew anything. Some of the people who were walking along the road knew who she was, but she knew only a few of them. Some were from Salem, others from Marblehead, Saugus, and points farther north and west.

Henry helped Jason to his feet and handed him a stout stick that he picked up in the woods. "Here, use this for a walking stick. We'll make it home in a little while. I will lead Sam; he is too hungry to carry us."

They slowly started out, but Jason hardly was able to stand up. He leaned heavily on Henry and the stick. He told Henry to whistle for Charlie.

"No use, Jason, he was in a hurry to get home."

There was a wobbly swinging footbridge to cross. It stretched across a rushing stream that ran through the woods. As Jason and Henry stumbled on to the bridge, Jason said he had to rest. He leaned against the grapevine rail while Henry held on to him.

"This stream is a runoff of the Saugus River," Jason said as he looked at the water flowing under the planks.

Henry, leaning over the rail with wide open eyes said, "Yeah, it is, but it is turning red."

"What do you mean, turning red?" questioned Jason, as he leaned out over the rail to watch a dead British soldier, still wearing his scarlet coat, floating along with the water under the bridge.

"We ought to get him out, oughtn't we?" asked Henry.

"No, let him be," answered Jason.

Henry carried Jason into the house and set him in the rocking chair. The fire had died out. The house seemed cold. Neither Clarice or Phinas were there. Jason called out, "Cee Cee." He got no answer.

Henry built a fire and soon had the place warm and cozy. Jason asked him to bring him something to eat. Henry looked around in the kitchen.

"Jason, I can't find anything but some sour milk. I know you don't want some of that."

The fire was so relaxing Jason had gone to sleep. Henry stretched out on the floor and was soon asleep.

Phinas returned, and his cart was loaded. He was surprised to see Jason and Henry and was anguished that Cee Cee was not there. Where can she be? Why did she leave? Was she accosted, harmed, or persuaded to go into Boston? His suspicions were running wild.

The only answer that Jason gave Phinas was, "I don't know."

Henry said, "Don't worry, I'm sure she's all right. My senses tell me she'll be here 'fore long."

Clarice decided to turn back toward home. She was too tired and hungry to go on, and she realized night was coming on. "What am I thinking about?" she said. "I am needed at home; I feel it in my bones."

Phinas's coming into the house had awakened both sleeping men. His questions about Clarice's absence had alerted their suspicions also.

Jason jumped from his chair, saying in an excited voice, "I have to go and find her."

Henry scrambled to his feet and grabbed Jason, shoving him back into the chair and buttoning his coat to make him warm. He said, "There, Jason, remember you have pneumonia. You ain't goin' anywhere. I'll see to that."

"Damn you, Henry, you're always butting in to stop me from doing what I want to do."

At that moment Clarice came through the doorway. She had gone around the house to the back door. When she saw the cart there, she knew Phinas had returned. She did not see Sam because Henry had stashed him away in the barn for fear he would be stolen, as his former horse had been, from in front of the McKenzie house.

Her joyous surprise at seeing Jason was almost overwhelming. She ran to him and threw herself onto his lap; her arms were around his neck, and she was kissing him all over his face. He put his weak arms around her and returned her kisses.

Clarice looked up at Henry, who was standing over them, and she said, "Pick him up," as she got off his lap, "and carry him upstairs to bed. I will be right behind you."

Phinas left the room. He could not stand to see the outburst of love and emotion taking place between Cee Cee and Jason. While putting away the vittles and other supplies, his eyes were drooping with longing.

As Henry straightened out Jason's legs, removed his boots, and pulled the counterpane over him, Clarice was shaking off her shoes and climbing into bed beside her husband.

She said, "Thank you, Henry, you are our very best friend. Now go downstairs and eat. Phinas has brought lots of food."

Henry asked Phinas, "How did you come by all this grub? I heered all the stores were closed."

Phinas replied, "There was plenty where this came from, and it was free."

Henry poured himself some more cider as he listened to Phinas. "There was a wagon loaded with grub and household supplies turned over in a ditch near the town square. Hardly anybody was looting it because most people already had a wagon load. They had all they could manage, not knowing where they was going. I helped myself until my cart was full. I also found the cart discarded into a creek. I waded in and pulled it out, thinkin' it might come in handy, as you see it did."

"You know, Phinas, I'm beginning to believe luck is on our side."

Clarice laid close to Jason with her arms across his body, whispering sweet words into his ears. She wasn't hearing any words from him but did see the smile on his face and the twinkle in his eyes. He noticed her sniffing and snuffing, along with her kissing.

When she asked, "Jason, when did you last have a bath and a change of clothes? You smell worse than Bessie's dung."

He squeezed her up closer and weakly replied, "It hasn't been possible. There were no facilities in my jail cell, but I will soon be up and able to wash and dress myself."

Clarice replied, "We're not going to wait." She climbed out of bed over him and went downstairs.

She soon returned with a large kettle of very hot water, a bar of soap, and a sponge. She placed the water on a chair which she pulled up to the side of the bed. She began taking off Jason's stockings, then his pants, then his underdrawers. Next came his three shirts, stiff with dirt from the jail's dirt floor and dried sweat and mixed with juice from the May apples. She put her arms under his neck and raised him to a sitting position on the side of the bed. He grabbed hold of the chair back. His eyes were crossed and his attempted talk was blurred.

"Hush up, Jason, don't try to talk." Clarice was not too gentle. She was wondering if he would ever tell her why he was put in jail. She began combing his hair with a fine tooth comb. When she saw lice rolling off his head, she reached for a jar of camphor and lard, which she used for lubricating her stomach to prevent stretch marks. She rubbed a handful of it into Jason's hair and scalp. She said to herself, "I will let it soak in for awhile as I wash the rest of him."

Jason was stark naked. He looked into her eyes and smiled as he placed his hands on her stomach. He felt little Jason Angus McKenzie moving around.

Clarice began with his face and neck. She dipped the sponge into the hot water and rubbed the bar of soap into it. Jason twisted and squinted, but apparently he enjoyed it because his smiles were showing wonderful approval. The touch of Clarice's hands on his body sent chills and hot flashes over him.

When she had washed him down to his privates, she pulled him to his feet. She said, "Hold on to the chair, honey; I'm going to renew your most vital parts."

This remark seemed to arouse Jason into a surge of strength. He burst out laughing and reached out with one arm and drew her up close to him. He held her to his naked body and kissed her lovingly. She returned his embrace and kisses.

She said, "I knew I could make you come alive again."

"Was I that far gone," he asked, "that I couldn't kiss you?"

Clarice called downstairs, "Phinas, bring me another kettle of hot water."

With the clean hot water she washed Jason's hair and vigorously rubbed it dry with a towel; then brushing and combing, she brought his honey-colored strands back to their lustrous natural beauty.

She finished bathing him, put a clean nightshirt on him, changed the linens, and helped him to lie down again.

Phinas was still in the room standing by the window. Oh God, he said to himself, what I would have given to have been in Jason's place for the past hour. He carried the soiled linens, clothing, and bath water downstairs and out to the back yard. He built a fire under the wash tubs and put Jason's dirty clothes in to boil.

Henry was still at the kitchen table staring at cartoon pictures in a year-old Gazette.

"Come here, Phinas," he said, "and tell me what this picture is about."

Phinas looked over Henry's shoulder, "Oh that...it's King George and Governor Hutchinson watching the Oliver Brothers and Lord North force tea down Boston's throat. I think I heard somebody say that Paul Revere is responsible for that picture. But heck, Henry, that is all over now; nothing was done about it."

As Henry got up from his chair, he said, "Like Jason said when we saw a dead soldier float way, 'That's water under the bridge'."

"Yeah," answered Phinas, "it's all over now."

"Well, I ain't sure about that, yet," said Henry, then added, "I guess I better get back to The Pig's Nose. I hope John is still there. He ought to know where we's goin' by now."

Clarice came into their presence just as Henry was leaving. She said to him, "You must not have told Jason about Panzy."

"No, I couldn't. He was too sick to have that sad story laid on him."

Before he left, Henry went up to Jason's bedside. He took Jason's hand and tried to engage him in conversation, but Jason was too incoherent to make sense out of what he was saying. Henry said, "Get well, old pal, I'll be back 'fore long."

Clarice went to the barn. Phinas followed right behind her. "Cee Cee," he asked, "is Jason going to be sick for a long time?"

"No, of course not. He is too strong-minded and determined to get up to stay in bed. As soon as he gets some nourishment soaked into his blood and bones, you'll see him up and taking charge. I hate to think of him finding out about Panzy. He's going to take her passing very hard. He grew up with that horse. You know she was twenty years old. Jason told me she was foaled right here in the old barn."

Phinas went over to the little filly and patted her head. He and Clarice squatted down in front of the baby mare and talked to her.

Clarice said, "I hope little Jason Angus McKenzie will grow up with you and love you like his papa loved your mama."

Next day Jason got up; dressed himself, and, after eating a big breakfast, informed Clarice that he was going over to Concord to look around. "Damn it," he said, "I sure am sorry that I missed the opportunity to kill some of those Lobster Backs."

"Jason…Jason McKenzie," Clarice yelled out, "that fighting was war…it was evil. It was murder. Why in the world would you want to kill my countrymen?"

Jason hesitated a moment, then said, "I thought you wanted to be an American."

"I do, Jason, because you are, but there is no American blood in my body."

"Oh, there is Cee Cee, about eight pounds of it, if my eyes are seeing correctly."

Clarice blushed and turned away, mumbling to herself, "Men…angry men wanting to kill each other. God, have mercy." She lifted her apron and wiped her tears away. Then she turned and ran back to Jason and held on to him. "Please, Jason dear, think of your son. He will need his papa. Please don't crave to fight."

"It's not that I crave to fight, Cee Cee, but it looks like that is the only way we will get our freedom from Britain."

Clarice took Jason's hand and said, "Please, dear, don't go out today; you might take fresh cold."

"Cee Cee, I feel fine. Your loving smile and wonderful scrubbing gave me a new lease on life."

"Maybe so, Jason, but I want you to stay here and talk to me. I have something to tell you."

"Can't it wait? I'm still on sort of a mission. The minutemen need to know where I am."

"What I have to tell you, Jason, is very important. Sad, but important," Clarice said. "First, we have a beautiful little filly, but we lost Panzy. She died while giving birth."

Chapter Thirty-Six

Jason sat down in the rocking chair. He said nothing for several seconds, then he spoke with a soft voice. "I thought she might die; she was just too old. I would never have let her foal again, but you know it was a sly act on Charlie's part. It must have happened in the dark of night, way back in the field. I will surely miss that old mare. Is the filly a healthy one?"

Clarice took his hand and pulled him up from his chair. "Come with me to the barn and see. She is doing well on Bessie's milk and soft gruel made with meal. I even mixed in a handful of cropped grass."

Jason and Clarice were met by the little filly.

Jason said, "She is beautiful, looks just like her mama." He continued, "Tell me, dear, where and when it all happened. How did you manage? Was Phinas any help?"

Clarice took the halter from the peg and slipped it over the filly's head. As if she had been trained to do so, the filly followed closely at her heels. She and Jason seated themselves on the bench at the barn door. The filly stood at their knees while Clarice told Jason the story of the birth of the filly, the death of Panzy, how Phinas ran off to Concord leaving her alone, and the arrival of John Slade and Henry.

"Jason," she said, as she laid her head on his shoulder, "I don't know how I got through it. I kept wondering what you would do and then realizing that I had to think for myself. There was no time for lingering to make decisions. Then, before I had time to rest, people began coming to the door, wanting something or asking questions which I could not answer. I could hear musket fire, the shots were deafening. Then wounded men began stopping for a drink of water or food. There were others in wagons and carriages, stopping, looking for someone. I began to be terribly worried about you…not knowing if you were dead or alive.

"Phinas came back not one minute too soon. He brought money, which I was completely out of, then he went to town to try to find some provisions. I haven't had time to see what he brought back. I think Phinas is wonderful help. I hope he will stay with us, but he seems terribly unhappy here."

"I will talk to him," said Jason. "What he needs is a friend to spark with."

"But nearly everyone has left Lynn. I doubt there is a young girl left that he could spark with." Clarice showed a pondering expression. She knew what was bothering Phinas, but she kept it to herself.

Jason sat very still in the chair near the hearth. It was late in April but not warm enough to do without a fire. Clarice went into the kitchen to take stock of her larder and to put away the provisions that Phinas brought.

Phinas was in the barn. Jason was just sitting there staring at the fire. Clarice was watching him through the kitchen door, walking past it more times than was necessary. Finally, she went back to him, carrying a mug of stew she had made. "Here, darling," she said as she sat on his lap. "What were you thinking? You were way off somewhere else, not here with me and your cozy home making plans for your son."

"No, Cee Cee, I was thinking about how I am going to find Adams and Hancock. I am sure they are hiding somewhere."

She held the mug to his mouth, "Here, taste this, and think how fortunate you are to have a wife who is such a good cook."

Jason sipped at the stew as she held the mug while he hugged her up close to his heart. "I love you so much, Cee Cee, I am willing to die for you."

She jumped up from his lap, spilling the hot stew onto his chest. She screamed at him, "Jason, you fool, I don't want you to die for me. I want you to live for me. If you die I will go back to England."

"Maybe that is what you should do now," he answered her in a loud voice, "and take Tom Fellows with you."

Clarice became angry. She threw the rest of the stew at him, but purposely missed hitting him. "Why do you bring Tom Fellows into this? He is a soldier and has a mission to keep. I have no relation with Tom except that I know him. Are you jealous of an old acquaintance? Jason, I'm appalled at you.

"Why are you so eager to be part of this rebellion? Do you want to be part of a revolution?" She answered her own question, "Yes, I believe you do."

She hastily left the room, ran up to her bedroom, threw some clothes into a blanket, and tied the four corners together making a bundle. She put a shawl around her shoulders. She tiptoed downstairs and out of the house through the back door, the blanket bundle under her arm.

Phinas was in the barn; he heard Charlie whinny, and he saw Clarice crossing the yard. Where was Jason? Where was she going? He followed her.

When she reached the road she stopped to buckle her boot, then she pulled a handkerchief from her pocket and sneezed into it several times. Phinas was coming up behind her. While wiping her nose she was turning her head left and right, looking over the road, as if she didn't know which way to go—and she didn't. She saw two horseback riders coming from the west. They were approaching her at a fast gait.

At the same time Phinas caught up to her. He placed his hand on her shoulder, "Cee Cee, where are you going?"

"Phinas," she answered him, "leave me alone."

Water Under the Bridge

He said, "Wherever you're going, I'm going with you."

The riders were right by her side, and she saw that one of them was Tom Fellows. She sighed in a disgruntled way. To herself she said, What an unsuitable time for him to call. I wonder what he wants with Jason, not thinking for a moment that it was her he wanted to see. Then she thought, Maybe he isn't stopping here. But he did.

When Tom saw that she was carrying a bundle and had been crying, he knew that she was distressed. He determined that she was leaving. Phinas, in trying to comfort her, seemed to be distressed also. He put his arm around her and guided her back to the house. Tom had dismounted and was at the door knocking.

Jason, still dizzy and wobbly, got himself out of his chair and slowly moved across the room and opened the door. He saw Clarice and Phinas coming toward the house.

"Come in, Tom. What are you doing way out here in Lynn?"

"I've come to talk to Clarice. May I speak to her for a moment, please?"

"There she is—right behind you, coming from an escape antic which she has given up. I suppose she got cold feet."

Jason had heard Phinas calling to Clarice when she was crossing the yard. With stumbling feet he had gotten to the window in time to see her blowing her nose and Phinas catching up to her. He made no attempt to follow because he knew he could not do it in his feeble condition.

Tom came in and stood with his back to the fire. "Too bad it won't warm up so we can do without warmth from the hearth."

"Yeah, it is," answered Jason gruffly, while watching Clarice and Phinas cross the room behind him.

Tom called out, "Cee Cee, may I talk to you for a minute?"

"Yes, she replied, "but only if Jason is by my side." She moved over to Jason's chair arm.

Tom said, "I have access to one reservation on a brig leaving New York for Liverpool in three weeks. I thought maybe you would like your baby to be born in England; I reserved the passage with you in mind. I think you ought to go home to your mother. This colony is in much frustration; it may be impossible for you to get a doctor."

Jason's eyes were beginning to show anger. "Tom," he said, "I can see you are encouraging my wife to leave me, but I don't believe you're going to be successful. Is he?" he looked up at Clarice, who looked quite bewildered.

She stroked Jason's hair as she said, "Tom, I do appreciate your concern of me, but I'm not going away from Jason. I also will appreciate it if you will leave me alone. Get out of my life. Go away and stay away. I hate the words I am saying to you. Can't you see I don't want to go back to England? I want to become an American," she added, "forever." Then she said, "I want my baby to be born here, right in the same bed Jason was born in.

"Please leave now, Tom. Good-bye." She bent over and kissed Jason as he shuffled around in his chair. Clarice then left the room and went into the kitchen.

Jason called out to her, "Wait a minute...where were you going when Phinas ran after you?"

"Nowhere, darling, just getting some air and exercise." She wondered why she did such a thing. She said to herself, Sometimes I do act a little crazy. I hope I won't be senile in my old age.

One morning early in the month of May, Clarice and Phinas were sitting at the kitchen table talking. Clarice could hardly reach her plate she was so big. Phinas saw movement under her garments.

"Cee Cee," he said, "Jason ought to be here with you. Do you know where he is?" He continued, "You look like you're going to have the baby very soon."

"No, not yet," she answered. "It will be about two more months. Don't worry, I will be all right. I'm going to send notice to Mrs. Jolly. I may even go there if it is possible. I haven't heard from her since I was there last fall."

Phinas said, "I will go and fetch her if you say so. Maybe Jason will let me drive the chaise."

Clarice smiled at him and said, "You are so thoughtful."

Jason had been gone two days. When he left he was carrying his musket and a bag of shells. Phinas asked him where he was headed. He replied, "Phinas, if you will ask me no questions, I will tell you no lies."

The fact was, Jason was on his way to Salem to try to make contact with Sam Adams to ask off from attending the Second Continental Congress, which was about to take up session in Philadelphia.

His recent bout with pneumonia and Clarice's pregnancy were the excuses he gave. The real reason was a rumor going around that the first order of business would be to call for a Continental Army. He vowed to be one of the first to sign up, to fight for his country.

May was a delightful month. Clarice felt good. Phinas stayed by the little filly and Bessie. There was plenty of food. The spring roses were abundant. The mint and other herbs were spraying their delicious aromas all around the doors and yard. Clarice moved a chair outside, near the front gate. She hoped that someone would come by and stop to talk to give her some news.

Phinas brought the Gazette whenever he could find one when he was at the market. But it was full of antagonisms and false reports, so she thought.

She sang lullabies to the baby she was carrying and talked to him as if he was already born.

She agonized over Jason's frequent absences. She knew he was war-mongering, but she vowed not to ask him any questions. It seemed to stir up his anger and set off his tirade against the British soldiers.

Phinas and Jason would talk while at the barn. Jason was teaching him the ballistics of musketry and warning him of probable serious and dangerous conflict in the near future.

Each time Jason returned home he would assure Clarice that he would locate a doctor to attend her delivery, but he knew it was almost impossible.

Later in May, Jason came home, and riding behind him on Charlie's back was an Indian girl, very young, probably fifteen. Clarice watched her swing her leg over the saddle and jump to the ground. She heard Jason say to her, "Come on into the house and meet your mistress."

Clarice backed away from the door and closed it. Jason held on to the girl's hand and kicked the door lightly with his foot. "Why did you shut the door in our face?" he asked of Clarice.

"Because I am afraid of Indians. Who is this one you are holding by your hand?"

"My dear, this is Shashaw's daughter. I have bought her to be your companion and the baby's nurse. You remember my telling you about Shashaw. She was my nurse and body guard until I was ten years old. She went away and married an Indian, and I never saw her again until I met up with her last week at the camp. She was in Cambridge looking for work and a buyer for Blue Feather here, to keep her safe from British soldiers and other mean men of sorts. I paid five pounds for her, for you. She is fifteen years old, and look how pretty she is."

Clarice didn't say anything, but she did take Blue Feather's hand and led her to the kitchen table. She poured tea into three cups. One for Jason, one for Blue Feather, and one for herself. Phinas had brought a whole bale of tea from the food he found in the overturned wagon. They sat at the table. Blue Feather and Clarice kept staring at each other while Jason gulped his tea.

After a few minutes, Clarice spoke to Jason, "I don't see how she is going to be much help if she can't speak English."

"Oh, she knows plenty of words, and she understands everything. I couldn't let her be bought by someone who would make a slave out of her. I believe she will learn very quickly to be your companion."

Clarice left the table and went to the barn where Phinas was currying the little filly.

"Phinas," she said, "I think Jason is going away again and I feel lonesome already. Did you see the Indian girl he brought for me?"

He answered, "Yes." After a moment of looking into Clarice's eyes, he said, "Jason told me to pack my things; he is taking me with him."

This news brought a sigh and big puff of breath to the astonished Clarice.

"Well, I won't let you go. I need you to look after Bessie and the filly, put in a garden, and to run the errands. Jason just wasn't thinking."

She sat down on the bench and gasped for breath. Phinas stood by her and patted her shoulder.

She said, "You are my best friend, Phinas. You must tell Jason that you can't go with him."

Jason came out of the house, and Blue Feather followed him. Phinas went into the barn.

Clarice looked at Jason with agony in her eyes. She stood up. "Jason, dear," she said, "Phinas tells me that you want him to go with you when you return to wherever it is you are going."

Jason stood by her but didn't say anything. He just looked at her lovingly.

Clarice, after a moment, asked, "Where are you going, Jason? And why? And for how long?" She continued, "I feel pretty close to delivery...I think if you love me, you will be here with me."

Jason put his arms around her and said, "Don't worry, I'm sending a messenger to Boston to ask Mrs. Jolly to come. If she can't come, here is," pointing, "the girl I've bought for you. She has brought many Indian babies into the world."

"Jason, I'm not an Indian woman." Clarice was indignant. She pulled away from Jason's arm and went into the house.

Clarice went to her bedroom and laid down across her bed without removing any of her clothes. She felt depressed and baffled at the thoughts of an Indian girl delivering her baby.

Blue Feather soon came to the side of the bed. She put her forefinger across her lips to indicate no words were forthcoming. She lifted Clarice's hand and squeezed it affectionately. Clarice smiled at her. Blue Feather loosened the buckles of Clarice's shoes and removed them from her feet. She massaged Clarice's feet and toes. It felt good. She stretched and twisted into a more comfortable position, indicating that she approved of the attention.

Jason entered the room. Blue Feather left and went downstairs. She saw Phinas at the hearth, so she stood beside him and watched as he covered potatoes with hot ashes.

Jason sat on the side of the bed and removed his shoes, then he laid back, taking Clarice into his arms. He whispered to her, "I love you more than anything or anybody in the world. I am glad you turned down Tom's offer for passage to England, but you ought to go somewhere for awhile. Boston and its suburbs are dangerous ground. Do you think that perhaps Parson and Sister Smith might take you and the baby for a spell? I think Connecticut will be safe from any conflict."

Clarice squirmed out of Jason's arms. She didn't answer him right away. He raised himself to his elbow and asked, "What do you think about going to the Smiths?"

She answered, "There isn't time. I don't want to go anywhere. I want to know where you are going. Why can't you stay here with me until my time comes?"

She got out of bed and went and stood in front of her mirror, sizing herself up and down. She said, "I hope Mother Jolly can come. She is good at midwifery."

Jason swung himself out of the bed. He walked over to the window and stood there looking out toward the road. He said, "We will know tomorrow when the messenger returns, but I won't be here tomorrow. I have to leave later today, and I have to have an assistant. That is why I'm taking Phinas with me."

The messenger that went to Mrs. Jollys' returned to the McKenzie home next morning with a letter from Mrs. Moody stating that Mrs. Jolly was in Provincetown because Dora was also having a baby. Blue Feather seemed to understand that the news was not good when she saw Clarice's eyes fill up with tears. The affection between the two girls was growing stronger.

Blue Feather took Clarice's arm and steered her to a chair at the table. She set a plate in front of the shaking Clarice with a nourishing breakfast served upon it. "Here," she said, then she said, "eat," and then she said, "good."

Clarice looked at the girl and said, "Thanks."

Blue Feather busied herself at the hearth. Clarice motioned for her to come and sit and eat. Blue Feather did sit and eat.

After the meal was finished, Clarice suggested they take a walk. "I want to show you our magic rock, Shiny Squatt." She also wanted to be away from the house when Jason and Phinas left. She said, "Goodbyes are becoming too much."

Jason watched from the barn door as the two women crossed the pasture. They were holding hands and smiling at each other, like two school girls.

"I've walked this path to the rock many times," Clarice told Blue Feather. "It is so big and solid, it seems to give me assurance that the future will be bright."

Blue Feather nodded her head up and down. There was a sparkle in her eyes.

Jason and Phinas left. They each had a blanket roll and a sack with potatoes and apples. Phinas was riding Charlie. Jason was walking and carrying his musket.

The sun was beaming down hot on Shiny Squatt. The warmth felt good to Clarice as she stood up close with her back pressed against it.

Blue Feather walked around the rock, one hand smoothing it. She said to Clarice, "Warm," then she said, "feel good."

Clarice slid her feet out in front of her as she slipped her butt along the rock and sat flat down on the ground. "Oh, my goodness," she exclaimed, "that was some bump." At that time her water broke and a sharp pain raced through her groin.

Blue Feather saw at once what was happening. She unbuckled her belt and let her skirt fall to the ground. She took hold of Clarice's feet and pulled her onto the spread skirt. She quickly examined the riling Clarice. She nodded her head up and down. She blurted out the words, "Baby come soon...be all right...soon."

Clarice was surprised at the words Blue Feather knew, especially in a moment of excitement.

In less than an hour, Jason Angus McKenzie the Third was yelling his head off. Well, Blue Feather had vigorously spanked his behind.

Clarice was in an emotional state. She asked Blue Feather, "What are we going to do now?"

The girl was a bit bewildered, at first, but she reached under Clarice's skirt and tore a big piece from her petticoat. After cutting the cord, she wrapped the baby in the piece of petticoat and laid him in Clarice's arms. She then put her arms under Clarice and lifted her into her arms. She took off in a loping gait, carrying Clarice and the baby. She reached the house in about twenty minutes.

The astonishing part of this birthing was the knowledge and speed with which the Indian girl used her expertise.

As soon as they were in the kitchen, Blue Feather made tea. She put a couple of spoonfuls into the baby's mouth. She set a large mugful in front of Clarice and said, "Drink now."

Clarice unwrapped the baby from his petticoat covering and examined his body; his arms, legs, ears, eyes, and penis. She bent over and kissed his stomach, then his cheeks. She said to him, "You seem to be perfect in every way. Your eyes are blue like your papa's, and your little bit of fuzz is blond. I love you and welcome you." She continued while the baby clasped her finger, "I know your papa will be overjoyed. I hope we can get word to him very soon."

Blue Feather came to the table with a kettle of warm water and a wash basin. She bathed and oiled the squirming infant. He fell asleep before she was through. She laid him in the cradle that Jason had made. Then she helped Clarice to the bed which had been put into the great room. Blue Feather was sleeping in the room that Matthew and Sally had used.

Jason Angus McKenzie the Third seemed to be quite pleased to be out and about. Blue Feather cuddled and carried him, even to the barn to show him to Bessie and Panzy.

Clarice spent part of the first week after his birth writing letters to her parents, the Smiths, and Julia, announcing the baby's arrival, expressing her joy and blessings. She heard nothing from Jason. Her heart was heavy for that reason.

Blue Feather was a constant reminder of her good fortune in having such a helpful companion. The girl's vocabulary was improving every day. She now could say, "Cee Cee", "baby", "Panzy", "Bessie", "cook", "eat", "wash", "clean", "milk", "cake", and others as they came to her mind. It was a joy to see her play with the baby and watch him hold on to her braids as she bent over him.

She was happy to be in a good home. She hummed a lullaby she knew, "Rock-a-bye baby in the tree top. When the wind blows the cradle will rock."

Jason was extremely busy at his station, a small shabby tent set up on the Harvard campus in Cambridge. His job was to record, muster out the minutemen, and enlist them into the Organized Militia. They were issued quarters and rations once they were in the militia. Most of the newly enlisted militia lived nearby and would go home at night. Tents were popping up all around

Cambridge, and activities pertaining to drilling, digging trenches, and musket fire were indications of things to come.

As days passed and Jason's thoughts got to wandering toward home and Clarice, he informed his superior officer that he needed to go home to see about things. He asked for permission for Phinas to also have a few days. The permission was granted, for three days only. Phinas was now a full-fledged member of the Massachusetts Militia.

When Clarice saw Jason approaching the house and Phinas loping along behind him, she quickly gathered the baby up into her arms and ran to meet them.

To say astonishment filled their faces would be putting it mildly. Jason had not expected the baby for several months.

Clarice called out on reaching him, "Darling, look who's here!"

Jason beamed at her; his face turned red. Before saying anything, he swooped her and the baby into his arms and began kissing first Cee Cee, then Angus. He moved the blanket off the baby's body and began looking him over. He asked, "Cee Cee, is everything in good condition?"

"Perfect," she answered.

He lifted the baby from Clarice's arms into his own and went skipping along, bouncing Angus up and down. Clarice was following at Jason's heels.

"Gosh," said Phinas, "I wish I had got a look."

"Oh, you will, Phinas, and expect to see the most beautiful and most perfect baby in the world."

Jason sat down in the rocking chair and began rocking and singing. Angus's deep blue eyes were sparkling.

"Look, Cee Cee, he's smiling. See how my finger tips fit into his dimples?"

"Jason, that's not a smile, that's gas."

He looked at his wife, "Anyway, I love it. Now tell me about the birthing."

"We owe it all to Blue Feather. It was a splendid performance. She was a wonderful midwife. It took place at Shiny Squatt. She did everything just right—and quickly—it took less than an hour. She took a buckle from my shoe to cut the umbilical cord. She tore a piece from my petticoat to wrap the baby. She carried me and the baby all the way from Shiny Squatt."

"Why were you way out there?"

"Just taking a walk, to get away from the house when you were leaving."

While discussing the birth, they saw two British soldiers coming toward the house.

Clarice took the baby from Jason and carried him upstairs. She placed him in the middle of the big feather bed. She threw a light cover over him, kissed him on top of his fuzzy little head, and told him to sleep. She returned to the great room. The soldiers were talking in abusive language to Jason, who was ordering them out of his house.

"I have orders to search this house for weapons," the largest of the two said. He flashed a search warrant into Jason's face, which Jason grabbed and tore to bits.

"Go upstairs and look around," ordered the large one to the smaller one.

"No, no," screamed Clarice, "we have no weapons in this house."

The soldier bounded up the stairs.

At that moment Jason jumped the other one. They began a real tough scuffle. They fell to the floor, and Clarice went down on her knees trying to pull Jason off the soldier. She tugged at him without success. The swearing and fighting went on.

Clarice got to her feet. The soldier came jumping down from upstairs. He jumped on Phinas who was trying to get to the kitchen.

The big one scrambled from Jason's grasp, grabbed the smaller one's hand and yelled out, "Come on, let's get out of here. There are no guns here." They ran down the road.

Clarice had returned to the upstairs and was screaming wretchedly. Jason ran to her. Clarice was on her knees in the middle of the bed, hovered over the baby, who was dead. She was rolling him from side to side, she held him up and pounded his back, she breathed into his mouth. She screamed and cried out, "Darling, darling, please come back; I love you."

Jason stood by her, horrified. He was trying to understand the actions of the moment.

Clarice cried out, "Jason, dear, that horrible soldier killed our beautiful baby. Angus is gone. I can't bring him back. Oh, dear God, I can't bear it." She rolled over on her back and cried uncontrollably.

Jason moved her over and picked up the baby.

Clarice cried out, "He's gone, I can't bring him back."

He could tell that the infant was quite dead. He begun shaking him. He asked, "How do you know that the soldier killed him?"

She answered, "Because he flipped the feather bed over, turning it upside down. I pulled Angus out from under the feather bed. I left him here sleeping. It must have been an accident. I do not believe a British soldier would deliberately kill a baby. It must have been an accident," she repeated. "He smothered the baby under the feather bed. Oh, God…have mercy."

Clarice's words were coming out irrationally. She was hysterical.

Jason was walking the floor with the baby in his arms, talking to him, "You sweet little son of mine, how can you leave us so soon? You just got here. We prepared for you. You were our long-awaited love gift. Please come back." Jason carried the lifeless body downstairs. He sat in the rocking chair and rocked him and hummed an old cradle song.

Blue Feather came and stood by Jason's chair. She tipped a cup of hot tea to his lips. He sipped it and nodded his head at her for thanks. Phinas had gone to the barn; he was good at escaping an ordeal.

Clarice stayed upstairs, lying across the bed, sobbing and talking to herself, Never again will I trust a British soldier. Nor ever again will I have respect for my country. This is dastardly, cruel, and inexcusable. There were no guns in or under this bed or in this house. It surely was an accident, but I have no precious son.

Jason placed the baby in the cradle by the window in the great room. He went upstairs and gathered Clarice up into his arms and carried her downstairs and placed her in the chair by the cradle. He asked Blue Feather to fix her some biscuits and jam. He donned his hat and said to Clarice, "I'm going to town to hunt down those sons of bitches who killed our baby. I'm heading straight for Gage's headquarters." He left.

Clarice spent most of the next two days sitting in the chair by the cradle or rocking the baby which she held close to her heart.

Jason neither ate nor slept. He went from camp to camp, looking closely into faces, trying to recognize the faces that rushed into his house looking for arms and smothering the baby.

Clarice called Blue Feather to come and squat in front of her. She said to the girl, "Have Phinas dig a grave under the tree where the school children's picnic table is. Make it three feet long, two feet wide, and four feet deep. Let no roots or rocks be growing in it. We will bury Angus this afternoon."

Phinas did a very neat job. Blue Feather lined the grave with rose petals and daisies.

Clarice put Angus's new linen dress on him, the one with his grandmother's petticoat lace around the hem. She pinned a rosebud on his shoulder. She wrapped him in the blue blanket she knitted last spring. She placed the lace cap on his head that his papa had worn for his christening. She kissed him several times, then slowly she carried him out to the grave.

She handed the little blue bundle to Blue Feather who dropped to her knees and placed it into the rose-petalled grave. She stayed on her knees and began an Indian lullaby chant as she bobbed up and down on the grass alongside the grave, keeping one hand on the little body.

Phinas, with Bessie on one side of him and Panzy on the other, stood back looking on.

At last, when the sun had gone down, Blue Feather began shoveling the dirt into the grave. After each shovelful she threw a handful of rose petals. Very soon there was a rose-covered mound.

Clarice refused to get up from the ground. She said to Blue Feather, "Leave me here alone; I'm going to stay here all night."

Chapter Thirty-Seven

It was after midnight when Jason came walking toward his house. He saw the faint flickering from a candle. It came from a mound under the picnic tree. He went to it and found the mound and Clarice lying alongside it. He stooped and lifted her hands and kissed them. He pulled her to her feet and hugged her up close.

"Darling, darling, my sweet, sweet baby...you can't stay here; the grass is wet, and the air is damp. I saw the flickering candle, and I thought it was a firefly."

He lifted her into his arms and carried her into the house. Blue Feather got up from the other side of the grave and followed them.

Clarice barely opened her eyes. She had sobbed until her eyelids were swollen and red. Jason held her on his lap and cuddled her until daylight came. He said to her, "I have to go back to Cambridge. I hate to leave you, but I must."

"Are you walking?" she asked.

"Yes, dear, Charlie was lame when we left. I hope he has been taken care of. That horse is too old to be working so hard."

Before the sun was high, Phinas built a picket fence around the little mound and painted it blue.

Jason and Phinas smelled the camp, even before they reached it. It had the odor of rotten potatoes. Boots had been kicked from sweaty feet and were lying around in the mud, while their owners tramped about barefooted.

It was sultry hot, and everywhere there could be found a scrap of food, there were also a million flies. Water was spilling over the troughs and barrels, making a muddy slush underfoot.

When the men saw Jason approaching, they ran to him and fell upon his arms and shoulders. The cry was, "Hey, captain, what in hell are we hanging around here for? Dismiss us and tell us to go home."

Soon they were in Charlestown. Jason felt heavy-hearted. He said to them, "I am under orders also. I have to obey the general."

General Putnam had given orders to fortify Breeds Hill—a wise decision. He called for Colonel William Prescott to unify the militia into squadrons and set them to digging redoubts. Breeds Hill was steeper and would be harder to get to. The British used their bayonets more than their muskets. They carried more equipment than the Patriots. What the British did not know was that the Massachusetts Militia, along with the help of the Connecticut Militia, had built a stone and rail fence along the Charlestown coast. This helped to turn them back for several hours.

Jason stood in the mud under a tree all night, handing out trenching tools and small packages of bread and meat to men who went trudging by cursing their plight.

Clarice and Blue Feather were having their morning coffee when they heard the noise. It shook the house and a large billow of smoke filled the air.

"My Lord, what's that?" screamed Clarice, as she ran to the back door, Blue Feather right behind her.

The British had discovered the redoubts being built and immediately opened fire upon it, by orders of General Howe from his powerful warship anchored just outside Charlestown.

That blast awakened everyone for miles around, even General Gage who at that moment decided to eject all those "damn Patriots from those hills." He entrusted the job to General Howe.

When Howe encountered the troops of Colonel John Stark with his New Hampshire soldiers, and Captain Thomas Knowlton with his troops from Connecticut, and the barrier fence they had built, he began the initial attack.

Clarice and Blue Feather were scared beyond self-control. Clarice took Blue Feather's hand and asked, "What are we going to do?"

Blue Feather answered in a quaking voice, "Run."

"No, no," replied Clarice, "let's go up to the lookout and see if we can see anything." Clarice ran to get the spyglass.

Soon the two women were squeezing through the narrow stairway. Looking through the spyglass, Clarice saw many British ships anchored offshore. Also many canoes unloading redcoats onto the sand at Charlestown. She saw them tearing down the fence and scrambling up the steep muddy hill.

There was so much smoke and fire, Clarice cried out, "Oh, my poor darling. May God protect you from all harm." She was crying and praying.

Blue Feather was cowering in the corner, whimpering and shivering. They stayed on the lookout for several hours. The sun got blistering hot, and they became thirsty and hungry.

Clarice turned the spyglass toward the mound under the tree in the pasture. "There," she said, "is my other darling. He is safe."

The noise did not subside until very late in the night.

Clarice took Blue Feather's hand and led her to her own bed. The two women lay there staring at the ceiling. Clarice was mumbling prayers, but Blue Feather was very quiet.

At the site of the finished battle there was much weeping and moaning, blood mixed with mud, broken muskets, bits of food and clothes. Contingents of men from both sides were cooperating with each other, picking up dead bodies.

Some six handsomely dressed officers from the Massachusetts Militia took away, on a stretcher, the body of Doctor Joseph Warren who was not a member of the Massachusetts Militia but a volunteer.

June seventeenth of 1775 will be a day to remember throughout posterity. There were 2,400 British troops engaged in the actual fighting. They had 1,500 casualties. The Americans had 3,200 troops in the battle proper, and had 440 casualties. These were caused mostly by bayonets.

Next morning Jason left his cot and proceeded to look around. He walked to the corral and spotted Charlie standing in the mud holding up one front foot. The old horse looked sad, and Jason knew Charlie's days were numbered.

There was a carcass collection sledge nearby, picking up.

"This is the time," said Jason, as he walked over to his old friend, patted his neck, and said to him, "Thanks, old boy, for a job well done." He lifted his blunder bust and shot Charlie right behind his ear. He watched the front legs wobble and crumple and the back legs fold and fall into the mud.

Jason's eyes filled with tears as he said, "There, old boy, you won't have to fight for your freedom." Jason took a few steps to the tiny tent which he and Phinas were sharing. He never looked back. He didn't see Charlie being loaded onto the carcass pickup.

Jason shook Phinas out of a deep sleep and said to him, "Wake up, get up, I need someone to talk to."

The boy sat on the edge of the cot. "What you want to talk about, Jason?"

"I don't know, kid, just about anything."

The atmosphere was noisy and smoky; Charlestown was smoldering. Not one house was left standing, and the air was full of ashes and smoke. Jason coughed and complained of a headache.

Phinas said his eyes were burning out. He reached for the tent flap and closed it. He asked Jason if he reckoned they would get anything to eat that day. There was some green apples and boiled potatoes spread out on a table about fifty yards away.

British soldiers and Patriot Militia were weaving around amongst each other, seemingly with not much animosity. British officers were yelling, giving orders of retreat. It took half a day to muster their regulars into formation and march them back to their ships or camps near Boston.

In about six hours Howe's army was all quiet, settled down for the moment.

Someone was scratching on the side of the tent. Jason pulled back the flap. Standing outside, muddy and worn, were Tom Moore and Henry Prentiss, two old teammates from the tea party.

"Hello, old friend," said Tom Moore. "We have been looking for you. Did you get into the fight?"

Jason answered, "Well, it was hard not to, but I don't think I hit anybody. The damned old rusty musket just wouldn't fire. Phinas here," he tapped the boy's shoulder, "thinks he knocked out a lobster back, but he doesn't know if he killed him. Come on in," Jason invited.

The two men dropped to their knees and crawled into the squalid tent. It was getting dark, and a gale was whipping the sides of the tent. The dim lantern was running low in oil, but the men kept wadding rags, their torn shirts, into wads and burning them for light so they could play pinochle. Sometimes there was laughter. No one knew what was coming next.

Tom and Henry had volunteered with the Connecticut forces. They had fought all day. They were so weary and hungry, and they fell asleep before they finished their card game.

It was six A.M., June 19, when Jason was awakened by the sound of a woman's voice. He crawled over the two sleeping visitors and opened the flap.

A woman with two large baskets of food hung across her shoulders with a water yoke was calling out, "Come and get it, chicken and biscuits." She was one of Charlestown's prominent women who, as she said, "Wanted to help the rebels."

Tom and Henry had also heard the call and were quickly scrambling toward the woman and her basket of food.

She slapped their hands as they attempted to reach under the covers. "Wait your turn," she scolded them.

She soon had two empty baskets. Tired, hungry militia men gathered around her greedily eating and asking for more. "I'll be back later with more. We women will cook all day. We want to help," she kept saying.

Jason, Tom, and Henry each had their share, and Jason had stashed away in his pocket a chicken breast and biscuit for Phinas who, in spite of noises of many kinds, was still sleeping.

Clarice saw John Jolly before he reached the gate. He was walking, carrying a satchel. Her heart skipped a beat, and she looked around to see where Blue Feather might be. She heard the girl singing as she pitched hay to Bessie and Panzy from the barn loft.

Clarice said, "Thank goodness she is busy." She opened the door to John Jolly. She noticed he had plucked a rose from the bush by the gate. Before she could properly greet him and invite him in, he had his arms around her and was tucking the rose into her hair.

"You look wonderful," he said. "I've missed you terribly." He was hugging her up close, and his eyes were beaming at her. "Cee Cee, where is Jason?" He had hopes that Jason was away somewhere.

"I wish I knew," she answered. I suppose he is in Cambridge working with the militia. We were scared to death during the big battle last Saturday, but we know very little about the outcome. I'm very worried about Jason and Phinas."

John asked, "Whom do you refer to besides yourself when you say 'we'?"

"Oh, I haven't told you yet about Blue Feather. I have an Indian girl companion. Right now she is working in the barn."

John said, "I am glad you are not alone here with a baby."

He did not know about the baby's death. When he said that, about her 'alone with a baby,' Clarice laid her head on his shoulder and began to cry. She tearfully told him about the British soldiers looking for arms and smothering the baby.

She finally got control of herself and said, "Let's sit awhile, John. Tell me about Dora. Has she had her baby?"

"Yes, she had a fine boy; they are doing well. She wants to stay in Provincetown. I'm going to let her do as she pleases because I don't want to be around her anymore. She is becoming like a witch." He hesitated, "Anyhow, Cee Cee, if I can't have you, I don't want anybody."

Clarice made no responsive remarks to John's words. She got up from her chair and started toward the kitchen. "I'll make us something to eat," she said.

John reached out to her as she passed him. He pulled her onto his lap and began kissing her.

"Quit it, John, I can't bear any affection from you right now."

"Don't you care for me just a little bit, Cee Cee?" John waited for her answer. She forced herself off of his lap. He tried to hold her.

She rushed into the kitchen and opened the door and called out, "Feather, come here." She left off "Blue." At that moment she was too excited to get everything right.

The girl came immediately.

"Make some coffee, dear."

John sat squelched in his chair, head down. Suddenly he picked up his satchel and exited the door, calling out as he left, "We'll have coffee another time."

Clarice cried out, to herself, Oh, dear, what have I done to my friend? I've hurt his feelings; I do hope he won't take it to heart. I need him at times. I believe he is a lonesome man.

Clarice was thinking and saying these remorseful thoughts when she observed Feather watching her. She said to the girl, "That man is a dear friend; his name is John Jolly. He lives at his farm west of here. He has been away, and I've hurt his feelings."

Feather nodded her head affirmatively and said, "Friend."

In a few days Clarice discovered someone had left a basket of fresh corn on the front door step. She knew it was John Jolly.

In the middle of July, Jason and Phinas came home. They were excited about the newly appointed commander in chief who was already busy recruiting men into a Continental Army. His headquarters had been established in Cambridge, on the Harvard campus.

Jason described him to Clarice. "He is rich. He is from the colony of Virginia. Was an officer in the French and Indian War. Has been a surveyor, a familiar with all the colonies. He is handsome, stately, friendly, and benevolent."

Clarice sat still and listened while Jason went on and on about George Washington. At last she broke into Jason's adulation, "Why did Congress appoint a man from Virginia? Why not Massachusetts? Why wasn't Mister Hancock appointed or Mister Adams?"

Jason pondered her question, then said, "It was because of his experience, his ability to get along with men. He did not want the command, but he realized the importance of the commander's expertise. He also was eager for freedom from England. He thought, in fact he knew, that he was the most qualified for the leader. Also, Mister Hancock and Mister Adams are needed in the Congress.

"George Washington left a fine farm, a wife, and two stepchildren. He had to make a big sacrifice to take over a very unpredictable and dangerous job.

"All of our militia men are rushing to sign up for six months in the Continental Army. By the end of six months we will be rid of the British plague."

Clarice was not as thrilled as Jason expected her to be.

He asked, "Aren't you happy that we have a real honest-to-goodness army with uniforms and artillery?"

She haughtily answered, "No."

"Why not?" he scolded her.

"Because you will always be gone. You may even get killed; let Congress settle the problem. I know that some of the soldiers on both sides will be children...look at Phinas."

Jason turned toward Phinas, who was nearby. He said, "He is in no danger. He is not a soldier. He will be with me as an assistant. We will protect each other."

There was a long pause before Clarice left the room. As she did so she said, "I'm going to see where Feather is. I'm worried that she might run away; she is so scared of the noise."

Jason called after her, "Are you leaving off the part of her name?"

"Yes," Clarice called back. "From now on it's just Feather."

She and Phinas came right back into the house. Feather stayed outside. Phinas looked into the kitchen cupboard, and Clarice was watching him.

He spoke to her, "Cee Cee, I'm almost sick with starvation. There is such a little to eat at camp, also we have no change of clothes. It's a good thing it is summer or we would freeze." He took from the cupboard some boiled ears of corn, some cold fried potatoes, and some jam.

Clarice watched him eat, she thought, He really is half starved. She got out a basket and began to fill it for him to carry back to camp.

Jason came into the kitchen and sat opposite Phinas. He watched Clarice filling the basket. He said, "Honey, do you remember where we got that basket?"

She ran her hand over it and replied, "Parson Smith left it on our door step the morning after our marriage."

She turned to Phinas, "Please bring it back the next time you come; I will fill it again."

Jason looked at Clarice with love in his eyes. "Dear, will you come upstairs with me for a little while, so we can talk privately? Also, I have to get some clean drawers and shirts from the bureau."

"Of course," she replied, "I have already patched and darned all the clothes you have. You are in short supply."

Phinas understood. He picked up his plate and headed for the barn. Feather was already there, bathing Panzy.

Clarice took Jason's hand and led the way to their bedroom. It was midday. The sun was streaming through the window. Clarice drew the shade. The air was warm and perfumed with mint and roses. It was the end of July. Angus would have been two months old.

At sundown the two men left. Both of them kissed and hugged Clarice and shook Feather's hand. She drew away from their hugging and kissing.

Phinas was carrying the basket of food. Jason was carrying the bundles of clothes across his shoulders, tied to the ends of a short pole.

The two girls wiped their tears as they turned back into the house. Some time in mid-August Phinas brought a letter from Jason to Clarice. It was not good news. Jason was sick with smallpox and was quarantined. He was in the camp infirmary and was not too bad off, but she was not to attempt visiting him. She would be turned back by sentinels.

This news sent Clarice into a frenzy. She stamped her foot. "They can't keep me away; I have to take care of him."

Phinas saw her emotional outburst, he said, "Cee Cee, consider yourself; you might catch it."

"No matter," she answered, "I'm going to him."

"It's a long walk and dangerous," said Phinas, trying to dissuade her.

"Hush up," she said.

She called to Feather, "Stay here and do your chores. I will be back soon. I'm going to Jason; he is sick. I'm going to bring him home." Clarice knew that she did not know how she was going to do it, but she knew she was determined.

She donned a bonnet and followed Phinas back to the camp near the burned down Charlestown. He led her to the infirmary and to Jason's cot. The sentinels were nowhere in sight.

In spite of being warned by an attendant not to get too close, Clarice fell on to Jason's chest and held his face between her hands and kissed him. He was too sick to pay attention to her, but he did manage a few words to ask Phinas why he allowed her to come.

"I told her not to attempt it. It's dangerous."

Clarice held Jason's hand as she said, "Darling, I'm going to take you home and take care of you myself."

In a weakened voice he pleaded with her not to do it.

She then frankly asked him, "Wouldn't you rather be at home?"

He smiled at her, "You know I would, but what about you and Feather?"

"We'll see," she replied.

She turned to Phinas, who was standing behind her. "Go out to that corral we passed and select a horse. A strong enough one to carry Jason, preferably a mare, young and healthy."

Phinas asked, "How will I know which horse I should take? Where will I get permission?"

Clarice looked sternly at him, "Phinas, we haven't time to fool around with permission. Just get a bridle somewhere, go to that corral, and borrow a mare. You can bring her back later."

He obeyed Clarice's orders and was soon back at the infirmary. There was a fine mare tied to the hitching post outside.

Clarice gave him a hug when he told her. She said, "Now, give me some help getting him out of here and onto the horse's back."

Jason put his arm around each and walked, dragging his feet, to the hitching post. Clarice and Phinas lifted him to a crosswise position on his stomach across the horse's back.

In about an hour and a half they were unloading him at his own house. They carried him upstairs to bed. Clarice called out to Feather to leave the house until they got Jason settled upstairs. Feather understood it was because smallpox was so contagious.

Phinas said, "I better be getting back to the corral with that horse."

"Never mind," said Clarice, "I think I will keep the horse. I need a horse. That mare is a real blessing. Yes, that will be her name—Blessing."

The disease got worse, Jason was near the point of death. Clarice was a constant nurse, and Feather placed food and supplies on the stairs, which Clarice picked up from the steps. The Indian girl did not have to be told what to do. She even went into the ice cellar and chopped ice. She made onion and mustard poultices. She cooked dandelions and strained the pot liquor for Jason to drink. Clarice bathed and massaged Jason daily. She watched over him through all the long nights.

In six weeks he began to recover. It was then the end of September. He was talkative and could walk around the room. Phinas had come and gone several times during that period, trying to keep in contact with activities at the camp and also help out at the house.

One day Phinas informed Clarice that he found out that if they hadn't taken Blessing she would have starved. She had belonged to an officer who was killed at the Bunker Hill battle.

As soon as Jason could manage himself without help, he returned to Colonel Prescott's company, still in camp at Bunker Hill.

Clarice and Feather cleaned and fumigated every nook and corner of the house. They burned sulphur in the fireplace and fanned the smoke throughout the rooms. Neither of them, nor Phinas, caught the dreadful disease. Jason survived it strong and unscarred. For this Clarice gave praise to the Lord every day, and others gave praise to her.

During the time Jason had been home, sick with smallpox, dangerous attempts to capture British forts had been undertaken. Fort Ticonderoga had been seized without a single fatality. The British garrison was then abandoned, leaving many cannon and other artillery in the hands of the Patriots (or colonials). George Washington spent many hours in desperation, especially at night when he couldn't sleep. He was having much trouble with the militia officers.

For a long time the siege of Boston was no more than a bluff. If the British had attacked the city, Washington could not have stopped them. The Royal Navy controlled the harbor and the sea.

The colonials had no heavy arms to shell the port. Washington had orders from Congress to send Henry Knox to Ticonderoga to bring back the artillery. Plans were to fortify Dorchester Heights from which the harbor could be shelled.

Henry Knox was a friend of Jason McKenzie. Knox had a book store on Charles Street. McKenzie had a bakery on Charles Street. Knox knew Jason had excellent skills as a cook and baker and also gunnery.

When Jason returned to camp, Knox went to Washington and requested Jason be assigned to his company as chief mess officer, also Artillery Captain. Washington acted affirmatively on the request.

Jason got permission for Phinas to go along as his aide, so long as he would provide for him and take responsibility for the boy's safety.

Phinas was delighted. He had always wanted to tramp in the woods. The 912 company that General Knox headed was made up of the strongest men. When Jason told Tom Moore and Henry Prentiss that he was going to Ticonderoga with Henry Knox, they too asked to be transferred to Knox.

Jason told Phinas that they must go home for a few days to let Clarice know and to make some plans for her.

Clarice had suspected that something was going to keep Jason away from her. Sometimes she cried; other times she bolstered her ego and pretended not to care. Once she said to herself, "I must get used to being without a husband, but I don't have to be without a man. I have John Jolly."

Then there came a letter, by way of stage; Feather picked it up at the stage station. It was from Julia. Please come and stay with me in New York. I hear there is much trouble in Boston. It is peaceful here. Boston under siege must put much hardship on everyone.

Clarice read the letter over and over again. She thought, Maybe I will go to New York, just for the winter. Feather will go with me. John Jolly will take Panzy and Bessie to his place. I will send the chickens to the camp; they need the food. Phinas said he was starving most of the time.

When Jason and Phinas arrived at home, before Jason took her into his arms, she knew that he was bearing heavy news. She saw that Phinas was happy about something and heavy-hearted about something else. It showed plainly on his face.

"Well," she said as she returned Jason's kisses, "tell me when you are leaving again. Will I have time to pack some food?" She turned to Phinas, "Did you bring back the basket?"

Jason thought she was acting facetious, but he knew she had a right to be frustrated. He was too much away. He thought, If she had known what the future would be, she probably would never have married me.

Clarice said, "Jason, I have made some plans. We have to talk about them. I need some advice." The two went upstairs.

"First," said Jason, "let me tell you what's happening to Phinas and me."

She answered, "If it is good news I will be happy to hear it, but if it's bad news I don't want to hear it."

"Well, dear, I can't tell you if it's good or bad."

"Then go ahead, tell me," she said.

Jason cleared his throat as he led his wife to the edge of the bed where they sat side by side. He began, "Phinas and I are going on a mission. I have been assigned to general Henry Knox's brigade to go to Fort Ticonderoga."

Clarice looked puzzled. She had never heard of Ticonderoga. She imagined perhaps it was far, far away and Jason would never get back.

He said, "I'm taking Phinas with me as my aide. We will probably be gone six months."

Clarice haughtily tilted her head, "Well, I'm also going away; that is what I have to tell you." She continued, "I'm going to visit Julia. I received a letter from her. She says there is no fighting in New York. There are many soldiers, but it is peaceful. I'm taking Feather, and we're riding Blessing."

"John Jolly will take Bessie and Panzy to his place. I may get back by spring. It all depends on your return. I don't want you to worry about me. If I write to you I won't know where to send it. I want you to take the chickens back to your camp, as there seems to be no food there. Chicken will taste good. Phinas told me he was 'sick with starvation'."

Jason said, "Then we will drive the chaise; we can take more that way. Phinas will bring it right back.

"When are you leaving for New York? You can drive the chaise if you want to."

"Jason, you know that I'm a poor driver. We will ride Blessing; it will be easier that way. We will make better time."

"Cee Cee, my sweet little wife. My heart will be throbbing for you every day, but I am glad you have decided to leave this angry place for awhile. I do believe that someday it will be a happy place again. Right now it is dangerous and impoverished. New York is a better place for you."

Jason and Clarice took a walk to Shiny Squatt. There was a full moon, the air was soft and fragrant. No sound was heard of distant drums or guns. Bessie followed them, lifting her head now and then for a low moo.

It was a wonderful harvest night, not much harvesting to do. Men had been too busy with militia and fighting.

Jason held on to Clarice's hand, which he squeezed in an affectionate way. She tiptoed to reach his cheek and kissed him each time she felt the squeeze.

She said, "I'm going to miss you, my dear. I can't tell you how much because I love you more than anything in the world."

He said, "When I return we will go and visit your parents."
"Jason, is that a promise?"
"Yes."

The sight of Shiny Squatt brought memories of herself and Feather scared out of their wits at Angus's surprising arrival. She leaned on Jason's arm and cried.

In a moment she asked, "Where is this place you are going to? How will you get there?"

He thought about it before answering her. "It's on Lake Champlain in northern New York. We will walk most of the way, canoe some, horseback some. It's a British garrison established for the protection of Canada. Recently it was captured by Ethan Allen and the Green Mountain Boys. The British abandoned it, leaving much artillery, even cannon there.

"Knox's men are going to bring that artillery back to Boston. Washington intends to fortify Dorchester Heights. I'm going to be the chief artillery inspector, also the mess sergeant. It will soon be winter. We have to hurry."

"My dear husband, I will pray constantly for your safe return." She put her arms around his waist and drew up closer to him.

They continued their walk home without any more talking.

There were only two more short visits home for Jason and Phinas.

On the last visit Jason discovered that Clarice had covered the old bureau with a sheet. She had greased all the iron kettles to prevent rust. The hearth had been swept clean. Curtains were covering the opening to keep birds that fell down the chimney from flying out into the rooms. All the shutters had been closed.

He said to her, "Looks like you're ready to go."

"Yes, my darling, we will soon be far away from each other, seems like only yesterday that we met. Time goes so fast. Feather is excited; she is the one who loves to travel."

"Do you have those little blue slippers in your satchel?"

"You can be sure of it," she replied.

"Who will leave first, you or I?" asked Jason. He had a desperate longing look in his eyes.

"I will leave first," said Clarice, "because I have already said goodbye to Panzy and Bessie. Feather has fed and groomed Blessing. She even polished the saddle. I am ready."

It was a very sad moment when she reached for Jason, who was crying like a baby. She said, "Don't fret, dear, think how wonderful it will be when we meet again."

Phinas was wiping his eyes, and he turned around and went out the back door. Feather went out also, taking a basket of apples to the animals. Blessing was waiting saddled at the front gate. Feather came back and picked up the satchels and went out.

Jason lifted Clarice into his arms and held her up, burying his head in her breasts. He gave her several kisses, then held a long, long one before releasing her. He said, "Go now and God be with you 'til we meet again. Someday these sad partings will be water under the bridge."

He watched from the front door as Blessing gave a long nicker and trotted off carrying Clarice in her sidesaddle with Feather riding behind her.

Clarice said to Feather, "In about two weeks we will be in New York."